Suddenly Rissa knew their terrible guess had been right—for Lena Hulzein did not flinch. Instead: "If you don't fear for yourselves, fear for this planet. For I've made sure it won't outlive me!"

All the way from the prison of Total Welfare, Rissa had fought the odds, setting her skills and fury against men and aliens alike. She had allied herself with the most dangerous man in space. . . .

And now—was it all to be for nothing?

Berkley Books by F. M. Busby

THE RISSA KERGUELEN SAGA

YOUNG RISSA
RISSA AND TREGARE
THE LONG VIEW

THE THIRD BOOK IN THE
3-PART SAGA OF RISSA KERGUELEN

THE LONG VIEW

F.M. BUSBY

BERKLEY BOOKS, NEW YORK

Again, for Michele

PRELUDE

SINCE early in the 21st century, the United Energy and Transport conglomerate has owned North America; gradually it has increased its sway over more of Earth. When Rissa Kerguelen is five, she and her older brother Ivan Marchant are railroaded into one of UET's Total Welfare Centers, which are little more than slave barracks. Eleven years later, due to backlash of a Welfare supervisor's illegal use of clients' credits to buy tickets in the state-controlled lottery, Rissa is unexpectedly freed, buying her way out of Welfare with part of the lottery proceeds. She undertakes survival training at the Establishment of Erika Hulzein in Argentina; then, disguised, she leaves Earth. UET gained star travel by murdering the Shrakken, interstellar aliens who had come to Earth, and copying their ship. So now UET has star colonies.

But not all human colonies are UET's; some ships have Escaped, and founded settlements on what are called the Hidden Worlds. On the minor UET world Far Corner, Rissa takes passage on such a ship—*Inconnu*, the only armed ship ever to Escape, captained by Bran Tregare, pirate and raider. Rissa's early acquaintance with this harsh man brings the two of them to mutual respect and a wary liking.

On the planet Number One, a Hidden World loosely governed on an oligarchal basis, Rissa finds one of the oligarchs to be Liesel Hulzein, estranged sister of Erika, who with her husband Hawkman Moray and their daughter Sparline control Hulzein Lodge. Rissa is surprised to learn that Tregare is Sparline's brother, but will have nothing to do with his family because they left him, when forced to depart from Earth, in "the Slaughterhouse," UET's brutal Space Academy. Rissa helps to heal that breach, and when she finds herself coerced by local custom into a duel with the spaceport's Provost, Stagon dal Nardo, Tregare is at hand, disguised in mask and hood. With she and dal Nardo fighting nude and weaponless by her own choice, Rissa suffers injuries from the man who is twice her weight, but kills him—and then is told that for political reasons she should marry the hooded man. Dazed, she agrees; later she accepts the marriage, and finds Tregare's goals worthy of her wholehearted support.

For the "pirate's" aim is nothing less than to "pull UET out by the roots like a rotten tooth." He is gathering ships—by purchase, by agreement, or by outright force—to build a fleet, then arm it. His first target is Stronghold, a UET outpost set up to guard the sector from which the Shrakken had come. And then to gather more ships and challenge UET on Earth itself.

It isn't all that easy; captains of Escaped Ships are apt to have a high degree of competitive pride. Jimar Peralta, a former friend of Tregare's, held seniority in the UET days; now, though it was Tregare who helped Peralta take the ship he captains, the man wants a share of overall command; his mutiny fails, but one ship and many lives are lost.

Six ships are Tregare's minimum, to move on Stronghold. He gets that many, but another threat looms: a Shrakken vessel comes to Number One. Tregare captures it, and the alien ship *Sharanj* is given no choice but to serve as decoy at the approach to Stronghold. Because Tregare's fleet is going in "camouflaged," pretending to be the group of UET ships scheduled to arrive shortly thereafter. That schedule, obtained by Tregare's old friend "Kickem" Bernardez, is the crux of the plan.

And Tregare needs all the odds he can get. The night before the ships lift from Number One, Rissa is hard put to quiet his last-minute misgivings. But she knows the plan is as good as can be done; there is no choice but to go through with it.

MORNING at Base Two—liftoff. To avoid sideblast at the ships around him, Tregare took *Inconnu* up gently. Vanois in *Carcharodon*, Limmer in *Lefthand Thread*, Gowdy commanding *No Return*—each followed his lead. Next came the Shrakken *Sharanj*, and behind it—together and now with no need for caution—M'tana and Krueger brought *Valkyrie* and *Graf Spee* up at full blast.

Watching the back screen as Tregare looked ahead, Rissa said, "The group forms, with the Shrakken at center as you designated." She turned to him. "Tregare—you have put together a very potent implement."

"Let's just hope it stays together and does what we need to do."

HOW long is a year—in space, while planets' clocks turn faster? Their best estimates of objective time, Rissa knew, were little better than guesswork. Only when the ships reached Stronghold could they anchor again to groundside chronology.

She worked, studied—became *Inconnu*'s Third Hat in fact as well as name, taking no advantage of her relationship with Tregare. One woman thought otherwise and resented Rissa enough to challenge her; Rissa held her anger and achieved victory without serious damage to her opponent.

Each ship's day she found a few minutes to talk with her brother and friends by viewscreen—choosing times when the intership circuits were not busy.

Turnover came and passed, and now time seemed to crawl—would this voyage never end?

And then Stronghold came in view.

"YOU there, groundside—cover me!" Hilaire Gowdy's voice carried urgency. "I have to land fast—alien attacker trying to cut me off. Only the one ship—the rest are ours, got drawn outside at first, but now they're closing—the alien must be crazy, to hang on like that. Don't shoot—we hope to force it down here. I—" As she zigzagged away from the Shrakken's harmless fire, Gowdy continued to call Stronghold. From the fortress came premature reaction, missiles that then destructed as their launchers heard her words. She said, "I'm coming down fast. Don't do anything. The other ships—coming up behind the alien—they'll take care of it."

A voice from Stronghold said, "But who are *you*?"

And Hilaire Gowdy; "You know who we are—we're maybe ahead of sked. Check your list, but *later*—our lives can't wait for your goddamned red tape!"

Stronghold said, "Put your computer on line to validate our checklist. Then we can—"

"It's not working—those bastards burned part of it out. Wait 'til we sit down, will you? And—oh, *shit*!" Gowdy dodged her ship, shuddering, out of the spectacular but harmless Shrakken beam that had found *No Return*, and dropped toward the planet. No Stronghold ship had launched.

On *Inconnu*, Rissa punched for Stronghold frequencies. "This is Fleet H-12 from Earth. As usual, there have been some changes since your advance notice. Now—*emergency!* We will contain the alien, force it down. Do not act against it—we want that ship alive! The Presiding Committee has so ordered."

From Stronghold, "There have been other incidents?"

"The Presiding Committee has so ordered. End of transmission."

She cut the circuit and turned to Tregare. He said, "You have them, I think—now let's play it out."

Fishtailing, *No Return* made a crippled-duck landing. Now *Inconnu* and the rest acted out their charade. They surrounded *Sharanj*, herded it with their projector beams, and forced it down, then landed encircling it.

Tregare punched the all-ships' channel. "Now we move *fast!*"

ALMOST, the plan worked. The attackers met less resistance than expected. Of the sixteen UET ships, none took off—and in the fighting only three were damaged.

Ivan Marchant led the assault on the communications center. When he came out, he had not bothered to wipe the blood from his knife. Rissa met him, and he said, "The ones I hate are those that quit without fighting—I have to let them live."

Rissa touched his cheek. "Consider, Ivan—many are not predators, but victims."

He nodded, but did not look totally convinced.

So far, so good—but Stepan Kobolak, it seemed, was a stubborn man. Twelve hours after the landing, he still held control of Stronghold's power systems. "I'll see you all in hell first," he said.

On the viewscreen Rissa and Tregare watched his taut, pale face. "That may well be," she said. "But might we not meet first, and speak together?"

"I don't trust you."

"And I do not blame you—all your life you have lived with mistrust. But may one of us come to you, under safeguards of your own choosing?"

Finally the man agreed. Tregare cut the circuit and said, "*You're* not going there without protection, Rissa—don't ever think that!"

"Would you prefer that he explodes his power plant, and with it this entire port? The way he talks, that is the alternative."

"Someone else could go. He won't see *me*, of course, but—"

"Bran—I could say many things. But all I say is that since—as you have pointed out—you are not eligible, I do not choose to wager *all* our lives on anyone other than myself." She reached to him; he held her. "Can you agree to that?"

When he released her, he said, "Sometimes you don't give me much choice."

GUARDS made certain she entered Kobolak's lair unarmed. Two more flanked the haggard man's desk. Watching his face, Rissa saw his jaw clench. She halted her approach and said, "I have no wish to harm you, Kobolak—nor to be harmed. But the truth is that no matter what you may do, Stronghold is no longer UET's. It is Bran Tregare's, or no one's."

Eyes wide, mouth now loose, the man looked at her. Finally he said, "Here—under my desk—my finger can blow us *all* up. What can you do against that?"

"Nothing, of course. I hope you will see no reason to do such a thing. May I speak?"

"Talk all you want—for as long as I leave us alive."

"But—why would you die? How does UET hold your very life captive?"

The man shuddered. She said, "Kobolak—UET does *not* own you. I—"

He reached under the desk. "Get out of here, or—"

His fear almost became hers also, but she shook free of it. "I have not finished! You must tell me *why* you take this insane position. Do you fear Tregare? He does not torture, and kills only in battle. He—"

"UET tortures."

"But you are no longer within UET's reach."

"My family—on the next ships from Earth, the ones we thought *you* were. When the Committee police on those ships learn what's happened?"

"But they will not—how can they?—until they too are taken. You do not understand Tregare's plan. He—" Then, afraid she might have revealed too much, she said only, "None have escaped to warn UET—and none will."

His hands clasped together, clenching and twisting. "You—he—can save my wife, my children?"

"Who can guarantee safety, if there is fighting? But *if* there is, no Committee police will live long enough to torture any."

He hesitated. Then, "I suppose that has to be good enough." He turned to his guards. "Put your guns on the desk." Rissa stepped forward and took the weapons.

"Tell the men outside," said Kobolak, "that we have surrendered to Tregare the pirate—on promise that our lives are safe." As the man moved to obey, Kobolak said to Rissa, "You *did* promise that, didn't you?"

"It was implied; I now make it explicit. But Tregare is not a pirate—he is the new commander of Stronghold."

The outside guards entered and put their weapons down. One said, "That's a relief—I didn't fancy going up as a cloud of ions." He looked to Rissa. "Our safety's guaranteed?"

"Yes. You'll be confined, until Tregare has time to determine who can be allowed freedom. Questioning under drugs is a slow process."

For the first time, Kobolak laughed. The sound was shaky, but in his face Rissa saw relief. He said, "You won't need drugs. The last ship here before you—it brought truth field equipment. Nobody's had time to set it up yet, but if the technician who came along with it is still alive—"

"We have our own technician," said Rissa. Then, "If you will call Tregare for me? I should report." She did so. Soon two from *Inconnu* arrived—one took station at Kobolak's desk; the other escorted the prisoners to temporary detention.

Then she returned to Tregare. Heedless of others present, he hugged her until her ribs creaked, lifted her off her feet in embrace, and kissed her until both were short of breath.

"You did it! And—a truth field, you say?" She nodded, and he said, "Good thing they *didn't* get it working—there'd have been a purge here like you wouldn't want to see."

"Or—if the news spread—perhaps civil war."

"Either way," he said, "we're lucky. Now, then—where's Felcie?"

"With Limmer's task group—identifying and classifying personnel. If you like, Bran, I can relieve her of that duty."

"Okay—sure, until I find someone else to do it. Hey—I'll bet you haven't heard! You know why there was so much less fighting than we figured on?" She shook her head. "Well, the commandant was asleep—the alarm woke him and he thought he had a mutiny on his hands. So—automatic response—he gassed the troop barracks!"

"He killed his own men?"

"No—just knocked them out for a while. But to be on the safe side, he hit the buttons for civilian quarters, too. Come to think of it, he *saved* a lot of lives—on both sides. But not on purpose."

"And this commandant—did he surrender?"

"Not so you'd notice. We took him alive but he's pretty badly wounded. I hope he pulls through—we need him."

At her look of inquiry, he grinned. "To appear onscreen—doped or hypnotized or whatever—when the UET ships get here. Otherwise they'd be suspicious. Hell of a job making someone up to impersonate him, let alone imitate his voice. There aren't many like Arger Korbeith—and thank peace for that!"

"Oh?"

"On my first ship, I served under him."

RISSA took Felcie's place with Limmer's identification group. When she saw the roster, the size of Stronghold's garrison surprised her; she wondered how Tregare had dared attack against such odds.

"Derek—we were outnumbered more than ten to one!"

"Closer to twenty," said Limmer. "But Tregare knows UET. You think their ships are run like ours, with practically everyone armed? Not a chance! Ships and groundside alike, only officers and Committee Police troops carry weapons. And Korbeith gassed out all his off-duty troops, at that!" He chuckled, and Rissa marveled that she had ever thought that scarred face ugly.

When Felcie had the truth field ready, a woman relieved Rissa to join Tregare in interviewing the captives. "About *time* we got started on this," he said. "Six hundred people, a little more, *can* keep the lid on nearly ten thousand—get them fed and all, using prisoner help. But I'd hate to have to do it much longer."

Rissa had helped prepare a list of questions for interrogation under drugs. The truth field simplified the task; Tregare scratched out more than half the list. "With the field we won't need to crosscheck so much."

●   ●   ●

EVEN in a wheelchair, Arger Korbeith loomed—a giant, with the exaggerated features of acromegaly. Under grayish blond hair his face had a yellowish muddy tinge. His voice grated as he said, "Tregare, eh? Been looking forward to getting my hands on your neck. Never thought it'd be like this, we'd meet. Should've spaced you the first week out, on the old *MacArthur*. Sixteen-year-old snotnose—even then I knew you were no damned good!"

Tregare grinned. "The sentiment was mutual, commandant—and still is. Now—do we get on with it?"

"You don't need that thing on *me*—or any Twenty Questions game, either. Quick and short—I hate your guts, I'll kill you if I can, you'll get no help from *me* in your damned treachery. I—"

"That's enough. You're a lot of things, Korbeith, but you don't bother to lie." he nodded. "Take him out—bring in the next. Put him in max security, and solitary for now—until we find another scorpion just as bad, so they can sting each other."

Rissa logged the instructions. When Korbeith was gone, she said, "Even drugged, do you think to use *him*?"

"Plus a little hypnosis. Easiest thing in the world—give him a happy-pill and tell him everything's just the way he wants it. His own wishes take over from gut level."

Seeing Rissa's frown, he imitated Korbeith's gravel tones. "Ahoy the incoming fleet! Good news! That bastard Tregare tried a sortie here—and we blew him to hell. About time, too! So skip the red tape and set down—we're *celebrating*, and glad to have your help at it."

Now laughing, she nodded. "You are right—that is how he *would* say it."

"Yes—and here comes our next. Your friend Kobolak." He motioned toward a chair. "Sit down, Kobolak. This is informal."

With the man seated, Tregare began his questions. After a few, Kobolak said, "This isn't necessary. Tregare, I'm with you all the way; there's no other choice. If UET comes and you lose, I'm dead—too many know I surrendered—and my family with me."

Watching Tregare, he paused. "That's not enough? All right—I'm *glad* you won. It's the first time I've ever been out from under UET's rotten thumb. If my family gets here—and survives—maybe we'll have a chance for a decent life. I—''

Tregare held up his hand. "Green badge, Rissa." She handed him one and he signed it. "Here, Kobolak—take this into the room to your left and get your picture on it."

Kobolak's brows raised. Tregare said, "Green badge means you have your job back, your quarters back, no restrictions on your movements, groundside. I'll want a talk with you—briefing me on the power equipment—sometime tomorrow. Good enough?"

Kobolak shook his head, but his face belied the movement. "And to think how close I came to pushing that damned button!"

By the end of that day, a pattern became clear. Among ships' officers and higher-ranking groundsiders, roughly half were hard-core UET loyalists. The rest were covert dissidents of greater or lesser degree—to these, Tregare's coup came as a great relief, since it saved them from truth field interrogation at UET's hands, and almost certain death.

Committee Police and their leaders were almost solidly UET's. Some few professed dissidence and asked to join Tregare, but the truth field indicators proved their words false. The higher ranks drew max security and the rest, for the most part, medium.

Ivan had taken charge of guarding the Police group. He said, "Tregare, why bother with these? Why not just lock them all up?" Tregare shrugged but continued his questioning.

The next subject was a tall, spare woman nearing middle age; she gave her name as Flaer Letiken, and said, "I don't believe this truth field hocus; I think you're guessing. So you're going to think I'm lying—but here it is, anyway."

She brushed back short, improbably vivid red hair. "I went into the Police because when I was just a kid—eight, maybe—I saw there were two ways to live. I could be a victim or a vulture. My parents were victims; I saw what it did to them. So I went the vulture route."

She watched Tregare until he nodded. "All right so far? Maybe the gadget does work, after all. Anyway—I've been in this rotten game more than twenty years. I've done things that would make you puke—and never got used to having to do them. Sometimes I'd wonder if it was worth it. Then I'd think about being on the other end—and go ahead with the next nasty bit of work they gave me."

She shrugged. "All right—vulture or victim. But maybe with you there's a chance to be neither, and just live and work and not *hurt* anybody . . . anybody . . . anymore!" Her hands covered her eyes; great, choking sobs muffled her next words. Then she wiped away tears. Her mouth twisted as she said, "Hell—what can you lose? If UET comes and wins, and you've recorded this, I'm dead—you know that. So where do I stand?"

After a moment, Tregare said, "With an orange badge." He signed one, explained about the picture, and said, "You're free of detention; you'll be assigned temporary work and quarters. Just stay out of green-coded territory; you're not cleared for that yet."

For the first time, she laughed. "I don't need to be. I've already seen it all—and it's not that interesting." She started away, then turned and said, "Thanks, Tregare—and I'm glad I was wrong about your gadget." Then she left.

Ivan touched Rissa's shoulder. "About the ones who didn't fight—I've changed my mind."

DETENTION was less problem than Rissa had expected. Stronghold, she decided, was *built* for policing. In many cases the people—especially families, though there were few children —could retain their own quarters or, at worst, move to similar ones. And as the interviews proceeded, more space was changed from detention status to the lesser restrictions of colored badges.

Shipboard and groundside, the lower ranks were nearly five to one in favor of the new regime. Here Rissa saw how UET held sway by fear, for many professed loyalty to UET—and the truth field showed them to be lying. Even when Tregare pointed out the discrepancy, some refused to change their statements. He could only shrug, confine them under minimum security, and hope that time would ease their fears.

• • •

AFTER the first day, interviews ran day and night—Rissa, Limmer, and Zelde M'tana worked relief shifts—working against time before the UET fleet arrived. At the end of it, Rissa summarized the results.

"More than a hundred green badges, nearly two thousand orange. The majority carries blue, of course—access to normal living and working areas only. Less than a thousand still in detention—eighty-seven max, the rest nearly even between medium and minimum."

"Some of the scared ones are deciding it's on the level," said Tregare, "and asking for new interviews. We can't spare anyone full-time to handle that kind of trickle, but—"

"I will schedule a time," said Rissa, "to talk with any who wish it, as the demand requires. Once the flow begins, it should not take long."

Limmer said, "You got more administrators, Tregare, than I'd have guessed. But ships' officers are what I'm happy about—we're almost half-strength for every hull we've got. Shuffle around, promote a few ratings, and we're covered."

Zelde M'tana spoke. "Only one captain came over, though —and a half a dozen First Hats. Mostly we collected Seconds and Thirds, a lot of them pretty green."

Looking at the tall, black woman, Tregare laughed. "It won't matter—by the time we can move, they'll be trained. And we'll have to get working on the squadron approach, Zelde—with you and Derek and Vanois, Gowdy and Ilse, each running a *group* of ships. I never thought UET made that work as well as it ought to."

"How could they?" said Limmer. "They can't trust each other. What kind of squadron is it—one or two armed ships riding herd on a flock of unarmed?"

The talk shifted to personnel assignments. Rissa was glad to hear that Kile Ressider now had his own ship.

"But I'll miss that palefaced stud," said Zelde, "when the time comes, we have to leave here."

TEN days short of arrival, the ships from Earth first called Stronghold. Tregare manned his screens with truth-tested Stronghold personnel whose names might be known to their shipboard counterparts; he or one of his captains monitored and guided the talk, but stayed offscreen. And he carried out his plan for Arger Korbeith.

He had changed the scheme slightly. Instead of Tregare's annihilation, the script featured a pirate raid beaten off—sent reeling, crippled, pursued by part of Stronghold's fleet. "That way we'll have those ships—plus our own, which would be a dead giveaway—out past detection range, but in position to head off any UET ship that gets halfway smart and tries to run."

"And what of the Shrakken ship?" said Rissa. The Shrakken had been restive, waiting Tregare's permission—and fuel —to leave. Rissa had promised Stonzai that he would meet with her when current crises had passed. "He has not the time now—you must see that. And your other supplies are replenished, are they not?"

Having spoken with humans, intership, almost daily during the voyage from Number One, Stonzai now spoke a less muddled version of the language. Still, Rissa thought, it was never predictable. The alien said, "Supplies, food, we have. Fuel not, drug to hold eggs back not—*time* not. We need to Shrakken homes go. *When?*" Rissa could only repeat that when Tregare could do so, he would meet with Stonzai.

Now Tregare said, "Maybe it's a good drawing-card, the *Sharanj*. We captured it, see?" He imitated Korbeith's voice. "In league with Tregare, I expect it was—dirty alien-lover, that one. Always said he was no damned good—should have spaced him off the *MacArthur*."

Laughing, Rissa clapped her hands. "Very good, Tregare! You have it almost perfect."

"But we won't depend on it. Not if the real thing's available."

THE detectors found UET's ships—nine, not eight. "And four of them armed," said Tregare. "More to gain, more risk to gain it." He called Limmer and left to confer with him.

This, thought Rissa, was Tregare's show. Less and less had she any part in it; Stronghold had become her rival, taking his time and attention. *Not until this crisis passes, but after it, I will redress these matters.*

• • •

SAFELY offscreen she stood beside Tregare and watched Arger Korbeith. Sitting in full uniform, the drugged, hypnotized man told the approaching ships how he had routed Tregare and captured the Shrakken. "Kept the filthy beasts alive this time," the grating voice explained, "to question them, one at a time." His laugh made Rissa shudder, as he said, "Under interrogation they last well enough. We'll learn plenty before it's done." He accepted congratulations with becoming modesty, she thought.

To Tregare she whispered, "He believes all that?"

"Sure. These wishful thinkers are all alike."

She looked at him. "Be sure, then, you do not become one of them."

He started to answer, but she nudged him; the commandant was departing from his script, giving an earlier version of landing instructions. Tregare signed to an onscreen aide, who leaned forward and said, "Sir? You changed that—remember? Because of the threat of epidemic."

Korbeith shook his head; Rissa held her breath—would the hypnosis hold? Then the man said, "Correct as hell, lieutenant—I did forget. All right, up there—land in B Circle, nearest my Headquarters building. Officers report to me there immediately; guides will take the ratings to get their shots elsewhere. And don't waste any goddamned time on red tape—you can't spare it. That's all; see you aground."

As the circuit cut, Tregare's sigh of relief echoed Rissa's own.

THE ships came down; personnel emerged. Tregare's own version of Committee Police—at least they wore the uniform—checked to make sure all had disembarked.

In guard's uniform, Tregare led the officers to the Headquarters building. By the door Rissa, also uniformed, sat by a desk; beside it was a checkstand with pigeonholes. As the group approached, she said, "All weapons are to be left here, while you meet with the commandant."

One man protested; Tregare gestured with his own gun. "No one enters the commandant's presence armed." Along with the others, the man deposited his personal armament. Lastly, Tregare did also. Rissa locked the stand and followed.

In the conference room Arger Korbeith sat, glaring about

him. Rissa knew he was drugged to semiconsciousness. As the ships' officers found seats, Tregare strode past them and stood beside Korbeith. Rissa took a position to one side, between Tregare and his audience.

"The fact is," he said, "there have been some changes. Commandant Korbeith is no longer in charge of Stronghold. So I feel we can dispense with his presence." A guard led the man away.

Tregare removed his uniform cap. "I now command instead." Several stood. "Be seated or be shot! This room is covered."

All sat but one—a tall man, older than most there. He spread his hands, saying, "If you're so scared you have to kill a barehanded man, shoot away. But I want a closer look at you." Tregare motioned to each side and nodded; the man walked toward him. Rissa moved closer also.

Two paces from Tregare the man stopped. "You may know me, you may not—Ildren Paszacker, first shipped out on the *Anslinger* when it was brand-new." Waiting, Tregare shook his head. "Well, I know *you!*" Paszacker clenched his fist and squeezed. Horrified, Rissa saw a blade emerge from between his middle knuckles as the man leaped, crooked an elbow around Tregare's neck, and held the knife to his throat. "If you shoot now, damn you, your pirate king is dead!"

No one shot—but as Paszacker moved, so did Rissa. Slowly —oh, so slowly it seemed to her, as time froze—she lunged and caught the knife wrist, kicking back to pull it with all her weight away from Tregare. Blood splashed her face as she fell away, momentum bringing Paszacker's arm toward her. She reached for a better grip but lost it; the knife came at her.

She slipped to one side. It grazed her and was past. She clamped the wrist in her armpit and strove to brace her other hand for balance, but Paszacker was above her and had the leverage. The wrist slipped—behind her shoulder she felt the blade's kiss. She clamped harder and now forgot balance, letting the man's weight crush her to the floor as her freed right hand stabbed and clawed at his dodging head.

Endless, endless—then two hands closed over Paszacker's face. Abruptly, the head turned to the right; she heard a sharp snap. Then—one spasm of muscles, and her opponent lay limp.

"Hold still so I don't cut your arm off." Tregare's voice—

and with only a slight twinge at her armpit the dead man's hand came out from under her, into view. "Are you all right?"

"I am not sure—I think so. Are you?" Now she saw—his neck ran blood, but it did not spurt; the splash she felt had been from his movement. And she said, "Bran—what took you so long?"

"*Long?* It wasn't three seconds."

"To me it was hours." Now, feeling her shoulder and finding less blood than she expected, she could laugh a little. "When one is losing, the gift of extra time is not an unmixed blessing."

"I'm not so sure you were losing—he showed no skill, only the knife—and he was tiring. But I wasn't going to wait to find out." Helping her up, he turned her and looked at her back. "It's not too bad. Can treatment wait?"

"If yours can."

"All right." He turned to the seated group; so far as Rissa could tell, none had moved. He said, "That's a new one—the knife *inside* the hand. Maybe more of you have such things. We'll find out—meanwhile you keep your distance. It's good you didn't try to mix in—you'd have been wiped out, the lot of you, before you took two steps." He stared at them, and to Rissa his look spelled death. "Anyone have anything to add?"

A very young man, wearing a barely visible moustache, raised his hand. "Captain Paszacker said he knew you. I don't. Will you name yourself, sir?"

Beside the boy, a man said, "Haven't you figured that out yet, Jamie? We're in the hands of Tregare the pirate."

The youngster shot to his feet, looked fearfully to each side, and sat again. Tregare said, "It's all right; there'll be no shooting, from here on, unless I order it. Now what's your problem, son?"

"Are you really Bran Tregare?" A nod. "Then—how can I convince you—to let me *join* you? Because the only reason I entered the Academy—curse that place!—was to try for Escape someday, the way you did. I—"

"You'll have your chance. And now—*your* name?"

"Jamie—I mean, James Pescadore, Third Hat on the *Saxbe*. That is, I *was* . . ."

"If you check out all right you'll probably end up Second,

at least. Now then—all of you—I'll cut the suspense. Strong-hold's mine now, not UET's—and it's going to stay that way. Those of you that I'm willing to accept can join me or not—and in any case your lives are safe. Worst that can happen to you is detention and maybe doing farm work—when I get that organized—how to get a little honest work out of the UET diehards among you."

He grinned. "Just so nobody gets any funny ideas, we've got truth field equipment here. Everyone on Stronghold's been through it and you're next. There'll be no UET under-ground running around loose—nobody joins me unless the field says you mean it."

"*I* mean it!" cried Jamie Pescadore.

"And that's why you'll get solitary detention—so nobody cuts your throat for saying so." The man beside Jamie glared but said nothing. "All right—that's it. Walk single file out the door you came in; you'll be escorted to your new quarters. Tomorrow we'll start finding out who's on which side." He clicked his heels and made a mock salute. "Dis-*missed!*"

Guards entered to escort the captives out; Tregare and Rissa followed, then went to the nearest medical station. Their in-juries were quickly treated.

Leaving, they met Stepan Kobolak. Tears ran down his cheeks; Rissa said, "Did something go wrong? I am *so* sorry!"

Kobolak shook his head. "No—no—I only wanted to thank you. They are safe, my family—a few bruises, a burn, but safe! I—" Tregare accepted the man's handshake, Rissa his embrace, and he hurried away.

Rissa smiled. Tregare said, "I'm glad of that; he's a good man."

Back in their quarters, dressing after a bath, Rissa said, "I wonder—how many off these ships will be like the young boy, and how many like the man who tried to kill us?"

Tregare shrugged. "The field will tell us. And in the long run, it won't matter—these ships were overofficered, with a lot of cadets doubling up and sharing jobs. We'll have enough."

He grinned. "You know? I *like* that kid!"

NEXT day, while Tregare began his truth field interviews,

Zelde M'tana came to Rissa. "You know what we missed, in all the arglebargle yesterday?" Rissa shook her head. "The ninth ship, the one we didn't expect—it's the original Shrakken ship, that landed on Earth and started everything!"

"But why—?"

Zelde shrugged. "Don't ask me. I shook down the people that came here on it—only five, just enough to pilot and maintain the drive—and they don't know much. Their guess is that UET wants to rig it that if the Shrakken ever show up again, the story is the ship came *here*, not to Earth—so Earth's not responsible for what happened. A little late with the thinking, I'd say, but any time UET thinks at all it has to be an improvement. Anyway—you want to look through the ship?"

"Yes, of course. And—no, I do not need to ask Bran. He is busy, and it is time again that I make decisions of my own. We will take Stonzai with us, also."

"The Shrakken queen bee? Hey, Rissa—you sure that's a good idea?"

Rissa thought, then nodded. "I am very sure. Let us go."

BEFORE entering the ship, Stonzai paused. "Long thought lost, this ship was. You say, to your home world it went?"

"Yes. Shall we go in?" Inside, Rissa said, "UET—the people we fight against—they killed everyone on this ship, to steal star travel from it."

The Shrakken stopped, and hissed. "This, to *me* you tell?"

"Yes, Stonzai. If you hate, you must know *whom* to hate."

"Hate we not know; only a word it is. But balance—that, redress we might can do."

"Comes to the same thing," said Zelde M'tana. "Let's go on in and look around."

The ship differed little from what Rissa had seen of *Sharanj*. Zelde gestured toward a row of storage cabinets. "A lot of the original Shrakken supplies in there, one man told me. UET put back stuff from museums and all, to make things look good."

Stonzai looked at her, then ran—toe-prancing gait, like a dog on its hind legs—to the farthest cabinet. She opened it, rummaged and reached out a large transparent container filled with gray pellets.

"The eggs—the eggs, to control! You, Rissa—home we could go, and *not* each other kill!"

Zelde said, "You know what that's about? I've heard rumors, but—"

Rissa nodded. "I know. And it is important." To Stonzai she said, "Keep what you hold, and anything else on this ship, that will be useful to you. About your going home, I will speak again with Tregare. And now let us leave here."

IN their quarters Tregare said, "I see your point, Rissa. But I'd been thinking—the Shrakken could be as good a decoy when we hit Earth, as they were here."

"That is not *fair*, Bran—it is cruel! How long before we go to Earth—how many years? And these poor creatures, who have never harmed us of their own will—all that time, suffering the violation of deep instinct."

She shook her head. "No, Bran. They must go home—I insist."

"Well—" He nodded slowly. "I hope they're not sentimental about their ships, though."

"What do you mean?"

"To fluster UET at Earth it's not really Shrakken we need —it's Shrakken *ships,* and maybe *films* of Shrakken to play over the viewscreens on the way in. We get Stonzai to design new insignia for the older ship, so UET doesn't recognize it for the same one they stole, and—"

"Yes, Bran; that is fine. But have you thought of all of it?"

"I—I think so. You gave Stonzai the true story—now I give her one of the new UET ships, unarmed but with a working projector in the cargo, along with instructions and spare parts. We send them on their way—with the drug they make it home just fine *and* have reason to feel friendly. Does that cover it?"

"Almost. You do not like the Shrakken, do you, Bran?"

A pause. "No—not really. Do you?"

"Yes—I think I do. And that with more acquaintance I would come to like them better."

"If you say so. But since they're leaving, anyway, what does that have to do with anything?"

"I should be the one to tell Stonzai your terms, and to bid them good-bye."

His frown cleared. "Maybe you're right—and I'm busy enough, as it is. I'll order them refueled and you take it from there. Okay?"

"Very well. Except for one thing."

"Such as?"

"As you say, you are busy. But either we find more time for each other, or we will find very much less."

He blinked, then said, "Trouble is, we've been splitting our work *too* efficiently. From now on, let's overlap more."

"That is reasonable," she said, and when he reached to her, she matched him.

BEFORE the Shrakken left, Rissa taped many reels of information, audio and visual, to send with them. "It is far short of complete, Stonzai," she said, "but I want your people to know *something* of us, more than mere events."

"Perhaps best, Rissa, that little contact we have. But some we will. And what to us you tell here, study we shall do, and troubles by every means avoid."

Rissa looked at the strange tall creature and reached to touch the alien's forehead as Stonzai touched hers in turn. With a feeling of regret, she watched the Shrakken enter the ship; then the ramp lifted and closed it. Stonzai held takeoff until Rissa was safely out of range, standing, seeing the ship rise and dwindle and finally vanish.

When she found Tregare and reported to him, she said, "It may be foolish, but I feel I have lost something—their leaving while I still know them so little."

Head shaking, he smiled. "Maybe so. But you ever hear of a three-ring circus? Everything going on at once—you can't *help* but miss most of it. I'm up to my ass trying to handle what I *need* to. You want the truth, the Shrakken are a big load off my mind."

Seeing the strain in his face, she smiled and agreed.

BY skill, main force, and good advice, Tregare reorganized Stronghold. A number of officers from the new ships joined him, including one captain—Terrell Ragan of the armed ship *Loose Goose,* formerly the *Trujillo.* Slowly the detention quarters continued to empty as Tregare's administrators found ways to make productive use of people he could not wholly trust.

The max-security prisoners made one bloody attempt to escape; Tregare shot his way out of their ambush. That same day he held drumhead court-martial of the four major ring-leaders—not for the attempt, but because they had killed several minimum-security hostages.

He spoke before the entire remaining detention group, surrounded by the armed guards who had assembled them. He wore no bandage; dried blood showed around the stitches in his shaved patch of scalp. He addressed the handcuffed prisoners.

"It's no news when somebody tries to kill *me*—I'm here, and that shows you what the try was worth. But you bastards killed some harmless people who had the job of bringing you your food—just because you could get your hands on them." Knife in hand, he stepped forward to the prisoners. "So now you follow them—and I don't ask anyone to do my killing for me."

He moved then, so fast that only one of the four had time to scream. But minutes later, in their quarters, away from blood of prisoners and vomit of spectators, Rissa held him.

"I *had* to!" His body started to shake. "Peace take me, Rissa! Now I know what you meant!" And when his sobbing was done, "You *do* have to grieve for your dead."

"That is true, Bran." Then, "Are you now healed?" And a little later, "I think we both are."

NEXT day Tregare met with his five original captains, along with Rissa, Ivan, Felcie, and Terrell Ragan. He said, "It's time we compared notes; we've been spread out too thin." He turned to Rissa. "You've at least sampled all the reports, which is more than I've found time to do. Could you summarize how the situation Earthside looks to you? Then anyone can add what else seems important."

She looked around the big table, visualizing Arger Korbeith presiding there. "We speak of Earth ten years ago—a hard thing to realize truly. It can be no surprise that UET, with its space monopoly, now holds most of the planet. When I left, it controlled only North America and, to some extent, Japan. Thirty-five years later, when this fleet left, Europe and most of Asia were engulfed, Africa neutralized—''

She looked around again. "A war is mentioned. Who knows of it?''

Ilse Krueger said, "A ship tried to Escape the easy way, by defecting to the New Russian Empire. UET wouldn't stand for that. When the neutrons dissipated, UET had Asia.''

"To cut it short," said Zelde M'tana, "what *doesn't* UET own?''

"The only major free areas," Rissa said, "are in the Southern Hemisphere—Australia and roughly half of South America.''

"That last," said Tregare, "would be the Hulzeins—right? Damn—I was sorry to hear about that old fox, Erika. Of course she'd be long dead by now, but still—'' He looked to Rissa. "How did it happen?''

She leafed through papers until she found a sheet in Felcie's bold handwriting. "A UET ambush in Madrid—only a few months, Ivan, after you left Earth.''

Her brother shook his head. "I wouldn't have expected it. I'd have bet—in her *sleep* that woman could outguess UET.''

"Maybe that's what she tried," said Tregare. "Or—even fools can get lucky sometimes. Now, then—what more do we know about the Hulzein situation?''

Rissa said, "Frieda inherited at thirty-three; she had held power for as many years again when these ships left. All else is rumor.''

"Such as?''

"That when she was about forty, Frieda produced a daughter. The story carries no details.''

"Well, *someone's* holding the fort, last we know of. Now —how did Australia manage to hold out?''

Rissa set down the papers. "This part I read carefully. The Australians invited UET to play Russian roulette. UET declined.''

"How's that?''

"A moon of Jupiter's was blown to dust. The Australians displayed an interplanetary craft they had built, and claimed credit. Then they told UET to stay off Australia, or Earth would suffer the same fate.''

Tregare whistled. "When the time comes, remind me to be *very* polite to Australia.''

"Yes," said Rissa. "But it will not be difficult.''

"Oh?"

"Tregare—they celebrate your birthday as a national holiday!"

When he stopped laughing, Tregare said, "First ship we send to Earth starts setting up liaison with those people."

"And how soon will that be?" said Limmer.

"Soon as we put our picture together enough to know exactly what we want that ship to do. Good enough?"

Limmer nodded. "Fine. One other thing, now—you have a timetable yet, when we expect to move on Earth in force?"

Tregare looked to Rissa, then said, "That depends on future news *from* Earth. The planet won't be undefended; we don't go until we think we have the firepower to make it stick." He stood, pacing back and forth behind his chair as he spoke.

The factors were these. Every two years, on the average, UET sent ships to Stronghold—usually eight, with three armed. For each two armed ships it sent, one was kept on Earth. Ten years ago, Earth's armed fleet had numbered twenty. "The way we beat that, of course, is arm everything we've got, same as at Number One."

Tregare had brought six ships, captured sixteen on the ground and eight from space, and given the Shrakken one. "And it turns out, theirs are almost impossible to modify, for a full crew of humans. And we can't afford empties, so I'm dropping the whole decoy idea."

Go now—when all Stronghold's ships were armed—or wait and capture one more fleet? Or still another? Every two years would change the odds. Now—after the routine courier was sent to Earth—meant twenty-eight against perhaps thirty-seven. "Not good enough. Two years from now it's more like thirty-six of ours and they're a couple-three better. If there comes up a *reason* to try that, I will. Otherwise we wait for second helpings."

"That's fine with me," said Limmer. "We're betting all of Earth; I'd like the odds good, too."

"Agreed. Now—Rissa, you had some questions for Captain Ragan?"

"I do." She looked at their new ally—thin, red-haired, of medium height. "Ragan—something puzzles me."

"Ask away, Ms. Tregare."

She did not correct his naming of her. "It is this. If Number—if a planet two jumps from Earth has truth field gear, and Stronghold too, why does not Earth have it also?''

His voice came softly. "But Earth does have it, of course."

"Then how do you come here, commanding a ship for UET?"

Ragan smiled. "Oh, yes—I see your question. Well, the field's only as good as the technician who operates it. And some years before our group left, the Underground got some of its own into that line of work. So—''

"Felcie!" Tregare grinned at Derek Limmer's wife. "Thank peace for *you*!" Her frown showed puzzlement; he said, "Stronghold's tech turned out to be solid UET. If *he'd* been running the field he could have sneaked us full of UET toadies." Felcie nodded; Tregare signed for Ragan to continue.

Rissa spoke first. "But at UET—when those techs themselves were tested—they could not be sure of friendly hands at the controls. So how—?"

"Now that *was* tricky. The UG set up posthypnotic triggers, so that under interrogation the person *believed* he or she was loyal to UET. And snapped back to normal, knowing what was happening, as soon as the danger was past."

"You bring anybody along who can do that kind of programming?" Tregare's voice held urgency. "Because if you didn't, school's out." Ragan shook his head, and Tregare said, "There goes any idea of sending ships back, let alone infiltrating. Sure as peace, UET checks all incoming ships. So—''

Rissa spoke. "Tregare! We have time for experiment—we have the field and Felcie to operate it. If with all that—!''

His scowl smoothed. "Sure—we'll get at it—the hypnotic drugs will help. And when one of ours can pass a UET-slanted questioning, we're in." Now he looked at Ragan. "Any chance some of the people in your fleet had that treatment?"

"I don't understand."

"I do," said Rissa. "Tregare—you mean some in detention may be there because their conditioning shows them as UET partisans, under the field, when they truly are not?"

"That's it. What do you think, Ragan? Any way to find out who might be set up that way?"

Ragan looked startled. "I have no idea. It's possible, of course, but I don't see any sure way you could find out."

Felcie said, "Wait a minute! Hypnosis—isn't that how you can make people think things are different? A friend is a charging bushstomper, maybe? So can't you tell 'em they're *not* under truth field, there isn't any such thing, and—?"

"I'm afraid not," said Ragan. "I know this much—the hum of the equipment, whether consciously heard or not, *plus* the interrogative situation—that's the trigger that sets up the false belief structure."

Felcie started speech, but Tregare said, "Ragan—you realize what you just told me?"

"I . . . no. What?"

"That maybe some of the people I've cleared—maybe *you*, for instance—could be hypnoed the other way around, by UET!"

Forcibly, the man shook his head. "That's impossible!"

"Like how, Ragan? And you'd better make it good."

Silence held until Ragan nodded. "Yes—I see. I *know*—but how do I prove it to you?" He paused again. Finally, "If I were what you suspect, I'd know enough not to tell you *any* of this—not to arouse your suspicions."

"Not good enough—Rissa asked questions and you *had* to come up with a story."

Ragan shook his head. "I'd have been provided with one —a good one, no loopholes. Now think a minute, Tregare. First—UET doesn't *know* of this trick. Second—they had no reason to expect the situation here, to prepare for it. If they had, the fleet certainly wouldn't have set down in your duck blind!"

He waited for Tregare's slow nod, then said, "I realize the stakes are too big for you to rely on my logic, let alone my word. You can check me out with any combination of field, drugs and hypnosis—so long as you guarantee me competent operators." He shrugged. "Otherwise, I suppose, I'm back in detention."

"And," said Rissa, "you do not object to that?"

"To what purpose? I don't really care for the idea, but—"

"Hold it!" Ivan spoke. "At Erika's—she had the field, of course, but she also used earlier types of lie detectors. I'm betting Stronghold has some, too."

"But if the *field* isn't foolproof—" said Tregare.

"Let me finish. Erika's other devices didn't really tell lies from truth—but they *did* show sudden changes in stress. Hitting a hypnotic trigger makes a distinctive pattern. So—" He looked at Rissa, then to Tregare.

The latter nodded. "You've got it—Ivan, you've *got* it!"

Ivan grinned. "Let's say—between us, we *all* got it."

THEY tried Ivan's plan. Under drugs Ragan was given several harmless short-term hypnotic implants. Unmistakably the polygraph indicated the activation or release of these. Then, under truth field, he was tested for previous hypnotic conditioning.

The result: Ragan was clean.

FURTHER checking found five from Earth's Underground among the apparent UET adherents in detention. Of the five, Lircia Gavaine was senior in the movement and best informed. Looking at the small, trim woman—tilted Eurasian eyes under closely cut black hair—Rissa guessed her bio-age at thirty.

"Closer to forty," the woman said. "And I'm second-generation UG—taught to fool authority before I lost my baby lisp." She leaned forward in her chair. "And—does this mean anything to you?—when I was twelve my parents smuggled me out for two years of Hulzein training."

Rissa smiled. "I had only one year, myself—starting at sixteen." On her notepad she marked an entry. "Did you—your group—retain contact there? For we badly need information, as to what has happened at the Hulzein Establishment."

"Well—what calendar do you use? Like it or not, I can think easily only in UET's 'New Years,' dating from when they took power."

"I no longer recall the older mode," said Rissa. "But by UET's reckoning I was born in NY23 and left Earth during 40."

"I was two, then." Gavaine laughed. "You must have traveled a lot—in space, I mean."

"Three trips—I have lived only two years, a little more, while perhaps forty-five have passed. But—the Hulzeins?"

"You knew Frieda succeeded Erika in 42?" Rissa nodded. "Things were bad, then, I'm told—Frieda so unstable that the UG expected the Establishment to go under. But it was a glandular imbalance—her doctors finally found and corrected it. By 50, when I went there, she had the place in control and moving well.''

"It is said, she produced a daughter. In the Hulzein fashion?"

"In what other? Yes—that was in 49; Frieda was forty."

"So at the time of your departure . . ."

"NY75, we left Earth. Lena Hulzein—Lena Diabla, she's called—was twenty-six then."

"The latest Hulzein—she is not popular?"

Lircia shuddered. "There's no sanity in that one, Ms. Kerguelen. Cunning, yes—maybe even brilliance. But—"

The copy machine effect. It has destroyed Erika's line—or it shall. Rissa said, "Specifics, please. What is the woman like? Appearance? Behavior?"

After a pause the woman said, "I haven't seen her myself—not even pictures. She's ugly, they say—somewhat deformed. Totally ruthless and impulsive, hungry for power—"

"That last is in the genes, I think. Is the woman . . . cruel?"

"I don't think the word—or kindness, either—applies to Lena Hulzein. Angered, she strikes without throught. Pleased —she once hugged a friend who brought good news, and killed him—she'd forgotten she was holding a knife. Other people simply aren't real to her." She made a one-sided smile. "My sister's boy trained there for a year. He was glad to come away alive."

"But does not Frieda—?"

Lircia's fingers riffled her short hair. "Frieda spent millions. A whole wing of the house was used for Lena and her needs—corrective surgery, training, mental therapy, glandular and chemical treatment, and—quite often—forcible restraint. And I guess Frieda thought it was working."

"Oh?"

"While my nephew Hiko was there, Lena was brought out to join the establishment. Cured, supposedly. But everyone—except Frieda—saw right away that Lena was as safe to have around as a hydrophobic cobra."

"I do not believe that disease attacks ophidians—but I understand you." She shook her head. "We had been pessimistic about any successful cooperation with Frieda. But *this* one—"

"Ms. Kerguelen, I'll tell you what I think. If Lena Hulzein ever gets her hands on the Australian Bomb—it's not one, but we call it that—Earth may not *be* there when you arrive."

". . . and that is what she said, Bran." Tregare's arms tightened around her; against the skin, below her shoulder blades, his fingers pressed. "But we go to Earth anyway, I suppose?"

"Sure." He laughed. "Right now, though, let's get up and go to dinner."

Now Stronghold ran smoothly to Tregare's routine; the work of arming ships and training men proceeded. It was not like Base Two, Rissa thought—for the work she had done there, she now had a trained crew, and needed only to make occasional spot checks. So for the first time she was free to explore outside Stronghold's fortress, out onto the planet of the same name.

It did not, she decided, compare at all well to Number One, or Far Corner or even to Earth. Its mountains were hummocks to one who had seen the Big Hills. Its two oceans were polar-centered; one froze while the other steamed—the life that swam in them lived by cycles no one understood.

Even the vegetation was drab and scraggly. Now, when warmth began at Stronghold fortress, gnarled, compact trees slowly put forth gray leaves with tattered edges, to draw sustenance from Stronghold's fierce, distant sun.

Kobolak, accompanying her one day, explained. "We have a short growing season, a quarter of our year. But that year—it's nearly fifteen of Earth's. And the winters—I haven't seen midwinter here, but what I did see was enough."

"Why did UET *choose* such a world?"

"Do you know your stellar charts?"

"Somewhat." But she raised her brows in question.

"Stronghold's almost directly on the line the first Shrakken ship followed, when it went to Earth. You see?"

She nodded. "UET must waste substance and effort in fear of consequence for its own deeds. Yes—that is fitting."

"I hear we don't have to worry about the Shrakken now."

"We hope not, Kobolak." Dusk brought chill, so they reentered the fortress.

Inside she said, "Now how goes it with you? And with your family?"

He smiled—how different from the frightened man she first had met! "It's a new life! I—we'd never lived without fear. Oh, sure—" He gestured. "What UET might do—someday. But that's a maybe—for now, we're happy, and I can sleep without taking pills."

His expression became serious. "The job's different, too. Tregare—I hope you don't mind my saying it—he's tough to work for. Demanding. But he's fair—you do your job, he knows it—you mug it up, he sets your clock back. Either way, you know where you stand." He looked worried. "No offense, I hope?"

"None at all, Kobolak. You summed it up well."

IN their quarters—the former commandant's, but much changed in decor—she related the conversation. Tregare laughed. "Don't ever tell Kobolak, but at first I took it easy on him. Now he's in better shape, he gets it just like everybody else."

"You find his work satisfactory?"

"One of the best—just needed a little time to shake down."

"Then why must you—how did he say?—set his clock back?"

"Because he's too easy. His people slack off, he lets it slide —does extra work himself, rather than gnaw them. So I gnaw *him,* and tell him to pass it along. You see?"

She nodded. "Yes—that is logical. Bran—never promote me to a position that forces me to do as you do to Kobolak."

"What's that? I'm not sure I understand you."

"Neither am I. I merely know—I would not like the task of prodding Kobolak to be harsher than his nature dictates."

He stared at her. "How the hell you think it was for him under UET?"

"Very bad. Remember—I met him before you did. And the change is good to see. But—still there is too much of putting someone in the middle, under pressure from two sides. I will not be put there—and I do not wish to do so to others."

"Yeah." Tregare drew a deep breath, let it out again. "I see what you mean. But somebody has to do it."

●　　●　　●

OCCASIONALLY Tregare and Rissa dined with some of his captains and groundside executives. Rissa most enjoyed the times with Ilse and Ivan, Limmer and Felcie. On one such evening Felcie was, for her, unusually quiet. Finally Tregare said, "You're not saying much, Felcie. Anything the matter?"

She started to speak but shook her head. Limmer said, "She's busting to tell you, but she's afraid you won't like it."

"Tell us *what*?" said Rissa.

"Derek and I—we're having a child."

Tregare burst out: *"Now?"*

"Why not?" said Limmer. "We'll be here awhile."

"But, a baby—at the battle for Earth? Or will you leave it here?"

"No." Felcie shook her head. "We take our baby—it won't be one by *then,* of course—it'll be running around like anything. No—don't interrupt—Derek and I don't have anybody but each other, and we'll be together—so if *Lefthand Thread* gets hit maybe we're safe anyway or maybe we *all* go, and—well, what's wrong with *that*?" Her face reddened; her breath came fast.

Tregare shook his head. "It's your decision; I won't argue with it. But—"

"You *can't* argue with it," said Ilse Krueger. "The birthrate always rises in times of war—that's instinct."

"All right." Tregare grinned. "Congratulations, then." He raised a toast; laughing, they drank.

The subject changed; a little later the party ended. But when the others had gone, Tregare said, "Well, Limmer made up my mind for me."

"Concerning what, Bran?"

"I'd been wondering who stays here, in charge, when we go. He and Felcie just bought him the job."

"Because of the *child*? Tregare—do you think there will not be other births? Short trips and groundside stays are one thing—but you speak of two years, or four. There *will* be children."

He rubbed his chin. "Sure—there's been kids on Escaped ships. Not many, because the parents—the mother, at least—usually gets off at the first stop they like. But that wasn't going into a battle situation—at least we always *hoped* it wasn't."

"You can order the children left behind, with the parents to stay also, if they so choose. But I think that choice would cause more trouble than the children would, aboard ships."

After a moment, he nodded. "All right—I'll leave all the choices up to the individuals. Just so they arrange—I don't care how—that child care doesn't interfere with anybody's real job." He poured himself more wine. "It's good this came up—so I'll have a policy figured beforehand."

"Yes. Perhaps it is."

"Well—thank peace, at least *we* don't have that problem."

She said nothing; he looked at her. "Rissa—we don't, do we? You'd have said—"

"I have not conceived, no—but I wish to."

"Just because Felcie—?"

"I had been thinking of it, but had not yet decided. Now, I have."

He shook his head. "It's out of the question."

"For you, perhaps—not for me. Though of course I would prefer . . ."

Now he stared at her. "You're *that* serious about it?"

"I am." She moved and touched his arm. "Bran—hear me out." He nodded. "It is as Felcie said—we accept the risk to our own lives. Then, why *not* to our child's? Would not such a child be proud, later, to have shared that risk?"

He frowned—but his voice betrayed no anger, only puzzlement. "I hadn't thought of it that way. You keep kids out of danger—"

"The Hulzein succession—you have your heirs—three icy little zygotes for Dr. Marco's zoom-wombs." She sighed. "Will we ever see those children? And that is *why*—" She gripped his arm until her knuckles whitened. "I had not thought myself to be maternal. But eighteen years, objective, since we left Number One—how many until we return? If we ever do—"

She released his arm, turned away a pace, and then back. "The processes of gestation and birth do not attract me. But I want to *see* a child of ours—and we have no zoom-wombs. So—"

"Of ours? A little while ago, you said—"

"Only if you refuse me—and that would be second-best."

After a moment, he grinned and embraced her. "Any idea where your gadget got mislaid to?"

"It is not mislaid—and the time is a week or more from

now. Still, it is a good time to release those flattened plastic tubes."

And when they had lain together, she said, "If we succeed, which do you choose to name?"

"Which what? You expecting twins or something?"

"Bran! No—male or female, you name one and I the other. It is fair—and I recall hearing that my parents did it so."

"Which named which, of you and Ivan?"

"They did not tell us that."

"Well, then—I choose the girl."

"And you would name her—what?"

"Let me think a little. And how about you? You have names picked already?"

"Yes. But not to influence you, I will tell you only the boy's." He waited, and she said, "David Tregare Kerguelen. David is for my father."

For a long moment he said nothing. Then, "I—I like that. And now, how about—Liesel Selene Moray?"

"Oh, Bran!" As she held him, she found no reason for her tears.

NOT at her first fertile period but at the second, Rissa conceived. When she was certain, she told Tregare. "And I am almost exactly two months behind Felcie—so in helping her I can learn what I will need to know."

"You've never been around babies at all?"

She shook her head. "In the Center the youngest girls I saw were perhaps three or four. And you?"

"Only Sparline—and I was still a toddler when she was born. But there'll be women here who can help you, give you advice."

"I am hardly acquainted with any groundside women. I have been too busy to socialize."

He thought a moment. "Haven't you met Eudyce Kobolak?"

"Briefly once—to speak to, only. Why?"

"Well—I forgot, but Stepan's asked us to dinner soon. Tomorrow night okay?"

After brief thought, she nodded. Tregare said, "Well, she's raised two. So if you hit it off—"

"I expect I shall like Stepan Kobolak's wife well enough."

• • •

EUDYCE KOBOLAK was as tall as her husband, but fair-skinned and thin in contrast to his dark complexion and stocky build. Her face was narrow. Above a high forehead, pale hair showing gray was cut very short in front; the rest she wore in a coiled braid. As she greeted Rissa and Tregare, her voice was soft. "Stepan is changing clothes. Our son and daughter will be a little late. Will you drink something?"

Tregare grinned. "Sure—thanks. Anything that pours."

"There is a native spirit—produced locally, I mean—that I've come to like. It's not really whiskey but they call it that. Do you know it?"

"I have tasted it," said Rissa. "Over ice it is very good."

Drinks poured, they sat and talked—of Earth, of Stronghold, of the differences between the worlds. Kobolak joined them, and soon the son and daughter entered—fraternal twins, nearly Rissa's age. Anders had his father's dark hair over a masculine version of his mother's face; Dacia—full-bodied with reddish hair and pixie features—resembled neither parent.

Dinner began—meat from a native herbivore, vegetables grown from Earthly seed. Rissa found some flavors different from what she had tasted before. "These seasonings are new to me, Eudyce—I like them very much."

"Thank you. It's native herbs. One of the women I work with—she's studied them, experimented, for years. I'll show you if you like."

"Show me, too," said Tregare. "Can't let her get ahead of me."

Like her voice, Eudyce Kobolak's laugh was soft. "Whatever you say."

The boy Anders, Rissa noticed, watched Tregare closely but never met his gaze. After a time Tregare frowned and said, "Something bothering you, Anders? Something about me, maybe?"

The boy's face reddened; he shook his head but said nothing.

Tregare scratched his chin. "You've been giving me the hawkeye all evening. No—" he waved a hand, "it's all right. I just want to know what's on your mind."

After a long pause Anders said, "Well, Captain Tregare—I

mean commandant—I'm glad to be here, see my father again after so long, but I've looked around—and I don't want to spend the rest of my life on Stronghold."

"I doubt you'll need to—you're young yet. But what's that to do with me?"

"You're moving against Earth—oh, everybody says so; they just don't know *when.*" *And so much,* thought Rissa, *for Security in this beehive!* "I want to go with you!"

Tregare looked to Stepan and Eudyce in turn, then back to Anders. "You're how old? Eighteen?" A nod. "Old enough to decide for yourself, then. But still I'd like to know how your parents feel about it."

Stepan said, "I'll miss you, son—again. But if it's what you want—"

Tregare looked at Eudyce. She said, "This would be—when?"

He shrugged. "*This* part, keep to yourselves—all right? Not sooner than two years—more likely, four and a bit."

Eudyce nodded. "I can guess why, but I won't. Well, Stepan? I think we can live with that; don't you?"

The boy's excitement showed. "Then I can go? Commandant—I can come with you?"

"Off duty, my name's Tregare. Phase out of whatever you're doing now—no loose ends; right? Meanwhile—" He paused. "Rissa, what have they renamed the *Saxbe?*"

She thought, then remembered. "It is now *Catclaw.*"

"Right. Anders—tomorrow you go to *Catclaw* and ask for Jamie Pescadore—*James* Pescadore. He's probably Second Hat—Second Officer—on her by now. Maybe First—I haven't kept track too well. Anyway—tell him I sent you and to tell his new skipper I want you trained for Third. You may end up serving elsewhere if *Catclaw's* fully officered, but that's where you'll train. Got it?"

Tregare looked at Kobolak. "The way I see it, any kid of yours is bound to be officer material."

The boy looked incredulous. "Third *Officer?*"

"If you qualify—all I'm giving you is the chance."

"Oh, *thanks,* commandant—I mean, Tregare."

"That's settled, then." Tregare raised his glass. "Let's drink to it."

For the first time in a while, Dacia spoke. "How about me?"

Her mother half-stood. "*You* want to go—to leave us—too?"

"I don't know yet. But if he can go to space, why can't I?"

Tregare laughed. "What have I let myself in for, here?" Again he looked to the parents. "All right if she tries it out, sees how she likes the training?"

Stepan nodded, not quickly; Eudyce turned to Rissa. "*You're* an officer, aren't you? On Tregare's ship?"

"Yes. And on three of the ships we came in, women command. *Not* as in UET."

"I see." Then, "Tregare? She would not be *committed* to go?"

"Course not—if she makes the grade she has her choice. For one thing, there'll be ships staying here—and they'll need officers, too."

"Then I agree. Not, as you say, that Dacia needs any permission."

"Then that's two drinks we have coming." In ceremonial fashion, Tregare sipped twice; the rest followed suit.

Dacia said, "Thanks, Tregare. Now who do *I* see, once I've cleared up the scut job I'm doing now?"

He turned to Rissa. "What do you think?"

"There is no need to think. Dacia, go to the ship *Valkyrie,* ask for Captain Zelde M'tana and tell her the same things Tregare told your brother to say."

Tregare said, "How did you decide between Zelde and Ilse?"

"This girl grew up free on Earth—no Academy, no Welfare Center—the word, Tregare, is *sheltered*. Zelde's life experience rubs off on her associates—and that may be as important as the formal training."

He grinned. "Now you spell it out, I don't see how I missed it myself."

Dinner ended; Eudyce said, "Rissa, I know ships' men and women don't segregate their discussions but I'd like to talk with you. Let's take some wine to my study." When the two were seated there, she said, "Tregare mentioned to Stepan that you and your friend—the truth field tech—are both into first preg. He didn't *say* you could use a friendly shoulder, but I thought perhaps—"

Rissa smiled. "You were right. I had wondered how to open the subject."

"Well, then—what is it you would like to know?"

"Everything, I suppose. My upbringing was not usual—unfortunately, on Earth it now *may* be." Briefly, not in detail, she outlined her early life. ". . . then, free of Welfare, in a certain place I was trained in many things—but not at all for what I now undertake. Of infants I know nothing."

Eudyce gave her gentle laugh. "Well, I know plenty. My two—I birthed them, nursed them, and sometimes cursed them. So—let me tell you a little about this whole baby business. To begin with . . ."

Rissa listened, asked questions and evaluated the answers. Eudyce Kobolak, she decided, should have been a teacher; she gave information in logical order, so that Rissa could see how one item related to the next. When Tregare looked in and said it was time to go, she thanked Eudyce and then said her goodbyes to the rest.

On the way home, she said, "We shall be good friends, she and I. She gives me confidence."

"Good. What do you think about both the kids signing on?"

"*If* they qualify, and make that choice. Well—they have capability. It is well that you give them the opportunity to test it."

THE next time Rissa visited Eudyce, Felcie Parager accompanied her. Over coffee, Felcie said, "It's not just the baby part that bothers me—I was up to here in babies, from when I still was one. I know it's different, most places. But on Number One, then, there were so many that if one died it was like somebody broke a dish—too bad but there's lots more." She turned to Rissa. "Well, *you* know—so many defectives—main thing was to find out what snicked it, and watch for it in the others. But any *one* baby—and no real parents for any of us—nobody could really care very much. Surprised me—it really did—to see how natural parents felt so different about their own. I was awfully young, see? And so—"

Eudyce shook her head. Her hair, loose today, shimmered with the motion. "I do find that hard to believe. Oh, I believe *you*, Felcie—it's the situation that's so incredible. But I can begin to see how it must have been."

Felcie leaned forward. "So the baby part's all snooky; noth-

ing shaken. It's the *parent* part—how do I learn to be one?"
She sighed. "Derek's never sired, that he knows of—Vanessa
Largane was pregging when UET killed her. If I can't do it
right—if something shakes with *his* child—I might just as well
cut my string. Not that *he—*"

Rissa took her hand. "You will do very well. There is time
to learn, and Eudyce will teach us both—will you not?"

"Well, I'll try to. But the fact that you're worried, Felcie—
that convinces me you won't be lax or careless."

"I hope not." Then, "Rissa, I liked the names you and
Tregare picked. That's another problem we had." Rissa's
brows raised; Felcie said, "You used names from both your
families. I don't *have* any—none of us zoom-wombers know
who we are, that way. I've always wished I did . . ."

Thinking of what Marco had said, how UET obtained its
ova, Rissa said to herself, *Be glad you do not know!* And
aloud, "But you have chosen names?"

"Finally we did. For a boy, Derek picked Arlen Limmer,
after his grandfather. Well, I'm Parager because the Paragers
mostly handled our creche, and I guess that's good enough. So
for a girl—I hope it's snooky with you—Rissa Parager."

Slowly, "I—am flattered. But why? I have done nothing—"

Felcie gestured. "I'd want her to be *like* you. Not like me—I
can't do anything really well—just a little of everything, well
enough to get by. But *you—*"

"Felcie—do not overestimate me. Please."

"I couldn't, ever. In the duel ring—Eudyce, do you know
about that?" And over Rissa's protests, Felcie told of the
killfight with Stagon dal Nardo.

Eudyce shook her head. "Rissa, you amaze me. How—?"

"Two factors won that duel for me." She explained her advantage in newer combat techniques, then the stress reaction
that stretched time for her. She shrugged. "The condition is
somewhat rare but not unique to me."

"Well!" Eudyce made a lopsided grin. "I can still learn
something new, it seems. Five years late, I owe Dacia an
apology. There was an emergency; she saved herself. When
she told us how, I thought she was making it up—but it was
much like what *you've* said."

Rissa's eyes narrowed. "Does Anders have it too?"

"I don't know. Why?"

"Then perhaps Dacia is best equipped, of the two, to go to space. Not that the phenomenon is necessary for that, of course."

Felcie spoke. "Does Tregare have it?"

"Somewhat, I think—perhaps more than he realizes. I cannot be sure."

Eudyce said, "At any rate—Rissa, I've *liked* you, and knew you were capable. But now I see what matched you up with a fire eater like Tregare."

Before Rissa could answer, Felcie said, "That wedding! You never saw anything like it. Right there in the duel ring—Rissa looking like what was left after the bushstompers stampeded, and—"

"Felcie—perhaps I should commission you to write my biography." Laughter.

WITH Felcie operating the truth field and Ivan the polygraph, Rissa and Tregare had experimented—learning how to set hypnotic triggers to protect persons against UET's investigations. With their first success—Terrell Ragan was the subject—they stopped work for the day and celebrated. As time passed, they improved their methods and results, checking under different conditions and after time-lapse, to see how well the protection held.

"Once the programming's in," said Tregare, "it holds up. But I wish I knew why it works perfectly on some—and not at all on others."

Ivan shrugged. "We're new at it. For now, we'll just have to use people it *does* work on."

For they were choosing a crew, preparing a ship to go to Earth, there to learn and to infiltrate. Reluctantly, Terrell Ragan changed *Loose Goose* back to *Trujillo*—for his was the ship chosen.

His crew—by necessity, but also fitting established UET procedure—came from several ships. Some were from the newest arrivals, but most had served on Stronghold. Rissa put each through a final check—all was well, for each tested solidly loyal to Tregare in normal circumstances and equally loyal to UET when the simulated situation required it. And the triggers, the knowledge of them—all was buried under at least three levels of code words.

At last Tregare showed satisfaction. "All right, Ragan. You're ready to lift tomorrow?"

"Yes. The reports are all ready and will pass inspection?"

"Falsified perfectly, I think. Korbeith—doped to the gills—gave his gravel laugh more than once when he signed them. So while I was at it I had him sign and thumbprint a stack of blank forms—just in case."

"Did he do the taped parts all right?"

"Some took several tries—dope and hypnosis mix him up a lot. But we did get them."

"Good," said Ragan. He asked a few more questions; then he and Tregare shook hands and he went to his ship.

And next morning the *Trujillo* lifted for Earth. Seeing its wake dwindle, Tregare said, "Rissa—I do hope we know the hell what we're doing!"

THE arming of ships neared completion. Two contingents went into space, where Limmer trained them in squadron maneuvers. So it was that when Felcie's labor began, a week early, he was absent.

Rissa sat with Felcie in Derek's stead, her hands aching in the girl's fierce grip as the pains came. Afterward she answered the dazed questions: "Arlen is of proper size and appearance, and if his appetite were any greater we might worry about Stronghold's food reserves." Felcie's unsure smile came stronger; Rissa patted her cheek. "Sleep now."

WHEN Felcie was, as Tregare said, "fully operational" again, the two families dined together. Afterward, nursing Arlen, Felcie said, "Isn't he a pretty one, though? Just like Derek, except the hair and skin a little lighter."

Without thinking, Rissa said, "Yes. I had always wanted to see how he looked, before—" Wide-eyed she clapped hand to mouth. "Oh, Derek! I did not mean—"

The scarred lips smiled; he shook his head. "As Felcie says, nothing shaken. Sure—I used to be bitter. But maybe you've noticed—since Felcie accepted me, and you two the same, a lot—it doesn't matter any more. I don't think of myself as—what did Peralta say that time?—a gargoyle, that's it. No—I'm just good old Derek Limmer, with one hell of a fine wife!"

His attempt to fend off Rissa's kiss was not wholly convincing.

RISSA'S own time neared. Striving for the best physical condition, she remained as active as she could, as long as possible. When she asked Tregare about medical arrangements—her doctor, the same who had tended Felcie, was abed himself with a persistent virus infection—her husband said, "Our ships' medics aren't the best for this sort of thing. I've checked around—there's two choices. Old Noridas used to be tops, but he's old and getting shaky. The other one—Correval—I don't know if we can trust him. He's a hundred percent UET, and living in medium-security detention."

She thought about it. "Let us speak with Correval and then decide."

TELIS CORREVAL—large, pale, approaching biological middle age—sat stiffly before the commandant's desk. "You're opposed to me," Tregare said. "I accept that." The man nodded. "You'll agree, Correval, that I allow your people as much comfort as I can reasonably provide?" Another nod. "The question is, can I trust you with my wife and our baby?"

"I hear that you make your own decisions. So make this one."

For a moment, Rissa thought Tregare would kill him out of hand. But, "All right—you won't make things easy, so we'll do it your way. I don't like playing tyrant but you force me. Here's how it is—if you preside at this birth, any harm that comes to woman or child you'll suffer yourself, many times over. While you live." He waited while Correval blinked, looked up and then away. "With that understanding—do you take the job or don't you?"

"And what if I don't?" Rissa thought, *I do hate a whiner —but maybe I need him.*

"If you don't," said Tregare, "nothing. Just back to the routine."

"No punishment?"

"No." When the man did not answer, Tregare said, "Well? Which is it?"

Slowly, pouting, Correval nodded. "I'll do it."

And when he had left under guard, Tregare said, "Are we doing the right thing?"

Rissa shrugged. "Even hate could not give that man the courage to defy you. But I wish we had a better one."

LYING belly-swollen, undignified, on the table, mind slowed by the injected sedative, Rissa waited. The contractions had come upon her prematurely; she had tried to call Tregare but could only leave word for him. *Felcie was early, too—does travel close to light-speed affect the body's clocks?*

Her body clenched again; she tried to do as Eudyce had instructed her. She heard someone—the man handling the anesthesia—say, "Dr. Correval! You've set this, on the card, at only half what she needs!"

"I'm in charge." Even commanding, the man's voice whined.

"But—"

Peripherally she saw Correval grasp the other's wrist. "Listen! This is Tregare's bitch! I don't dare harm her or the child—nothing that would show—but I can make her hurt, and I'm going to! When Tregare arrives, he'll be just in time to see her writhing and screaming—and no fault of *mine,* you see? But all that I can hurt both of them, I will! And don't interfere—or *Korbeith* will hear of it."

This cannot be real! But it was—before Tregare arrived and long after. The drugs in her blood blocked coherent speech; she said only his name. Pain grew until death-fear slowed her time and made the ordeal endless—but grimly she refused to scream, to writhe, to show her agony in any way she could avoid.

And finally it was over, the baby out of her and lying on her flaccid belly. With effort, she smiled at Tregare and carefully mouthed a few words. "Who—who is it, Bran?"

His grin stretched his lips. "Say hello to Liesel Selene Moray."

She did, and he kissed her. Her mind came clearer; she said, "Get Noridas. I want him to check me—what was done, whether it is all right."

CORREVAL was gone; others tended her. Old Noridas found

some work done not to his taste, and corrected it. Tregare looked questions but she shook her head and did not answer. "It will be all right, Bran."

Eventually she and "Lieselene" returned home. To Tregare she reported nothing. But when she was healed and could exercise again, she went—in Tregare's absence and without his permission—to the detention quarters of Telis Correval. Using a master key, she entered without knocking and found Correval lounging in an easy chair.

She moved quickly to stand over him. "You need not rise."

"What—what do you want?" His lips twitched, sneering.

"I have learned from you, Correval. Now *you* will learn." Axlike, her hand's edge chopped; too late to catch the spurting blood, Correval's hands went to his smashed nose.

"Lesson one: do not boast in the presence of one you have denied adequate anesthesia. Such patients still hear—and remember." She struck again, jarring the protecting hands; Correval whimpered.

"Lesson two: do not give pain to one connected with Bran Tregare." She pulled one bloody hand away, chopped to the clavicle, and felt it snap. The sound the man made, she could not classify.

"Lesson three: whatever else, do not think to victimize Rissa Kerguelen." He gestured feebly; the flattened nose was unprotected, but her slashing hand had no mercy.

When he could stop his screaming—a wet, spongy sound —he mouthed words she could barely understand. "Why not just kill me? *He* will. Go away—you've done enough."

She sat on the arm of his chair. "I have told Tregare nothing—but perhaps I have not begun, with you. We will see."

"What—?"

"Now we come to the real point of this meeting." She took one hand and twisted its wrist just short of breaking. "If you wish your hands to be fit to hold a broom, let alone a scalpel, you will tell me why it is that anyone on Stronghold should fear Arger Korbeith."

The answers were not long in coming.

"HE'S got his own Underground going? Rissa—how did you find this out? And what were you doing, running around when you're still supposed to be resting a lot?"

She thought. "Bran—if I tell you, will you consent that I settle my own scores? For I have done so."

He nodded, but before it was done she had to shout against him, until he would agree that Telis Correval remain alive. He still glowered as he said, "And you wouldn't tell me about it, would you? You had to do it all yourself, when you're not really back to scratch yet."

"If I had told you, you would have killed him. And we would not know the machinations of Arger Korbeith."

"Yeah—there's that. Sounds as if he's got quite a network building. You got any ideas?"

"If I see this rightly, Bran, it is simple. He works by intimidating the lesser prisoners who serve him."

"So?"

"Isolate him—in a separate section, and served by our own free people."

"Yeah. And first chance we get, interview that old bastard again."

"Both of us? Then not immediately. This day *has* drained me."

SITTING quietly, nursing Lieselene, one hand caressing the dark-fleeced head, Rissa wondered about herself. Sane persons were consistent in their behavior, were they not? But here, now, she was all gentleness, all love and tender feelings—and three days earlier, with Correval, she had been totally ruthless and even sadistic. How could these things be reconciled?

She shrugged. At all times she was herself—that would have to do. When Tregare came home, Lieselene was asleep and Rissa welcomed the chance to indulge another facet of herself—it was not long since passion had again become permissible.

ARGER KORBEITH flexed his oversized hands as if planning to take Tregare's neck in one and Rissa's in the other. *And probably he is—but he cannot do it.*

Tregare said, "We haven't pulled your group in yet, Korbeith, but we've got it pretty well pegged. A little while longer . . ."

"You're crazy, always were. They'll get me out of here. Takes a little time."

Tregare laughed. "But you're not here, Korbeith—far as your troops know, you're still in charge of your conspiracy. Oh, the double's not all that good, for voice—so you've got a cold, and we've dubbed in some tapes for viewscreen contacts. But give another ten days, your kite's down."

In his chair, Korbeith straightened; behind the yellow overtinge his heavy features showed ruddy. "No guts—never had any! Ship to ship—how about that? Just you and me, Tregare! I can take you—always could."

Rissa saw her man go taut. She said, "He wants a chance he has not earned. Do not be foolish."

"I—he—I *feared* him. A chance to wipe that out—"

"You'll never do it!" Harsh cackle. "Snotnose Tregare! Always will be."

"Bran!"

"Not now, Rissa—this is *mine*. Now just a minute, Korbeith—let me think."

"All the cowards say that, trying to wiggle off the hook. Yes, *think*—for what good it does you."

Rissa did not find Tregare's laugh convincing. "You wouldn't know, Korbeith—UET did all your thinking for you. But *I've* thought now, and I'll tell you."

"Speak up, snotnose!"

Tregare began a word then shook his head, scowling. "No—I fought free of that shitbag; you won't talk me back into it. You like that kind of talk—if I'm snotnose, you're the snot. Stupid, *stupid*—that's all UET is or ever was. And you're a damned good example."

"Tell me your terms, you were going to. What's your wait?"

Rissa saw Tregare hesitate. "Figuring. I can't waste ships —forget *that* big idea."

"No guts. I always knew it. Should have spaced you. I—"

"*All right!*" Tregare turned to Rissa. "Sorry—I *have* to do this, for myself." Then, to Korbeith, "Armed scoutships is the best I can do. Suit you?"

"I can inspect? I get my choice?"

"Yes."

Korbeith laughed. "Have to, then, I guess. But on top of all else, Tregare, you're *cheap*!"

Drawing breath, Tregare shuddered. "Sure. Look who's giving you a chance you couldn't make for yourself." And before Korbeith could reply. "When I've killed you, I'll be a whole person. Take that thought with you, when it happens."

As they left, Rissa said, "Bran? Are you sure you can win?"

"Of course not."

"Then why—?"

"I—you heard—I *have* to."

"UET's mark on you—it runs that deep?"

"Maybe—but there's more to it, than that."

Until they reached their quarters, he said no more. There he poured himself a drink, raised his eyebrows, and at her nod poured for her also. When both were seated, she said, "Will you tell me?"

"All right. When Korbeith talks about spacing me—wishing he had, back then—I suppose you take it for bluster?" He shook his head. "It's not. Standard practice, on UET ships— if a new cadet wasn't measuring up, out the airlock, as an example for the rest."

"Bran!" Until she felt the pain, she did not realize her hand was to her mouth, teeth biting knuckles.

"Oh, it was rare on most ships—the threat was enough, and knowing it *had* happened. But Korbeith—every trip, at least three!" He gulped half his drink, turned and poured more.

"Every few days, the lineup. All cadets—stripped, male and female alike—in the corridor by the airlock. Korbeith going down the line, two guards with him—stop and look at you, move on—and *maybe* jerk his thumb back. *That* one, he'd say, and just keep moving. And then—"

"Bran—you need not relive this, now—you—"

"Let me finish! The first time—a girl, it was—the guards grabbed her. I *saw!* Her eyes rolled up in her head and her legs shook—they started dragging her to the lock—and—and—she *pissed* herself. And worse—spewing, both ends—that's when Korbeith started laughing. That goddamned gravel laugh of his—the last thing she heard before they threw her in the airlock and opened it to space!"

He wiped sweat from his forehead. "They had a camera on her, when the vacuum hit and the air blew her outside. And still on her, dead, turning and tumbling. They marched us up, naked still, to view the tape—over and over, until *we'd* puked enough to suit Arger Korbeith, and then cleaned up our mess, and hers."

Rissa could not speak; she waited. Tregare said, "That was the first one; there were four more, on that trip. And every time, even the ones when he let us all stay alive, I expected it to be *me!*"

His face was pale, his grin a parody. "Now do you see why I have to kill him in combat?"

She reached for his hand; it trembled but soon steadied. "I see why you must—but I wish it were not so."

"All right." Now his voice was brisk. "One more thing—in case I lose, you'll have to—"

"I?" She shook her head. "No, Bran—I will not carry out the plan, to move on Earth and oust UET. If your captains wish to do so, well and good. But just as you have your imperatives, so have I my own. I would take one ship—I believe I have earned that much—and return to Number One with our daughter and any friends who wish to accompany me. There I would tend to the raising of the three children who wait in the Hatchery. And that is *all* I would do." She paused. "Except, of course, to see to the death of Arger Korbeith."

Long he looked at her. "You mean that, don't you?"

"When will you realize I mean *everything* I say?"

Scowling, he said, "I know you do. It's just that I *have* to do this thing."

RISSA watched the viewscreen. Side by side, two scoutcraft stood. Neither carried official names, but one bore the insigne *UET Forever* and the other, *The Hell You Say*.

Dust rose; the scouts prepared to lift. Rissa's breath caught —how could she *stand* it—the battle in space and no way of knowing its results until one vessel returned?

Then as both began to rise, *The Hell You Say* tipped to the side and rammed *UET Forever*—the two fell, rolled, and came to rest. A hooded figure emerged from one and clambered up and into the other. A few minutes later the man reappeared; blood stained his coverall. Others ran to meet him, and now Rissa could gauge his comparative size.

It is Tregare! Rissa watched no further; she was hungry, and so was Lieselene.

• • •

SOME of Tregare's bandages showed bloodstains. "Bran! Your injuries—are they serious?"

"The cuts? No. What you *can't* see—some bruises—they're what hurts. Korbeith—it was like being hit with a maul."

"Then you have done for him?"

"Yeah. You want to hear about it?"

"The details of his execution, no. But I was most impressed by your strategy at takeoff."

He grinned. "Yes—well, while we waited the signal, the idea struck me. The bastard called me cheap—so I figured I'd show him what cheap *meant*!"

"I do not understand."

"If we'd fought in space, at least one of those scouts would be total junk—and maybe both. This way, neither's damaged much. I've already got repair crews on them."

"I see." She frowned. "Tregare—I do not criticize you— but had you not promised to fight the man in space?"

"No. I thought back, exactly what I'd said—armed scouts, was all. Not a word about space. Well, my scout got his, right? And boarding is good traditional navy tactics—even if not much used these days."

Her brow cleared. "Very good, Bran. And—and I am glad I did not have so long to wait, and worry of you."

"Worry? About *me*?" Now he could laugh. He came to her. "Hug me gentle, Rissa—I think Korbeith cracked some ribs."

IN Tregare's office, Korbeith's gangling "double" rubbed his face. "Glad to be done with it, Tregare. Ticklish job—expected my throat cut any day. And that makeup—damned uncomfortable."

Rissa chuckled. The man looked at her; she said, "You still speak in his patterns."

"Oh. Take me a while—I mean, *it will* take me a while, to get over that."

"Sure," said Tregare. "Now—these twenty-eight names— they're all you know of, who were in it with him?"

"May—*there* may be more." Self-conscious now, the man spoke slowly, carefully. "*I* didn't hear of any; there might be a few, though."

"All right—we'll find out. Thanks, Cardinger; you did a good job. Take a few days off now, if you want—say, four, not counting today."

"I will—and thanks, commandant."

The tall man left, and Tregare called in his guards officer. "Here's a list. Have these people picked up from detention— quietly, one at a time—and brought over for truth field questioning. Keep them isolated from each other before *and* after the interviews."

"Yes, sir. Anything else?"

"Uh—yes, there is. The prisoners shouldn't have heard, yet, that Korbeith's dead. See that no one tells them."

When the man had gone, Tregare said, "The field hasn't been used since Felcie last adjusted it—right?"

"That is correct," said Rissa.

"Then you and I can run the thing ourselves."

QUESTIONING produced seven more names; Tregare interviewed those persons also. At the end of it, he said, "Of the lot, five were purely scared into it. Three more I'm not sure about, so they get max security just like the hardcores." He stood. "Now it's time to announce their boss's death."

"Do you think the more fanatical ones will believe you?"

"They will when they see his head on a stick."

AT times, the restrictions of motherhood galled Rissa. She loved the baby fiercely, protectively. She did not mind waking for night feedings. But the new limits to her freedom she found hard to accept.

She and Felcie took turns caring for both children, and occasionally Eudyce Kobolak sat for the two of them. But not until Arlen and Lisele—her new, shorter nickname—were crawling, would Rissa and Felcie entrust them to anyone else.

Felcie showed no sign of discontent. "How do you do it?" Rissa asked her. "You are accustomed to as much freedom as I, yet you go along cheerfully, most of your time taken by one or both children's needs. After all your worry beforehand, I think you are a better parent than I am."

"I don't know, Rissa—as soon as Arlen was born it just

seemed natural." She paused. "Does Tregare know you're chafing? What does he say?"

Rissa shook her head firmly. "He does not know and you must not tell him. Bran has never said he told me so, about *anything*—and I do not intend that he have the opportunity!"

"Are you—you're not *sorry,* are you?"

Rissa looked at Lisele, busy chewing the ear of a stuffed animal and at the same time trying to pull its legs off. She smiled. "No—never that. It is merely that there is no time to do many things I wish to do. And then I feel guilty about resenting this—resenting time spent with *Lisele,* who is so precious to me. Do you see?"

"I think everybody feels that way sometimes. Rissa—you worry too much."

"Perhaps. Certainly, in the past, I was well trained to worry. Except that then, it was called forethought . . ."

AT the far side of a tillable plain below Stronghold fortress, at the edge of desert, minimum- and medium-security prisoners erected prefabricated quarters for themselves. When construction was finished, a training program began. As Tregare had promised, those persons became farm laborers.

Seeing the facilities, Rissa asked, "And where are the guards quartered?"

Tregare shook his head. "No guards 'way out here—just back at Stronghold itself."

"These, then—they can escape?"

"To where? Coming near the base in prison clothes without a pass, that's an easy way to get shot. And it's a long haul going around, up through the hills on either side, to reach country anyone could live off. I don't patrol there—in case of an escape it's simple enough to send a couple of squads out. Or maybe, not even bother."

"But one could carry food—I saw, you store great amounts here for them. Even across the desert, perhaps—a strong person—"

"Across the desert I don't give a damn—they'd never get back, anyway. But food's not the catch."

"Oh?" She waited.

"Water—water fit to drink, that won't kill you. I have each

day's supply brought out the day before. And distributed—everybody has a two-day canteen so nobody runs dry." She began to speak but he waved a hand. "Nobody's going out carrying more than one, either. Because if you don't have your own, with your name on it, you don't get your water."

Rissa shuddered. "It seems—so grim." She looked around. "But you have arranged that your guardless prison is comfortable enough."

"Sure. Why not? These people aren't safe to let run loose on base and I want good work out of them. So I give them decent living—here, where it's damned near impossible to get away."

"Still—it must be a monotonous life."

"Anybody wants out, it's easy. Ask to ride the water truck in to base, you get a pass that same day. Then it's up to the truth field."

After a time, Rissa nodded. "I find no fault with this planning, Tregare."

ARLEN LIMMER'S first birthday—by Earth time—had been celebrated; Lisele Moray's was not far off. It was then that the next UET fleet was detected, nearly a month ahead of "schedule."

Changed names or no, sixteen of Tregare's ships still bore UET insignia. While the rest lifted, these stayed aground. Of the departing ships, Tregare said, "Just like before—out of sight, but in distance if needed. Now we wait."

The incoming fleet numbered ten; three bore weapons. Tregare had elaborated on his previous methods: "Squads in Committee Police uniforms board each ship and pull the plug on its drive," he said. "Then we bring the personnel out—small groups—in our own good time, for questioning."

Rissa frowned. "May not this tactic cause tension? Trouble?"

"The line you used when *we* landed—remember?" She shook her head, so he quoted, "The Presiding Committee has so ordered."

THE ships landed. Busy, and with no viewscreen near to hand,

Rissa did not see what happened. Home again, she found Tregare talking with Zelde M'tana. "Some trouble," he said. "Could have been big, but wasn't. Tell her, Zelde."

The tall woman's glass—straight spirits, Rissa guessed, except for one small piece of ice—was half-empty. Her wide grin emphasized the swollen bruise over one cheekbone. She said, "Second ship I boarded, somebody got the itch—took off before we got to the drive. So we fought upship and took Control. Tried not to kill any unarmed—but at a time like that you can't be too nice about things."

"And so then," said Rissa, "you brought the ship down?"

"Not so quick as that. The Committee Police aboard got desperate and began arming the crew to storm us. In tough like that, I flip a coin in my head. It came up take the chance, so I did." She took a full-throated gulp. "I'm running dry, Tregare." He poured the large glass full again.

"The chance?" said Rissa. "What was it?"

"I broke all the rules and told the *truth*. On the horn, all over the ship—that Stronghold is Tregare's and that we were his people." She shook her head. "I thought I'd seen some fighting—but when *those* folks started, between themselves—"

"And UET lost. But what a risk—if they had *won*! A ship escaping us, with *that* news . . ."

"You don't get it," said Tregare. "Zelde still held Control. If UET had won, she'd have crashed the ship—right into this planet." He took one of Rissa's hands and one of Zelde M'tana's. "Why the hell you suppose she needs such a big drink right now?"

EARTH'S Underground still had a hand in UET's truth field operation—barely twenty percent of fleet personnel, largely officers and Police, were hardcore UET adherents. Using the techniques that Ivan had suggested to test Terrell Ragan, several hypnotically programmed Underground representatives were discovered.

But from Earth the news was sparse; in the two years between departure of one fleet and the next, little of importance had happened.

"The major change," said Rissa, "is that UET no longer

pretends to appoint the Committee—the Committee *owns* UET. And the occasional vacancies, as often as not, are created by assassination.''

Tregare said, ''Stagon dal Nardo would feel right at home.''

''Must worlds be governed so?'' Rissa shuddered. ''Bran— perhaps I am not, as I had hoped, done with killing.''

He did not answer. She said, ''Bran, what do you think of?''

''Whether we could go to Earth with what we have.''

''THE trouble is,'' he said at next day's conference, ''we can't leave Stronghold bare of ships. Too risky—next fleet from Earth would smell the biggest rat you ever saw.'' He grinned. ''You know—I'm having second thoughts about the Shrakken ships.''

''I sees no way to use them,'' said Raoul Vanois. ''You has a thought, there?''

Rissa saw Tregare shake off irritation at the man's lapse into dialect. ''Local defense,'' Tregare said. ''Wouldn't have to remodel too much—just Control and a few bunks. Full arming, of course—but we've got that down to routine.''

''We've plenty of UET ships' names to spare for them,'' said Ilse Krueger. ''I like that idea.''

''Another I like,'' Limmer said, ''is what Zelde suggested. Remember, Tregare? Heft up every scoutship to carry one full-sized ship's projector—and use them for action, not just for scouting.''

Tregare nodded. ''The need, near Earth, would be local and fast—no fuel problem. And we have—how many, Rissa?''

''Including your own, twenty-five.''

Limmer slapped the table. ''In terms of projectors, only, the equivalent of six ships!'' He looked across the stack of planning sheets. ''Tregare! You want to go with it?''

''Peace knows it's tempting, Derek. But—you mind if we kick it around first, try to spot all the strings?''

''Sure—sure. Anything special you have in mind?''

''We have sent only one ship to Earth,'' said Rissa. ''To follow UET's routine and avoid suspicion, we must send an- other—long before we can be prepared to go, ourselves.''

''Leaving us what?'' Limmer said.

Tregare squinted, then nodded. ''Thirty-seven, plus the two

Shrakken. But the minimum to leave *here*—I can't figure it less than four, to match or top the armed ships in the next load from Earth. And even so—we'll need a good story, if we expect UET to bite on *that* hook."

"Peralta's trick!" At Tregare's frown, Hilaire Gowdy said, "No—not *that* one. I forget the planet and the details don't matter—but UET was coming, armed, and we couldn't get off in time to miss them completely. So he had the crew build a dummy hull—crude job, fabric over a wood and wire framework."

She grinned. "He fooled UET—not that it has any bearing on *this* case—by putting our spare emitter in the dummy, with a timer. When it went off, it made a *beautiful* ionized dustcloud, exactly like a ship starting to lift. So UET blew hell out of the dummy—and we got away clean."

Tregare shook his head. Gowdy said, "You don't like it?"

"I like it fine; let's build six. Hilaire—you're in charge—okay?" He paused, then said, "I was just thinking, there—what a damned shame that Jimar Peralta couldn't wait for command."

THE second ship—the *Committee's Pride,* which for a time had been renamed *Committee's Fall*—left for Earth. *De facto,* Coryle Hagenau commanded—but since UET allowed women no rank above First Officer, *de jure* command would go to Rocklin Caine when the ship neared Earth.

Again Tregare voiced misgivings. Rissa squeezed his arm and said, "Bran—we *have* to send these ships. And the hypnotic protection is as perfect as we can make it—you saw that."

"Yeah." He grinned. "Well, this cooks it."

"What do you mean, Bran?"

"We *have* to go before we're due to send another ship. Because I don't have enough forms left, with Arger Korbeith's prints and signature, for another load of fake reports!"

ARMING the scouts was simpler than arming full-sized ships. No aiming controls were needed; the pilot aimed the scout itself, and its smaller computer had only to rule on that aiming and on range—convergence and heterodyning.

Relaxing at day's end, Tregare said, "The programming's tricky. The smaller projectors—the ones we're replacing—didn't have those features."

"Then they could not," said Rissa, "have been very effective." She paused. "Yet at Base Two yours seemed powerful enough."

"Against groundside, sure—look what Peralta did with maybe one-tenth power, at Base One. These projectors we're pulling out carry about four times that. But against ships, forget it. Besides, scouts' guns have fixed convergence—apertures set closer together to make a skinnier angle, so the range isn't so critical—fairly short range, at that. And fixed heterodyne. Adding the extra control circuits is what takes most of the time."

"And what about training?"

"Two scouts set up for simulations; Limmer's feeding the programs from *Lefthand Thread*. His computer tech's cussing a lot—he thought the change from turret to scout aiming would be easier to program."

"And you need monitor feedback to control the firing."

"Right—that wasn't too hard, though. Anyway, the job's in good hands." He poured his second drink of the day. "Where's Lisele? With Felcie?"

"No, she's napping. I had Arlen here; the two kept each other awake longer than usual. Now she catches up on her rest."

"She really goes, that kid. I hope she wakes up for a while—I don't see enough of her."

"When we are in space your time will be more your own."

Tregare frowned. "Yes—but I've been thinking about that."

Guessing what was to come, Rissa waited. He looked at her, then said, "I still don't feel right about it—taking Lisele to Earth this way. Listen—what if we *lost*?"

"You would *leave* her—all those years? And if we lost, UET would come here and exact its revenge; she would be none the safer."

As he shook his head, his impatience was evident. "UET's lost Stronghold for all time. Think about it—five more fleets in the pipeline for Limmer to snap up before we reach Earth. And *if* we lose there, how many ships will UET lose in the doing? They wouldn't have a lot left, is my guess."

"But the *time,* Bran—the child separated from us—"

"Let me get to my main point—which has nothing to do with Stronghold. It's Ivan's idea, by the way. We leave one scout unchanged, UET standard. We drop it free, three months' decel time from Earth. A scout's long-term deceleration is about half that of a ship—so *we* get there six weeks ahead of it, and get the shooting over with before it arrives."

"And Lisele is aboard it? But, Bran—what if we have lost?"

"The scout's apparently UET—remember? A gang of UET loyalists that got off with a ship, hoping to warn Earth, but were caught—well, where we let the scout off. Ship blown up—only these few escaped. All protected by hypnotic triggers, of course—and Lisele with a false ID as well." He waited. "Can you buy the idea?"

"I—am not sure. Her young mind, muddled with hypnotism?"

"Not muddled, damn it! Was Terrell Ragan muddled? Just a few implants for her own protection. And set to erase completely when one of *us*—and maybe a few more key people, in case our side wins but we don't, personally—says the right words."

"And if we have lost, Bran? What of Lisele then, in UET hands? What hypnosis will keep her out of Total Welfare?"

He grinned. "Arger Korbeith's granddaughter? He had a son—my reports to Earth show him married instead of dead. It fits like a glove."

"You would have her raised to be one of *them*?"

"*If* she has to live in UET's world, it might as well be on the best terms we can manage. So—what do you say?"

She looked down at her clasped hands, then up again. "Bran—I will think about it. But if I do not agree—?"

He stood. "If you *insist,* Rissa, Lisele goes with us, live or die. But I want—like all hell I want it—to avoid that risk."

She went to him. "Yes—I understand. Do you understand how *I* feel?"

They held each other, kissed, and then leaned away enough to see each other clearly. "I think so. You grew up to depend only on yourself. You did your own fighting—and then some of mine, too. So now you feel you have to do it all. But you forget one thing—UET isn't Stagon dal Nardo. Or Jimar Peralta, for that matter. You *can't* deal with it, alone."

"No." She moved away and sat again. "Bran? Who would be in charge of the scout? Whom would I be trusting with Liesel Selene?"

"I was thinking of Dacia Kobolak. That suit you?"

"Dacia? She does well, then? She says nothing of her training."

"She wouldn't, until she's sure she's made it. Well, she has —but it won't hurt her to keep sweating right down to the end of the string. She'll learn more, that way."

For the first time, Rissa smiled. "Unfeeling though it sounds, you are probably right. And you have almost convinced me. But still—may I think on it further?"

"There's no hurry. Ivan's starting hypnotic indoctrination on the scout's crew, but either way it won't be wasted—I've got a couple of other good ideas for that kind of decoy, if we don't need it for Lisele."

She laughed, and he said, "What's that all about?"

"Your Hulzein genes—as your mother said, *everything* a Hulzein does serves many purposes."

"Oh? I can think of something, right now, that wouldn't. Unless you're too hungry."

Deliberately she paused, then smiled and said, "No—our dinner can wait a bit."

BEFORE dawn, one morning, the viewscreen sounder woke them. Tregare scrambled out of bed. "That's alarm mode!"

Rissa followed him. The screen lit, showing a frightened face. "A ship—it's UET's, not scheduled. Refuses to land without talking to the commandant first. I've programmed enough missiles—I can blast it if it stays close enough—I—"

"Loosen your string, man!" Tregare shook his head, rubbed a knuckle across his eyes, blinking. "This ship give a name?"

"Yes—the *Hoover*. That's a fast one, you know—if it runs we'll never catch it. Wait—it's coming closer—I'd better fire!"

"Hold it, you damned fool! That's Bernardez—he's *ours*."

"But—"

"Do as I say! First, put me through to the *Hoover*."

"Are you sure, sir?"

"I'm sure you've worked your last shift on that job if you don't get your ass cracking. Now *move!*"

The picture wavered, dissolved; then another's face appeared. The image shook and jiggled, colors shifting continually, but Rissa saw a ruddy, bearded man with bushy hair. Was it brown? Probably, she thought.

Tregare shouted, "Bernardez! Tregare here—and all's solid at Stronghold."

Circuit distortion could not disguise the deep chuckle. "Well, now—it's good to hear that. Your tame rabbit who first answered me—I had to stay loose, ready to dodge—the way his shoulders twitched I knew he was playing with the shoot-down button. Hey, now—Tregare, man, it's good to see you—even though on this thing I hardly can't."

"Good to see you, too. Just a minute now—*you in the middle of this,* give Captain Bernardez proper landing instructions. Set him alongside *Inconnu,* to your—let's see—to your left. Got it?"

Subdued now, the voice said, "Yes, commandant. Understood and executing."

"Right after this," said Tregare. "Bernardez? I'm coming to greet you personally."

On the screen, heavy slanting brows lifted. "Well, I should purely hope so." A laugh. "Last one there buys the drinks."

The screen blanked; Tregare turned away and began dressing. "You want to come along, this time of night? I think you'll like Bernardez."

Half-dressed already, Rissa said, "I think I already do. I would not miss this reunion." Then she paused. "Oh—but what of Lisele?"

"She'll be—no, you're right; we *don't* leave her alone. So— I was thinking to reunion aboard the *Hoover,* but I'll bring him here instead. All right?"

"Yes. I will make myself presentable and set out glasses and —how many bottles?"

Halfway out the door, he turned. "A lot. And—no, we'll call Derek later. He'll hate to miss any of it, but one household's enough to wake up while it's still dark." The door closed and he was gone.

•   •   •

WHEN he returned, he said, "Liesel and Hawkman came along all right, in freeze. I have his letter; we'll get to it in a little while." He gestured toward the man beside him. "Right now, I want you to meet one thirsty ship's captain."

The brown hair and beard showed some gray, but Bernardez moved like an athlete and his deep voice was vibrant. "Tregare's been telling me about you—and you needn't deny it, because I always discount everything he says."

"In this case, don't," said Tregare. "I broke all the rules and told the straight truth." He poured glasses full and handed them around.

Under Bernardez's gaze, Rissa felt somehow impaled. She said, "I hope it is well that Tregare tells truth of me. He has told me little of yourself." She raised her brows and waited, silent, her stare holding his.

He blinked first, and said, "All right—I'll tell you my deepest, darkest secret—Rissa Kerguelen, proscribed on Earth and earned it rightly." *Bran trusts this man wholly.* "Do you find it believable that an Escaped Ship—one of Tregare's own —is captained by *Cecil* Bernardez?"

She saw the amusement in his face. "You do not, I gather, use your given name in daily activities?"

She waited until his laughter came. "Well, it did make life difficult for a time—until I beat the grudging bejooks out of my Second Hat for calling the *Hoover* the *Cecil B.* But once he was again fit for duty—though not entirely of his original appearance, mind you—somehow I was spared that sort of harassment."

"Well, I'd think so," said Tregare. "But, Bernardez—you said you had serious news?"

Bernardez's smile straightened. He said, "I could have used another drink before telling you, but here it is. They got Malloy."

Tregare half-rose. "UET? *How?*"

"At Johnson's Walk, his message drop. I know because I stopped there, coming from Number One—that's what took me so long, the extra decel and accel time. Well, UET had two ships at the Walk—just stopping over, nothing special—and Malloy came in careless. Didn't even bother, on a colony world—or else forgot, is more like it—to paint on his old UET insigne. What was it, now?"

Tregare shook his head. "I don't remember. The first I ever

heard, Malloy had already renamed it *Pig in the Parlor*." He drank. "So—what happened?"

"He landed, you understand—and UET tried to jump him, groundside. Imagine?" Bernardez shook his head. "Malloy rightly shot their ass off."

"Two ships, though, you said." Now Tregare did not smile.

"And one armed, and beat Malloy to takeoff. When most of his people—and I hope the rest found safe hideouts—when most were aboard, Malloy went straight up at max blast. But the armed ship was above him and the other went up straight alongside."

"And Malloy—?"

"And what would you suppose, Tregare? Malloy rammed the armed one—blew it wide apart—and aimed his dying carom for the other. That one survived, worse luck—though not without a meritorious amount of damage."

Tregare stood. Rissa saw that he weaved a bit. He raised his glass. "And here's to Malloy! *And there's only one latrine in all of U! E! T!*"

It was not time for Rissa to ask her own questions. Later, when Bernardez slept blanket-wrapped on the sofa—he would not hear of her making up the guest room at that time of morning—she followed Tregare to the bedroom. For undressing he needed only a little help, and he slept immediately.

DESPITE loss of sleep, Rissa woke in time to give her daughter breakfast. Almost a year old, Earthstyle, Liesel Selene was a responsive child. When Rissa pointed to the sleeping man and "ssh'd" her, Lisele put her own finger to her lips and repeated the sound—and only occasionally needed reminder.

There was no doubt, thought Rissa, of her parentage. The black hair, wavy around her face while Rissa's was straight and Tregare's downright curly—Tregare's high forehead and strong cheekbones somehow blending well with Rissa's complexion. Rissa nodded. *She will be taller than I.* And Tregare had said, "I think she'll be smarter than both of us—and in your case, that's going to take some doing."

While the child ate, Rissa decided it would be unfair to expect her to be quiet until Bernardez slept off his drinks. In a low voice, she said, "Lisele—would you like to visit Aunt Felcie this morning?"

"Aunt Felcie!" The little girl nodded. "Arlen, too!" She had few words as yet, but those she did know she pronounced clearly.

"All right. I'll call her." And a few minutes later, with Lisele's visiting-bag made ready, Rissa admitted Felcie. Finger to her lips, she pointed to the sleeping man and led her friend to the kitchen.

"Who's that? Friend of Tregare's, I suppose? New here, isn't he? I heard a ship landed last night. Where—"

"That is Bernardez of the *Hoover*. Liesel and Hawkman are aboard, in freeze. I do not know yet whether they will be awakened here or wait until we reach Earth—Bran has a letter but he and Bernardez were too busy celebrating, to open it. Well—to be fair, it was not entirely a celebration." And seeing Felcie's questioning look, she told of Malloy's end.

"Oh! I hate to have to tell Derek! He's said lots about Malloy—how they shipped together once and planned to take the ship, but Derek was transferred before they were ready. Oh, what a foul snick!"

"Yet he will be proud of his friend. Against two UET ships, after all—he took the armed one with him and tried for the other, also."

"Rissa? You know what ought to scare me sweatless? That *our* men would do the same thing. But, you know? It doesn't, somehow."

Before Rissa could answer, Lisele tugged at Felcie's sleeve. "Go Arlen?"

Rissa smiled. "Yes, dear." And to Felcie; "She has been very good, being quiet. So do let them be loud for a while if they wish."

"That one of mine? There's no letting to it, peace knows! Well, all right then—let's go, princess."

WHEN they had left, Rissa sat with a final cup of coffee. She felt restless but had not the heart to wake Tregare. She went to her study and began crosschecking progress charts against planning sheets—yes, she decided, it was moving well.

She finished the chore and was trying to choose what next to do when Tregare entered. "Everything all right? Where's Lisele?"

"After I gave her breakfast, Felcie came for her—so that

she need not tiptoe with silent lips while you drunkards get your sleep."

"If you weren't smiling you'd have me worried. Well, it's past mid-morning—time we got the day started." He left the study, Rissa following, went to the sofa, and shook Bernardez' shoulder.

"Up and hungry! You want to sleep all year?"

Bernardez turned like a cat and caught Tregare's wrist, then blinked and shook his head. "You always did take chances. All right, then—a moment, and I'll be ready to eat your cupboards bare." Draping the blanket around him, his clothes over one arm, he disappeared into the bathroom. A few minutes later he emerged, looking not at all like a man long on drink and short of sleep.

Rissa began to set out food but Tregare said, "No, sit down —I'll feed us. You've eaten?"

"I have. But I would rather cook while you read Hawkman's letter and tell me what you can of it. I—"

He rummaged in his jacket pocket and produced an envelope. "Here—you read it." She sat, opened it and read. "Well? What's it say? Do we wake them up?"

"I—I am not sure. It says, if all goes according to plan they wish to stay in freeze until we all reach Earth. But that if new developments have changed those plans, we are to wake Hawkman. He in turn will decide with regard to Liesel."

"Well—a two-year update isn't enough change to call for a conference, so I guess we let them sleep. Too bad—now we're all family again, I miss them."

"But, Bran—we *must* wake them."

His tone was quiet. "I don't think I get your meaning."

"Do you think they would wish to miss their only chance— for we all know what risks we venture—to see Liesel Selene?"

"Yes—there's that. But—"

"Now there," said Bernardez, "*I* can help. When Hawkman Moray gave me the letter, just before preparing for freeze, we talked a moment. And what that giant of a man said to me was that he hoped there *would* be reason to wake him here. And that although Liesel Hulzein, his wife, said differently, he knew she felt the same."

"Then why—?" Rissa's question went unfinished.

"Because, Rissa Kerguelen who married Bran Tregare who always did have more luck than he deserves—because Hawkman wrote that letter from his business head. But to me he talked from the heart of a strong, loving family man. And there it is." He spread his arms wide. "Do with it what you will, but at least you have it."

"Bernardez—" Tregare's laugh caught in his throat. "How have we ever done without you, all these years?"

"Oh, the best you could, I suppose—and not half-bad, considering. But now you do have me." His voice took an edge. "And now, Bran Tregare, it's time to talk terms."

"What terms?" Tregare's voice also held tension. "We agreed—you're here as my ally, independently except for over-all command. Something more you want?"

Bernardez shook his head. "Not the way you're thinking. Oh, I heard about Peralta. But, realist that I am—though romantic, mind you, as well—I have no such ambitions."

"What, then?" A little, Rissa saw, Tregare relaxed.

"You'll be organizing by squadrons—four?—five? However it may be—not as demand nor either as begging, but as earned right, I do believe, I'm wanting a squadron command. And what that may lead to, later."

Tension left Tregare, visibly. "Is that all? Man—you had it as soon as I saw your rascally face!"

Bernardez's expression was serious. "Truth?" Then he smiled. "Oh, surely—of course it is. Tregare—will you have my apologies? 'Twas merely—arriving so late and all of it, for reasons I'll tell you later though they're of no great interest—I feared those commands were all taken, that Bernardez with all his craft and talents would be doomed to a lesser role. Unless he spoke up plainly and made his wants known . . ."

"I see. Well—just a minute; food's ready." When the two were eating, Tregare continued, detailing the size and disposition of his proposed fleet.

When he came to the plan to use ships' projectors in the scouts, Bernardez whistled. "Another of your sterling qualities, Tregare—besides your reluctance to avoid risk, you were never one to think small, either."

"Whatever. Now, then—"

Bernardez raised a hand. "A moment. Twenty-five scouts, you say—and fifteen ships equipped to carry two each. Scout berths are no more than converted cargo holds—why don't we convert a few? One each for squadron command ships, at least, I'd think."

Tregare grinned. "Hell, yes! Equalize the load capacities a lot, too—for personnel *and* supplies. We'll get on it."

"Fine, fine! And now then, as you were saying—"

Tregare nodded. "Squadrons. Five, I thought, to divide thirty-four ships handily. But Stronghold's costing me two of my five captains—Limmer in overall charge when I leave. And Vanois—he wants no part of Earth—detests it—commanding the ships. Even though there's plenty of trustworthy people here, I want two of my own in those jobs."

He paused. "Which reminds me. I sorted all of Stronghold out under truth field. So don't take it wrong, but just to keep the records straight, you and your people go that route also. All right?"

The other frowned. "*Everyone* else has submitted to it?"

"That's right."

Bernardez shrugged. "Then I'll overcome my natural aversion to such measures and be my best cooperative self. But now, your other captains—would I know any of them, do you suppose?"

"Ilse Krueger. Hilaire Gowdy. Zelde M'tana."

"Krueger, yes—on *Graf Spee*. Not the others."

"Both promoted on Number One. Gowdy was Peralta's First and Zelde my own Second."

"Good enough. And now where does our story go?"

"To right here—you make a fourth and I'll run the fifth myself, basically. Seem reasonable?"

"Oh, eminently. And is there more of this oddly textured, delicious meat?"

"Sure. Here you go." Bernardez finished the added helping and sighed, smiling. "Enough?" said Tregare, and the man nodded.

Rissa said, "Bran? There is more to Hawkman's letter."

"Oh, sure—what's it say?"

"Business matters—we can discuss them later. But—you might be interested to know that you are an uncle."

Tregare laughed. "Well, I'd *think* so, by now. So tell it."

"Sparline was pregnant when the *Hoover* arrived. And when the ship was armed and ready, Liesel insisted on waiting until Sparline's time."

"She did that. A formidable woman, your mother, Tregare. Not that the similarity should surprise anyone."

"*At any rate*—" Despite Bernardez' smile, the interruption

irritated Rissa. "Ten months, about, after our departure, Ernol and Sparline had a son." She looked at her husband. "He is named Tregare Lonbuno Moray."

Sober-faced, Tregare nodded. "A little later in the day, I'll drink to that." Then, "Peace be perpetrated! You realize, Rissa—that kid, biologically, is nearly as old as you are?"

For a moment she did not comprehend. Then shock struck, and she could not hold back her sobbing.

Tregare came to her and held her. "What's the matter?"

Shaking her head hard against his chest, "The long view—it costs us too much. *Sparline*—she was ten years older than I—now it is nearer to thirty. Will I ever see her again? Or Ernol? Oh, Bran—it *is* too much!"

"I know," said Tregare. "But I'm afraid we're stuck with what we have."

Bernardez cleared his throat. "If I might add a word, well chosen or not as the case may be?" Rissa wiped her eyes and looked at him. "I have in my own way been faced with this problem—oh, many's the time. As a young—well, fool is not a bad word for it—I once married, groundside and leaving soon after, hoping to return."

"And—did you?"

"Oh, yes—the very first place I went, after the *Hoover* was mine. But it had been a time. I found my bride—it was not easy, you understand, for things had changed—and she was an old woman; our one child was middle-aged while I was yet young. Rissa—I cried then as you did a moment ago."

"I am so sorry."

"But you needn't be! You see, that's the thing of it—I cried in the arms of her who'd been my young, dear love, and she stroked my head and soothed me, and when I was done she said to me—"

"Yes?"

"She said—I remember this well—she said, 'But what disturbs you? For I've lived a good life, more than fifty years of it since you left,' she said, 'with two husbands, and I soon got shed of the bad one and found the good one, and four fine children. And you,' she said, 'Cecil Bernardez,' for I told her my true name also—'you've been spacing and saving up your life so you have it all ahead of you.' And she kissed my forehead and said, 'So why in all the worlds are you grieving? We had what we had and I treasure it, and I regret nothing in

my life and wish you all good in yours to come.' " Bernardez
smiled. "I'm afraid she didn't say it all quite that well; I'm
given to poesy, as you may have noticed. But that was the
gist."

"And then?"

"And then, since time and space had unsuited us and
besides she had a pleasant liaison with her gardener—'Well,'
she said, 'my son by you is a joy to me and my youngest
granddaughter relates to you not at all and was kissing your
picture good morrow when she still wet at night, and is of no
mind to marry but still has the child want, so—' "

"So?"

"So the dear girl came to my room, and we talked and
drank and other things you might expect before the bed drew
us to it. And she was all as sweet as her grandmother before
her, and the two weeks before the *Hoover* should have left
were not enough—I held it there six more."

Smiling, he shook his head. "But I didn't go back again—
and I never will."

Rissa could not speak. Tregare cleared his throat and said,
"You see?"

She paused, and said, "Yes, I think I do. I will misuse a saying from the old sacred book of the Christian sects: the long
view giveth, and the long view taketh away."

RISSA needed a brief time alone; when she rejoined the men,
Tregare said, "Rissa, we're going to the ship and start Hawkman thawing."

"And I? I would be there when he wakes."

Tregare shook his head. "You've never seen anyone coming
out of freeze. You wouldn't want to."

Annoyed, she said, "I have *ridden* in freeze. And I have
killed, and looked upon my dead. Yet now I am a fragile
blossom who must not see a dear friend in less than best
health?" She shrugged. "Oh, go away, both of you! I suppose
I can find something to do while I wait, that will not wholly
waste my time."

Tregare began to speak, but Bernardez tapped his shoulder
and said, "Rissa—it's not from outdated male pride that
we're giving you short shrift. Tregare, despite his many flaws
which of course don't detract from his brilliant leadership—

Tregare is in this case quite correct."

"What do you mean?"

"The *first* time you see someone being revived from freeze, I do recommend that it not be someone you have a care about. Have I by luck made this any more clear?"

Slowly, she nodded. "Yes. All right. Bernardez—" A thought came to her. "Surnames seem so formal—yet you dislike your given name. Have you a nickname, used by your friends?"

Tregare whooped. *"Kickem!"*

"Bran—what—?"

Blank-faced a moment, then Bernardez laughed. "Committee's bloated bowels! Tregare—I'd forgotten—no one's called me that since the Slaughterhouse!"

She looked to Tregare. He said, "The Academy—we called it that."

"Yes." And to Bernardez, "Kickem?"

"Well, I was a young lad, you see. This was before the killing bouts. Tregare—?"

"It's all right; I told her about those. Anyway—let *me* tell it." He gestured. "Your first year, the forced fights weren't to the death—but the sooner you were out, the worse punishment you drew. You're getting this?"

"Of course, Bran. Please continue."

"Well, this not-so-young lad here started cocky; somebody had trained him fistfighting, of all the useless things. So first time out he broke a hand, and next time or two he got hammered pretty good. But then he learned to use his feet, and got good at it. The trainers thought it was funny; any time he was in there they'd holler—"

"*Kickem*, Bernardez! They shouted that to me, so it came to be what I was called. Nothing to do with my brilliance or good looks, you understand, but—"

"And—did you mind? Would you like or dislike that name, now?"

Bernardez paused and cocked his head. "Kickem, eh? Yes. It wouldn't, you gather, have been appropriate in intervening years, for I was dodging more than striking. But now to move on UET—I'm glad you should have reminded me, Tregare—for the long and longer of it is that going to Earth, Kickem it is!"

Rissa's hand reached out. "Then hello, Kickem."

The handshake over, he said, "Tregare, we'd better get to the *Hoover*."

Tregare looked to Rissa. She kept her face blank. He said, "Kickem, you know your way back to the ship?"

"Oh, yes—once guided, I can find my way again through any labyrinth."

"Then you mind if I follow on a little later?"

"Not at all. Shall I begin resuscitation on your father?" Tregare nodded. "Then I'll see you aboard at your convenience."

LYING quietly as Tregare still held her, Rissa said, "Bran? Do you know why I could not let you go now, without this?"

"Maybe—but tell me anyway."

"Because—on Number One you would have left me behind. And I thought of being like the woman that Bernardez—Kickem—returned to, fifty years later in her own life."

Her head thrashed on the pillow. "I could not—I could not *stand* that. The long view, yes—we have to take it, there is no choice for us—but whatever happens, Bran, we must take it together!"

"Gently now," he said. "You convinced me of that, sure as peace you did, back on Number One. And it gets me, too, about Sparline—I'd just got to *know* her again. But you heard what Kickem said—people live good lives even when we're not around to share them."

Now she lay quiet. "Yes. I must remember that. My parents—killed when I was five—but I know they were happy while they lived." She looked up at him. "Does that thought apply here?"

"Yeah—I'd think so—sure it does." He began to move free of her. "Okay if I go now, and see how Hawkman's coming along?"

"Of course, Bran. And when he is well revived, will you bring him here—or shall I go to the *Hoover*?"

"Depends; we'll see how fast he comes out of it. I'll call you."

"Very well. If it is to be here, I will have Liesel Selene ready —bathed and brushed and glowing, to meet her grandfather."

"I'll bet you will." He laughed. "You know? There's a pair that's going to get along just fine."

• • •

WHEN Tregare had gone, Rissa arranged their guest room for
Hawkman and—she hoped—Liesel Hulzein. She checked her
watch—nearly midday. She called Felcie, saying, "I am restless here. I am fishing, shamelessly, for an invitation to join
you for lunch."

"Sure—that's snooky. The kids were running like bush-
stompers for a while but they've calmed a little, now. Say—are
Liesel and Hawkman coming out of freeze? Or are they out
already? And what's new on Number One? I—"

Rissa shook her head. "No, Felcie—if I tell you everything
now, we shall have nothing to talk about when I get there."

Felcie laughed. "Then hurry," and she cut the circuit. Rissa
punched the code to relay incoming calls to reach her, and
walked to join her friend. After greeting the children, she sat
with Felcie to eat.

"Now," she said. "Hawkman is being awakened, and will
probably have Liesel wakened also." She told of Ernol's and
Sparline's son—and of her feelings about the long view. "But
it is as Bernardez says—" and she told his story also.

For a moment Felcie kept silent. Then; "Tregare warned
me, didn't he? But I didn't see—how could I?—what it really
meant. Arni Gustafson—I *liked* her. She's old now—if I
started back this minute, she'd be dead before I got there. And
Sparline . . ."

"Oh, stop it, Felcie! You are pushing me right back into
black depression." Then, rueful, she took the girl's hand.
"No—you cannot help it, your reaction—any more than I
could help mine. But we must ask ourselves, is it worth it?
And my answer is yes."

"Mine, too, Rissa—Derek, and Arlen, and you and Bran
Tregare? I guess we have to make choices, don't we?" She
paused and poured coffee; then she smiled. "I'll always be
glad I chose to go with Derek Limmer."

"And I with Tregare. Oh—the laws of time and space,
Felcie, cost us dearly. But is it so different, really, from long
ago on Earth, when men exploring in sailing ships could be
gone for years?"

Felcie's frown, Rissa thought, was like a child's. The girl
said, "But at least they all aged at the same rate. Do you think
it was easier for them, that way?"

Rissa shook her head. "I cannot know." With effort, she smiled. "At least, Felcie—we who ride the ships, chasing light but never quite catching it—we span more time than we could ever experience. Perhaps that is good."

"Rissa? I was barely seventeen when we met. How old am I now? And you—what's *your* timeclock age?"

Rissa needed to consider it. "Biologically, you are perhaps halfway from your twentieth birthday to the next—and I a year older. By planet time—let me see—this guess will not be exact, but close—you were born thirty-seven years ago, plus a few months."

"Oh! That *knucks* me, you know? And you, Rissa?"

"Well—so far as the concept of simultaneity can apply at all—if I were on Earth and had never left it, I would be slightly over sixty-four years old."

"*Really?* Oh, I believe you, all right—except, how *can* I?"

Rissa laughed. "I cannot either—but I do. For I know I will find it true, and more, when we reach Earth. Tregare has experienced return to the same places—and so, as I told you, has Kickem Bernardez."

"I think I'll never go back to Number One—so I won't *know*—"

"You need not decide now, Felcie. You—" Interrupting her, the viewscreen chimed. When the screen lit, Tregare's face appeared.

"Hi. Hawkman's awake but still connected to the pumps. He'd be in shape to come visit this evening, but Liesel won't be until tomorrow—and he says she'd skin him for his pelt if he jumped the string and met their grandkid ahead of her. So the party's tomorrow night—okay?" She nodded; he said, "You want to come here about dinnertime and say hello?"

"I would love to, Bran."

"See you then." The screen dimmed.

Felcie said, "This party—Rissa—why don't you let *me* do it, here? You have so much to do—correlating reports for Tregare, and still helping part-time, several places, when you can get loose for it? So why not?"

"Felcie—you and Derek are invited in any case, you know."

Felcie laughed. "Maybe I just wanted to be sure! No, really—isn't it better if I do this part for you? Now—how many do you think there'll be?"

Rissa counted fingers. "Adults, at minimum—you and we —four. Hawkman, Liesel, Bernardez—seven. Ivan and Ilse— nine. Oh, I would say anywhere between ten and twenty. Depending on how late Hawkman and Bran Tregare drink together this night."

As she expected, approaching the *Hoover*'s galley Rissa heard cheerful discussion. Then, "Hawkman!"

"Rissa—looking better than ever!" Rising, he moved a little slowly, she thought—but his embrace lifted her high to his kiss.

Breathless, back on her feet again, she said, "You look and seem most well yourself, Hawkman. And what of Liesel?"

"Sit down, sit down—here, beside me. Liesel—she'll be all right. At her age—or mine, for that matter—recovery from freeze after a haul of this distance, it takes a little longer. But worth it—I told her as soon as she could hear and know, of our granddaughter Liesel Selene. She said—still gasping for her breath, mind you—she said, 'Damn good thing you woke me—never forgive you if you hadn't.' "

"You see, Tregare?" said Rissa.

"I know." He looked at Hawkman. "What she's on about, I wanted to see you both and thought I couldn't, so I tried not to think about it."

Rissa's eyes narrowed. "You pretended indifference—is that it?"

"Yes, that's how it was."

"Then I can understand and forgive you. For a time I was almost angered."

"Here, now!" Hawkman gripped a shoulder of each. "No arguing—not this day. Rissa, Bran Tregare's been telling me his plans. How do you see them? Good, I hope?"

"As good as all, working together, can make them. The unknown factor, of course, is Earth itself—the time-lag. What may be new there, and unexpected?"

"We've taken two fleets sent from Earth," said Tregare. "The latest left there forty years after I did. And I didn't find much new on it—just minor changes. Seems to me that on Earth nowadays, it's the Underground that's making all the progress."

He turned to Hawkman. "I haven't told you about that."

And he explained how UET's truth fields had been circumvented, and how, if need be, they might again.

"More complex all the time, isn't it, son?" Hawkman smiled. "I'm looking forward to tackling Earth again—even though it scares me."

Rissa stared at him. "*You*, frightened?"

"Oh, I frighten easily. I find it helps to keep me alive."

Before she could answer, Bernardez said, "So we don't all wither away out of sheer stark famine, I've ordered food brought and here it comes now. Drink, also, is included—for knowing Tregare I assume that thirst is a family trait."

During the meal, talk became more general—dealing with events long past and far. Afterward, drink was taken in steady fashion, but sparingly. At an hour early enough to surprise Rissa, Tregare said, "For me, it's a night. Hawkman—you and Liesel visit us tomorrow, then? Old Kickem here will bring you—right?"

Bernardez gave half a salute. "Name the hour—and Bernardez, whose fine mind puts many a computer to shame, will arrive with companions. Assuming a reasonable tolerance, of course."

Rissa laughed. "Mid-afternoon—will that suit you, Bran?" He nodded, and she said, "For dinner we are all invited—I had not thought to remember this before—to meet with Felcie and Derek. My brother Ivan, and Ilse, also are expected."

"Good!" said Hawkman. "And how many others?"

"I told Felcie this might depend on how late we drank."

Tregare laughed. "I know what you mean. But for this time, I think that's about right."

Tregare and Rissa said good-byes and left. At home, with Lisele retrieved, bedtime-talked and asleep, they sat for a time. Tregare said, "Hawkman—he looks good, doesn't he? A little shaky from freeze, but coming out of it fast."

"Yes. Will Liesel be all right? I did not know that bio-age made so much difference—in my own case I had very little after-effect."

"You had a shorter haul, too—that helped. Sure—Liesel's doing well. Tomorrow she'll be her real self." He yawned. "Let's go sleep, shall we?"

LIESEL HULZEIN, next afternoon, was first in the door.

"You've got a hug like a bear!" Tregare said, laughing.

Rissa exchanged kisses with the older woman; then she was released and Liesel squatted beside Hawkman to meet their granddaughter eye to eye. "Hello there, Liesel Selene. My name's Liesel too—did you know that?" The little girl shook her head. "Well, I'm your daddy's mother, and Hawkman here is his father."

After a moment Lisele, grave-faced, moved to kiss her grandmother and then Hawkman. Heedless of formality, the two sat on the floor with the child between them. Liesel looked up. "She takes after both of you, all right. And a little, around the eyes, after the Hulzeins." Then she was back to talking with Lieselene.

For the first time, Rissa noticed that beside Bernardez, still standing in the doorway, was—well, either a young girl or a small, slim woman. Bernardez brought her forward. "She's been abed these past days with an attack of some impertinent virus, but now I'd like you to meet my freemate Aedra Leng."

Exchanging greetings, Rissa studied the girl. Chinese?—probably. Above delicate features, expressive even in repose, her head seemed almost overbalanced by the mass of blue-black hair, smoothly coiled. "I'm sorry I couldn't meet you earlier," Aedra said, "but it's only this morning I tested non-contagious." She looked to Bernardez. "And he told me you had young children here, so I—"

"You are thoughtful," said Rissa. "And we are glad you can be here now."

"Right," said Tregare. "Are you up to a drink? I'm pretty sure everybody else is."

"Today I'd better settle for half-strength." Tregare nodded and moved to serve the group. Only Liesel Hulzein waved him off; she was intent to talk with her grandchild.

When everyone was settled, Tregare said, "Kickem, how come you didn't tell us about Aedra, before?"

"Why, because you couldn't have believed me—could you now? My poor powers of description—I wanted you to see for yourselves."

"You're right," said Tregare. "I *wouldn't* have believed, without seeing. For one thing she's much too lovely for an old crock like you!"

Bernardez's face lost all humor. "You think I don't know that?"

Aedra touched his hand. "We settled this, my love—long ago—that we are for each other." She turned to Tregare. "He's not that much older, and I'm not the child I look."

"Hey—" Tregare waved a hand. "I didn't *mean* anything—"

Bernardez gestured all-clear. "I know—I know you didn't. Tregare, in the three years bio-time—more like twenty-five, by planets' clocks—Aedra and I have been together, there've been some who tried to part us. So it may be I'm too sensitive, in the matter of age."

Rissa spoke. "Tregare said—at the Academy you were the younger."

"Yes. I had the bad luck to spend more time groundside, waiting chance for Escape. After two runs on fink ships, no prospects at all, I bided and wangled for assignments like old Machiavelli himself—who if truth were known, lent his genes to a little-known branch of the Bernardez family. Little known, I mean, until now."

Tregare laughed. "Right enough. Well, *you're* back to normal. Another drink? Not yet? Well, pour it as you like—and when."

The talk continued. Lieselene became sleepy; Liesel helped Rissa put the child to bed and then joined the group. Bernardez, his hand on Aedra's shoulder, was saying, "Stranded on Terranova, she was—no money. Came aboard the *Hoover*—we were short of crew—and wanted to sign on."

"I had no spacing experience, of course," she said, "except as a passenger. And I'm too small for heavy work, or unarmed combat. But fairly competent with weapons, and—"

"*Fairly* competent! Friends—my indispensable one seeks to delude you. She—"

His boasts on Aedra's behalf were strong, but Rissa was inclined to believe them. "Projectors? Give her chance to train, and she'll go against anyone. There's been some, hinted—none more than once, you'll understand—that she's my First Hat for reasons other than ship's business. Well, were that the case, I'd kept her a rating, so we'd not have to stand different watches so much. Isn't that right, Aedra?"

The small woman looked at him. "Bernardez—it's time you changed the subject. I don't embarrass easily, but you're coming close."

Noting the time, Rissa said, "Our hosts will be expecting us.

Perhaps if you finish the drinks you have now—there is no hurry; mine is empty and I will fetch Lisele—we can go shortly. They are on this same level; it is not a long walk.''

ILSE KRUEGER and Ivan were there before them. Ilse greeted Bernardez with a handshake, saying, "I'm glad you made it," before Limmer gave a roar of welcome and the two men embraced with great resounding backslaps.

Finally breaking away, Limmer said, "How long's it been?"

"If—if you'll allow me to draw breath, Limmer—" But Bernardez was grinning. "Since the Slaughterhouse—it must be more than forty years, planet time. I've lived close to fifteen. And you?"

"Something less, I think. Can't be sure—I lost my timer in a fracas on Hardnose and jumped ship before I could get it replaced. And on worlds with longer and shorter days—tried to keep track, but I get busy and forget." He shook his head. "Some of us don't know each other yet. Tregare?"

"All right." Tregare performed introductions and soon the group settled into general talk. Felcie asked several questions about events on Number One, but when Liesel mentioned that the answers were nearly two decades old, Felcie's face went solemn and she asked no more.

Limmer spoke of progress in work and training. "I've set up simulations for projector gunners in five ships. Tregare, how does the manning problem look?"

"Like not much of a problem. Nearly all the captaincies are firm—most of the First and a few Seconds. We'll go with some pretty green Thirds—but then, we always did." He looked to Rissa. "I don't mean *you*." She smiled at him.

Limmer said, "That's command—how about engineering?"

"Even better—technical people don't tend to be so damned political."

"Good. I—" Limmer paused. "Enough business—Felcie wants to feed us now."

During dinner and after, talk was of other matters. The two children drew their due of attention until their bedtime—and a certain amount, in comments, after it.

And later, before leaving, Rissa said, "This—with all of

you here—has been the finest evening I have had on this planet!"

THE next day, Tregare took Hawkman, along with Bernardez and Aedra Leng, for "the deluxe guided tour of Stronghold. You want to come, Liesel?"

"No, thanks—not today." She wiped a smear of cereal from Lisele's chin. When the others had left, she said, "Rissa, we hadn't decided, Hawkman and I, how long to stay out of freeze here. We can't afford too long, I know—but now I'm up, I'd hate to waste the waking on just a few days."

Rissa thought. "You must stay at least for Lisele's second birthday, bio-time, and counting by Earthdays. That will be in twelve more of ours."

"Good! We'd thought either a week—make it quick—or a month. You've decided for us." Watching the little girl, she smiled. "This one—in her ways, more than looks—reminds me a lot of Sparline at the same age. I wish Sparline could see her—and that you and Bran could have seen her young Tregare."

"Yes—Tregare Lombuno Moray. Who chose those names?"

"Ernol insisted on Tregare, and Sparline on Lombuno. They both agreed the surname would give the boy proper status."

"I see." The door chime sounded. "Just a moment."

She opened the door to Felcie and Arlen. Felcie said, "Am I late? Liesel—you're so good, to look after these little bush-stompers for us. Are you sure you know what you're getting into?"

Liesel waved a hand. "The short time I'll be awake here, I want to get to know these two kids as much as I can—along with seeing the rest of you. And this is one good way to do it, so I can concentrate on 'em."

"Well, they're a handful, sometimes."

"I am sure," said Rissa, "that Liesel Hulzein can cope with two small children. But we do appreciate it, Liesel!"

"Sure. Now get your string moving."

RISSA had planned—and Felcie was agreeable—to spend the

day inspecting programs that for some time she had only been able to spot check. They visited the ships set up for weapons practice, and Rissa noted the average scoring progress at each—as well as taking one half-hour practice session herself.

"Sixty-eight. I had better come here more often."

The woman on duty as instructor said, "Why, that's the best score I've seen here!"

"But I have done better—and I will again." Then, "It will not be enough, I see, to train turret gunners *before* we leave here. I will suggest to Tregare that *each* ship have one position set for practice, to keep skills honed during the journey."

As they left, Felcie said, "You're really expecting a big battle at Earth, aren't you?"

"I do not know—but if there is one, I intend that we win it."

RISSA boarded *Inconnu* on whim; she had no real business there. She found Gonnelsen in Control; the tall blond man nodded, smiling, but said nothing.

She said, "Well, hello—I did not expect to find you here, for I heard you are to have a ship of your own."

He swallowed; then—low-toned, as usual—he spoke. "Ms. Kerguelen—you've got to speak to Tregare for me."

"I do not understand."

"I've told him—I don't want command—it's not in me. But he won't listen."

"Tregare says, and I have noted also, that you are very capable."

He shook his head. "Not to command—not that. I'll go groundside first. It's—the deciding."

"But all of us must make decisions. You make them *now*."

"Not the same. Once I—people died of it. Not again!"

Seeing the strain in him, she touched his hand. "I will speak to Tregare."

The only thanks he gave was another nod.

"Gonnelsen—you have spoken to me more, just now, than in all the time I have known you."

His gesture stopped midway. "I had to."

•   •   •

HOME again, after dinner she told Tregare. "He means it, Bran."

"I know. But damn it—he's *wasted* in a subordinate job, working under someone who knows less than he does."

"Under *you*, Tregare?"

His headshake showed impatience. "I can't keep him on *Inconnu*—I have to spread the talent thin; you know that." He rubbed his forehead. "The man *owes* it to me to hold down a bigger job."

Rissa smiled. "You have said he is a good organizer, once someone sets policy. Are there not subordinate jobs on a larger scale?"

Tregare's finger stabbed air. "Right! It's making death that bothers him, is it? Though he's never shown squeamish in a fight . . . well, Limmer needs a top aide, to help run Stronghold when we've gone, and neither of us are all that satisfied with the possible candidates." He moved to the viewscreen. "I'll call Gonnelsen."

Suddenly busy with her daughter's needs, Rissa heard only the last of Tregare's side of the call and none of the other man's. "That's right, and Fleet Liaison's a big part of it . . . no, you'd work *for* Limmer and *with* Vanois, on that . . . sure, in space some of the time; how else? . . . All right, and when you come to Earth I'll buy *you* one . . . first of the week, I'd think, if that gives you enough time . . . yes, sure, I'll tell her."

He cut the circuit and joined Rissa. "It's all set, and Gonnelsen says to thank you a lot." He kissed her. "That last, though, was my own idea. You've cleared up something that's been bothering me."

"I am glad. And there was something more—" She told him her idea for weapons practice in space.

"No reason why not—I'll get it started tomorrow."

Hawkman and Liesel entered. "Business twenty-seven hours a day," Hawkman said. "But that's what wins wars."

Tregare laughed. "It had better." And then, "Just one more item. Rissa—you knew you're moving up to Second Hat? And Hain to First?"

"I had not thought—but, very well, I accept. And do you have a new Third in mind?"

"Not from *Inconnu;* we've pretty well picked over the executive talent aboard." He stared at nothing, then grinned.

"How about Anders Kobolak?"

"I have noted his progress. He becomes competent—a good choice."

"Yeah. I'll tell Stepan—no, I'll tell the boy tomorrow and let *him* do the announcing at home."

"Ah, Bran," said Hawkman. "If only we could have got you away with us, to Number One! We'd own the planet by now."

"But as it is," said Liesel, "it's a bigger prize we're going after."

ON the morning of Lisele's birthday, Rissa and Liesel sat, making preparations. "It is like two birthdays for each child," said Rissa. "On Arlen's, Lisele was—you might say—crown princess to his king. Today it will be the other way."

"Sure—with the two kids so close, you have to give both a good play." Liesel sighed. "It's been so damned long—Hawkman and I used to do it about like that with Bran Tregare and Sparline, when they were small."

Rissa still shrank from thinking of Sparline, aging while she herself had not. She said, "Liesel—you have told of personal happenings, but nothing of how your plans for Number One were developing."

"Haven't I? Oh, yes—I started to, the other day, but Lisele banged her head and I forgot. Well, then—no, I need a cup of coffee first." That need filled, she said, "It *was* moving. I hated to leave just then—but Sparline has a sound head and Ernol was coming along like a good kite in a strong wind. He could even *lie* by that time—so long as it was merely business."

She sipped her coffee. "Well, let's see now—you left before Fennerabilis pushed at the wrong oligarch, finally. Crandish, it was—you may have met him, I don't recall. So control of Fennerabilis' interests was our price for protecting him. Once the shock was past, he settled down well."

"First Bleeker, then Fennerabilis. You do gather the reins of power."

"Not *first* Bleeker—remember? Sixth, or maybe seventh. But then—Crandish was overextended, too, we found. So we let him waste substance against Fennerabilis until we could grab *his* string."

She paused to sip again from her steaming cup. "Right after that, it got snicky. Everything we tried, we ran into stone walls. Finally—you know what it turned out?" Rissa shook her head. "Well, you see—we weren't the only ones with the same idea."

"Of gaining control of Number One?"

"Of gaining control to stop the peace-spattering cutthroat infighting! We'd been suspicious of Harkeen and the No Name Cooperative but we couldn't prove a damned thing— any more than they could on us. Then our strings crossed, and for a time it looked like civil war coming up, or close to it."

Rissa said nothing. Liesel set down her cup. "Ernol presided at the meeting we called. It was time to push his status— and he had a cue box, just in case. Not that he needed it."

"And everything you do," Rissa murmured, "is multipurpose."

"Of course! Well—everyone jockeyed a lot, and right quick it came clear we all held more cards than showed. So right in the middle of Harkeen's ultimatum Ernol asked him—and not off the cue box, either—how many votes he controlled."

"Harkeen had five. The No Names, after stalling a while first, admitted to four. So—it took a while, but we made a pact."

"You have a majority—that you can trust?"

"I think so. Harkeen and I had been at odds for years— nothing personal, just two dogs after the same bone. So when it came clear we each wanted to save Number One from tearing itself apart—"

"Liesel! Why have you not told of this before?"

"Too far away—here was more important. Anyway, it wasn't strung solidly when we had to leave. But working at it, we were. So if Ernol and Sparline can keep the string tight—"

"I wonder that you dared to leave, at all."

Liesel Hulzein laughed. "Wasn't a matter of dared—I've got confidence in my daughter and in Ernol. But I do hate to miss a good ruction."

THE party, thought Rissa, succeeded totally. Arlen took his secondary role as well as Lisele had done two months earlier. The adults set their own concerns aside, for the time—*and for Hulzeins, especially,* Rissa mused, *that takes some doing!—*

and gave the children full stage center. The two were let to overstay their bedtimes; only when they clearly showed fatigue were they bundled off, undressed, and tucked away in bed.

Then, and only then, Limmer said, "Tregare? Let's talk schedules." Over Felcie's protest, he continued. "I've asked before—when do you leave? I'm not all that happy about staying behind here but—"

"I *told* you, Limmer—I need one of *us* to hold the fort here. Vanois stays, true—but he can't handle *people*. You can. Sure as peace I'll miss you folks, but there's no help for it."

Scarred lips twisting, Limmer smiled. "I didn't ask all that—just, when do you leave?"

"He says more than you asked," said Rissa, "*because* we will miss you."

"Yeah, yeah—they know that." Tregare waved her words away. "All right—I've had to stretch schedules more than once, but now I think I can set it. By Earth count, we're nine days short of eight hundred here on Stronghold. Another three hundred, minimum, plus ninety or less for leeway, we lift. That good enough?"

Limmer frowned, then nodded. "I guess it has to be. Let's see—that puts us barely into NY88. So—now the *big* question."

Tregare's brows rose. "Like what?"

"Like how long after you leave are we stuck here? Who takes over from me, and when and how?"

With both hands Tregare pushed those questions back. "Wait a minute, Derek." Now the hands rubbed his face. After long moments, he spoke. "Yeah—I see it. And I think you gave me the answer to something."

"Oh? I didn't notice, Tregare—and I'd like to hear it."

"Let me figure, a minute—I can't do the long view in my head." On a scrap of paper he scribbled, scratched out, and wrote again. "All right, here it is—we hit Earth. Win or lose, Stronghold's no more use to us—except as a place to collect ships as long as UET sends them out. You agree?"

A pause, then Limmer said, "Damn all, you're *right*! But how—?"

"But win or lose, you won't *know,* here, until NY109—and that's too long to wait."

"You're sounding good, so far. I'm still listening."

"All right. You stay here long enough to swallow two more

UET fleets and arm them—or three, if you'd rather. And pick your successor—someone Vanois can work for without too much trouble."

"He gets along with Kobolak as well as not."

"Kobolak it is, then—unless you get a better idea." Tregare looked at what he had written. "*Then*—leaving about as much defense here as we're leaving you, you pull string for Earth."

Limmer's mouth twitched. "And when we get there?"

"If you need to ask, I picked the wrong man. You tell *me*."

"Okay—yeah, Tregare. If you've won, no problem—*only one latrine in all of U!E!T!*—every hour, on the hour. And if, peace forbid, the bastards get you or chase you off—"

"You know what to do, don't you?"

"Have a shot at it myself—but get out if it doesn't look like working. And scatter, and—those who get away without a UET tail on them—regroup at Number One."

"See?" said Tregare. "You didn't need to ask."

THE days passed, and one evening Liesel Hulzein said, "Our last night. Bran—Rissa—you can't know what this month means to me."

"I can guess," said Tregare. "You sure you wouldn't rather stay up—and warm—a while longer?"

"If we did," Hawkman said, "we'd end up riding live, overcrowding you on *Inconnu*." He laughed. "Life, if you hadn't noticed, is a contagious habit."

Tregare grinned. "I don't know—I've never been in freeze. Rissa?"

"Merely the one time, Bran—as you know. For utility, only. The philosophical side escaped me."

"Just as well," said Liesel. "Save the philosophy until you need it. And give me another drink, Bran Tregare. I'm of no mind to go sober into freeze—and of little mind to go at all. But I must—I must—"

Later, good-bye kissing, Rissa said, "We *will* be together, on Earth. Do not doubt it."

And Hawkman. "If there were any reasonable way to stake a wager on this outcome, I'd bet high on it."

FOR several days afterward, Rissa felt depression. "And Lisele does not help," she told Tregare. "Always asking 'Where Liesel?'—and of course I cannot explain to her."

He looked up at her. "You think it doesn't bother me, too?"

"You have said nothing—but then, you would not."

"That's as may be. But still—Rissa, would you rather they'd stayed in freeze? Or that the *Hoover*'d been too late to come here at all? Gone straight to Earth, instead?"

"No. No, I do not wish either of those things."

"Then be glad of the time we did have—and look forward to the next."

She shrugged away tension. "You are right, Bran. I will try."

AEDRA Leng lived up to Bernardez' claims. Rissa instructed her in projector gunnery, and soon they were fierce competitors, as well as friends. And after one such session, the two of them visiting with Felcie, Aedra told her personal history.

Born on Earth a year before Rissa, Aedra left that planet when she was twenty-two. Her father was in civil service, in a grade safely below political levels—but from his student days he had worked with the Underground, and from childhood Aedra had known his dual role. When one day he announced that he had procured a job for Aedra with the colonial government of Terranova, she knew he was getting her off Earth for her own safety. And at Terranova she found that he had not wholly succeeded.

"I'd enjoyed the trip—about fifteen months subjective—we couldn't afford freeze, you see. And a good thing, too, it turned out. I found a new lover—the ship's Third Hat—to console me for the one I'd left with more tears than I really felt. And he—Miklos—was the one who saved me."

She went groundside and reported to the agency that was to employ her. She met with blank stares; no jobs, she was told, were available. Frightened as well as puzzled, she started back to the ship. But on the way, Miklos intercepted her. He told her that a faster ship from Earth had brought word that she was proscribed.

Her money, in the ship's vault, was out of his grasp, but he had brought her cabin luggage. And in the lining of one suitcase was hidden Aedra's jewelry. "So—a fugitive, on a new world. It was a bad few days, hiding in cheap inns until I found someone who recognized one of the passwords my father had told me. I got half price, a little better, for the jewels—and lived reasonably well, in hiding, the months before the *Hoover* came.''

Rumor said the ship *might* be Escaped and keeping cover, but she had no certain knowledge. She watched—only a few came groundside from the *Hoover,* and always the same few. And finally, when her money was nearly gone, she went to the ship and said she had a message for its captain. ''—and they let me go upship.''

''A bad risk, you took,'' said Rissa. ''I think you must have great skills.''

''I don't know. When I saw Bernardez I said I had to speak to him alone. Then I looked at him and decided. I said, 'If you're not Escaped, I'm dead—because *I'm* Escaped—can I find a place here?' ''

Felcie gasped. ''Just like *that*?''

Rissa said, ''At such a time, having gone so far already, there was no other way.''

''But I liked the look of him, you see—*before* I spoke up, I was almost sure. And he glanced around quickly, asking if anyone knew I'd come there, then said I could stay aboard, safe. I didn't even return groundside for the things I'd left.''

''And how did—'' Felcie blushed. ''I mean, did you take to each other right away?''

''His quarters were off limits to groundhogs, even UET—so I stayed there. But when I—he said I looked twelve years old, and it took me a time to convince him I wasn't!'' The small woman sat erect. ''And I've never regretted any of it, and I never will!''

''Well, I'd *think* not,'' said Felcie. ''Uh—you ever find out what became of the other one—Miklos?''

''Nothing solid—no word of him personally—but it's rumored that the ship Escaped, later. I hope it's true and that he's prospered.''

Rissa nodded. ''You care about those your life touches. One must, to have a life at all.''

''Yes,'' said Aedra. ''For a while, Bernardez was nearly all of my life—but that can't last, not and be healthy in the mind. Now we're maybe half of each other.''

She stood. ''I have to go now. I need to wash my hair, and

my dryer's working at only half efficiency, so it takes forever.''

Felcie ran fingers through her own pale hair. Since joining Limmer she had let it grow and now kept it trimmed a bit longer than shoulder length—in the style, Rissa noted, of Limmer's pictures of Vanessa Largane. Felcie said, ''Why not wash it here? *My* dryer's in good shape.''

''I'll take the offer, and thanks.'' Then, as Aedra loosened the coils atop her head and shook the mass free down her back, Felcie gasped—for it reached below her knees.

''Rissa! Did you ever see anything like it, in your *life?*''

''No—and I had thought *I* was doing well, finally fulfilling the boast I made on Earth.'' For Aedra's benefit, she related it. ''Well, it *is* down to my butt—but only barely, since I trimmed ragged ends a few days ago. And it seems to wish to grow no farther, or not by much.''

''Natural limit,'' said Aedra. ''It varies with the individual. My race seems to have some advantage there, and since I'm a lot shorter than most . . .''

Rissa smiled. ''Well, I will not envy you—but only admire. And now—Eudyce will be bringing the children soon, so I must go.''

WHEN she told Tregare the story, he laughed. ''Don't worry—win or lose in the great scalp contest, you'll do.'' Then he said, ''Aedra—what she told you—lots more there than meets the eye, wouldn't you say? Little thing like that—but a real tiger.''

After dinner, and with Lisele in bed asleep, he spoke more seriously—of the fleet's progress, of the plans for Earth. ''Because something's *always* overlooked—only question is, will it turn out to be vital? I've been over the whole thing with the others until we all think alike—but you've only seen it on paper, mostly. So run the situation through as you see it, will you?''

''Very well.'' She rose and poured more coffee, then sat and looked through the planning sheets he handed her. Arming, manning and training—progress was on schedule. Fuel and supplies—check. Rearrangement of quarters, full use of freeze-chambers—the fleet would carry more than five thousand, nearly a thousand more than normal capacity. Takeoff date not yet set, but firming. Yes—

Now to choose the course, their path to Earth. Limmer's was shorter, but the difference was at high speed and saved little subjective time. Tregare's avoided not only the UET fleets coming from Earth but also any unexpected ships arriving from major colony planets. "Check, so far," said Tregare. He poured more wine. "And then?"

Lacking fresh news from Earth, they must be prepared for total hostility. The planned attempts at subversion *might* be effective—hypnotic protection *might* keep the passwords, arranged with Terrell Ragan and Coryle Hagenau, uncompromised over so many years. Or they might not. . . .

"So there will be," she said, "fully or to a lesser degree, a battle of ships."

She looked for another sheet, found it. If defeat were inevitable—the remaining ships to group, regardless of damage they might incur, and make one concerted firing pass at UET Headquarters Base. "Oh, Bran—that would make what happened at Base Two look like a child's bonfire! So terrible . . ."

"I know. That's the idea—if we can't win, we tear up UET so much that maybe the locals will have a chance, in the confusion."

Then—collect as many scoutships as possible, fire all remaining missiles at pursuing UET ships and scatter at top acceleration. Eventual rendezvous—well, she knew that part—ships that could shake off pursuit, at Number One.

She paused. He said, "Can you improve on any of it?"

"It seems doubtful that many scoutships could be saved."

"That's the hell of it. We've got two-way locators for each ship with its own scout, but a ship may be knocked out or in the wrong place—no chance to connect. And there's not enough computer circuitry—let alone trying to interpret the Tri-V display—to locate *all* ships and scouts to each other."

She thought. "The limitation is in the scouts' computers?"

"Mostly. Why?"

"How many ships could one such handle, on its locator?"

"Oh—four, maybe five. You got something?"

"You had fifteen ships equipped to carry two scouts each; Kickem is converting ten more to carry one each. There are twenty-five scouts; all these factors are evenly divided among your squadrons. Can you not provide each *squadron* with full two-way locator capability? The odds, then—"

"Yeah!" He frowned for a moment, then nodded. "Eight

berths possible for each five scouts—I like that!" He stood.
"Here. For that one we deserve a *real* drink."

And for that evening, planning ended.

STRONGHOLD'S long, slow spring waxed into summer. The
changes, when she had time to notice them, intrigued Rissa.
For weeks or months one kind of flower might bloom, then be
replaced by another. It was, she thought, as though between
March and June on Earth a dozen generations of plants—each
of its own kind at its own time—bloomed and fruited. Except,
she knew, that on Stronghold the progression lasted nearly
four Earth years.

Occasionally she and Felcie took the children out for pic-
nics. Sometimes Eudyce Kobolak accompanied them, and
twice Aedra Leng. One breezy day Aedra loosened her hair
and ran into the wind, the long, incredible mass whipping
behind her. From the side, Felcie photographed her in motion.
Breathless, cheeks flushed, Aedra rejoined the group and said,
"With all that exercise, I hope Bernardez likes the picture I
saw you take!"

"If he doesn't," said Felcie, "he needs his eyes tested!"

When Bernardez saw the picture, his eyes passed inspection.

RISSA had studied Tregare's escape-hatch plans rapidly.
Despite his attempted hurrying, she took more time over the
contingencies of success. Finally—and again, on an evening—
she felt ready to discuss these.

She looked from one to another of the papers before her.
He waited, and she said, "You try to provide for *every*
possibility—and you cannot. The combinations are too
many."

"What else can I do? So many parts to it, and none
solid—"

"Yes. The Committee, its Police and remaining ships if any
—the Underground, the New Mafia, the Hulzein Establishment, the Australians—these factors cannot help but interact,
I know. Yet I think our plans must treat them separately.
Or—" she gestured at the papers—"by the time we learn the
situation it will be too late to sort through all these, and find
the plan prescribed for it."

"Zelde M'tana said something like that—but when I asked what better she had in mind, she couldn't say." He leaned forward. "Can you?"

"I think so—perhaps—a start, at least. Assume we have won in space." Tregare nodded. "The one constant is that UET groundside is still our major enemy and will require the most of our force and effort. The other groups—we devote small segments of our strength to scouting them—adding more where it will gain us and dropping contact where our efforts are wasted." She paused. "Yes, I think that is it—five or six *basic* plans, separate and parallel, rather than the hundreds you've tried to perfect in detail."

"Oh, hell—it's not hundreds; you're exaggerating."

"It would be, by the time you covered all possible combinations separately."

"All right—if you write up a rough on it, I'll put it to Captain's Council tomorrow."

"The next day, Bran—it is much too late to finish such a thing tonight."

WHEN Rissa's personal timer registered a thousand Earthdays spent on Stronghold, she calculated. "—and not counting the eight months in freeze, to Far Corner—then, *yes*!" And when Tregare came home she told him, "Five days from now I would celebrate, as an approximation, my twenty-second birthday. I know we have not done this before, but I find I would like to."

"Huh? Oh, sure—fine by me. Who's invited?"

Counting on her fingers, Rissa soon lost track. Limmer and Felcie, Ivan and Ilse, the four Kobolaks, Kickem and Aedra, Zelde and Kile—"How many is that?"

"With us, and the kids, fourteen. Who else you want?"

"Hain Deverel and Anse Kenekke—they fought for us, and I have seen so little of them here. And Hilaire Gowdy? But that would make it so pointed, to exclude Vanois—and I am sorry, Bran, but although I respect his competence and loyalty, I cannot *like* Vanois. So—"

"Nothing shaken. He's taking some people up for maneuvers, about then—and he can be in space that evening as easy as the next day, which is what I'd planned." He grinned. "One thing, though—along with Gowdy, these days, comes

Elrain Hardekamp. Remember him?"

After a moment, "Yes—the man who spoke up to you, under truth field, and earned First Hat on *No Return*. He spoke straightly; he will be welcome."

"Fine. That's eighteen grown folks and the kids can make enough noise for six more, if they try hard. So we don't have the party here. Too crowded."

"Then where, Bran?"

"On *Inconnu*, in the galley. Where else?"

TREGARE and Rissa were the last to board; Rissa suspected that her husband had purposely delayed their arrival. Entering the galley, she gasped—the plain hues of walls and ceiling were covered by brightly colored swirls and sketches, a huge "Happy Birthday, Rissa!" in red across the ceiling, and line drawings—each clearly labeled—of herself, Tregare, Lisele, and others.

Ivan hugged her. "Didn't know we had a bunch of artists here, did you?"

Then Limmer kissed her, and Stepan Kobolak and Bernardez. Elrain Hardekamp held out his hand instead. "I don't feel I know you well enough, Ms. Kerguelen."

She embraced him anyway. "Now you do!" Nor did she spare Kile Ressider, Deverel, Kenekke, young Anders Kobolak, or any of the women. "Have I missed anyone?"

"Only me," said Tregare, laughing until she sealed his mouth with hers. When she was done, he said, "We'll have drinks and then bring the children in and sit to dinner. Who's tending bar?"

"Displaying yet another of my many skills," said Bernardez, "I'll have a turn at it." Then, with some sitting, others standing in groups, the talk and drink began.

Rissa stood with Zelde M'tana and Kile Ressider. "Zelde—how do you like being a squadron commander?"

"Bothered me at first, keeping tabs on six ships besides my own—not to mention the five scouts when they're out loose. Then Kile told me, quit trying to run *Valkyrie* personally—forget I'm on her, treat her just like the rest. Well, it worked."

"And in essence," said Ressider, "she'll use two First Hats on *Valkyrie*—one to run the ship and the other to handle the squadron's scouts in action. This part was her own idea, and I think the other Tops are adopting it."

"Tops?"

"Top Hats, Rissa," said Zelde. "Bernardez' term, I think."

"Yes—it would be." She had another thought. "How does Dacia Kobolak progress?"

"That one?" Zelde made an emphatic nod. "She's a pure natural—learns it the first time and moves like a cat. I was thinking of her, young or not, as backup to run the scouts. But Tregare says he's got another job for her—didn't say what."

"Last call for drinks!" Bernardez announced. "Then we sit." Rissa went to refill her empty glass, then found her seat between Lisele and Felcie, across from Limmer and Tregare.

". . . well, I don't care which order they come in, Tregare, but you've got to number the squadrons."

"*You* don't care, Derek. But some might—so we're naming them, instead."

"Yes—that's all right, I suppose. What names?"

"I'm leaving it to you Top Hats, each to name your own. Zelde's is *Parnell,* after the captain she learned from. Kickem's named his for Malloy. Ilse calls hers *Falconer*—he was the man that led *Graf Spee*'s escape, and died in it. Gowdy!" He called over to her. "You decide on a name yet?"

The woman raised an eyebrow. "Tregare—would you mind—*Peralta*?"

"*Peralta?*" Limmer's voice showed disbelief.

"Why not?" said Tregare. "He went wrong at the end, sure. But, before—well, few men twisted UET's tail more and better than Jimar Peralta. Agreed, Hilaire." He turned again to Limmer. "And yours, Derek, here at Stronghold?"

"I'm thinking—you're all commemorating people; right?" Tregare nodded. "Then mine is *Largane.*"

Rissa reached across and touched his hand. "So that she will have a part in our endeavor."

"Right—she will." Then, "And your own, Tregare?"

"A first name, this one. My grandmother who died fighting UET when they drove the Hulzeins out of North America. *Renalle.*"

Rissa stood. "I raise a toast—to the squadrons of our fleet." Holding her glass toward each commander in turn, she called the squadron name, then sipped. At the end she said, "And to all of us, present or absent here, who will ride them," and drank the glass dry.

Before she could sit, Tregare caught her hand and pulled her, both leaning awkwardly over the table, to kiss her. "That was perfect."

Now galley personnel served food; for the most part, talk quieted. Afterward came the traditional cake. "The candles— I did not know, Bran, that there were such things here."

Tregare grinned. "Hand-rolled—Anse made them." The tapers sputtered rather than burning smoothly, but Rissa did not mind. She winked at Kenekke and smiled. Then all of them sang to her the old, old song and she blew out the flames, needing her last bit of breath to douse the final one.

When she could speak, she said, "Thank you, everyone! This is—I had not had a birthday party since I was five. I had forgotten how it would feel!" Felcie led the applause; then came coffee and liqueurs to accompany the cake. Rissa was served the first piece—then Lisele and Arlen, then Tregare; after that, Rissa did not notice—only that all received portions eventually.

Another hour and Limmer said, "Work comes early tomorrow. We'd better go." Others followed suit; soon, as Rissa exchanged goodnights with departing guests, the galley began to empty.

To Kennekke she said, "The candles, Anse—I had not expected any, here. Thank you very much."

"My pleasure."

"And how goes your work?" Kennekke was now in charge of testing the drives of other ships.

"The latest drive's giving me problems. It's nowhere near up to *Inconnu*'s yet—but it will be!"

"I am sure of it." And she bade goodnight to Deverel also.

A few minutes more, and all others were gone. Tregare picked up drowsy Lisele and carried her. When they were back inside their quarters, Rissa hugged both man and child.

"And thank *you*, Bran."

"Any year you say—just speak up."

"My next birthday—if at all—will be on Earth."

"It *will* be on Earth."

• • •

As new, unexpected delays plagued Tregare's schedule, Rissa came almost to doubt his assurance. "I don't know," he said, one evening, "who slipped up, on spares for the turrets. Doesn't matter—I should have checked it myself. But they're in production now, and we can make up the time." She looked a question and he said, "Something we can do now and save time later. All personnel, including us, move aboard and live shipside from now to takeoff."

Not until they moved into the cramped space now available on *Inconnu* did Rissa realize how much she had enjoyed their roomy groundside quarters. "But," she said, "it is only two months more—three, perhaps—besides the six or so from here to Earth."

She and Lisele visited groundside daily—her ship's duties, now, took little of her time; she took advantage of her temporary freedom. One day, at tea with Eudyce Kobolak, she said, "Is it well now with you—accepting that Dacia and Anders leave with us soon?"

The tall woman smiled. "Yes—Stepan and I see how they *grow* with the training they've had. They're Earthraised; they never really acclimated to Stronghold. Coming here—if Tregare hadn't taken the place, our son and daughter would be watching their every move and word for fear of Committee Police, the same as on Earth." She spread her hands. "Rissa —do you see what I mean?"

"I think so—but there is more, is there not?"

"That's right. Now you and Tregare—all of you—you go, hoping to do for Earth what you've done for Stronghold. I can't blame Anders and Dacia for wanting to be part of that."

"Perhaps, later, you may come also."

"No." Eudyce shook her head. "It was hard, moving here. Unless my thoughts change later, one uprooting is all I can take. Dacia and Anders say they'll try to come back someday; I'll have to pin my hopes on that."

Rissa found little she could say. Finally, "And I hope *we* will see you again, also."

Time passed—Arlen Limmer's birthday came and then Lisele's —each briefly celebrated by the two families. Between those dates came Tregare's 300-day minimum for earliest takeoff. He told the assembled captains, "I said, no longer than ninety days after this. But that was just *me* talking. Now I'm asking *you*—can we make it?" He looked around. "Anybody have a problem that might hold us back?"

Tentatively, a few raised their hands. One by one he queried them—two were merely overcautious, one he agreed to confer with afterward, and the rest he was able to refer elsewhere for needed aid.

"All right. Then we leave in ninety days—or preferably before that. When I know, you'll get at least three days' notice."

The group dispersed. Tregare stood, and Rissa beside him. He said, "Just a minute, Derek."

"Yes?"

"I want to say—I appreciate the way you're lending your own people, as many as you can spare—stretching yourself thin, to help."

Limmer smiled. "After all, I'm working for my own command—isn't that right?"

Tregare snapped his fingers. "Oh, sure—why didn't *I* think of that?" The men laughed, and Limmer hurried to his next task.

BY six days Tregare beat his maximum. When Rissa's timer showed her 1,170th day on Stronghold, he gave his notice—not three days, but five "And get your partying over," he announced, "in the first three. Last day here will be solid checklisting; you won't want to be doing it hung over."

Rissa declined to hold or attend any large farewell gatherings. She said, "I wish my leavetakings to be more personal. But you go to whatever festivities you choose, Bran—it is all right."

He frowned. "Well—a couple, I have to. And you should be at the Top Hats' bash—you really should."

"Yes—very well. I will attend the dinner and stay a short time after, then excuse myself. For I planned to spend part of that evening with the Kobolaks."

"All right. If I get loose reasonably early, I'll pick you up there."

• • •

THE remaining work could be done at a reduced pace. Now only half the fleet's personnel had duty each day—and at night, only a skeleton force. Rissa checked schedules and arranged—sometimes with Tregare and sometimes alone—to find her visiting times with those she needed to see and talk with, both friends she surely would not see on Earth and also those she *might* not see.

A full afternoon with her brother, part of an evening with Deverel and Kenekke, a morning with Aedra Leng—somehow she found time for everyone. On the final evening, Tregare said, "I'm free until morning. Who do we see tonight?"

"I had thought—the three of us only. And when Lisele sleeps, just each other."

PERALTA squadron lifted first—gently, to avoid damaging ships closely grouped around its own. Then—also with care— *Falconer* and *Malloy*. *Parnell* was grouped at one end of the port with no ships near it—Zelde M'tana needed less caution and used the bare minimum. Tregare grinned. "In a hurry, that one."

And now *Renalle*, well clear of Llimmer's defensive fleet and the dummy hulls—Tregare whooped and slammed the power control against its stop. *Inconnu* growled and shivered; for the first time, Rissa felt the ship's full power. In seconds the sky was black; ahead she saw the leading squadrons spreading into formation. Then Tregare eased his controls back, and *Inconnu* and the other ships of *Renalle* coasted into position.

Grinning, he said, "How's that for a liftoff?"

"Recalling your departure from One Point One," said Rissa, "I hope all below were safely inside. And this was *six* ships."

He laughed. "Oh, sure—I told Derek this one was going to be worth watching, and he had the orders out." He looked at the screen. "Fine. Formation's a little ragged—matching velocities and then accelerations, but it's shaping up."

Rissa looked. Centered on *Inconnu* the configuration was that of a bowl, rim forward. Tregare flipped his talk switch. "Squadrons report." One by one his commanders reported all ships operating in good order. He breathed deeply, exhaled a gusty sigh. "Tregare to all squadrons, all ships, every man and woman aboard. Congratulations—well done."

He cut the circuit and turned to Rissa. "Peace take us— who'd have thought it? Rissa, we're on our way!"

SIX months to Earth, while that world's clocks ran twenty times as fast. She would be returning, thought Rissa, to an Earth that had seen fifty-eight years without her—while she herself had lived less than six, and more than half that on Stronghold. The long view . . .

Ship's routine was not arduous, its monotony broken by practice sessions. Near light-speed, the fleet's separate drives needed little adjustment, but the ships could simulate low-speed combat as though their relative velocities were not tiny vectors added to their mutual greater one. In turret practice, Rissa found that the minor changes of acceleration affected her coordination—but with practice she adapted to the new factor and her scores rose again.

But in combat she would not be operating a turret. Tregare told her, "I need you here in Control for about three jobs— and I'm still inventing two of them."

"Inventing? Do not *make* work for me, Tregare, to keep me safe."

He shook his head. "No such thing. These squadron maneuvers showed me problems—I'm working on ways to handle them with the fewest people. Trouble is, UET didn't have a real squadron system, let alone trying to control *groups* of squadrons. So—"

Except in stable formation, one ship's computer could not feed wide-band, detailed information to another—or control the other's weapons. As speeds and accelerations changed, the wide-band circuits needed to carry complex information in real time fell prey to Doppler shift. "The error rate gets unworkable," Tregare said. "There's circuits that could compensate, I'm told—but UET didn't need them so we don't have them, or the drawings to build from."

He shrugged. "It doesn't matter—with all the drivewakes crisscrossing, we couldn't punch a complex signal through all the ionization, anyway. *But*—cooperation's still what we need."

"So—what kind of answer are you seeking?"

"If we can't centralize control in fine, we'll have to do it in large. Coordination officers alongside commanders, here and in each squadron—and same from Top Hats to each ship. I haven't sorted it out yet, who does what and how many it takes. I see three functions I'm trying to reshuffle into only two—so that here, for instance, I can do one of them and you the other."

She looked toward his scribbled notes. "May I study these?"

"If you hadn't asked that, I would have."

The answer, developed over several hours by both of them together, turned out to be the more simple than Rissa expected. Finally Tregare pushed the papers away. "We'll work out the details later. There's more to it, of course—but what it boils down to, I tell them where to go and you tell them what to do when they get there."

WITH a few changes, the system adapted well to squadron level. Tregare and his Top Hats worked out contingency plans, each based on one of several possible combat situations, to be used when direct communication was lost. Rissa devised shorthand codes for all orthodox or expected tactical moves. And one day, about two-thirds through the voyage, Tregare declared himself satisfied.

"I can't think of any chance we haven't allowed for," he said. "All we need now is more practice."

"Yes, Bran—but do you mind if I continue to look for things we may have missed?"

He laughed. "Sure, go ahead—you will, anyway!"

SHIP'S work was not all of Rissa's life. Liesel Selene, close to halfway through her third year—and Arlen Limmer, thought Rissa, would be nearly nine!—was a considerable part of it. And to not much lesser extent, of Tregare's.

Looking to the time when Lisele would leave with the scout-ship, Rissa or Dacia—sometimes both—often took the child there to play. Gradually, more and more of her toys and other belongings were kept there, and occasionally she and Dacia slept aboard the small vessel. Convinced, eventually, that Lisele would accept the separation without too much difficulty, Rissa lost her anxiety about the matter.

INTERSHIP communications were not all business. Tregare had arranged for a few small viewscreen terminals to be set up in each ship's galley, and earmarked several frequencies for "chatter circuits."

"All scrambled, of course," he said, "just in case. But no reason folks can't talk to their friends, while we're sailing out here in no place."

Usually Rissa had no long wait for a clear circuit—the more usual obstacle was finding that the other party was on duty. One day she tried three times without reaching her brother. Shortly after the third attempt, he returned her call.

"Hi, Rissa—sorry I was held up so long. This squadron coordination job—I don't know how you manage it, for the whole fleet. Sure knocks me out of my coffee breaks, these days."

"But you are now free for a time?"

"Sure. Why? Anything urgent?"

"Merely that we have not spoken together for more than two hundred hours. I like to know that all is well with you."

"Oh, I'm fine." But his face was taut. She waited, brows raised, until he said, "Can't fool you, can I? Maybe that's why I haven't called." He shrugged. "All it is—the closer we get to Earth, the tighter I wind up. Can't seem to relax, at all."

"The outcome worries you?"

"Not that much—I've chanced my life before, in lesser causes. No—it's that we're going where *they* rule."

"They?"

"UET—the ones who—"

"But they are *dead,* Ivan—remember?"

"The new ones, they'll be the same—they're *all* the same." His head shook back and forth.

"Ivan!" Until he looked at her, she waited. "Ivan—if you reach Earth alive they will be in your power, not you in theirs. Is that not correct?"

He frowned, then nodded. "Yes—yes, sure, that's right! Ilse—she'd never surrender, she'd ram the planet first." He breathed deeply and exhaled with a shudder. "Thanks, Rissa." Now he grinned. "I've been jittering myself into a first-class case of the heebies—I won't do *that* again. Now, then—anything else?"

"You might think to ask after your young niece." And she told him the latest family anecdotes, listened in turn to *Graf Spee*'s shipboard gossip—heeding it little, but watching her brother's face lose tension with the telling. Finally she said, "I must go now—Lisele will be hungry. To talk with you, Ivan —it has been good."

"That goes double here. All right—I'll give Ilse your best —you do the same for us, with Tregare."

"Yes." She watched the screen go blank, and nodded. "Yes."

TREGARE said, "You sure he'll be all right? Squadron coordination officer—if *he* cracked—"

"Ivan? In action? Never. I was concerned of his feelings, not of his performance."

"Yeah—I expect you're right. But check back now and then anyway, will you?"

"In light of my concern, of course I shall."

TIME came to jettison the scoutship, Liesel Selene's passage to Earth. Dacia Kobolak's crew had been chosen carefully, including a man to assume nominal command in case the scout arrived to find UET still controlling Earth. "They won't believe anything without a man in charge of it," Tregare had said.

So Starbur Clegg, a senior rating in Navigation, agreed to have another centimeter pared from the stump of the arm he had lost in storming Stronghold—so that the wound would seem fresh, sustained in the battle UET must be convinced to believe. "Just make sure you don't short me on pain shots for the first three weeks . . . ."

The scout, carefully damaged and then patched, carried the scars of authenticity. Rissa and Tregare inspected it thoroughly; inside and out they found nothing to belie the planned deception. "All right," said Tregare, finally. "But we'll have the good-bye party on *Inconnu*—so's not to have to give this bucket the inch by inch, all over again.''

Afterward, the celebration of departure finished and the taste of Lisele's final kiss fading from her lips, Rissa watched the screen as the scout dwindled and its faint drivewake was lost in distance. Tregare said, "They've got an extra week, remember—to stall or maneuver if they need to. But it doesn't make a lot of difference—they get there, either we've won or we haven't.''

"Of course, Bran.'' But she thought, *Will I ever see her again?*

ANOTHER crucial time approached; Tregare spoke on the screen with his Top Hats and other critical personnel. Wavering, their faces appeared on segments of his primary viewscreen—other ships' captains were on voice circuits only.

He said, "If we were UET we'd begin decel in two weeks— I'm starting a week early, to give us leeway to maneuver with if we need to." Rissa nodded; Lisele's scout had the same option.

"We'll be slowed down a lot farther out," said Zelde M'tana. "Is that good, Tregare?"

"I think so. Near Earth we can speed up again if the tactics say to, without piling up so much Big Vee that we overrun the planet.''

"But when we meet UET's fleet—" Kile Ressider was not on the screen, but Rissa recognized his voice. "—we'll be going slower than usual. Why give them more time to shoot at us?''

Tregare shook his head. "Other way around, Kile—I'm giving *us* more time to shoot at *them*." He waited, but the other did not answer. "UET's projectors don't have heterodyne control—standard practice is waste a shot or two, warming up, then keep firing while the heterodyne drifts through effective range. It's good for fast passes and cooling down in between—nothing else. We *do* control heterodyne—once we last out their effective bursts we can cut them up, while their turrets make pretty flares and not much else. You see?''

The other's "yes" sounded reluctant. Then, with enthusiasm, "Yes—I *do* see it. And have you thought to get more contact time, still?" Now he talked rapidly, describing a new maneuver.

Tregare's brows lowered, then raised. He listened, then said, "You've got a good idea, Ressider—I think I see a variation or two. Tell you what—when this is over, take ten, then let's you and I talk with our hands and show diagrams back and forth. Okay?"

The other agreed, and Tregare concluded his announcement of plans. He met few questions and answered those quickly. He ended by saying, "Kile and I may take some time putting the best polish on his scheme, so let's adjourn until—oh, tomorrow, same time."

He cut the circuit. "Rissa—if only that man had armed ship experience! I could have used a sixth Top Hat—smaller groups, easier to handle . . ."

"Once we reach Earth, he will have the experience. At that time you can promote him."

"Sure. Now I've got to leave for a minute and then get back to him."

"Yes. Will you need me?"

"Not for now—we can talk it over later."

"Very well. I will have some coffee and try a call on the chatter circuit."

AT first attempt, she reached Zelde M'tana. "Zelde! Are you not proud of Ressider? Although inexperienced, to make a plan that impressed Bran Tregare?"

Fingering her lobeless ear, the big woman grinned. "Oh, I knew all along, that bleached-out stallion has more to him than usually shows, in bed *or* out. Just glad Tregare sees it too, now."

"Yes. It is too late, now, to reorganize our fleet in space. But on Earth, Tregare plans to give Ressider a higher place."

Zelde made a grimace. "So maybe I'll get to see him, sometimes—and maybe not."

"Oh . . . it is unfortunate that you must be separated. But still—"

Zelde laughed. "Rissa—before I was half-grown I learned never to let my wants go where I can't follow. So—well, here comes my new coordination officer, just appointed. Maybe you know him?" And turning aside, "Come say hello, will you?"

The boy hadn't grown so much, thought Rissa—when first

he stood and pledged to Tregare, he had been tall. But now the moustache looked appropriate and the face showed mature outlines.

"Hello, Ms. Kerguelen—do you remember me?"

"Of course. It is good to see you again, James Pescadore. You have come a long way, from Third Hat on the *Saxbe*."

Before Pescadore could speak, Zelde said, "*Catclaw*, you mean, it is now. But Jamie couldn't get above Second there, and I needed a First. Then it turned out he's good at keeping things straight under pressure, and we worked together more, and—"

"And I know very well," said Rissa, "that you would never confuse one type of merit with another."

As Zelde grinned, Rissa saw the young man look from one woman to the other. Then he said, "Thanks, Ms. Kerguelen —and when the time comes, I'll do the fleet a good job."

"Of course you will, Jamie Pescadore—I am sure of it."

TREGARE said, "Oh sure, I knew about that—didn't I tell you? Thought I did." He laughed. "There's one lucky kid— training with Zelde M'tana won't be easy, but he'll come out fit to be top man in anybody's game."

"Bran—which way do you mean that?"

"Both ways. How did you think?"

"As you do. But I wished to be certain we thought the same."

OUTSIDE Pluto's orbit Tregare expected no sign of UET—and found none. "Somewhere between the Jupiter and Mars slots," he said, "is their optimum for first interception. They patrolled as far as Jupe when I was in the Academy—pulled back a ways later, to save expense. Still, we'll keep our eye-balls loose."

He and Rissa went to the galley for coffee. She said, "I noticed we changed course. There is a reason, I suppose?"

"Sure. We're angling over to keep Big Jupe between us and Earth. That way, even if UET has ships farther out than I think, they can't be sure of us until we pass the big fellow. He puts out too much interference of his own."

"And we will pass closely? But, the radiation belts, around a body of that size—"

"Well, it's no place to lose your drive at planetary speeds. But our field deflects the heavy stuff, and at this speed we wouldn't take much damage, even coasting—not close enough for long enough. But back in Number One's system, orbiting a big one, *Inconnu*'s drive field was on at all times."

"Then how could the ship hold orbit?"

"Putting out minimum thrust—a gentle spiral out for a while, then reverse to drift back in. Besides, it gave the watch something to do."

She nodded. "And when, on this changed course, will we pass Jupiter?"

"Not long now. We can check, exactly, in the log."

SMALL groups of ships approaching at standard decel, Rissa knew, could be detected ten days out—something over a quarter-billion miles. For Tregare's fleet, his best guess was perhaps a third greater. "Actually," he said, "any time after Jupe." And as soon as they cleared the signal-smothering fields of that planet, the screens showed a ship ahead, suddenly in frantic acceleration toward Earth.

"Do we try for it?" said Zelde M'tana.

"Hold course and decel," Tregare said. "Let's do a computer check first." And, a few moments later, "If yours says what mine does, that ship's trying to match velocities with us, at our present decel."

"One ship wants to fight us all?" Zelde laughed. "UET gets more stupid all the time."

"Or perhaps," said Rissa, "the ship is no longer UET's."

"Maybe." Tregare frowned. "Or just maybe they've got something new—say, a doomsday bomb to use in space, so one suicide ship could take out a whole fleet." He paused. "Just in case—spread our formation—keep the depth the same but triple the radius. And be ready—on command from me or anything that looks funny from that ship—to get directly the hell away from it and regroup farther in. Meanwhile, in a little bit we'll be close enough to call to it. Everybody's welcome to monitor, but *Inconnu* does all the talking."

Into the computer Tregare punched the dual problem: given

initial distance and velocities of fleet and ship, add current decel and accel respectively—at what point in space and time could they meet *and* match speeds? Still far from Earth, the distance mattered little; the time would be slightly under three hours.

As the range closed, Tregare called to the strange ship—in the clear. "You, up ahead there—I want to talk to you. Come in, please." At first the screen stayed dead; when it lit, its wavering shadows showed no recognizable picture.

The voice came faintly, then louder. "If that's you, Tregare, go to scramble. It cleans up the—" Signal faded again. Tregare switched to scramble-code; in a moment the picture cleared enough to indicate a face but not detail.

Now the voice came steady. "Yes, that does help—I can almost recognize you. When we're a little nearer—"

"You have the advantage of me," said Tregare. "Who are you?"

"Terrell Ragan, with the *Trujillo*. Thank peace you got here before our patrol tour ended—we had only another month to go."

"Ragan! Thank peace, right enough! Rissa—pass the word on the all-ships channel—they won't be getting this." He turned back to the screen. "Now then—what can you tell me?"

"I've a great deal of news, Tregare—but there'll be time for that when we rendezvous. Just now I'm rather busy."

"Busy? With what?"

"I'm afraid we've had a bit of a mutiny. I couldn't control all the personnel assignments, you see. And when I set course for rendezvous instead of running for Earth—and refused to allow warning to be sent ahead—we had to have it out with the UET hardcores aboard. There were more than twenty, and—"

"What's the situation now?"

"Eight dead—five theirs, three ours. The rest of them confined and being questioned under drugs, along with the other new people I hadn't checked personally—I got the drug supply from the Underground, before we lifted. So now I think I'd best get back to that job."

"Sure—okay, Ragan. But call me as soon as you can—I need to know what the hell's been happening on Earth!"

"I can give you the background now; I've taped it. Of course it only brings you up to several months ago. But if you're set to record, I'll shoot it high-speed; I think we're close enough."

"Just a minute." Tregare moved switches. "All right; let it come."

"Ragan out, then. Tape starts—*now*." Picture and sound became total jumble; Tregare cut the screen, leaving only the recorder on circuit. When the "End Message" light blinked, he cut power to the unit. He turned to Rissa.

"Let's eat. I can't concentrate with an empty stomach."

AFTER dinner, each making notes, they heard the first of the tape—putting it on voice feed to the other squadron command ships as well. The listening gave them little cheer.

Approaching the ninety-eighth year of UET's reign, most of Earth was divided into two groups—slaves and masters. Nearly seventy percent of the population was under Total Welfare, "owned" by UET and supervised by its Committee Police. What remained of a free citizenry was almost wholly employed in serving, one way or another, the Welfare system.

"Australia and the Hulzeins, it looks like, are the only major holdouts," Tregare said. "A few other pockets, like Israel—but they can't do much."

"And Frieda has been dead nearly a year." Rissa shook her head. "Do you think it is true, the rumor that Lena Diabla has moved her headquarters to Australia?"

"No way of knowing. The South American operation's still hanging on to its territory, the last Ragan heard; that's all we know. And does it matter?"

"Perhaps not, Bran. Let us hear the next section, which he says deals with Earth's armament."

"All right." They listened. Ragan told of thirty-eight armed UET ships. Then the voice level changed. "Splicing a piece in for you. I just heard—this is ten months out—one's down for damage repairs, and it might be rather a long job of fixing."

A pause, with only background hiss. Then, "But there's a new tactic you'll have to watch for. One of the Underground rumors backfired—for an unwelcome change, it brought action. UET's dummy-armed some ships and improvised a few with fixed-mount turrets. I've seen some wargames plans —not officially, I might add—they specify unarmed and dummy-armed ships for screening, for decoys and for ramming. So instead of thirty-eight ships, start thinking in terms of perhaps sixty. Old Ozzie's going to have a time trying to coordinate *that* batch. Pardon me—I mean Admiral Osbert Newhausen the Third, no less.''

Stopping the tape, Rissa caught Tregare's arm. "Newhausen!"

Over the command circuit, Ivan spoke. "He's *mine,* Rissa! You got the first one—this one's mine!"

"If he lives, and we also, I will not dispute your claim."

Tregare interrupted. "Sure, sure—but I'm worrying about maybe sixty ships and you're arguing over one man. Let's get on with it."

Again the tape started, now with report of Ragan's own activities. Bribery had gotten him patrol duty in Stronghold's direction for the year Tregare might first arrive. As backup, for the next opportunity, he and Coryle Hagenau had obtained the assignment for the *Committee's Pride.* "A man and woman of initiative, Tregare," said Rissa. "As well as ingenuity."

"Yeah." Tregare grinned. "We do get good people, don't we?"

The tape moved again. "Infiltration and sabotage began slowly, but they're moving. We kept the two packages as separate as possible—only the necessary minimum of liaison. Sabotage—mostly in defense missiles—it's the New Mafia's specialty. Our top contact there is Wroade Gameel." He spelled the name. "Infiltrating our people into decisive jobs —as I told you on Stronghold, we work with the Underground. They're a secretive bunch, naturally enough—I don't think I've met any of their top echelons—but Laje Markine speaks for them, and so far his word has always been good."

They heard Ragan clear his throat. "Now, about our plans for UET's fleet, itself—which should make a considerable difference when you arrive. In sum, here is the last version I heard . . .''

THAT section concluded the tape. At its end, Tregare said, "Let's break for coffee. Top Hats' conference in half an hour." In the galley, he said, "That part sounds good, Rissa. Only trouble is, we won't know how well it worked—until UET's in space and coming at us."

"But long before they *meet* us. It is a good plan—one hour after liftoff, mutinies on every ship where the conspirators feel they have a reasonable chance. One hour—how far from Earth?"

"Oh—half a million miles, roughly, and with good safe outbound vectors." They talked further, then returned to Control for the conference.

After initial discussion of what all had heard, Hilaire Gowdy said, "If mutiny's successful, the ship turns and flees, right? If its drive goes dead, that's a stalemate. I'd like it better if the successful ones stayed on and fought for *our* side."

Tregare shook his head. "Can't be done—there's no sure way to keep UET's skipper from getting off a mutiny warning. And with fighting aboard, probably, our people can't defend against retaliation from solid UET ships. They *have* to run. And if they stayed against those odds—more chance than not that our people wouldn't know who was who and wind up shooting each other."

Ilse Krueger said, "I like the double approach. No good for a simple Escape, alone in space, but for this situation it's great."

"I do believe I missed that part," said Bernardez, "—being momentarily called away, and constitutionally incapable of occupying two places at once."

"They go for the drive first," said Tregare, "secure it, *then* tackle Control. If the second move fails they kill the drive —and threaten to blow the ship if attacked. That gives time to parley, betting on the outcome between us and the rest of their fleet."

"What I see," said Rissa, "is that on many ships the conspirators will be undecided. The first few attempts will be decisive—if a good number of ships flee or drop behind without power, others will be encouraged to take the chance and follow suit."

Tregare nodded. "That's right. We'd better hope the first results look good, is all."

Zelde M'tana said, "Maybe I missed something, but I didn't hear anything about battle formations."

Tregare answered. "You didn't—Ragan didn't say. We can ask when we rendezvous—which isn't long from now." He turned to his watch officer. "Hain? How does it look? Do we need to change decel, to match up?"

"No." Deverel shook his head. "Ragan's figured it perfectly. About fifteen minutes now—where do you want him?"

"Where—? Oh, yeah. With me—*Renalle*'s a ship light." Then; "Formations, Zelde? UET never used anything more than unarmed ships shielding armed ones, which doesn't help us much, here. But I've thought about it—" He sketched on the back of a log sheet and held it toward the screen.

"Here's why we're going with the bowl idea. Meeting head-on—and I expect we will—you can't use a flat front because the center cuts your communications. A globe's no good because only half your ships are up front and shooting. That leaves you a concave or convex pattern—facing forward, I mean. I picked concave because that gives us the outside—if we have to, there's room to move."

He put the log sheet down. "But I'll see if Ragan knows anything that might change my mind."

HIS ship in formation, velocity matched, Ragan brought his scout to *Inconnu*. Rissa and Tregare met him—after greetings, the three went to the galley. "Let's talk a little, here, first," said Tregare. "We'll broadcast to the squadrons in the morning."

Rissa said, "I see the *Trujillo* is once again *Loose Goose*."

Ragan smiled. "Yes. Once we had the odd ends tied up, I sent a man out in a power suit to change the insigne."

"Odd ends?" said Tregare. "Oh—questioning the ones you weren't sure of. How did the score turn out?"

"None who stood with UET could be trusted—and I found two sleepers among the untested who'd fought on *our* side."

"Why—? Oh, yeah—" said Tregare. "Suicide missions—right?—in case of successful Escape."

"Precisely. Both were lower ratings in the driveroom—not trained to work without supervision in the ordinary way, but well enough instructed to blow the drive. And hypno'd up to the gills, so that they'd *do* it."

Tregare paused. "This leaves you shorthanded, doesn't it? Some dead—others locked up and needing guards?"

"No," said Ragan. "For a long haul—yes, I'd be short. But this near to Earth, we can manage. And we're not guarding the prisoners, you see."

Rissa said, "I had not thought you a man to kill his captives. But if you found it necessary—"

"If I had to do it, I would," said Ragan. "But I didn't. I've only one scout, so I locked them in the extra berth, displacing cargo from it to the empty quarters. They have water and emergency rations—a portable toilet, for that matter—but no place to go except *out,* and no tools to manage that."

Tregare laughed. "It'll serve. But—you sure it was a good idea, changing your insigne so soon? If things go bad—"

"Melt back into UET again?" Ragan shook his head. "It's not possible, even if I'd consider it. Circumstances too fishy— I'd have to kill the prisoners for certain, and the odd coincidence of all UET's prime plants being killed in action—no, it won't wash, Tregare. And for the sake of fighting morale, I'm glad it won't."

RAGAN slept aboard *Inconnu.* Next morning, on squadron command broadcast, he answered questions. To Zelde M'tana's, he answered, "UET started playing with formations not too long ago, when the rumor came of a big Shrakken invasion." To Tregare; "There isn't one, is there? I mean, at Stronghold . . ." Tregare shook his head and shrugged; Ragan continued. "They had groups out maneuvering against each other—all fairly close to Earth and at slow speeds, to keep the costs down, and of course—"

Zelde said, "So—what d'you think they'll be *using*?"

"The argument, I'm told, was between closed formations— spherical—and open ones like yours here. The latest compromise, before I left, was a sort of cone pointing forward— open, you see, but showing closed toward the enemy. Ozzie really likes that cone, by the way."

Tregare said, "Any special reason, you know of?"

"Surely. He bunches the unarmeds and dummies, with a few real shooters for appearance, to form his point—and himself hides behind it with a picked escort. The bulk of his armed ships make up the rest of the cone."

"Tregare." Rissa caught at his sleeve. "Does that give you a thought?"

"Let's see if it's the same one. We take *Renalle* out of the middle of our dish, put all five squadrons on the perimeter—

still holding about the same overall shape as now. They come with the cone—we open out, let it go through our empty center and rake hell out of it on an outside pass. And then—"

"That is what I had thought, Tregare. But—there is more?"

"We want even slower relative speed than I'd intended—well, Ressider's plan just might get it for us. Because—then we turn back to the cone as quick as we can. Before they can invert it, with luck—and catch Ozzie *without* his screen of unarmed expendables."

Ragan nodded. "If you're fast, you could do it. So far as I know, he maneuvers his formations as units—which is to say, rather than invert his cone, he'd try to turn it."

"Which will take him hell and forever!" said Zelde M'tana. "Ragan—anytime you'd like to come have a drink here on *Valkyrie,* don't wait for an invitation. You've got it!"

FOLLOWING lunch, Ragan returned to *Loose Goose.* In Control, after ordering max decel, Tregare fidgeted. Rissa asked, "What is wrong, Bran? Have you thought of something we overlooked?"

"No—no, it's just that we *must* be in detection range by now—from the Luna spotters, if not from Earth. But—nothing's happening."

He called *Loose Goose* and put his question. Ragan said, "What did you expect? Ozzie to spot us and lift fleet five minutes later?"

"Peace take it, that's what we'd have done at Stronghold!"

"Earth isn't Stronghold, Tregare—and Ozzie Newhausen isn't you. Don't worry—a few more hours and you'll see the hornets swarming from their nest."

"Well, I wish they'd get to it. Anyway—thanks, Ragan."

The screen went dark. Rissa said, "You are so eager for the fighting?"

They walked out of the Control room, and downship. "Eager? Hell—I'm scared enough to piddle!"

"You, Bran?" She looked at him. "When Peralta attacked, tried to cook you like a sausage, you wasted no thought on fear. Nor at the ambush on Stronghold. I—"

"Wasn't time for it then, either case. This waiting . . ."

"Is it—like Ivan, perhaps—the going back to where those who hurt you—?"

"No. That ghost died with Arger Korbeith—I told him it would." He frowned. "It's—there's so damned *much,* riding all on this one try."

"But all along, you have known this."

"And was working for it—preparing—busy. Now it's done, all I can do is wait—and wonder what mistakes I won't discover until too late."

His laugh carried no amusement. "Tregare the pirate, come to challenge all Earth? Little boy grown up to tackle his wildest dreams—or *did* I grow up? I wonder . . ." He shook his head. "Oh, let's go get some coffee."

She took his arm. "Not coffee—for now, wine is better. In our quarters—I will open a fresh bottle, I think. And then, perhaps . . ."

He looked down to her, and now he could smile. "Yes, Rissa—you're right."

And after the wine, after the love, he said, "You ever think you should've been a doctor? Your prescriptions really do the job."

"You feel better now, do you, Bran?" Smiling, seeing the relaxed vigor of his face, she said it.

"I feel so good you wouldn't believe it. Until a little later, maybe."

MORE than a day later, ships rose from Earth. No accurate count could be made—individual blips were indistinct, fading in and out—but the screen shimmered and the shimmer moved slowly out from the planet. Tregare watched closely, occasionally glancing at his watch.

The crucial hour passed, then another minute, and part of another. Rissa bit her knuckles. "Bran! None have turned aside—has the plan failed?"

He took her hand. "Wait—we're still not down to planets' time—not quite." Then: "There they go! Peace under pressure, some are Escaping! Look, Rissa—can you get any idea how many?"

"No—not really. But—another, and two more! It is not finished yet, Tregare. And on those ships, men are dying . . ."

"*Have* died," he said. "Minutes ago it happened, what we're seeing now." Still they watched. Belatedly, two blips left the shimmering cluster—and one more, and then none.

Now they waited for sign of ships dropping behind the fleet, coasting with drives silent. "We won't see those for a while," said Tregare. "Ozzie's coming almost straight at us—any that stalemated are hidden behind him."

"Is it too soon to begin Ressider's plan—make them turn to chase and meet you? The dead ships, drifting straight ahead—"

"Sure—that's it. Let me check." He punched keys and scanned the readout. "We can start it. Have to keep varying the thrust angle anyway—I'll start heavy and ease off later, as need be." On squadron broadcast he gave orders; on the screen Rissa saw how the entire formation, still pointing toward Earth, began a sidewise drift.

"We're heading straight up," said Tregare. "North from the ecliptic. Easier to keep track of Earth that way, than if we went to one *side* or the other."

"Tregare—what of our planned timing?"

He looked at her. "What? Oh—I get it. Don't worry—there's plenty of leeway before Dacia arrives in the scout—with Lisele."

"Then as you say, I shall not worry."

Two fleets swinging to the "North"—Tregare's slowing, UET's gaining speed—their velocities, originally opposed, now vectored at a narrowing angle.

Tregare jockeyed to increase the tendency. "I want as close to a rendezvous situation as I can get. It won't be that, of course, or even close—but thanks to Ressider, it'll be a lot better than I ever expected."

"In essence," said Rissa, "by turning the courses nearer parallel than opposing, you have traded distance for time."

"That's one way to put it. We couldn't slow enough on a straight approach—not enough *time*—so we've *folded* our paths together."

"And we meet—when?"

"Depends. Ozzie's fiddled his accel a couple of times. I'm not sure why. But at present rates—less than two days."

Their count of stalemated ships had been no more accurate than that of successful Escapes. No matter—the remaining

UET fleet was now close enough to show distinctly. "I make it forty-two," said Tregare. "I wish we could tell from here, how many are armed."

Rissa said, "Would it change your plan in any way?"

He laughed. "Course not. It's just—I'd like to *know*."

"I would guess that the unarmed ships, the expendables, would be most apt to attempt Escape."

"Yeah—I'm afraid you're right." He turned to Anders Kobolak at Control. "Latest time to contact, and relative speed?" The boy read off the figures. "Not good enough—or rather, we can do better." To Rissa, "Broadcast—standard max decel."

She relayed the orders. Then, "What improvement will this make?"

"Ozzie's caught on, I think—he's pouring on more punch, trying to overspeed us at meeting by more than I'd like. I want to close faster, before he can build it much. And then—Kobolak! Stay on that computer. What I need now is optimum time to switch to *accel*—half-max, say, to give us leeway—to meet at the least relative speed. Can you do that?"

"Yes, Tregare. It will take a minute to program, but—"

"Good. Get on it." He spoke to Rissa. "Nothing's going to happen for a while. Within the hour, sure. But—hey, Ozzie's just realized he has to turn his cone or we'll get him near to broadside. See?" She nodded. "So let's hit the galley for a while. Kobolak—call if there's any change."

"Right, Tregare."

IN the galley they found Deverel and Kenekke, and joined them. Kenekke poured coffee and said, "Like old times, skipper. Remember, off Shegler's Moon?"

"Some ways," said Tregare, "I wish we were back there. Three UET ships, but only one armed. Small actions give more room to improvise in a hurry."

"And you know what he did?" Deverel said. "They came at us even-on, a triangle. Tregare went for the middle of it, full blast—chanced their missiles and his turrets got 'em—fired none of his own. Then he flipped ship and went through them *again*, and popped two missiles into the shooter on our way past. He—"

"—and I caught a turret shot across the drive nodes; it cut

us to little more than half power. The other two ships got away and we had to limp back into Shegler's. So you see, Rissa—these hooligans remember mostly the parts they *like*."

"Lucky shot," said Kenekke. "That's all they got us with."

"Maybe," said Tregare. "But that's all it took, too."

BACK in Control, Tregare said, "Pretty close, aren't they?"

"Approach speed's lower now," said young Kobolak. "Another five minutes, I'd have called you."

Tregare looked from the screen to a readout tape. "Yes. Good estimate. All right—" He sat at his command console, Rissa at her coordinator's panel beside him; he opened the broadcast circuit. "Tregare here; prepare for battle stations. Don't jump off the throne or anything—five minutes to get there with whatever you need, another five for checklists. Be sure of your communications—when I sign off here we go fully to squadron relay and coordination. Ten minutes from now all circuits are operations—*only*." He breathed deeply. "All right—this is when we have to do it. Tregare out."

He said then, "Rissa? You've got your tandems set? For when *Falconer* and *Malloy* are out of sight behind Ozzie's cone?"

"Yes, Tregare—since this morning. Through *Valkyrie* to Ilse and through *No Return* to Kickem."

"Good. I—oh? Something, Kobolak?"

"Optimum time coming up, for accel change. Two minutes from . . . *now*. And it's from our neg max to plus four-tenths."

On the squadron circuit Tregare gave the orders. Then to Kobolak; "Estimate, time to contact?"

"Between seventeen and eighteen minutes after the flip, if Ozzie stays constant. But—" the boy's voice rose in pitch—"shouldn't you, or somebody, *check* this? I mean—the whole thing, on just *my* calculations?"

Tregare reached and touched his shoulder. "Anders—for months I checked your figures, or had somebody else do it. Until I was sure I didn't have to, any longer. Now—the time for flip?"

"Yes. Fifteen seconds." They waited, and Anders Kobolak made the change. Even through the drive field's shielding effect, Rissa could feel the wrench of it.

Tregare nodded. "Good sync—see it, on the screen? A little wobble, not much, over in *Falconer*. Now we watch it—the way Ozzie's cone drifts, looks like, sidewise to us and closing—you wouldn't know, would you, we're *all* going like a bat out of hell straight North?" On the command circuit, "Attitude change, to face them, exactly seventeen minutes after flip. Accel or decel for slowest pass—Kobolak's feeding you the starting readout, you take it from there. Turret gunners attempt firing as soon as you're faced into position. Use your override pedal until they shoot back, to spook them—but not afterward except at need. We want Ozzie to waste his heterodyne as quick as possible. And hold your missiles unless you get a *sure* one—there'll be more than one pass, before we're done here."

Now, to Rissa, time stretched without benefit of adrenaline. She saw and felt the ship swing—toward them, crabwise, came UET's coneshaped fleet. Suddenly she laughed.

"What's funny?" said Tregare.

"The cone—pointed toward our dish formation. The symbolism—there was a man named Freud—"

Tregare laughed. "Yeah—I get it. Even in a battle, UET has to be the one to do the screwing. I bet that's *why* Ozzie chose the inside formation!"

"And if you chose rightly, Tregare, it may be his undoing."

"Yes. *Hey!*" From *Parnell* squadron, nearest the enemy, a turret spat, then more. "Rissa! Get set—just a few seconds and we open the dish. Hold it as long as you can—we want a *close* pass, maybe even knock a few out of that tip."

"Yes." Now UET ships fired and she saw the cone's tip carried few weapons. When projector fire lit nearly the whole display she turned aside for a moment.

"Tregare—I love you!"

Then she opened the coordinator's circuit and said, "Prepare to open center—side vectors . . . *now!*"

Brilliant flecks obscured the screen's pattern. Squinting, she glimpsed *Parnell* sliding down the cone's flank—*ramming distance,* she thought—*get back, Zelde!* To her other side *Peralta* moved, not so dangerously close, but in good range. While under Tregare's hands *Inconnu,* leading *Renalle's* veeformation, dipped toward and then away from enemy fire, sometimes closer than Zelde M'tana.

Seconds seemed like hours; then space ahead was clear. The squadron circuit babbled, several talking at once. "Hold your reports!" Tregare shouted. "Casualties and damage have to wait. Max thrust *toward* those bastards—keep open formation. I'll take reports when we're turned, not before."

Silence, until the screen showed enemy ahead and the distance slowly beginning to close. Then Anders Kobolak said, "We took a hit ahead of the driveroom. Two dead, the rest walking—they didn't say how many. Operation not affected. And one more of our ships was hit—three dead there."

Tregare shook his head. "I got too fancy—too close. Thought they'd lost heterodyne by that time, but some smart snicker down the cone must have held his fire a while." He checked the screen again. "All right, the others are mostly turned now." He looked at Rissa. "Hey?"

"Yes, Tregare?"

"Just before you gave the order to open—what's the idea of putting personal messages into the command net?"

"But it was *not* on the circuit—and I wanted to tell you—"

"I wish I had your reflexes—you beat me to it by about half a second."

"Bran—" She reached and squeezed his hand. Then the squadron circuit began again. Rissa set the order of reports.

"M'tana from *Parnell*. Lost one ship—not total, but the drive's shaky and three turrets gone. Killing North speed, best it can, hoping we can pick it up later. Casualties bad. The rest of us—two unscratched, the other four caught minor damage —some casualties but nobody dead."

Then her voice rang. "And Jamie blew a ship in half!"

"My congratulations," said Tregare. "To Jamie and to all of you."

Next, "Gowdy here. I'm missing a ship. No clues—maybe Control's knocked out and it's on its way to Polaris. Have to wait and look later, if we can. One more beat up a lot but it can go with the next pass, anyway. I don't have details on the rest—just that they're in good enough shape and working like crazy to repair minor damage."

More faintly came Bernardez' relayed voice. "Tregare, it may be that my strategy—invented on the spot, mind you— was too advanced for its time. But in tribute to our friend Malloy, who—"

"Peace take you, Kickem—get on with it!"

"Well, if you wish only the drab facts, so be it. Seeing an ir-regularity, a hole in UET's formation, and being ever on the alert, as you know—well, I took *Malloy* squadron through and inside the cone. And then back out through it. I regret to say that it cost me two ships—one caught in crossfire and the other by ramming." For a moment, silence; Rissa watched Tregare but he did not speak. Then Bernardez said, "But for those two, UET paid with five. Aedra got one and shares credit for another. And the rest of *Malloy* is as healthy as you could ask for."

Still Tregare did not answer. The faint voice said, "Your comments?"

Tregare shook his head. "What am I supposed to say, Kickem? Your people knew the odds and went along with them—and you know I can't fault five for two. But keep in mind now—this battle's not just for itself, it's for Earth. And we still have to get to groundside with enough force to handle what we find there." Then, after a pause, "Hell—you did a damned fine job and you know it!"

"True—yet a little appreciation, Tregare, is not spurned."

"Oh—go polish your well-earned halo!" He sat back and glanced over to Rissa.

"Bran—there is no word from *Falconer*."

"Ilse? Here, let me try. *Graf Spee,* come in—Tregare call-ing."

Again the voice, relayed through *Valkyrie,* was faint. "Sir, we took a hit in Control—a bad one. The skipper—her man's with her—"

"Who's speaking? Identify yourself."

"Piet Voeren. I'm—Second Hat, I guess, now. Well, sir, the repair crew got this circuit working first, and they're rig-ging new controls now, what they can, so we'll be—"

A harsh voice, tight-edged, broke in. "All right, Piet—thanks." Then, louder, "Ivan Marchant for *Falconer,* from *Graf Spee*. The rest of our ships, all right except for grazing shots—casualties minimal, no dead. But—" The voice broke into racking sobs.

"Ivan! This is Rissa—what has happened?"

"Rissa! We—we caught it, here—they got *Ilse*—she's not dead yet, but I think she's dying. And—and others—I haven't been able to check."

They heard choking sounds, then; "Oh, don't worry—I'm on the job now. *Graf Spee*—she'll be ready, when we catch up. But—" The voice changed, and Rissa could not interpret that change. "Our squadron command circuit, it's done for. You'll have to—"

"Ivan—how can that be? Your alternates—"

"Just take my word for it—*Graf Spee*'s not a command ship now. You'll have to go on broadcast and reassign all of *Falconer,* because—"

Tregare said, "Because *what,* Ivan? I don't understand. It's not clear—"

The sound, before Ivan spoke, might have been a laugh. "You know something, Tregare? If I'm not clear—well, that's just too fucking bad, isn't it? I've made my report and now I have to get back to Ilse if she's still alive—and the rest of it's up to you. Piet, he'll pass the orders to me."

"Ivan!" But the circuit was dead. Rissa looked to Tregare. "If she dies—"

He scowled. "Peace knows I value the woman and I'm sorry for your brother. But the way he's talking, just as well we do break up *Falconer* and get him out of the line of command. We don't have *time* for how anybody feels about anything!"

"Do we not, Bran?"

She saw him shudder and relax. "All right—I *wish* we did. Now then—Kobolak, how long until we overtake? Do you know?"

"Of course—I'm monitoring continuous readout. A half hour, a little more. And you said you wanted a slow pass—this time we'll really get one."

"Yeah? How slow?"

"Could be as much as three minutes—five, total contact."

"That's slow enough to use the scouts. Get them out—each to stay with its own squadron."

TREGARE assigned four *Falconer* ships to the adjacent *Malloy.* "Kickem's short two, and peace knows what he'll try this time." The other three, *Graf Spee* included, went to Zelde M'tana's *Parnell.* Then, still on squadron circuit, he said, "Change of plan. Shift to orginal dish, centered on *Renalle* again. But with M'tana on *Valkyrie* commanding the outside squadrons. Because while everybody else makes the outside pass, same as before, I'm taking *Renalle* up the inside. And, Kickem—don't come through this time, or we might mistake each other for somebody else.''

"Why, I wouldn't dream of it, Tregare—you're too fast a shot.''

When the circuit was closed, Rissa said, "Bernardez sounds most independent of late. Are you sure—?''

"You mean, like Peralta? No.'' He paused, features relaxed. "With Kickem—when he blows his ego out through his ears, all good-humored this way—it just means he's happy with himself.''

"If you are certain . . .''

"I am, Rissa. And another thing—he's not one to hunger after someone *else's* place. He enjoys making his own—and then making the most of it.''

She thought, then smiled. "Yes. That fits what I have seen of Kickem.''

"Just so he doesn't get any more expensive bright ideas . . .''

OZZIE had lost ships; the cone looked ragged. Tregare's dish formation spread to contain it while *Renalle* stayed on center course. The cone had begun to turn sideways, but the angle, Rissa saw, was not prohibitive.

"Zelde,'' she said, "in a few moments we will be cut off. Your relays are in order?''

"It's all working—the new ships you assigned, and everything. We're ready—even the command circuit, though frankly I'm not sure Tregare made the right choice. Never thought I'd be doing such a thing.''

"I am sure you and Jamie will handle the outside squadrons well.''

"Well, the plan's clear enough—and don't worry—I won't take *quite* the chances I did last time. Damn near lost my ass.''

"That would be a tragic loss, Zelde. And now—we meet the enemy.''

SLAUGHTER, she thought—ahead, the UET ships still turning, their formation hanging quartered away from Tregare's attack. But as the range closed, first one and then more of the enemy swung to face the threat.

"Somebody realized what was happening," said Tregare. "And look! They're trying to close this end of the cone. But too late now, Ozzie! Another minute and *Renalle*'s inside you!"

Rissa watched. *Inconnu,* the six other ships almost abreast, passed the tightening circle, exchanged a few shots—she saw no damage to either fleet.

"Up this side and *rake* 'em!" Tregare shouted, and *Renalle* veered left. Projector burst dotted the screen. Then, when they were nearly halfway along the cone, Rissa saw something appear alongside and flash ahead, its projectors in continuous fire.

"What the hell is *that*?" Tregare scowled at the screen. "It's not part of ours." He opened the broadcast circuit, motioning to Kobolak to hold course.

"You up there—who are you? Why aren't you on station?"

"No time, Tregare! Squadron *Falconer*, what's left of it— *Graf Spee*, Ivan Marchant commanding." And then, "Rissa? It's good-bye, I think. Sorry—but I *told* you Newhausen was mine!" His voice gentled. "And Ilse—she'll live long enough to see it."

"Ivan!" Rissa screamed it. "Pull back—go in with the rest of us. We can—"

Ionization scratched random sound over his voice before she heard, "—she's got to know he's dead—I owe her that. Ivan Marchant out."

Rissa called; her brother did not answer. She said, *"Renalle!* Close with *Graf Spee!* We go in together." Turning to Tregare, "If you wish, you may countermand."

He shook his head. "I'll go with your hunch."

"With my *need*, Tregare."

"That too. Now then—give me the circuit. I've got to change some orders."

He spoke only a few moments, as *Renalle* shot ahead. The squadron pulled free of the cone wall, out of projector range; a few turrets still spat flickers of glare, but futilely.

"Ivan—he's got to slow now," said Tregare. "I don't know if we can catch him, but maybe—"

They waited; slowly the distance closed. Then, ahead; "Tregare! Newhausen's ship, it must be, with three others around it. And Ivan—he intends to *ram!*"

"He—no, we *can't* reach him—peace help him, Rissa, maybe he *has* to. But we'll—"

"No! *Look!*" On the screen *Graf Spee* blew one guarding ship apart and closed on the protected one. The images blurred together; a burst of light obscured them, and then —"Tregare! See—the other ship is gone but *Graf Spee* survives. How—?"

"Later, Rissa! The closed tip of the cone—not much room there. We—"

But as *Renalle*, moving too fast for such close quarters, entered that blind alley, the ships ahead parted and opened a way. And Tregare said, "I think we've won. Let's find out."

ON squadron circuit he said, "All ships and scouts turn to close again, but don't be in a hurry." Then on broadcast, in clear; "To all surviving UET ships—Bran Tregare offers amnesty for surrender. If you don't I'll wipe you out. But we need you, to help round up our cripples—on both sides—and save lives the best we can. I think your commander's a pile of plasma by now—who's next in charge? Answer on open frequencies."

Answer came. "Vice-admiral Jarlson speaking. What do you mean by amnesty? If you satisfy me I can speak for the entire fleet."

Tregare laughed. "That's easy to say when I can't spot you. Fire a projector to identify yourself." He waited. Then, to *Inconnu*'s right and below, came a flare. "All right, Jarlson. Amnesty means you stay alive and go to Earth under guard. There you get a chance to join me or go groundside, however it turns out."

"Your offer's not all that attractive."

"Neither is death; you have your choice." Then; "Squadron circuit—prepare for another pass. Destroy any ship that doesn't kill its drive in token of surrender."

"Wait, Tregare!" Jarlson's voice came hoarse. "You've gutted us—have some mercy!"

"I thought that was what I *was* doing. Look, Jarlson—I don't have a lot of time. Either accept terms or we'll get on with the killing. And—for several reasons—right now I don't give much of a damn which you do."

The pause was not long. "All UET ships! Acting in lieu of Admiral Newhausen I surrender all of us to Admiral Tregare under the terms of his amnesty. Any breach of this surrender will be a capital offense."

"You're right," said Tregare. "But that's my department now." Then; "Zelde, you're in command again—take charge of the surrender festivities, will you? Set the scouts to work —each side checking its own wrecked ships—to rescue survivors. You can help UET out if they need it, but make it clear that treachery gets *no* mercy."

"Sure, Tregare—we can handle it. But why not *you?*"

"We've got a ship to find. See you later."

ALONE, *Inconnu* searched Northward for *Graf Spee*—and found that ship near to drifting, its drive working feebly in deceleration. Rissa's calls brought no answer; when the two ships neared, she saw the reason. "Tregare—the antenna systems are melted to rubble."

"Yeah. Kobolak—close and match velocity to rendezvous. Near as you can get without actually rubbing noses." And to Rissa, "At that range, voice will get through anyway."

It did, Ivan answered. "My screen's shot, but that's you, isn't it, Rissa? Tregare?"

"Yes, Ivan. What happened? Is Ilse—?"

"Still alive—barely—and conscious. Our medics—out of action. Can you—?"

Tregare said, "Kobolak! Get a medic team on the scout and over to *Graf Spee* about five minutes ago. Ivan—if your equipment's damaged—okay to bring her aboard here? You come, too, if *Graf Spee* can do without you."

Ivan's laugh was shaky. "What *Graf Spee* needs just now is a drive tech, not me."

"We can fix that. Anders—you heard?"

"Right."

Rissa could wait no longer. "But, Ivan—what *happened?*"

"Tell you when I get there. Rissa—right now I need a drink."

HEAD bandaged, tapped with tubes for blood and glucose, Ilse Krueger was not the healthiest-looking person Rissa had ever seen. But Ivan said, "She's coming back so well—I wouldn't have believed it."

Then, in the galley—not only wine but spirits supplementing the coffee—Tregare said, "All right, Ivan—tell it. What the hell did you *do*?"

Ivan tipped back a shotglass; his face was regaining normal color. "Well, I went in berserk, you know—our missile circuits were out, so ram and have done with it. Ilse was good as dead, I thought, but she'd live as long as Newhausen. So I brought her over where she could see the screen, and told her. She couldn't talk but she shook her head, just barely—and I thought, no, she shouldn't let death make her afraid, so I said it again. She started to fade out and I gave her a hype-shot—she had to be there to see it, you understand. Then she came awake and told me what to do."

Rissa interrupted. "*She* told you?"

"Ilse, awake and in good sense, still had command. She said ramming was stupid. So what we did—went in close enough to throw rocks, almost—then launched the scout on drone, with drive set to blow at collision—and fired ahead, max accel."

"Well," said Tregare, "you got Ozzie, all right."

"And the blast wrecked *our* drive, mostly—but not before it threw us out of there. And then I waited, and hoped—and then you called. And now Ilse—she'll *live*."

"Right." Tregare nodded. "And peace knows we're glad of *that*. Now then—the drive techs said they could cobble up controls and get the ship working?"

"Yes—two days, maybe three."

"All right. We'll be longer, getting UET's ships—*our* new ships—under control, and searching for the missing ones. Let's head back and get started."

Now both fleets—Tregare's squadrons surrounding their defeated foes—used thrust to slow their Northward motion. As yet the two groups stayed apart. Then, after dinner of the day *Inconnu* rejoined his fleet, Tregare said, "It's time to tell everybody how we're going to work the changeovers. Let's go to Control."

On the way Rissa said, "You have planned it, how to handle the UET persons?"

"I think so." He told her.

"I would not have thought of that. It is harsh, but will save much time."

In Control, Tregare arranged for general broadcast and for acknowledgment from all ships. When he was satisfied, he said, "Tregare speaking, to every ship and person here. Record this; everybody has to know it."

He waited, then said, "You UET people have my amnesty for all past actions. There's no grudge that you fought me; that was your job. But from now on, any act against me means death. Behave yourselves and you keep alive—at Earth you can join me or leave space. A lot of my people here came to me that same way."

He sipped coffee. "But for now, until I have the chance to check you out, I can't leave a UET officer on an armed ship. So you'll be moved to the decoys, and my own people will officer every ship that has weapons."

He frowned. "I know damned well, some of you out there still think you can beat the surrender. I'll tell you why you can't."

He consulted his notepad. "Here's how it works. One of my scouts comes to your ship and takes aboard your officers, leaving a few of my people in their place. They'll board you unarmed, take control, including ship's weapons—and you'll give them all personal arms, to lock up. You won't do anything cute like trying to take them hostage—because at *any* sign of ship personnel acting against me, that ship is dead."

Faint with distance, a voice said, "You'd kill your own?"

"Think about it. I could send armed parties in power suits, board each ship in force and search it, face you down with guns. Sure I could—but it'd take me months. This way we'll be done with it in about a week, by the time we're headed back toward Earth pretty well." He grinned. "There's just one thing."

He waited nearly a minute. "Don't let anybody sell you the stupid idea that Tregare doesn't mean exactly what he says. Because if you do, you're dead. Which doesn't bother me a lot, except that I'd hate to lose *my* people—and the ship—along with you. But you'd best believe, I'd do it. Don't try me out."

Another voice. "Terrell Ragan here. Channel K. Patch me into the broadcast?"

Hain Deverel threw a switch, looked up and nodded.

Tregare said, "You're on it. You have something to add?"

"Yes." Then, "This is for the UET people. I'm Captain Terrell Ragan; I commanded the *Trujillo* in the NY66 fleet to Stronghold. When we got there it was Tregare's planet; we landed and he took us without a shot. We had the choice—join him and mean it, under truth field, or go to detention. I joined and was glad of the chance—and I've never regretted it."

"Acting commander Jarlson here! You mean—when you returned to Earth, and all this time, you've been Tregare's man?"

"That's right. And that's why I wangled outpost patrol when he was due to arrive."

"But—on Earth, how did you get away with it?"

"Trade secret," said Tregare. "Which reminds me—anybody out there that's on my side but don't think you could prove it, under truth field—don't worry. You'll ride the decoys, I'm afraid, but once groundside we'll get to you as soon as we can—and you'll check out all right. Until then, keep your string loose."

He laughed. "Sorry—that's a Hidden World term. Just keep cover and relax."

Jarlson's voice. "Tregare, you're a madman! Do you think you can take *Earth*?"

"Peace and population, man—what the hell you think I *came* for? And right now, what's to stop me?"

From Jarlson came no answer.

THE work continued. A scout located *Parnell*'s missing cripple, drive jury-rigged, limping back to rejoin the fleet. No one found trace of the ship vanished from Gowdy's squadron. On Squadron circuit Tregare said, "It's been a rough five days—six?—I've lost track."

On split screen he viewed his Top Hats. Ilse, still aboard *Inconnu*, was replaced in the picture by UET's Jarlson. Ivan had protested but Tregare said, "We have to coordinate some of the information with him. It's not as if we're telling him anything he can't find out."

Now he said, "Time for an overall summary. Squadrons, record for transmission to all ships. All right—out of thirty-five ships we lost ten—three destroyed, two missing, five crippled too bad to salvage—and we're going back with two that aren't in shape to fight. That one of yours, Zelde, and *Graf Spee*. And we lost six of our twenty-five scouts, on that second pass.

"That's roughly thirty percent losses. We're lucky, though —we lost *people* in less than half that proportion. The rescue operation was damned good, is why."

Zelde M'tana said, "What's the figures for UET? From where I'm sitting, I can't get a count."

Instead of answering, Tregare said, "Jarlson—you got here with forty-two ships. How many were armed? And how many of each kind took off from Earth?"

The UET man said, "We started with sixty, thirty-eight armed. In your surprise mutinies—I *assume* you set those up, somehow—we lost eight armed and ten of the others, either Escaped clean or went dead on us. So we met you with thirty armed and twelve decoys. Is that what you wanted to know?"

"That's right. Thank you. So—that means we got thirteen of the armed ones and four decoys, either pretty well destroyed or no trace found at all. And personnel losses almost as bad as ship losses—near forty percent, even with good rescue effort."

"Nearly two thousand people," said Jarlson. "Proud of yourself?"

Tregare's lips parted, snarling. "Don't bait me, UET man! But since you asked, I'm hardly ever proud of giving death— even when it's deserved, and I know a lot of those people were here because they had no choice. I'm proud of exactly one of those deaths—or rather, I'm proud of the man who got it for me. That's Osbert Newhausen's. I'd like to have got him myself, but somebody here needed it more."

"You gloat over killing a great leader—the third in a line of fine commanders?"

Now Rissa spoke. "The first of that line—such a brave man he must have been—to gain fame by gassing to death whole blocks of helpless people." Her eyes narrowed. "Do you know how he died?"

"Why—yes, I know of that tragedy. The admiral's grandfather was stricken by a loathsome, disfiguring disease— highly contagious. He spent the last twenty years of his life in aseptic isolation, slowly going insane. No one knows how it happened."

"You are wrong! *I* know—for I hired it done. Because two of those he killed with his cowardly poison were my parents —and as a consequence I spent eleven years in Total Welfare!"

Anger shook her. "I regret that he—as well as the grandson—died without knowing the truth."

On the screen, Jarlson fidgeted. "I—we all know mistakes were made. But it's not healthy to brood so long." His expression changed. "Why—that's nearly sixty years ago—and you're only a young girl. Who *are* you?"

Tregare gripped her arm. "We won't go into that just now, Jarlson. She's the wife of Bran Tregare; leave it at that."

Silent, Jarlson nodded. Tregare said, "Back to business. We've abandoned the derelicts; a few hours more and we'll have our Northward momentum killed and be on our way to Earth. And when we get there—" He reached for a switch. "The rest's private, Jarlson. Glad you could join us." He paused, then said, "One thing—you did a good job during rescue and transfer operations—kept your head level, and your people's, too, so we didn't need any more killing. I'd expected to have to blast at least one ship. I'm glad I didn't, and it's to your credit."

Jarlson's half-smile looked grim. "I had a few hotheads, but they still took orders."

"Good. That's all, then, and thanks." Jarlson's face faded from the screen. Tregare said, "That man may possibly come over to us—if he does, he'll bring others with him. That's another reason I wanted him on here, for the open stuff. I—"

"Bran—then I should not have vented my anger."

"To tell the truth, Rissa, at first I wished you'd said none of it. But—"

Ivan spoke. "No. She was right. Reminded him that UET does things he can't approve—and also that it's not invincible, and hasn't been for a long time."

"That could be," said Tregare. "And at any rate, Rissa, you had the right to speak your mind." He smiled briefly. "Now then—when we approach Earth . . ."

HAMPERED by the limitations of the two crippled ships, that approach went slowly. The combined fleets' drift had overshot Earth, radially; Tregare put a slight skew in the course to compensate, and to near Earth—when the time came—from "behind." "The planet's orbital velocity doesn't sound like much," he said, "but it's roughly a hundredth of one percent of light-speed—and on the slow end of the trip, it does save a bit of time."

"Time—Bran, I have lost track. Taking the battle so far above ecliptic—are we much behind our schedule?"

"Not bad—two weeks, maybe a little more."

"Good. Then we should be well able to receive Lisele in safety."

CURVING into the ecliptic plane and still decelerating, the fifty ships followed Earth in its path, always gaining but ever more slowly. Still at a distance, Hain Deverel sighted a group of ships. "Seventeen, I make it, skipper—looks like they're riding Trojan position ahead of Luna."

"Good safe place," said Tregare. "UET on Earth must be gone bushstomper. Let's call those ships. In clear—peace take me, I want UET to know what they're up against!"

Deverel arranged the circuit, then nodded. Tregare said, "Ahoy, lunar contingent! Combined fleet calling. Who speaks for you?"

Distance made the voice waver. "Who speaks for you?"

Tregare failed to contain his laughter. "Bran Tregare speaking. You hear that, you on Earth? Bran Tregare Moray! Thirteen years ago I took Stronghold from you; I've taken all the ships you've sent me, since. I command those and what's left of Ozzie Newhausen's fleet. And now here, I think, are seventeen more to join me!"

Again he laughed. "UET on Earth, get ready to surrender —or to die!"

He waited. The first voice spoke again. "Tregare—thank peace it's you! This is Coryle Hagenau on *Committee's Fall*. We're—Ragan's told you about the Escape plans, I suppose? Well, eight of us made it clean and ten more stalemated and killed drives until things were settled. One group had to blow their ship—then the rest of the UET people listened. We—"

"What's your situation now?"

"Low on supplies, some ships—half rations, or worse. The loyalists destroyed food to try to force us to land. And a tense balance, too—some UET fanatics are armed, hold parts of several ships, still think they can recoup. Get us down safe, Tregare! And get some food to us!''

Rissa said, "Bran? The food comes first, I think. Can we meet them?''

His fist thumped the control console. "Sure—we'll put scouts over to them, when we're close enough. But you heard —no trust this time—our people go with power suits and heavy guns. Order it out, will you, Anders?''

WHILE they waited, still approaching, a call came. Rissa was sure she had never seen the man on the viewscreen, yet he looked familiar. He said, "I am calling Bran Tregare Moray.''

Tregare answered. "Who are you?''

"Kane Altworth." *Altworth?* "Currently prime minister of Australia.''

"Glad you called—I'm honored. What can I do for you?''

"I wish to explain something. UET keeps its forces out of this country. Do you know why?''

Tregare grinned. "I've heard, yes. Anyway—rest assured, *my* forces will visit Australia only by your invitation, and in friendship. We do want contact, naturally, after the shooting's over—assuming we win. You agree?''

"Surely—and good luck.''

Before Tregare could cut the circuit, Rissa said, "Sir? I knew a Camilla Altworth once—and she went to Australia. Are you—?''

The man smiled. "My grandmother. But—*you* knew her?''

"I have traveled in space a great deal. But—someday, when there is time for it, I would like to talk with you about Camilla Altworth.''

"My pleasure." And with that, the call ended.

SLOWING, the fleet reached and passed Luna, and made rendezvous with Coryle Hagenau's ships. As agreed, Tregare saw to the transshipment of food to those in need of it. At the same time, all ships were cleared of UET holdouts—not always peaceably. The mortality rate on UET's side was close to half.

And when Jamie Pescadore, wearing a bandage on his shoulder, reported the last ship secured, Tregare said, "Good job. And now I guess it's time to go."

As the screen dimmed he turned to Anders Kobolak. "Any answer yet from the Hulzein Establishment?"

"No—we've been running the loop tape, calling them, for three days. Still are, in fact. But there's been no response."

SIXTY-SEVEN ships now approached Earth. Tregare called, "UET, North America—HQ Port, whoever you've named it for by now. Tregare speaking. We're landing—your choice is, do we land quiet or shooting? Answer—and when you do, speak up and name yourself."

A voice said, "I'll do better—I'll show myself. Tune your screen." The screen showed flickering light—then a woman's face, harsh-lined below short gray hair. The lips parted. The woman said, "All right, I see you. I'm Ingrith Hannulan, deputy port commander. You don't look so much, Tregare, but I can't argue with sixty-seven ships. Not when two-thirds of my goddamned defense missile sites don't respond, I can't." She shook her head. "Now how the hell did you manage *that?*"

"I'm the questions, Hannulan—you're the answers. You got room for us?"

"Yes—barely." Her hand moved; at one corner of the screen a map appeared. "North is up. The HQ building, where I am, it's middle of the west end. How do you—?"

"Just a minute." On ships' circuit: "Coryle? Is that straight?"

"She's told you the truth, so far. But—Tregare, watch out for that one!"

"Naturally—and thanks. Any special reason?"

"No. Just that—nobody gets as far as she has, in UET, by being easy."

"Sure. Tregare out—but keep listening." Back to Ingrith Hannulan: "All right. Turn on some landing markers, spaced as wide as you have room, like this: one group, circular perimeter, west half of the port, seventeen ships. Those land first. Another circle, same way in the east half—twenty-five in that one. You got it so far?"

"It's clear enough; you're hardly overloading me. And the rest?"

Rissa nudged him, and whispered, "This is still a battle.

Keep some aloft, and all the scouts, and do not say how many.''

Tregare nodded; he turned and winked at her. Then, to the screen; ''Hannulan, you're smart enough to guess what I'm doing so I'll tell you. Mostly so you don't try something fancy and make me wreck this port. All right—the seventeen are Escaped and stay buttoned when they land, until I have time for them. The twenty-five are what's left of the sixty Ozzie started with. My people are in charge of those, but they stay closed until I say so, too.''

''I understand.''

''All right, then—around those two circles you spot fifteen sites in a figure-eight—forty-five degree intervals. That's for *my* ships—except the ones I keep upstairs with me a while.''

''What—''

''Tell anybody you want to, Hannulan—I hope you do. Before *I* land, I'm neutralizing any threat that's more than a popgun.''

''On the whole planet? With ten ships, maybe twelve? You're crazy.''

''Sure—and I couldn't take Stronghold, either, with only six. And when I was with UET it wasn't possible to Escape; right? But we did, and here I am. How many ships doesn't matter—it's that many more than *you* have. And you forgot about the scouts—you know scoutships?''

''Enough to know they're not that formidable.''

He laughed. ''*Mine* are— they mount ships' projectors, fully powered.''

Silence. Then; ''You're lying—you're bluffing!''

''You ever hear of Jimar Peralta?''

Hannulan gasped. ''Escaped Target Number Two?''

''Number Two? Who's Number One?''

''Why—*you* are, of course. I—''

''That's good; I wouldn't want you to get your priorities mixed. Anyway—you can forget about Peralta. He tried something and it got him killed. But the point is, he loaded a ship's projector into an *aircar* to make his try. If he could have carried a bigger power pack, he'd have won.''

''I don't see—''

''If Jimar could do that with an aircar, what makes you think I can't soup up a scout? You want a demonstration or something?''

The woman shook her head. "No—no, I don't. Not me. But—I think you'll find somebody, someplace, who will."

"I expect so," said Tregare. "There's always some fool who insists on getting killed to convince the rest. If you want to hold down the slaughter, keep Channel J clear to me, to record and broadcast. And I think that's all, for now."

As he turned to Rissa and began to speak, the screen dimmed and then lit again. Ingrith Hannulan said, "Tregare! I have word from—from the Committee. An offer—from the Chairman himself. You'd better listen—"

Tregare looked to Rissa; she nodded. "It cannot harm, to see and hear him."

The screen blurred; then a man's face appeared. Rissa looked, and was repelled. "What decadence, Tregare! See? The tattoos, the gems inset on the forehead and—it must be—on posts piercing the cheeks. A ring through a *tooth* —who chews his food for him?" She laughed shakily. "The *least* of it is the brows, plucked into dotted lines. Bran—is *this* what governs Earth?"

The man's voice came deep but soft, almost lisping. "Ah— Tregare, isn't it, my good colonial? Shall we parley, then?"

Tregare grinned. "You know my name—what's yours?"

"Oh, of course, my dear lad. Gairn Forbisher. I had forgotten—you provincials, out of time and far behind it—how could you know? But now, without the amenities, unfortunately—you'd *love* my villa and its charming denizens, I assure you—I'll make peace with you."

"That's good," said Tregare. "Tell me just how."

"Even for a crude outworlder, I should think it were simple enough. It—"

"You better make it crude, Forbisher. And quick."

"Oh, very well. No finesse—I shouldn't have expected it, I suppose—but well enough. I propose unity again—the ships returning to our jurisdiction with you commanding as our deputy—in return for appointing you to the Committee with a twenty percent interest. That is one-fifth share of UET worldwide, you understand, and of offworld holdings."

Tregare cut voice-transmit as he said to Rissa, "What do I *say* to this creature?"

"Let me say it." He nodded and restored transmission. Rissa said, "Do you hear me, Gairn Forbisher?"

"Of course—but I had in mind to arrange terms with Tregare."

"And that is what you are doing. I will now tell you, on behalf of Tregare and myself, what you may do with your offer."

In a few brief words, she told him. When the screen showed Forbisher no longer, Tregare said, "That wasn't very original, was it?"

"Perhaps not. But neither was the situation."

Now, on the screen Ingrith Hannulan spoke. "I hoped you could agree. *Now* what do I do?"

Rissa said, "What do you suppose? You are acting under our coercion, are you not? So keep Channel J open to us—and for the rest of it, act as you think best."

Hannulan scratched gently at her forehead. "As *I* think best? You know, I get the distinct idea you're running a play you've done before—and that I haven't."

Before Rissa could speak, Tregare said, "That's right—and don't forget it." Then, "By the way—if you're deputy commander, who's commander?"

"Here at the port, I'm as high as it goes. Overall command is vested in the Presiding Committee."

"*Was*, you mean. As of now, it's vested in Squadron Commander Zelde M'tana, speaking for Bran Tregare."

THE ships grounded as arranged; *Parnell*, *Falconer* and *Peralta* made up the guarding figure-eight. Zelde M'tana reported that her port command circuits were connected and working, and said, "The truth field gear's on its way—we'll start vetting the Escaped ships first, soon as we can. Now then—these seven scouts you're leaving me—all right to keep only two aloft at any given time, with the rest primed to lift on order?"

"However you want," said Tregare. "And keep this channel open, Zelde. I'll have someone hanging high enough to relay to me, anywhere on this continent. Anything else, now?"

"Not that I can think of—watch yourself, is all. M'tana out."

Rissa said, "Bran—these ten ships, yours and Kickem's—

they seem few to cover UET's major bases, even in North America."

"Plus eleven scouts, don't forget—not counting the one topside. But we're not trying to cover everything yet—just the really big stuff. Right now, for instance—" He activated a circuit. "Kickem? You set to go?"

"As ever, Tregare. Check me now—Ragan's mapped me the four regional Police troop bases. A ship and a scout to each, with stalwart Bernardez reserving the command base to himself, since you insist on taking the administrative Headquarters. Oh, I don't begrudge you—except, I wish I could be there to see it. I—"

"Good enough, Kickem—and remember to relay the action through here. Now let's move it—I've got other calls to make."

He flipped switches. "Ahoy, Hannulan—Tregare here."

The woman looked tired. "What do you want?"

"Peace and quiet, but I don't expect to get it for a while. No—can you arrange Channel J, any time a signal comes over it after this discussion, to preempt all Tri-V outlets you can reach?"

"I—the eastern half of the continent, I can get you. It may take some time to get trunks to the west."

"All right—record what you get, and feed it west when you do get the trunks. Clear?"

"All right." She hesitated. "Tregare—will you let me join you?"

"You'll have your chance. But why now? You think I've already won?"

She shook her head. "I don't know—but if you *don't* win, I'm dead. Forbisher called—cooperation, even under your guns, is treason."

"Typical stupid UET policy," said Tregare. "But you're safe where you are."

"No. And—I might as well go all the way—neither are your ships, here."

"What do you mean? UET has a hideout fleet someplace?"

"Not the way you mean. But I know how Forbisher thinks. At Hokkaido there's at least one ship—maybe more. He'll have it sent here with a suicide crew and—"

"Sure—ram dirt and blow the drive! Hold it a minute." He switched circuits. "Kickem—and all ships and scouts now aloft! You see anything of UET's, armed or not, heading into this continent—give it one chance to turn back or surrender, then blast. Got it?" He listened to the acknowledgements and returned to Hannulan. "Okay—I've alerted my people; it should be all right. And thanks, Hannulan."

When he cut the circuit, Rissa said, "Here, as on Stronghold, UET drives its capable persons into your fold. And perhaps that is the Committee's undoing."

"Let's hope. Now one more thing." He called Ragan. "The Underground—you have any contact yet?"

"Not yet—I'm working on it."

"All right—keep me posted, when you can. Now it's time for our bunch, here, to scatter." He gave orders, sending his five remaining ships each to a major administrative complex. With two he sent accompanying scouts; the other three smaller vessels he kept with him.

"And now," said Rissa, "we go to the heart of this monster?"

"The top HQ? Call it the head—UET has no heart and never did. Here we go."

UET's headquarters were vast; buildings soared and sprawled, and among them Rissa saw signs of missile installations. She said, pointing, "These are less likely than most, to be neutralized by infiltration."

"I know. That's why the scouts are going in low—to scrub a few of those without damaging much else—before I start talking."

High enough to dodge, low enough to strike fast, *Inconnu* moved back and forth, never repeating a pattern. Rissa saw the scouts converge, then separate again. They rose—barely clearing a concrete cube, monolithic, windowless—and dipped again to paint fire across the launching sites. Several exploded; one missile lifted to fall away and crash outside the complex. A second shot toward *Inconnu*, but halfway up, bloomed flame.

"Another pass," he ordered, and the scouts turned and repeated their attack. Meanwhile half a dozen missiles had launched; *Inconnu*'s projectors spat until the last warhead exploded. "Too close, that one," said Tregare. "Now I'm cutting Channel J in, and—"

"No!" Rissa saw a turret's searching flare reach from the grey cube and wave across a scout's path. For a moment the small craft sought to evade; then its drive blew and the wreckage fell.

Without words, Tregare shouted; *Inconnu* dipped and the ground seemed to leap upward. Rissa saw his hand reach and said, "Not the bombs, Bran!"

"All right—a countermissile, then." Ahead loomed the gray cube—then a corner and half its top fragmented and sprang away. *Inconnu* rose and turned. "The red building, all spread out—executive wing—*there!*" Full-out, full-firing, *Inconnu* cleared buildings by mere feet as its turrets cut smoking swathes. The wing Tregare had pointed out erupted into smoke and fragments, dimming vision as the ship drove through it. And now Tregare pulled up again.

"Hannulan! Did that get on the Tri-V?"

"It—yes, Tregare, it did. You—that was *Headquarters!* The exec wing—"

"That's right," said Tregare. "And unless the rest of HQ wants to surrender, right now, that's just for starters."

"Wait—you knocked out their communications center; I'll try to reach the backup."

"Just tell them I'm not much for patience."

ABOVE any projector's range in atmosphere, *Inconnu* circled. A screen lit, and Bernardez said, "Tregare, you're looking at Committee Police command base. You might well take a good look, for its commander declines to surrender."

Tregare activated Channel J. "Get this on Tri-V, Hannulan. Committee Police command—about to give up, or *go* up." Then; "Ask them once more, Kickem—just for the record." He grinned. "They can't check with Headquarters, you might add—the exec wing isn't there any more."

"You've just told them; you're patched through, here. Well—you, down there—you've heard what my boss did to some of yours. Now then—is it necessary for Bernardez to do the same to you? Or will you see reason?"

Another voice, fainter. "Tregare? This is Kilgain, commandant. It's true I can't reach Headquarters. You've wrecked it?"

"I've made one pass, only. I'll make some more if the rest don't surrender damned fast. And Bernardez is ready to do the same, there. You want to live, give up."

"Go to hell!" From groundside, toward the *Hoover*, fire spurted.

"Ah, the sneaky ones!" said Bernardez. "They've been holding their turrets at low power, hoping to lure me down— and now they've tried to bag me. No luck, they had, as you see. But, Tregare—unless you say otherwise, I'm making an example of these."

After a moment, Tregare shrugged. *"Kickem,* Bernardez!"

On the screen, relayed, Rissa saw the same kind of swoop *Inconnu* had made. But Bernardez had cleared no missile sites, and now retaliation sprang at him. The view jerked and swung as the *Hoover* dodged through the barrage; it jarred as he took a hit. And then the entire command base vanished in a ball of flame that swung offscreen, leaving only sky showing until Bernardez switched views to face them himself.

"Primary warhead," said Tregare. "Wasn't that a little excessive?"

"Well, you see—it struck me they had more missiles than I'd thought, and that even if I made my pass successfully they might put one in my drive, going away. So not wishing to deprive this underprivileged world of the rare talents of Bernardez, I—"

"All right—I see your point. Now—check how your other ships are doing with *their* bases. Surrender might look a lot more appealing there, now, than it did five minutes ago."

"As you say, Tregare. Bernardez will apply himself diligently. And by the way—two ships *did* appear, on course from Hokkaido to the port."

"What happened?"

"Ressider got one of them. The other tried to ram him, and crashed."

ON Channel J, Ingrith Hannulan waited. "Tregare, I've got somebody on circuit, speaking for what's left of Headquarters. He wants to know your terms."

"Show me him." The picture wavered but Rissa saw a slim

man, not young. Tregare said, "Who are you and what's your job?"

"Albert Kybel. I'm—so far as I know—you made a pretty mess of things here—I'm the senior surviving administrator. I'm unable to reach the Committee and I can't speak for them —only for myself and the personnel under my supervision."

"So speak."

The man ran fingers through longish wavy hair. "You're demanding our surrender. On what terms?"

"I could say I don't have to give any—except quit or die— but I'll make it easier. Amnesty—you keep your lives, and for the time being, at least, your jobs. There'll be a lot of reshuffling later, but not punitive."

"You mean—this isn't just a raid? You intend to *replace* the Committee?"

"Stick to administering, Kybel. Now then—do you surrender or don't you?"

"I—I don't seem to have a choice, do I?"

"Sure you do—you can go up like the exec wing did, and Police command base."

"Then I surrender—myself and this entire Headquarters. And now what happens?"

"I land. And there's one catch to the amnesty."

"Perhaps I was premature? You weren't telling the truth?"

"Sure I was. The catch is only this—amnesty's for *past* actions. Treachery—resistance of any kind—means death. Death right now, no questions. You got that?"

"I—I will see that all personnel are informed. You realize I can't vouch for each of several thousand people, not to take ill-advised action?"

"And I don't vouch to hold down the scope of retaliation, so we're even." Tregare waved a hand. "All right—we know where we stand so I'm coming down. I'll land in the square— alongside where the exec wing used to join the main complex. Get some circuits ready to connect this ship with your main computers. I've got a lot of work to do in a hurry. And as soon as you can, report here in person—bring an aide or two if you need any."

The screen dimmed. Rissa said, "You mean, *we* have a lot of work to do."

"I know. I get carried away sometimes, Rissa—but I'm not

really dumb enough to think this is going to be any kind of one-man show."

"Of course. And I suppose we may as well land now."

HAIN DEVEREL led the first landing party, Anders Kobolak the second. Rissa watched as guards put down their weapons and were herded inside. Kobolak's voice came from a speaker. "As soon as all these are rounded up, Hain's taking over their weapons control and I'll salt the prisoners down in the bottom sub-basement. No stairs to it—all we have to do is control the elevators." A tiny figure on the screen, he waved to the ship and followed the rest inside.

Now, as Anders' party or Deverel's encountered other groups, only occasional remarks were heard. Once a shot sounded, then a volley. Deverel said, "The fool cost two other lives along with his own. And missed, besides."

Albert Kybel called. "Tregare—would you ask your technicians if your computer inputs can handle twenty megabit band-width? Or fifty? Perhaps a hundred? And your antennas, also—running cables would take longer, so the men are hanging a dish out a window for you. But we need to know your capabilities, so if you'd ask—"

"I don't have to ask—I know. Use fifty." He grinned. "And in case anybody has a bright idea, the input I'll use deletes command codes."

"Why—I wouldn't *think*—I—"

"Somebody might. Somebody better not, though—because the deletion process also brings up an alarm, and I'd have to . . . *talk* to somebody."

"I—I'll go make sure." The screen darkened.

"He goes to change the plans, Tregare."

"I figured—and warning's less work than punishing." He turned to the intercom. "Galley: send up a couple of lunches and a pot of coffee." And to Rissa; "Might as well snack here, I guess."

THEY had finished eating when Ragan called. "I have Laje Markine for you, speaking for the Underground. The picture's not half bad for a bootleg circuit. Incidentally, don't bother asking where he is; he won't tell you.''

"All right." The picture shifted; they saw a gaunt, balding man who wore a patch over his left eye. "Markine? Bran Tregare here.''

"Yeah." Gap-toothed, the man grinned. "I caught your act on the Tri-V. Not bad—but what do you plan for an encore? And where do we fit in?''

"That's going to take some figuring. I don't know what you can do because I don't know how many you are or how you're organized." Markine frowned. Tregare said, "Hold it! I'm not asking for your secrets—not until you decide they're safe with us. We'll do it the other way—tell you our ideas, and you can say if they'll work. But we've got a lot of talking to do, I think. Can you come here—not right away, but in a few days?''

"If I decide to, sure. Now what's your plans?''

"I want to round up the entire Presiding Committee. Can you find them for me?''

"Locate them, yes—but you'll have to dig them out yourself, physically. Or arrange for the New Mafia to do it—that's probably better.''

"Agreed. Now this next is your pitch, Rissa. Markine—my wife, Rissa Kerguelen.''

"Kerguelen?" Markine frowned, his single eye narrowed. "Yeah—the millionaire Welfare Kid, the one they never caught. You any relation?''

"I am still remembered here? It has been a long time.''

"What—? Oh, sure—you must have been in space a lot. Straight time, here, you'd be—oh, seventy-five, maybe.'' He shook his head. "Who'd have thought it? Well—what's on your mind?''

She paused. "Assume that we overcome UET—on this continent, at least. The problem—what to do next—is not simple. Much as we would like to, we cannot merely open the Welfare Centers and release everyone. At the start we can work only through the existing structure, changing its worst features as quickly as possible. I know this may disappoint you, but—''

"Disappoint me, hell! I'm glad you know you can't just barge in and kiss it and make it well—snap, like that. Seventy percent of the country in Welfare, five percent in UET, in the repression business—and the rest, nominally free citizens working to keep the wheels turning. I—we hate to admit it, but a lot of Welfare clients won't *ever* be fit to run loose. It's too late to teach them.'' His face twitched. "Hell—it's too late for some of *us*.''

"Do not be so certain. What we cannot accomplish quickly, we may eventually. We intend to put programs on the Tri-V, to teach illiterates to read, for example. And I have thought—those who were Welfared most recently—we can begin releasing them as soon as we control and understand the administrative apparatus. We—''

"Right." Markine nodded. "A lot of them are doing the same work as before—not getting paid for it, is all, and quartered in those damned Centers. But that's nothing *we* can help much with. So—''

"Another problem," said Rissa, "is that we cannot abolish the Committee Police, outright. But we can *command* them, change their functions and practices. Of ourselves, we are too few to monitor these changes. But you—carrying ID as free citizens—can perhaps manage that supervision.''

Markine grinned. "You've got it. And we have files on the worst of the bastards—the ones that really need killing.''

"Hold it," said Tregare. "I feel the same as you do. But we can't punish anything—no matter how bad—that wasn't a crime under existing law. I don't like it, but I *have* to give amnesty on those terms if I don't want to have to fight for every inch of this planet.''

"Our people aren't going to care much for the idea.''

"Can't help it—that's how it's got to be. And another one you may not like. The amnesty for *your* people—it covers all activity against UET, of course. But if a man's hiding out for —say, rape or murder on the civilian side—he'd better stay hid. Because if it's on the record, sure as peace he'll stand trial.''

Markine stared. "Trial? There's no real courts any more.''

"There will be. It may take a while, but there will be.''

Markine spoke slowly. "That takes some thinking about. Not just our few really bad apples, but—we've done things, sometimes—the only way to strike at UET was terrorize the folks who do their work for them. Might be hard to justify, if you didn't know the circumstances.''

"I am certain," said Rissa, "that such matters would be taken fully into account."

"Don't forget," Tregare said, "*we* grew up under UET, too."

"All right—I don't promise anything but I'll put it to the Council. I can reach you again through Ragan?"

"Right. And—as soon as you can, Markine?"

"Sure." He smiled. "Wait'll I tell 'em I talked with the all-time Welfare Kid herself!"

A FEW minutes later the computer terminal blinked a light. "They've got the circuit up," Tregare said. He looked at a screen showing the outside view. "And here comes Kybel, I'd guess—he's got two others with him. Look—you want to make the first data searches? I'm overdue to check groundside here, make sure our people hold all the important spots."

Rissa said, "Of course. I am curious to see how accurate Markine's information is."

"Then I'll send someone up to stay with you."

"Why?"

"I doubt they'd try anything *here,* Kybel's people. But just in case—well, it is three to one and you'll be wanting to concentrate."

She nodded and he left. Shortly, Anse Kenekke entered. "Skipper says you can use a bodyguard, Ms. Kerguelen."

"A precaution, merely, Anse. I hope you were not taken away from important work."

He laughed. "Fact is—if I checked drive balance once more, when we haven't used it since last time—well, I was getting bored." He looked behind him. "Here they come now. I'll sit over there, out of the way but in good position."

Albert Kybel, Rissa saw, was not much taller than herself. Behind him came a younger man, plump and breathing heavily. And finally—Rissa gasped. The slim girl wore a gray-blue jumpsuit, and her pale hair was clipped to plushlike stubble.

Kybel gestured toward the man. "Eyron Langer. And—my other assistant."

"Kybel! What is this? The girl—"

"Oh, she was Welfared last month. The usual thing—treason—I forget the details. I leave such things to others. But I need her so they left her on the job."

His thin lips pouted. "It's a nuisance—they deliver her late and pick her up early; she has to work through lunchtime to keep pace with her tasks. But I suppose I'll adjust to the added burden."

"*You* will adjust?" With effort, Rissa refrained from striking the man. Eyes narrowed, she said, "She has a name, does she not? I wish to know it."

"She was Aiela Lindstrom. Now she's Client—oh, I forget the number, it doesn't matter; she knows who I mean when I speak to her."

"How fortunate for you." She turned. "Anse—watch these two. Keep them here and see that they touch nothing. Aiela Lindstrom—you come with me." Kybel tried to speak, but Rissa chopped with her hand—deliberately missing his face by only millimeters—and he held silence. Rissa took the girl by the arm and led her out.

"I—ma'am, is it all right if I speak to you? I don't understand—"

"Of course you may speak, but come along."

"What are you doing? Administrator Kybel—"

"Administrator Kybel may be Welfare Client I-cannot-remember-the-number before this day ends—I have not decided as yet. Now—here we are, my quarters." Inside, she closed the door. "Now take off that jumpsuit."

"All right. I—I haven't had to have sex with women before, but I'll try."

Rissa stared, then remembered Welfare Supervisor Gerard. "Peace take you, girl—*I* want nothing from you!"

"Then why—?"

"Because, as of two minutes ago you are no longer a Welfare Client, and I wish to provide you with more suitable clothing. We are nearly of a size; for the moment, my garments will do." She took underclothing from a drawer, then rummaged in a closet and came out with green slacks and an orange top. "Do you like these?" The girl nodded. "Then put them on, please."

While she changed clothing, Aiela said, "But what will happen? They'll come to pick me up, then report me missing to the Center, and they'll be one short—I don't know—" Tears welled. "And there's no place I can *go*—"

"Perhaps—as I mentioned—Kybel may take your place. It will be a nuisance, of course, but he will know who I mean when I speak to him. And he can work through lunchtime to keep pace with his tasks."

Aiela Lindstrom stared. "Why, you mean it! You do, don't you?" Rissa nodded. "But—they took everything, all I owned, and my room—someone else has it, I suppose. What will I do?"

"Well—for starters, as my husband says—you will live here, on *Inconnu*." Seeing the girl's bewilderment, "That is the name of this ship. Its captain is my husband, Bran Tregare. And I think we can find room for you with no difficulty."

"*Tregare?* Kybel didn't tell me—"

Kybel now, thought Rissa—*not Administrator Kybel. Good* —She said, "Here, let me straighten the top. Yes, the colors are right for you. Now you look almost as you should."

She stroked the stubble, half soft, half prickly, on Aiela's scalp. "The hair will take longer, unfortunately." Now she touched the coil atop her own head. "But it will grow. Mine did."

"*You* were in Welfare?"

"For eleven years, from when I was five."

"But how did you get out?"

"The lotteries. I won a top prize."

"Lotteries? But those were stopped before I was born—for Welfare Clients, I mean."

Rissa shook her head. "The bastards! So they no longer feel the need even to hold out *hope!*"

Aiela touched Rissa's hand. "I don't understand—but it's all right. Shouldn't we go now, though? Admin—Kybel gets impatient."

"What I care about Kybel's feelings you could stuff up his nose. But a good man named Anse Kenekke is probably becoming quite bored, so let us go."

They went upship to Control again. "Any troubles, Anse?"

"No, Ms. Kerguelen. The Administrator here, he asks a lot of questions, like when do we get on with it. Too bad I don't have any answers." His mouth twitched but did not quite smile.

"Thank you, Anse. I should have thought to provide a few, should I not?"

Kybel stared at Aiela Lindstrom. "What does *this* mean? Speak up!"

"I will speak for her," said Rissa. "Aiela is the first of many who will be released from Total Welfare. She is no longer your assistant, but mine instead, and she is quartered here on *Inconnu*. Have you other questions?" Then, not waiting, she said, "Put on your Administrator hat, Kybel. Get on the appropriate circuit and cancel all current *and future* Welfaring actions—except those approved personally by Tregare or myself."

"I can't do that! The Committee—"

"To the Committee, by being on this ship you are a traitor to be executed. I trust you know Gairn Forbisher?"

"I—yes, you're right. I have no choice, have I?"

Why—he's relieved! "I would say not. Get on the circuit."

WHEN the man was done, Rissa checked computer readout to be certain the new directives were clear. Then she questioned Kybel, crosschecking Markine's data and ascertaining that UET's computer confirmed it also.

Markine's percentages—Welfare, UET, and a quarter of the populace caught between them—were quite accurate, almost exact. The population of North America—and of Earth, for that matter—was much less than Rissa had expected.

"That's why they leveled off," Kybel told her, "nearly ten years ago, and haven't Welfared so many since then. And sterilization of Clients isn't automatic any more. The top-testing ones, physical and mental, are given reversibles so they can be bred together, the children raised outside Welfare. No point in wasting a traitor's genes if the traitor has ability."

"Very sensible," said Rissa. "There will, of course, be a few changes now."

"I don't understand," said Kybel.

"And it is not necessary that you should. But tell me one thing—was Aiela sterilized?"

"How would I know? I don't keep track of minor details."

Rissa looked to the girl. Aiela said, "Yes. I was off work

several days—and penalized for it, of course."

And Rissa said, "Kybel, I hope you look well in a jump-suit—for tomorrow you will be wearing one."

TREGARE, when she told him, said, "You're moving a little fast, aren't you?"

"Perhaps. But it strikes me that by using their own machinery with its known penalties, we can make such people serve us without fear of treachery."

"You going to have Kybel sterilized?"

"I shall leave that up to the standards of his own procedures. *I* would not want his genes in my garbage can!"

But when Rissa thought to check the records, and found that Aiela's sterilization was reversible like her own, she relented. "I have ordered that he be left intact and a portion of his holdings kept for him. If his attitude changes for the better, he will be freed again. But he is not to know this, yet."

Tregare laughed. "Your trouble, Rissa, is that you're not really half as mean as you think you ought to be."

BY next mid-afternoon, command communications were reestablished. "The network's jerry-built," said Tregare, "but we can reach nearly anyone we need to. I've already ordered *all* Space Academy training halted, until I can inspect in person and set up a new system of regulations." He frowned. "One thing bothers me—a whole group of priority trunks is dead. It's not tagged, so I don't know where it's supposed to go."

Rissa said, "Possibly to the individual Committee members?"

"That's my guess, too—but everybody pretends not to know. Kybel really doesn't, probably—you said he likes to leave details to others."

"How has he adjusted to his changed status?"

"You haven't seen him? No, I guess not. Well—he's a little subdued. Sullen at first—then I told him his fertility was riding on his grade of cooperation, and he snapped to, a lot better."

"A good Hulzein move, Bran—multipurpose."

"Yeah. Oh, say—Kickem found the Committee Police

backup command base and took it without resistance. Got on their comm net and convinced the other major bases to surrender to the ships we sent to each. Then he lined out the new Interim Regulations and called Ressider to relieve him, so he can go to the port.''

He grinned. "So now we can get Liesel and Hawkman out of freeze!''

"Oh, Bran! Through the fighting—Kickem going through UET's cone, and attacking the Police base—not once did I think of them on that ship, in such danger!''

"Your mind blanked it in self-defense, maybe. *I* thought of them—but I didn't want to say anything. Besides—from experience I'll go with Kickem's luck over someone else's caution.''

"But why the port, Bran? Why not here?''

"Because now *I'm* getting cautious. We've got pretty good control here, but for now the port's still the safest place.''

ZELDE M'TANA reported on the screening of UET personnel. "The seventeen Escaped ships, we're nearly done. Most are ours, all right—they check out fine. We've run into some that probably have the hypnotic-implant protection. Can't be sure because the tech who handles that special gear we brought—he doesn't seem to know if it's working right or not.''

"Can't Ivan check on it?''

"Ivan's having a hard time right now—Ilse needed surgery and she's not doing too well.''

"Poor Ilse!" said Rissa. "Bran—I have worked with the equipment—and I want to see Ilse. I could go in the scout.''

Tregare scowled, then nodded. "All right, but not tonight; tomorrow's soon enough. And not in the scout. I'll have a ship come pick you up. Zelde? Who's available?''

"Ragan wants to see you in person, anyway. Okay?''

"Fine. Tell him, get here early, he can breakfast with us.''

RAGAN landed *Loose Goose* well away from *Inconnu*. On screen he said, "I'm not being standoffish—merely leaving room for fast lift if need be. I'll be with you as soon as I give a few instructions here.''

"That is agreeable,'' said Rissa. "I need to speak with my

assistants now, anyway." Kybel had entered Control and stood, waiting.

She looked at the man and hardly recognized him. His face was drawn, and now she saw why he had worn his hair long—clipped to stubble it no longer hid the jutting ears. *Like two antenna dishes,* she thought. The changes of proportion—head, face and ears—transformed him utterly.

She said, "And how does it feel to be Client whatever-your-number-is?"

He looked at the floor; she could not see his eyes. He said, barely loud enough to hear, "If I'd known what it's like. But Welfare's a fact of life—you take it for granted. To lose everything you have—" Now he looked up. "I had no *way* to know!"

Rissa felt pity—but no, it was too soon. "You are fed adequately? You sleep well?"

He shook his head. "I haven't slept. The food—it's edible, I guess."

"I am sure you will adjust—and meanwhile there is work to do. I have listed the information I wish and indicated the way you are to organize it. There is perhaps two days' work outlined; if you finish before I return, report to Tregare instead."

She paused. "Kybel—you see, I break custom and use your former name—remember, work done well can never worsen your condition."

"You mean—?"

"I mean what I say—nothing more. And now, to work." She left him.

OVER breakfast, Terrell Ragan reported. "I didn't want to put this on the air, even scrambled—there's no telling what kinds of decoding gear the Committee has available." He took second helpings. "Early rising—pardon the pun—gives me an appetite." A sip of coffee. "Now then—Laje Markine's coming. Not here, but to the port; I don't know why. You won't recognize him—he's good at disguise—but he'll use the same initials and expects you to know who he is."

"Why all the string-slipping?" said Tregare.

"String? Oh yes—I recall now. Well—if you'd spent your life dodging UET on its own home grounds, Tregare, you'd slip a few yourself, perhaps."

Tregare shrugged. "Sure—I see it. I didn't get over their

Space Academy all that quick, come to think of it."

Rissa said, "Do you know what Markine wishes, at the port?"

"Not a clue. But he'll tell you when he's ready."

"You trust him?" said Tregare.

"His problem's whether he can trust *us*." Done eating, Ragan poured more coffee. "What worries me is—Tregare, there's still no response from the Hulzeins. I've tried through Markine, through the New Mafia—any bootleg circuit I could get a line on—nothing. And something else may be wrong, too."

Tregare leaned forward. "Like what?"

"The Australians. As you asked, I've tried to set up contact. Well, Altworth—to hear them tell it, he's always busy. Just once he came on the circuit—for about ten seconds, and all he'd say was that he'd get back to us in a few days, but that right now—"

Tregare said, "He's stalling. I wonder why."

"Perhaps, only waiting until the outcome is clear," said Rissa. "But I wish we could be sure that were all of it."

"I agree," said Ragan. "Well, I guess we're ready to go."

"Yes. I will call, Tregare, when I have news."

RAGAN made a smooth takeoff. As *Loose Goose* rose and turned southeastward, Rissa used one screen to scan the terrain. Below she saw farmlands, cities looking almost deserted, and always the vast ugly blocks of Total Welfare Centers. "Housing may be a problem," she said. "If they have let the emptied citizens' quarters go to ruin—"

"A lot of them are still occupied, I'm told," said Ragan. "Converted to Welfare operation, though, mostly."

"How to *undo* this damage? It will not be easy. I only hope it is possible at all."

Now the port lay ahead, and Ragan's landing was as gentle as his liftoff. Rissa complimented him, then said, "Would you call the *Hoover* for me, please?"

Ragan shook his head. Before she could speak her puzzlement, he said, "No such ship—not any more. What you want is *Hobnails*."

"*Hob*—oh, I see! Kickem Bernardez—and *Hobnails* to do it with."

"Right. One moment—there's your circuit."

She called for Bernardez; after a short wait he appeared. "Congratulations on your new insigne, Kickem. It is an excellent choice."

"I thank you. And what you're after, I expect, is word of Liesel and Hawkman. Well, they're coming up nicely, Liesel taking a little longer about it as she did at Stronghold. They might possibly be ready to see you this evening—but actually, were it up to me, I'd advise a night's natural sleep first."

"Yes—by all means. Shall I visit you in the morning, then?"

"Unless they decide to disregard the sage advice of Bernardez—in which case I'll let you know. Or they will."

"Very well. Thank you, Kickem. And how is Aedra?"

"Fine, as usual—she's in charge of the resuscitations."

"Then they are in good hands. Please give her my love."

As soon as the call ended the screen lit again, and Zelde M'tana said, "Hi, Rissa—there's some people here, want to see you. I'm set up in the HQ Building. The guards out front—they're off *Valkyrie,* they know you—just ask for my office."

RISSA signed off, thanked Ragan and went groundside. As she walked to the building, sunshine took some of the briskness from morning autumn air. From Stronghold days she knew the faces of both guards but only the woman's name. "Garnet Spence, are you not? And—I am sorry—you are—?"

"Dalton Heindekk. I don't think we've met, actually, to speak."

She smiled. "Well, now we have. Can you tell me the way to Zelde's office?"

"I'll take you," the woman said. "She's not using the old Command office in the penthouse—said it was too much of a nuisance getting there." They walked inside, along the major corridor. "Captain M'tana had some walls knocked out here on the first floor—made several smaller rooms into one big one—alongside the auditorium where the truth field's set up. Not much farther now. Here—this door and through the anteroom."

"Thank you."

Garnet Spence turned back and Rissa opened the door. The man behind the desk said, "Good morning, Ms. Kerguelen. Commander M'tana's expecting you."

"Thank you." Then; "I do not seem to recall you. Have we met?"

"That's not only unlikely, it's impossible. You left Earth some fifty-eight years ago, I understand. I'm only thirty and I've never been off Earth."

"Then—you are of UET?"

"I was—hanging onto my job and hoping the next day wouldn't find me working in a jumpsuit. I asked to join Tregare—I was one of the first—and the truth field confirmed. So —Tanner Havelock, at your service."

"I am pleased that you are with us, Havelock. Now I must go to Zelde M'tana."

She passed through the next door and closed it. Zelde said, "Glad you're here. Those three in the side office—" She looked to her left. "They're getting antsy. But I have a couple of my people in there, so nobody's going anyplace until you say so."

"Three? Who are they?"

"One says he's Leonard Masterson—he wouldn't show ID, but the initials on his briefcase fit. The other man, and the woman—they didn't give names."

"I see." *At least, I hope I do.* "Well, another minute's delay should not harm them. How well does the screening go?"

"Faster. We moved in here because the equipment next door has multiple inputs and indicators—we can run through twenty at a time."

"That is good news. Now—do you wish to interview these people, with me?"

"I think they'll want privacy. You may have to send my men out. But there's no other door to the room, so unless you think you might need help—"

"I will see them first, then decide." She moved to the door, opened it and entered.

"Well, about time!" The man who spoke had bright red hair above a thin face. He tapped his briefcase and Rissa saw the gold initials—L.M.—that Zelde had mentioned. "You know who I am?" His grin showed perfect teeth.

Markine? No longer bald or gap-toothed, with two good eyes? "I think I know. Do you have proof?"

He motioned. "Send those men out—you're safe enough." When they had gone the red-haired man—red-*wigged,* she reminded herself—put one hand to his mouth, then the other.

Now his grin showed teeth missing, and in one hand lay the flawless denture. "All right?" He reversed the exchange.

She nodded. "Do you still wish to be called Leonard Masterson?"

"Outside this room, yes. In here it doesn't matter."

"Very well. And who are the associates you bring here?"

"Those names don't go out the door, either. Okay—you know who Wroade Gameel is?" He gestured toward the plump, ruddy man, who smoothed back his blond hair. Rissa looked at him, then at the thin, graying woman who had not been introduced. Markine said, "She's for later."

"Yes. Well—Mr. Gameel, I understand you have represented the New Mafia in negotiations with Captain Ragan."

"That's right." The man's voice was shrill. "But for this job I want to talk with the boss. Where's Tregare?"

"At UET headquarters, taking charge of it. You knew that, Markine—why did you come here instead?"

Markine shrugged. "Maybe Tregare's got HQ nailed down solid and maybe not. Here I *know* it's safe."

"Then you must deal with me. I assure you that I speak for Tregare—and we can confirm that on a circuit if you like. In scramble, of course."

Gameel said, "The Committee can decode any scramble I know of."

"If we word our talk discreetly, it will not matter. Tregare and I are accustomed to doing so, when necessary. And now—what is this job you speak of?"

"The Committee itself," said Markine. "What else? Our people have them spotted for you—all but two, and they're off Earth. But we can't grab them ourselves—we're not set up for that, and I don't think you are, either. For that job you need Gameel's outfit."

"And it's going to cost you," the plump man said. "And not just in money."

"Then what do you want?"

"Our sharc, is what. We talked about that, in High Council. A long time ago our outfit was called 'organized crime.' Things changed; a hundred years ago we were just about like any other big company—bid in elections a couple of times, even. When UET squeezed us out—us and everybody else—we were outlawed again, and ended up doing everybody's dirty work to make a living. And fighting UET, when we could, working with Laje's gang. But now that's not going to work so well, for us." He smiled. "If you don't see what I mean, you're not as smart as I think."

"I see part of it—but so I do not misunderstand, say it all."

"If the Underground's on your side, that crimps us right there. And the way you're starting out, where's the graft? Peanuts, that's where—lower echelon stuff, not worth bothering with." He sighed. "When I think of losing all that blackmail —for not telling one Committee member's dirty secrets to the others, and vice versa. Oh, well—times change, we have to change with them."

Rissa frowned. "Committee members squeamish about the details of their private lives? I have seen and heard Gairn Forbisher, and—"

"No, no—it was their conniving against *each other* that we played on. A little spying, a discreet hint—and now—"

"Yes—under Tregare there will be no such opportunities. But you take a very long time, Wroade Gameel, to come to the point. What is it you want? Your share of *what?*"

"Control—what else? Goods and services our outfit used to handle—came to more than four percent of the total, this continent. Now, working other ways and squeezed, our holdings are down to half that. And frankly, the way you'll be changing things, we're in trouble—unless we can make a deal."

"Which we may be able to do," said Rissa, "if you can bring yourself to clearly state your terms."

"All right." He waved a hand. "I thought we needed the background. Well, then—you want the Committee, we can get them for you. Our price is, we'll group our holdings—our credit—in the total pot and you assign us four percent of the overall package. Plus a seat on the Committee, to vote it."

"And all of you will sit back and live off that?"

He shook his head. "Not me, and not a lot of others. What I own isn't what I do—there'll be jobs out *looking* for me. Now, then. Four percent—how about it?"

Rissa thought. "We may not continue the Committee structure itself. The corporate governmental system, however, must remain for an indefinite time, since none of us is experienced in a better alternative. If Tregare approves, your group may have its four percent of control and ownership in that system. One moment."

She moved to the intercom. "Zelde? I wish to call Bran Tregare. Is the terminal in this room equipped for scramble?''

"Not with his codes. You'll have to use the one in here."

"Very well." And to the others, "Come with me, if you wish."

They went into Zelde's office. Rissa sat at the terminal; behind her stood the three. *I still do not know about the woman —Markine and Gameel have succeeded in keeping me off balance.*

She completed her circuit selection; the screen lit. She asked for Tregare and was transferred, at the distant end, to another local trunk. She saw him smile in recognition.

"Rissa! What's developing? Who all's that with you?"

Carefully she chose her words. "I am told that this circuit may not be secure." When he nodded, she said, "The redhaired man is Leonard Masterson, the one I came here to meet. Concerning the location and procurement of several unique and valuable objects—the project we discussed not long ago with an associate of his—he tells me that he has located all but two. You understand?"

"The two are sort of unavailable?"

"It is probable that they are not presently on this planet."

"All right—what else?"

"The other man represents the procurement group. He is the one Captain T.R. has spoken with. His price is high but—I believe—fair."

"Then let's hear it."

"It is not money as such, but a—a merger, it could be called. Following the conclusion of this project, his group would be granted four percent of the total holdings achieved, with appropriate voting rights."

Tregare whistled. "That's a lot—but maybe worth it, to eliminate—uh—competition in the field." He squinted. "You —the procurement man—step up where I can see you better."

Gameel moved forward. "Sure—I'd like a closer look, too. You're Tregare, huh?"

"That's right. And I've heard your name from the captain Rissa mentioned."

"I imagine so. Let's get on with the deal, shall we?"

"All right. You can deliver? How soon?"

"Within a week, I'd guess—except for the two. Condition as good as can be managed, I suppose you want?"

"Yes—try not to damage the items. Now, then—you're asking four percent of the takings on this project, with voting rights. You accept that this means no competitive activity in future?"

"On our side that's been agreed. So what do you say?"

"You've got a deal. Now—Masterson, anything new on your end?"

"Besides this project, I've been passing the word you gave me, about a lot of new assignments coming up. You have anything more on that?"

"Not yet—but soon, I think. Your contact will be—no, continue to go through T.R. for now. Until the current project's completed."

"Sure—that makes sense."

"Fine. Anything else, Rissa? The woman—what's her part?"

"Different project entirely," said Markine. "We haven't discussed it yet. Nothing that needs negotiation, anyway. Okay?"

Rissa said, "I will call you, Tregare, if there is reason."

"Okay. Good-bye for now. Nice talking to you all."

THE screen dimmed; Rissa turned to Zelde M'tana. "As soon as I am free I will look at the equipment that is hampering the truth field work." And back to Markine; "Is there anything more we need to discuss? Or would you like luncheon before you go? Incidentally, how did you get here?" *I sound like Felcie!*

Gameel said, "Aircar. Safe passage cleared with Ragan."

"Lunch sounds fine," said Markine. "Other business? Well, we may have some help for you. This equipment you're talking about—that's what you use to check for hypnotic implants?"

"Why, yes—but how could you help?"

"Let's see it first."

"Zelde? This is your jurisdiction—"

"If it's all right with you, Rissa, it is with me; let's go. It's in a different room, down the hall. Come on."

They followed her. In the room were the woman operating the truth field, a young man sitting before the polygraph gear, and two guards—all attention focused on the man who sat, shaking his head.

"I tell the truth, but the field calls me a liar." His voice rose. "My name is Borg Hasson—I hate UET's guts and I want to join Tregare!'' His shoulders slumped. "And there goes that goddamned alarm again.''

To the polygraph attendant, Rissa said, "Let me see that. On Stronghold I have worked with these processes.'' And to the troubled man, "Hasson, we understand the problem. It is to find the triggers for the hypnotic implants that protected you from UET's probes—and then the slower job of deactivating them. We—'' Suddenly she saw the error. "This connecting cable!''

"The only spare I could find,'' the young man said. "The other one—it got a short in it.''

"But this is an older model,'' said Rissa. "See the designation? The internal connections are different—no wonder your results have been inconclusive.''

Wide-eyed, the boy shook his head. "I didn't know. But I can fix it—I know how to make wiring changes and the drawings are in this carton. Let me—''

"Very well—the fault is not yours, but you may have the credit for correcting it.'' And to Zelde; "Well—the work will still be slow, but now it can be sure.''

Markine said, "It doesn't have to be slow.''

"Oh? You are experienced? We have found it to be most painstaking.''

He gestured toward the older woman. "We got word you were having trouble, so that's why *she's* here—Melya Corradone, studied under Dr. Sandissen who invented the method. Thirty years ago UET Welfared her, and it took us five to get her out.''

"I can sympathize,'' said Rissa. "I spent eleven years in a Center. But I do not understand—Melya Corradone, how do you plan to help?''

For the first time, the woman spoke. Her voice rasped; looking closely, Rissa saw scars on her throat. "Your equipment detects the hypnotic implants, doesn't it? Then you have to probe with questions until you deactivate them.''

"That is correct.''

"We can bypass a lot of that. I have a list of who was treated; I can spring the triggers and all you have to do is check, make sure they're gone. And then your field will work the way it's supposed to.''

"And how can you be so sure of releasing all the implants?''

Markine laughed. "Hell—she's the one who put most of 'em *in!*"

WITH the wiring changed, the polygraph gave definite results. Quickly, Rissa asked Borg Hasson the standard questions; the triggering of implants registered clearly. Then she watched, fascinated, as Melya Corradone said, "Hear me, Hasson. The time's come to end the masquerade—know that, deeply. No other with these words could open your mind, but now it opens. You remember. I will say the key words that implanted your protection against UET, and now they will unlock that protection, for it is no longer needed." Then, slowly, she said a series of words, random-seeming but carefully pronounced. She turned to Rissa. "Now try him."

"Yes." Again Rissa asked her questions—and now the polygraph gave no untoward sign, and the truth field verified what it had denied before.

Rissa said, "It worked—it worked perfectly. Hasson, you're cleared—and I welcome you." As the man came to shake her hand she saw tears in his eyes. A smiling guard escorted him from the room.

Rissa turned to Melya Corradone. "Can you stay, and help us with the others? How many, do you think?"

"That's why Mar—Masterson brought me. How many? Thousands, over the years—but many are elsewhere, or dead. I have the list; we'll see. But—"

"But if you're as hungry as the rest of us," said Zelde M'tana, "it's time to stop and eat."

THEY lunched aboard *Valkyrie*. Careful of her words but being as frank as possible under the circumstances, Rissa found herself liking all three guests. An idea came to her; thinking about it, she fell silent. Finally Gameel said, "Something wrong?"

She shook her head. "Not really. But I have a thought—if you will not be offended—"

"Allies can't afford to be offended," said Markine. "They do have the right to say no."

"Have you, then, read my mind? Well—my thought is this.

We accept or reject recruits by truth field evidence. Would *you*—?

Gameel's violent gesture rejected her words; Markine said, "Gently, Wroade. Now, Rissa Kerguelen—I see your point, but there have to be safeguards. We don't turn you loose on our minds in all areas—we have our secrets, even from you. But—"

Gameel said, "No part of it, I'm having!"

"Wait—listen—" Markine spoke softly. "A list of questions, in writing—we check the ones we'll answer. And you *tape* them, and with the field on, you play the tape—no impromptu additions, you get me?" He paused. "Well? Both of you—does it work?"

Rissa said, "I accept those restrictions."

"But what we *don't* answer," said Gameel. "That could tell you a lot."

"If you feel, on seeing my questions, that such is true, you may refuse entirely."

"And then what happens?"

"Nothing—except that I must then trust you less than I would prefer."

FOOD was done with, but not coffee, when Jamie Pescadore joined them. "Rissa! It's been a long time."

Catching Zelde's look, seeing her obvious pride in the young man, Rissa stood and kissed him. She saw Zelde grin and wink at her, and she said, "Are you James or Jamie—now that you have become a man who blows UET ships in half?" And he *had* grown, she saw—not so much in height, but in the assurance of maturity.

"Zelde calls me Jamie—and so do half the crew. You might as well."

They sat. "I see—you no longer need formality."

He laughed. "I don't need much of anything except what I have—including the chance to keep learning." He looked closely at Rissa. "I'll never forget—when I stood up, right after Captain Paszacker tried to kill you both. I was so scared —and Tregare steadied me, I knew I could trust him. And then later he assigned me to *Valkyrie*, and—"

"No." Rissa shook her head. "Zelde herself chose you for *Valkyrie.*"

He stared. "Then it's you I owe, Zelde—for being here in the first place, besides all the rest?" He shook his head. "How can I thank you?"

Never before, thought Rissa, had she seen Zelde M'tana embarrassed. Aloud she said, "Oh, quite easily." For a moment she let him puzzle. "Just continue being Jamie Pescadore."

And now Zelde laughed. "She told you, Jamie—I hope you listen."

MELYA CORRADONE'S system worked rapidly. The words varied, but the results were consistent; one after another, men and women were cleared of implants and passed as trustworthy.

Between cases, Rissa asked, "But you say you are the only one who can unlock their minds. Supposing you were not available?"

The harsh, croaking voice said, "I'm the only one who can do it *with these words.* With someone else—and we did set up alternates—the words would be different. It's all part of the method. Dr. Sandissen worked it out—I merely apply it."

"That's horse puckie," said Markine. "Sandissen did the pioneer work, sure—but Melya's improved on it and refined it a lot. Modesty's her worst fault."

"And yours," said Melya Corradone, "is talking when I'm supposed to be working."

IN the side office Rissa worked at her list of questions—adding and deleting, trying to cover every possibility. Markine, watching, grinned at her. "Not so easy?"

She looked at him and crumpled the paper. "I have been using the wrong approach. Details are not important here." She stood.

"You've figured something out, then?" said Gameel.

"Yes. To each of you I shall outline the terms of our agreements, then ask two questions: Do you offer these in good faith? And; what limits have you set, to your cooperation?"

She waited. Neither man spoke, so she said, "Will you answer these? And is it necessary that I tape them?"

Markine said, "I'll answer; forget the tape." Gameel looked dubious, gave no answer for nearly half a minute, then slowly nodded.

"All right," he said. "But I get to ask you the same questions."

"Agreed. Shall we get on with it? We may have to preempt Melya's work, briefly." But Zelde guided them to a machine being used for lesser-priority subjects. They waited until the current group was finished—most passed but some went to detention—then had the room to themselves.

"Me first," said Laje Markine. To her first question, he said, "Yes—in good faith, from our side." To the second, "Well, we're not giving up our protections until we're *sure* you're phasing out Welfare and giving as much freedom as possible—that you don't bog down and decide it's too much work, and leave things pretty much as they are. In a few months we should know.

"I don't mind telling this because there's nothing you can do about it—and in fairness, you have to admit it makes sense. Until we're sure, we keep our cover—just in case. Our people who come out to help you, don't get too nosy about their IDs —maybe they're phony, or maybe they have still other names to hide under if anything goes sour. I guess that's about it. Satisfied?"

"Yes. And convinced that you are as valuable an ally as we had hoped."

"Oh? How's that?"

"Had you *not* arranged to protect yourselves, I would doubt your capability."

Markine moved to another seat; Gameel took his place and again Rissa spoke. The man's first answer was, "That's right. For our percentage we're with you all the way." Then; "Limits? About like Markine's, I guess. You don't see our books until our contract's signed and completed. And no ID at all on our hideout people, until they're ready to give it. That bother you?"

Rissa moved a switch; the field's hum stopped. She stood and moved away from the equipment. "The field is off, so I may ask another question. How long, before these people come out of hiding?"

"Like Laje, again—a few months, maybe. High Council will vote it, actually." He moved to the operating position and sat. "Now I'm in a hole—I don't know how to work this gadget. Can we get Corradone here?"

Markine said, "I know how. You ask; I'll interpret."

The men changed places. Gameel said, "I don't have to repeat the agreements again, I guess. Are you and Tregare dickering in good faith?"

"Entirely." Gameel looked to Markine, who nodded.

"And like you said to us—with what reservations?"

"We, also, withhold information you will not need in our joint efforts. You do not, I am sure, expect to know *all* our plans. You will know all that concerns your activities with us—which is to say, we will not attempt to use you for aims you do not know about."

"There was a flicker there," said Markine.

"I had not finished; what I said was ambiguous without what I say now. *Of course* we will take precautions. It is conceivable, Gameel, that your High Council might change its mind and decide to try for a larger slice of the pie—or even for dominance. Naturally, we shall see to it that no such opportunity arises."

"All in the clear this time," said Markine.

Gameel nodded. "That's straight enough. All right—I guess we're done here." He stood. "Corradone's staying for a while —right? Okay—let's go, Laje. Pleasure dealing with you, Ms. Kerguelen."

"And my pleasure also. I will convey your regards to Bran Tregare."

". . . and I did not bother to mention, Bran, that the truth field console was the recording model. I will play the tape for you."

When it was done he said, "Good enough—everybody's using precautionary common sense and making no bones about it. That's a good way to start off." On the screen, he grinned. "And the polygraph trouble was nothing but a wrong cable? It's good you spotted it so fast. And this Corradone woman—Markine gets points for bringing *her* along, all right."

"She has speeded the work greatly. There were more implanted persons than we thought—including some who had gone to detention without trying to clear themselves, since they did not know this was possible."

"How many *total*? Roughly . . ."

"Of the more than five thousand on her list, many are else-where—on UET ships years from here, or dead. Nearly seven hundred are here and alive. We had cleared less than a hundred—in a few more days she should be through the lot."

"Fine. Tell her she's on the payroll, special consultant to the Port Commander, as long as she wants. Now, then—what else are you doing?"

"Waiting to see Liesel and Hawkman tomorrow morning—unless I hear from them, earlier. And Ivan, and Ilse—I have not had the time, as yet. And—I have been missing you, Bran."

"Yeah—I miss you, too. But you've done a real day's work, there. Any chance you can bring our unfrozen family out here tomorrow?"

"I will ask. Aedra Leng is working with them and I have had no opportunity to speak with her. But, Tregare—it is wasteful to use a ship to move three people. And I can fly a scout. All right?"

"UET—"

"No UET ships have been sighted since Ressider met the two from Hokkaido. And if one appeared—and was not intercepted, and by wildest chance detected me—how would its captain know my scout was of any importance?"

"They wouldn't have to—they'd shoot just to be shooting. But you're right—the odds are with you. Just stay low and keep a sharp lookout."

RISSA called *Graf Spee* twice; neither time could she reach her brother. She gave it up and took Melya Corradone with her to dine aboard *Valkyrie* with Zelde and Jamie. The older woman spoke seldom, until Zelde said, "The Underground broke you loose from Welfare?"

Melya looked at her, then nodded. "Yes. And it wasn't their fault it took them five years. But two weeks earlier and I'd still have a voice that wouldn't hurt your ears." She waited, then said, "Our floor heard an escape rumor—when nothing came of it, they rioted. I caught two slugs through the neck. When Markine's people—though he was just a recruit then—got to me, I was in an infirmary bed. The first time I'd slept in a bed for more than two years.''

''What—?''

''Economy—in space and fixtures. Ms. Kerguelen—as a child, I suppose you thought *your* dormitories were crowded.''

''I did not think of such things—it was so totally different from what I had known—''

''Before I was Welfared I saw it explained on Tri-V how forty persons could sleep just as well in a hundred twenty square meters as in nearly two hundred. And that is how I slept, at first. Then someone realized that cots need more space than people do—so they took out the cots and padded the floors. It more than tripled the capacity of the dorm.''

By conscious effort, Rissa relaxed her clenched jaws. ''This still exists?''

''Worse, in some of the Centers. Sleepers don't have to stand up, do they? So the dormitories, some places, are subdivided vertically—one meter high—you *crawl* in. Forced ventilation, so you don't quite suffocate.''

Rissa gasped. ''Under those conditions—seventy percent of our people—''

''No—just the more crowded areas. And they've quit building Centers some time ago. Cheaper to transfer people between condominiums, and then when UET's ready, change a whole condo over to Welfare. Cut off services, move in Committee Police as guards—move out people's possessions, put up the fences. Instant Welfare.''

Silent for a moment, Rissa then said, ''The worst of it—those in the most terrible of conditions, they will be the *last* we can help.''

Zelde M'tana reached and squeezed her hand. ''You'll be working on it. And where we can, we'll *all* help.''

Rissa tried to smile, but her thoughts were grim. And later, sleep did not come easily.

ZELDE woke her, next morning. ''Hawkman Moray called—you're invited to breakfast aboard *Hobnails*.''

Rissa got up and began dressing. ''How does he look?''

"A little pale, but same old hearty smile. Voice, too. And said to tell you Liesel's fine—has an appetite like a horse, so hurry along."

Rissa laughed. "All right; tell him I will." Zelde left; Rissa prepared herself quickly. Wearing a light jacket against morning chill, she went groundside and walked briskly to *Hobnails*.

Upship, short of the galley, she met Aedra Leng. "Aedra!" She hugged the smaller woman. "Liesel and Hawkman are waiting?"

"Yes. Oh, it's good to see you, Rissa! Come along. I'm afraid Kickem's gone groundside already." And in the galley Hawkman cut short her embrace with Liesel, to lift her high and kiss her himself.

When she had breath again Rissa said, "Well, you both look well enough. Zelde said you were pale but I do not notice it." They sat; a crewman brought food and coffee.

"Oh, we're fit to travel," said Hawkman. "Whenever you're ready."

Liesel said, "Funny thing—recovery this time seemed faster than at Stronghold."

"It's a shorter haul, for one item," said Aedra. "We don't know why, but it seems to make a difference."

"Well, it sure feels that way." Then, to Rissa; "Where's our granddaughter? With Tregare?"

Rissa explained. "And it will be—oh, I have lost track of time—a few weeks more, before Dacia arrives with the scoutship."

Hawkman said, "Well, we'll just have to wait, then." And; "I hear we missed a good fight, in space. But no one's told us the details."

Between bites of food, Rissa described the battle. "—so, riding with Kickem you broke *through* UET's formation— twice." Hawkman grinned and shook his head. Rissa went on to tell of the hit on *Graf Spee,* Ilse's injuries and Ivan's destruction of the UET command ship.

"A deadly young man, your brother," said Hawkman.

"And how's Ilse now?" Liesel said. "Have you seen her lately?"

"No—and I must. I will try to again call Ivan."

Taking coffee with them, the four went to Control. The woman at the comm-panel soon had Ivan on the screen; Rissa asked her questions.

"It's been bad, Rissa, but she's coming out of it—physically, anyway."

"What do you mean? Can I come see her?"

"I—I'll ask. If you do—well, be careful how you react. Her appearance—"

"Ivan! What has happened? Bran mentioned surgery, and—"

He shook his head. "That's not it; the latest operation was mostly to pin her shoulder together better, and some of the bones around it. She suffered shock from that, sure. But her face—maybe she won't want you to see her without the bandages. I'll go find out." He left, but the screen stayed lighted.

Rissa turned to the others. "I had not known. When I saw her, her head was bandaged, but no one said—"

"Maybe they didn't know, yet, how bad it was going to be," said Liesel.

"But how bad *is* it?" Rissa said. "I—oh, here is Ivan again."

Her brother was frowning. "She says she'll see you—that she can't hide forever."

Liesel moved forward. "Can I come along? I'm her friend, too." Hawkman began to speak but Liesel motioned him away. "I think—just Rissa and I, for now." He nodded and gripped her shoulder; she patted his hand.

Ivan said, "I'd think so. If Ilse says no, our galley can keep that coffee cup full for you."

"Very well. We will be only a few minutes." Rissa signed for the technician to cut the circuit.

Aedra said, "Perhaps it's a hurt that looks terrible for a while, but only until it heals."

"No," said Rissa. "I cannot think so. Ilse—she is tougher than that." She breathed deeply. "Well—let us go."

SINCE LIESEL'S vigor was still below par, Aedra called a groundcar for them. Walking up *Graf Spee*'s ramp, though, the older woman moved briskly enough.

Ivan met them. "She's had a trank shot to relax her, so if she's a little erratic, don't mind." He led them to the quarters he and Ilse shared, and they entered.

Rissa, determined to show no reaction, was hard put to keep her resolve. *I had not imagined it would be this bad!* The right

side of Ilse Krueger's face—more than half, over to the line of
the left cheekbone—was unharmed. But the left side—from
near the mouth's corner to within inches of the top of the head
—was covered with massive scabbing. A burn wound, Rissa
guessed, and saw that it was cut by a slash of deeper scar—
pointed near the mouth and pulling it up and wider, pointed
again high on the side of the head, and widening to nearly an
inch where it crossed—

"There wasn't enough left of the ear," said Ilse, "—just a
little tag at top and bottom, no point in trying to save it. I'm
deaf on that side, too." She tried to laugh, choked on it. "I've
always been vain of my face, my body, and my competence.
Well, I can forget the face, can't I? And for catching this,
maybe the competence, too."

"It was a freak chance!" said Ivan. "You know that." He
turned to Rissa. "One in a billion—I investigated it, later. A
turret blew—faulty component, I guess—you hear of it now
and then. And three to one on us, they were, Ilse—remember
that. Caught in crossfire and still you got one of them—and
got us out of there, *after* the hit." He was nearly shouting;
now he lowered his voice. "Plain bad luck they hit the hole the
turret left. And someone fleeing that blowup opened a bulk-
head door—there wasn't much left of whoever it was—and
one lousy flash of their beam reflected off it. Less than half a
millisecond, or her head would have been taken clean off—but
she got the flash burn. The deep scar, almost to bone, was the
beam itself; the rest is side-dissipation."

"Yes," said Ilse Krueger. "They put the right things on it,
your medics, when they arrived. So maybe I've got skin re-
growing under these scabs, or maybe scar tissue and I'll need
skin grafts. Either way I suppose the hair's gone on this side,
but they've been making wigs a long time. But this—" She
pointed to the deeper slash. "I think it's too deep; a graft
won't help, even if there's enough left over the bone for a
graft to grow to."

"We had a groundside doctor look at it," Ivan said. "A top
man. He says, once it's healed, at the least he can take out the
lower end of that scar, where it thins down—"

"So I won't have to go around the rest of my life with this
idiot half-grin. Well, that's something, I guess."

Rissa knew she must speak. Finally; "The loss of hearing
—you are sure it is permanent, not correctible?"

Ilse stared at her, then broke into real laughter. "Rissa—I love you! Because—I think that's the same question you'd ask if *you* were lying here." She waved away Rissa's attempt to answer. "Oh, it's permanent, all right—no eardrum and damned little middle-ear apparatus. In fact, they closed the passage off—too good an access for infections, otherwise."

Liesel spoke. "That's sound practice. Now, then—how's the rest of you?"

Ilse said, "You two do make a pair. Well, the beam flash didn't do anything below the neck. But getting out of there we took another hit—a dud missile, I think—and it threw me halfway across Control and smashed this shoulder into gravel, mostly. Also broke some ribs and my right thigh. I'll be slow getting back to any kind of good coordination—if I ever do."

"You will," said Ivan. "You won't let up until you're satisfied with yourself."

"Now *that*, I'll never be again. Don't be foolish. And—" She looked at him, then said, "I appreciate what you're doing; don't ever think I don't. But once I'm up and around, and don't need somebody to hold my hand—well, if you want to leave *Graf Spee*—"

"Ilse! I—"

"No—don't say it! Not now, when you *have* to tell me it doesn't make any difference. It does, and it will—you know that as well as I do. Just promise me, Ivan Marchant—that when you've given it a fair try and found you need a woman with a whole face—you'll tell me straight out, not try to hide it. All right?"

Ivan looked to Rissa. She said, "It's a fair thing, that she asks. Only to know how it stands between you, not to have to wonder."

"All right," said Ivan. "*If* ever I want to go—I'll tell you, Ilse."

The mutilated face smiled. "Good—I'm glad that's settled. Now—I'm afraid I'm getting tired; I'd like to sleep a little. Rissa—Liesel—thanks for coming. And later, any time you're not too busy. And Ivan—wake me maybe half an hour before lunchtime?"

"Sure." He bent to kiss her, straightened and escorted the two women out. Downship a little way he said, "You did it— you really did it. I don't know how you knew what to say, both of you. But this was the first time she'd talk about her—

damages—and the first sign she's shown of any interest in her future. I don't know how to thank you."

Liesel stopped, pulled his head down and kissed him, long.

"That'll do for me." Rissa reached out and squeezed his hand.

She paused, then said, "Ivan—the promise you made—you must keep it, you know. If, when her present need of you is less crucial, you find that her maiming comes between you, you cannot try to pretend otherwise. For she will *know*, and—"

"Peace be swallowed! You really think I'd leave Ilse? For *what?* A scar down her face—and I expect there's makeup will cover it for social occasions—and the loss of an ear, hidden by a wig?" He put his hand over that part of Rissa's face and head. "*That* much of Ilse, disfigured—you think it's going to change how I feel about her?"

He laughed. "You might as well think the scars she'll have at the shoulder, and around it—that *those* would turn me away."

"I had not thought, Ivan—and I am not sure what you mean."

"I guess you've never seen Ilse without clothes. Well—Tregare and I went swimming once; I've seen his scars."

"What—?"

"Ilse went through UET's Academy, too."

Speechless, Rissa could only nod.

BACK aboard *Hobnails*, Rissa called Tregare. He expressed sympathy and concern for Ilse, wanted to know if Liesel and Hawkman were ready to travel, and was pleased to learn they were.

"But not in the scout," he said. "That's off. No, I'm not being supercautious—I need another ship here, is all. Not Kickem's—I'm naming him strike force commander in case of action from outside. I had in mind Coryle Hagenau—she did a good job, coordinating the Escaped ships. She's on—what's it called now?"

"*Committee's Fall*. Have you sent orders, or shall I call her?"

"She has a tentative alert, through Zelde, so she could pick someone to stand in, there. If you agree, you can confirm it."

"I shall. But why do you need another ship?"

"Well—it's all moving. Enough so that now I can get around to pulling the Space Academy apart. And I'm not going there in any peace-splattering little scoutship."

"But *Inconnu*—all the administrative circuits—"

"We'll take the *Fall*; Hagenau can sit in, here. Now then—quick summary? Ressider's getting a handle on the Police system. You remember the woman on Stronghold? Flaer Letiken? Policebitch all her life and glad to get free of it?"

"Yes. Tall, thin—I did not ever believe that bright red hair."

He grinned. "She's on Ressider's ship—that's why I picked it for the Police job. She knows the system inside out, and that's just about the way she's starting to turn it."

"That is very good news, Bran. And what else?"

"Nothing—*zerch!*—from the Hulzein Establishment, any branch. Maybe it's gone out of business, which I don't believe. Or else Lena Diabla—my first cousin once removed, isn't she?—is waiting to see how everything turns out.

"The Australians—Altworth came on the screen once. All he said was call back when things were settled, better. I don't know—"

"And elsewhere, outside this continent?"

"Feelers, is all—they're waiting, too. And I'm hanging from a tight string on Markine's project. But that's why now is a good time—tomorrow or next day—to proof out the Academy."

"Yes. Then if nothing goes amiss, Tregare, we will come to you today."

"I was hoping you'd say that."

BOARDING *Committee's Fall*, Rissa thought back to what little she knew of Coryle Hagenau, from the time the woman had arrived with UET's second fleet until she had taken her ship back to Earth. A crewman met Rissa and escorted her to Control; there Hagenau greeted her.

"Welcome aboard, I've been making the arrangements; we can move today, if you want."

She has not changed so much . . . slightly taller than Rissa, perhaps five years older biologically, slim to gauntness—her dark hair now worn somewhat longer, and curling. Rissa said,

"Good—we can be ready soon." She looked around; Control was in good order. "All your Escaped ships have been cleared, I understand. Who will be in charge of them while you are away?"

"Yes, we're cleared—our bad UET apples are in detention, or maybe Welfare by now. You wouldn't know my deputy— Carsh Rodelle—he's never been off Earth long enough to give him two ages. He's only a figurehead, anyway—the same as I've been. Zelde M'tana's running this group herself, through James Pescadore."

"You resent the situation?"

The woman shook her head. "No. It's interim; I realize that. We're not needed just now, and M'tana has no time for us. She said she'd get to us when she could." Coryle raised an eyebrow. "You know what I think of that one? If Tregare hadn't pulled the whole trick off, she's the only other who might have."

"No. I agree, she has the ability—but not Tregare's incentive."

"You mean—it's true, the story that she didn't come up through UET at all?"

"Correct. Zelde began her career, on an Escaped ship, as captain's bedmate. When the man succumbed to drugs and sickness, she learned quickly enough to handle the ship while he lived and take command when he died. But she did not inherit control, and others bought her out. Soon after, she joined Tregare on *Inconnu*."

"Captain's bedmate, again?"

"I have not asked. If so, each had a worthy companion."

Hagenau's eyes narrowed. "I see. Well, the first man, the one who died—*he* must not have been very much."

"I do not know what his troubles may have been. But years afterward, Zelde M'tana named her squadron for him— *Parnell*."

Exhaling a deep breath, Coryle Hagenau shuddered. "Kerguelen—I don't know why I keep trying to fence with you. I—"

"Perhaps you feel I hold a position I have not earned."

"Maybe I do."

"If the matter needs settling, how should we go about it?"

The woman shrugged. "There's no way, I guess. I'm a primitive, I suppose—if it weren't for Tregare I'd fight you, assuming you knew how. Nonlethal, of course—just to first disablement. But—"

Rissa laughed. "If it were not for Tregare? Tregare has stood aside, as the local rules provided, and watched me fight. On our wedding day, it was. And when I had killed the man—but I will tell of that, another time." She paused. "Would a practice bout satisfy you?"

Hagenau stared. Finally; "No, it wouldn't. But your offer does."

"I do not understand."

"Not much, you don't—but all right—you wouldn't offer if you couldn't back it. Which says I've been wrong, thinking you're a parasite on Tregare's power."

"You thought that? Well—I do not know—I had not considered our situation in such terms. But I have worked alongside Tregare, and sometimes fought, also—and once to save his life I killed a man neither of us wished dead. I would think it enough—"

"That's twice in as many minutes you've talked of killing. Trying to scare me? I thought I made it clear; you don't have to, now."

"Then loosen your string, Coryle Hagenau! Which is to say —in no way that I can imagine, am I a threat to you. I have never killed—and I hope I never will—unless forced to it. And even then—it costs me grief."

After a moment the woman held out a hand; Rissa grasped it. "Sorry, Kerguelen. Sometimes it takes me a while to get to know people right."

"Then you should know that my name is Rissa."

"All right, Rissa. Could you use a drink? *I* can."

BEFORE leaving the port, Rissa called to check developments with Zelde M'tana, with Melya Corradone and with Ingrith Hannulan. The last said, "I wouldn't have believed how smooth this takeover could go, so fast. Here at the port, anyway—I don't know how things are, outside."

"There is much to do, sooner than we can reasonably expect to do it. Have you lost many of your people to truth field screening?"

"At the political levels, yes. It helps a lot—I can promote capable persons into those jobs. Commander M'tana—she's a good one to work with—she's screening only the top five levels, for now. Except security forces, of course. Says we can do the rest later. I don't know—"

"We will overlook some, I suppose, who might be threats. There is not *time* for all of it. You will simply have to keep tight security, Hannulan. At Headquarters we have the same problem."

"I suppose." The woman grimaced. "Forbisher—he called me yesterday. He—"

"Did you trace that call?"

"Can't be done; those trunks are blind coded, incoming only. But he—my God, I didn't think a human being could *imagine* some of the things he said he was going to have done to me!"

"You can trust those who guard you?"

"Yes, they're all cleared. But—"

"Then you are as safe as any of us, perhaps more so. And the threat will not last much longer."

"I purely hope not. Well—thanks for trying to help. Anything more you need?"

"No—merely that you continue your work, as I know you will."

"Sure. Hannulan out, then."

CORYLE HAGENAU flew low and fast to Headquarters. Like Ragan, she landed a civil distance from *Inconnu*. She said, "Give me a few minutes to button things up here, and I'll walk over with you. Or—Ms. Hulzein, would you prefer a ground-car?"

Liesel said, "I'm up to walking now, I think. Let's give it a try."

"All right." Hagenau made a few intercom calls, instructed her First Hat—a thin, dark young man who never said one word where none would suffice—and led the party ground-side. Looking at Tregare's ship, she said, "You really took one, didn't you? Lucky it missed the drive."

Rissa said, "Is there such a thing as luck? What happens, happens."

"There speaks the girl," said Hawkman, "who came out of Welfare against odds of more than fifty million."

Impatient, Rissa shook her head. "I said it at the time, on

the Tri-V. It would happen to someone, that month or another. And that time, I was the one—but except to myself, what difference did it make?"

Liesel grasped her arm but did not slow their pace. "That's the thing about you, Rissa. I mean, I don't know anyone else who'd see it that way."

"I can find no other way to see it. Am I, then, wrong?"

Hawkman said, "No—maybe you're the only one who sees it right."

Now they climbed *Inconnu*'s ramp. At the top, entering, Rissa met Tregare's kiss and rib-creaking hug, then stood aside while he greeted Liesel less violently and exchanged back-pounding shouts with Hawkman. At the first pause Coryle Hagenau said, "Is it all right if I only shake hands?"

Tregare broke into laughter. "Welcome aboard, Coryle. Don't worry—just the family has to put up with this sort of thing." He shook her hand, then ushered the group inside and upship. "It's a little late for dinner, but I figured you wouldn't be eating on such a fast jaunt, so I waited. Okay?"

A few minutes later they sat and ate. Tregare said, "Coryle —you know this already, but it never hurts to make sure. Anything said here, you tag it Top Silence. Okay?"

Before she spoke, she looked at him. "Yes. Of course, Tregare. I won't tell your secrets."

Now it was he who paused. "Anything eating on you, Hagenau?"

"No—it just seems to be my day to run crossgrain to the Tregares."

His brows raised. "Something I ought to know?"

Rissa touched his hand. "No, Bran. Coryle and I—we took a little time to reach understanding. That is all."

Tregare looked at Coryle Hagenau; she said, "I didn't know you people, really. I still don't, but—I had some wrong ideas. Rissa took time to straighten them out."

"Well—everybody satisfied now?"

"I am," said Hagenau.

"And I," Rissa said.

"All right then." He brushed air away from him. "If all the small stuff's out of the way, here's what we're up against." He looked to Rissa. "Your red-headed friend with the interchangeable teeth—that's a nice touch he has there—he says the procurement department wants to make delivery three days from now—but at night, and separately. We're supposed to use a scoutship for each item. How does it sound to you?''

As Rissa thought, Coryle said, "*That's* Top Silence? Why don't you just talk Greek? I don't understand that, either.''

Tregare's fist clenched, then relaxed. "Any particular reason you want to know something that doesn't concern you and could be dangerous?'' He stared at her until she looked away, downward.

Rissa said, "Coryle is in charge of a major subfleet. If you do not trust her, then relieve her of command.''

"Wait a minute—I didn't mean—''

Hagenau spoke. "No—it's my fault. I've been edging people all day—first Rissa and now you, Tregare. Comes, I guess, from sitting in space too long, not knowing who I'd have to deal with when somebody showed up. And then squatting groundside with nothing to do.'' She shrugged. "All right —tell me or don't. I'll accept it either way.''

Tregare grinned. "Now there's an answer I believe. Okay—the package we're talking about is the Presiding Committee itself, delivered one by one. We—''

Coryle gasped. "Peace push a pencil!—and I guess you know where.'' One hand rubbed over her nose and mouth. "That's Top Silence, sure enough.''

As though there had been no interruption, Tregare said, "Rissa? What do you think?''

"Do not agree to simultaneous pickups. They do not know how many scouts you have—say that there are less, and for every one that risks landing, have another aloft, on guard. There is no reason to expect treachery, but still—''

"The New Mafia, isn't it?'' said Coryle. "Couldn't be anyone else. Well, you can trust them—as long as you have their balls in both your hands and squeezing hard!''

Rissa said, "I think our grip is firm enough.''

Tregare nodded. "They cross us, they get nothing and they know it.''

"What have you agreed to give them?''

Not hard but audibly, Tregare's palm slapped the table. "Now *that*—it's outside the scope of this talk. We're getting above Top Silence and into policy.''

"Of course.'' The woman nodded. "Tregare—you haven't told me yet, what *I'm* doing here.''

"All right. The situation here is stabilizing, and at the port and the Police bases. And we can't start on anything long-range until we've settled with the Committee. So you're here to sit in for me, on *Inconnu*, for the next two or three days. While I go—in your ship—and overhaul the Space Academy to my own specifications. And I've waited one peaceloving hell of a long time to do *that* job!"

Hagenau half-stood, then sat again. "Tregare—I wish I could go with you on that one. You think *you* had it bad—but the girls—"

"I know. We didn't have that part when I was there, but I've heard. Don't worry; I'll take care of it. No vengeance, though—you don't punish people for following a system that's already there. It's hard, agreed. If the same people were still alive who—when I was there—I don't know."

"Some are still alive from when *I* was there."

"That's why you're not going."

AFTER Hagenau returned to her ship, the discussion turned to family matters. In answer to Liesel's question, Tregare said, "Another four weeks, I think, before Dacia could bring the scout in. But I've sent two patrol ships out—one to take station where we met Ragan and the other to meet the scout and fetch it quicker. So knock off maybe a week."

"It'll be good to see Liesel Selene again," said her grand-mother. "How old will she be, bio-time?"

"I cannot be sure," said Rissa. "Time-dilation on the scout will have varied somewhat, from ours on the ships."

Tregare said, "We'll get a reading off Dacia's personal chrono, when they get here. Offhand, Lieselene'll be about two-thirds through her third year. A little more, maybe."

"And we last saw her," said Hawkman, "when she was barely a year. We can expect some changes, Liesel."

"I always expect change, and so do you. But, Rissa—are you *sure* you can clear the child's mind of all that hypnotic clap-trap?"

"The release is as simple as possible. And the polygraph will confirm that it is complete."

"All right—but I won't be satisfied until I see the job's done."

Tregare laughed. "If *you* were ever satisfied with anything, Liesel, I'd start worrying about you. Now, then—you want a job?"

"What kind of a job—besides baby-sitting?"

"You and Hawkman are the managers in this family—not me. Well, we have a management problem—how do we start a fiscally sound program of turning people loose from Total Welfare?"

Liesel Hulzein leaned forward. "Tell me about it."

BETWEEN them, Tregare and Rissa explained. When someone was Welfared, that person's assets—living quarters, personal possessions, financial holdings—all went to the State Bankruptcy, Tregare pointed out, was no longer the criterion—if UET wanted you, UET got you. You ceased to be a name and became a number. No record was kept of the sources—individuals or families—of the confiscated assets; they appeared in UET's books as Miscellaneous Income.

Money saw little use, even in credit-entry form. As Rissa said, your *level* entitled you to acquire thus-and-so—or did not. Status limited your permissible acquisitions and way of living, and these were seldom tallied in Weltmarks. It was possible—but unless your political standing was above question, not advisable—to borrow against future quotas.

So how, Tregare wanted to know, could you restore a man's holdings when you didn't know what they were? Maybe his former condominium was now Welfare barracks, maybe not. His name's wiped off the records—how do you know who he *is*, let alone what's coming to him?

There was more, much more. At the end of it, Liesel said, "You can't climb a broken kite string and splice it. Forget about trying to put things back as they were—can't be done."

Her solution was simpler—continue the present "levels" system, but reduce its inequities, using credit vouchers to keep tabs. Accept whatever name a Client gave and issue ID accordingly, assigning levels by skills and knowledge. And certainly UET held enough real wealth to pay citizens' wages to Welfare Clients immediately.

Q.E.D.

Hawkman laughed. "It takes a Hulzein to set things straight."

"All right, Liesel," said Tregare, "you're in charge of it. Whenever you're ready, get started."

HAWKMAN and Liesel still slept when Rissa and Tregare, carrying light baggage, went early to *Committee's Fall*. They breakfasted with Coryle Hagenau. Toward the end of the meal, she said, "How much personnel do you want to exchange between ships for this job?"

He handed her a folded sheet of paper. "We're bringing along about fifty ratings who double as security people—combat types for groundside work if UET tries any surprises. I'm sure yours are good, but mine are used to me. Here's a list of their regular jobs, so you can transfer their counterparts to *Inconnu*."

"Thank you. How soon do you plan to lift?"

He looked at his watch. "Two hours suit you?"

"I can arrange it faster, if you'd like. I'll go start on the assignments."

"Then whenever you're ready. Let me know when your people are set to move and I'll have mine coordinate—so we don't have a jam at one of our entrance ramps."

"Fine. Did you bring my operating instructions also?"

"Taped them—just punch for the daily suspense file. Any questions, ask my First Hat, Hain Deverel."

Hagenau nodded and left. Tregare said, "Nothing for us to do for a while. We can sit and take it easy."

"Very well. Will you pour me more coffee, please?"

THIRTY minutes short of the two hours, Coryle Hagenau's people began to disembark. Tregare called *Inconnu*. "Okay, Hain—send the troops on over." And shortly he lifted ship and headed it northeast. "Not a long hop." He turned to the ship's lanky First Officer. "You know where the Academy is, from here—you want to fly it?"

The man shook his head. Tregare looked at him, checked his controls and nodded. "Okay, she can fly herself for now. Now, then—you're First Hat on here?" A nod. "You got a name?" Another. "What is it?"

It seemed the man was not going to answer, but eventually he said, "Garn."

"First name, is it?" Garn shook his head. "You have one, though?" Nod. "Well, in the name of peace, what is it?"

Again a pause. Then, slowly; "Jevers."

"Jevers Garn. That right?" The nod again. "Well, tell me something, First Hat Jevers Garn—why didn't you say so in the first place?"

Finally the man said, "Hard . . . talking. *Excused!*"

Tregare began to speak; then his lips closed. He smiled instead, and slowly nodded. But when Garn turned away, he called after him. "Garn? I'm not after giving you trouble; I ask questions only when I need answers."

The man looked back, smiled, and nodded again.

"But when I do, don't make me ask four times when once would do."

The smile faded; Garn looked away and left Control.

"Rissa—how does a man like that hold his job?"

"Gonnelsen held his—and he spoke little more."

"Yes—but when you asked him something, he gave good answers."

"Perhaps Coryle knows better than we, how to interpret his responses."

APPROACHING the Academy site, Tregare said, "First I'm making one fast pass. Tape it, Rissa." She nodded, and the pass he made was fast indeed.

Aloft again, they ran the tape and agreed that the picture showed little in the way of weapons emplacements. "So now you will go in slowly, I suppose—almost hovering, ready to shoot or run if necessary?"

"Yes—but more likely shoot than run. They know who we are. I told them when I was coming. All right, let's go in."

Under Tregare's hands *Committee's Fall* drifted gently toward the Academy's landing space. There two ships sat— old ones, partially disassembled. Tregare hovered, and no weapons emerged from camouflage; no shots came. "Good enough—we sit down." And on the ground; "Let's see if anyone comes to meet us."

They waited. After perhaps ten minutes, a few people appeared at the largest building's huge, ornate entrance. They stood for a time and then, with apparent reluctance, approached. Watching, Tregare said, "All right—they're halfway." He gave orders on the intercom; when he and Rissa left the ship, his security troops were aground to escort them.

He said, "Watch the buildings as well as that group ahead. When we reach them, surround the lot of us. And then we'll see."

ANTICLIMAX the meeting was—the eight who met them carried no arms, and their snug uniforms left no room for concealment.

Tregare wasted no words. "Who commands here? I want to see him."

A fat gray-haired man spoke. "I'm in command. General Archifal."

"Point us toward your office, general. We'll talk there."

At the building's entrance and at each checkpoint inside, Tregare left two guards, covering all approaches with their heavy, twohanded guns. At Archifal's office twenty were left. Tregare said, "Six of you stay here. The rest—scout around a little, in pairs. Don't start trouble—but if it happens, finish it." He turned to the general. "All right—inside."

The office, Rissa thought, was more like a stage setting—with a massive desk at its far end. Tregare, striding faster, moved to sit behind it, leaving the general standing. Rissa picked up a chair and moved it to sit beside Tregare. The other UET personnel, looking uneasy, stood to either side of their commander.

Archifal said, "Tregare—until you relieve me of command, that's my desk."

"I've borrowed it. Now, Archifal—what's your space experience? What ships have you served on? How did you qualify for this job?"

"Why—I was appointed directly, by the Presiding Committee. I didn't waste my time in space."

"Then you're relieved—and this is *my* desk. You're also under arrest—no charges yet—just investigating. Now, then —somebody show me your table of Organization. Who's senior here, who's been through the Academy *and* ridden ships?"

After silence, a stocky woman spoke. "If you want what I think you want—I'm senior in rank, of those who have two ages." Rissa looked at the woman, seeing a round face, firm-jawed, under short graying hair.

Tregare said, "For the time being, then, you're in charge here as my deputy. Tell me your name and I'll put it into the computer terminal."

"I'm Arden Craistell—but you don't know the input coding; you'd put in gibberish."

"No hurry—show me later. Now—how many other politicals outrank you in the Academy?"

"All the rest here—and three others, maybe four. But—"

Tregare said, "Come around here, to the terminal. Punch the data, and speak it for the recorder as you do so—I'll want to check it over later—on all the ranking political appointees. And schedule them, temporarily, for detention."

Archifal snorted. "Just as I'd heard, Tregare—you're a maniac, unrealistic. No detention facilities are available. Think of something else."

Tregare's eyes narrowed. "No cells? You've abolished them?"

"Of course not. As usual, they're filled."

"With whom?" For a moment standing, Tregare sat again. "You got my orders—stop the Academy routine until I got here. Why didn't you?"

"I obeyed orders. Those waiting confinement still wait. Those confined already, stayed there."

Tregare's fist struck the desk; Rissa winced, but he showed no sign of pain. He said, "Craistell, clear the cells—we're going to need them." The woman punched codes into the terminal. When she was done, Tregare said, "Archifal—do you still have the Special? With the cold, and the random shocks?" The general nodded. "That one's yours—until I happen to think to get you out of it." He turned to Rissa. "I spent a lot of time in that hellhole—when I was maybe thirteen, fourteen. I never thought I'd get the chance to use it on the Academy Commander."

"Tregare! You said—no punishment for acts that were lawful . . ."

"Course not." He grinned. "But until I change the regulations, this *is* lawful."

WHEN the Academy cadets were released to their barracks and the Committee's appointees confined in their places, Tregare questioned Arden Craistell.

"I won't pretend to you," she said. "I spaced twice and hoped for Escape—but nothing happened, so I settled down to what I could do. If you hadn't come, I'd keep on working for UET and hope to stay out of trouble. But I'm glad you're here."

Tregare nodded. "I'll settle for that, the truth field willing. But you don't necessarily get permanent command. Depends on who else I happen to find."

"I don't need command; I've never had it. I'll settle for what I can get."

And afterward, Rissa said, "Tregare—they beat the strong down, into less than they could be."

With his free arm, the other hand punching data into the terminal, he hugged her. "Yeah. But you notice? Like it or not, some of us they push into *more*."

AT mid-afternoon, back on Hagenau's ship, they had a belated lunch. "Or early dinner, maybe," said Tregare. "I lose track."

"So that you keep control of essentials, Bran, it is well. Your men, groundside—can they contain this vast enterprise? It must have resources we have not seen."

"Just barely, they can—working shifts to cover all the key bottleneck spots. But the string's loose. Whatever resistance is here—and I bet there's plenty yet, nobody'd put *all* their money on that fool Archifal—they won't try to buck this ship. Especially since—well, how do they know how many scouts we're carrying?"

"And I do not know either, Bran. How many?"

"None—they're both out working for Kile Ressider, helping civilize the Police. But what UET doesn't know, won't hurt us."

NOT until the next day did they return groundside. After meeting with Arden Craistell, Tregare suggested a walking inspection tour. "You won't like this, Rissa—but maybe you'll have some good ideas, how to change it." She agreed, and they began.

In the first barracks they entered, filled with young boys in their early teens, she felt wrongness. Not relief, as she might have expected, but tension. "Bran? I do not like this."

"I told you, you wouldn't. You don't have to continue if you don't want to."

"I do not mean that. Something is *wrong*."

"With UET, something always is. You coming?"

She nodded and followed him, six of Tregare's men bringing up the rear. They entered the next building. Older boys here—about twenty of them—suddenly moved to surround the small group. And then the knives appeared.

"Tregare! They shall *not* kill us!" She moved without thought; time slowed. Adrenaline shock took speech away; she screamed a battle cry. Almost calm, while her mind watched avidly—she grasped a knife hand and brushed it across the wrist of another—both knives dropped. A gun—she pushed it into the face of the wielder and did not pause to see if it had fired. A guard's gun spat, and space before her was clear.

Tregare! One attacker fell away from his thrusting arm; now two more came at him, one from behind. With another great scream, Rissa launched herself—she missed the first but it did not matter—her foot caught the second squarely in the throat. She crashed into Tregare, and the two fell.

"What the hell—?"

Panting: "Bran! There are not so many now!" She scrambled up. A knife reached for her—she broke the wrist that held it. Turning, she saw Tregare—hand like a blade felling his assailant, then his foot striking. Under the jaw—*dead, that one*.

Then it was over and they stood, facing. Rissa felt his grip hurting her arms and relaxed her own. "Thank you, Bran," as he relaxed in turn.

"Ambush," he said. His men, the four who still stood, held guard.

"You must not punish these children, those who live."

Frowning, he shook his head. "No—course not. This wasn't their idea; they were set up for it." He wiped blood from over one eyebrow; more blood came. "Maybe we can find out who did it."

WOUNDED and hale alike, the captive boys faced Tregare. Seated behind his desk, he said, "Who speaks for you?"

A tall youth, cradling a broken forearm, stepped forward. "I'm senior, I think. What are you going to do to us?"

"Depends. Who set up the ambush?"

A headshake. "I don't know. The word came through Trenery—and the weapons—but he's dead."

"What was the word?"

"To kill Tregare—because if you won you'd make us slaves instead of officers. And if we failed and then you lost, *we'd* be killed."

"You believed all that?"

The boy began to shrug, then groaned at what the movement did to his arm. "In the Slaughterhouse, who believes *anything?* But what choice did we have?"

"About as much as we did, when you attacked."

"I know—I'm sorry. We—what happens to us now?"

"You, and the rest who need it, the infirmary—I assume there still is one. The rest—confined to your barracks. No—" He shook his head. "Circulate—and pass *my* word. Anybody still has weapons, turn them in voluntarily and no penalty. Anyone *caught* armed, after today—no, make that tomorrow—it's death." He started to dismiss them, then said, "You won't be slaves, by the way   I'm not even filing charges for the ambush. Whether you stay in the Academy or not—you do if you want to and if my truth field likes your answers."

He chuckled. "To help you make up your minds—space training has to be tough, but it doesn't have to be a hellhole. And from now on, it won't be."

He motioned for his guards to take the group out. At the door, the boy who had spoken turned and said, "We should have known UET was lying—they always do. Tregare—my name's Hask Ornaway, and I hope I pass your truth field."

As the door closed behind them Tregare said, low-voiced, "So do I, son—so do I."

TRENERY'S death left no further clues to the ambush; they dropped that investigation and turned to correcting abuses in the Academy. Again, responsibility could not be defined—at each level of command, questioned parties cited higher authority for their acts. After a time, Tregare said, "Then it's like Liesel said. We can't put it back, so go from here. All right—Welfare all the Committee's people, the general and right down the line, and we'll sort it out later when we have the time. You agree?"

Rissa thought about it. Then, "Yes, Tregare—fully. And in Welfare, those are among the persons least in need of early release."

AIRCARS came to remove the Committee's minions; Tregare's guards completed their shakedown. A number of cadets voluntarily surrendered weapons. One barracks refused to open to search; Tregare had the building sleepgassed. When the gas cleared he entered to check personally; after searching, he said, "Hell, the kids weren't even armed—just scared, is all. Let's get back to work."

In his office he made final revisions to his new Academy Regulations. "The present ones don't look so bad on paper," he said. "It's the loopholes—the way they can be interpreted."

Rissa looked over to him. She was calling selected fleet officers, offering them positions on the shorthanded Academy staff—but now, over the fleet broadcast circuit came Tregare's voice, loudly if not tunefully informing all concerned that there was "—only one latrine in all of *U!E!T!*" Smiling, she shook her head.

"You don't think I sing pretty?" He was grinning.

"Let us say, Bran—your rendition is spirited."

"Okay, okay—how's the recruiting business?"

"You did well to list many more than will be needed. Only about half—a little more—are accepting."

"Have you reached Gowdy?"

"Not yet."

"Damn—I *want* her for Commandant."

"She is a good choice—if she wishes to take the job."

"Yeah. Well, keep trying."

Finally Tregare called in a young staff member and held out his revised draft. "Have somebody do this up neat and run me off about a hundred copies—one for each barracks room and a few over. I want them as soon as possible."

"Yes, sir." The aide made a rapid exit.

Tregare said, "Time to talk to the whole outfit—I need to clear the air." He put his intercom on All-Points. "Now hear this—Tregare speaking. You know anybody, staff or cadets, who's out of range, get them. Three minutes." When the time was up, he said, "I'm changing this place so you won't know it. You'll see the new Regs by evening; meanwhile, here's a summary.

"Combat training: no more forced fights to death or disablement. Anybody gets killed, accident or not, the instructors answer for it. If it couldn't be helped, no penalty—but usually it can be.

"Discipline: only for real offenses—disobedience, theft, unauthorized fighting—that sort of thing. And you'll get your chance to tell your side of it.

"Punishment: mostly restricted to loss of privileges, confinement—and that's simple confinement, no more torture cells—or expulsion. If the offense is criminal under Outside law you stand trial as a civilian.

"Sexual exploitation of cadets—male or female—by the staff or other cadets, is a criminal offense and will be so treated.

"Duty hours: except for endurance training or emergencies, it's eight hours a day, six days a week.

"Furloughs: Most likely you don't know the word. It means you get up to three weeks per year to go outside the Academy —home if you have one, or wherever you want—with a little expense money provided. Failure to return on time can get you confined or maybe expelled, depending—but nothing more than that.

"Release from contract: When you've seen how the new system works here—say, a month from now—anybody wants out, can go. I—"

Rissa tugged at his arm. "Bran! They will think that means Welfare!"

"Oh—yeah—" Back to the intercom. "Release does *not* Welfare you. You'd be at least a basic-level free citizen— maybe better, depending on what you were before.

"I think that sums it up. Read the new Regs tonight. If you have questions, get them together. Tomorrow I'll see one spokesman from each cadet squadron, and answer the best I can."

He grinned and shook his head. "Don't get the idea you won't be working your tails off, still—because you will. Maybe even harder—since you won't have to waste so much energy being scared.

"All right—Tregare out." To Rissa, "Did I get most of it?"

"I think so."

"Then let's call it a day and go to the ship. I'm hungry—and I could use a drink, too."

THE first few cadet spokesmen, next day, seemed merely to need assurance that the new Regulations meant what they said. After the fourth, Tregare said, "The way these kids have been treated, they're a real mess. Rissa—you think more than half of them are worth training?"

"Give them time, Tregare, to readjust. Do not expect too much from them, immediately."

As the next cadet entered, he nodded. A girl, this one—tall and muscular. She would have been pretty, Rissa thought, save for the angry scar that split an eyebrow and crossed the forehead to disappear into short black hair. After paying official respects the girl said, "What the Regs say, about exploitation—is it just that we don't have to spread for anybody senior, any time they say? Or does it apply to the official stuff, too?"

Tregare frowned. "Official stuff? Explain it a little."

"I mean, taking our usual turns Friday nights for gang sex in some squadroom."

Slowly, he shook his head. "Now that's new since my time." He looked at the girl. "The regulation means you don't have to do *anything*, in the way of sex, that you don't want to. If the Reg isn't clear, I'll amend it. Friday-night gang sex just now stopped being official."

The girl grinned; she had lost a front tooth. "That's going to disappoint a friend of mine. Friday's her favorite night."

Tregare's brows raised. Rissa said, "There is no intent to enforce celibacy. If your friend wishes to volunteer, no doubt she will be quite popular." But when the girl had gone, she said, "The friend does not sound suitable for this training. A person who *wishes* to be treated like an object . . ."

"Yeah. Like I said—some of them, they're beaten down too much ever to grow back from it."

THE rest of the interviews were routine. At the end, Rissa took Tregare's notes to an aide for transcribing. When she returned, he said, "Gowdy called; she's taking the job. Coming up in a scout tomorrow or next day, soon as she's squared away with *Peralta* squadron."

"Who takes her place there?"

"Hardekamp, for now—she vouches for him, and that's good enough."

"But they—he and Hilaire—"

"Not any more, it seems. Still get along, but not sharing quarters now. Could be—she didn't say—she's moved somebody else in."

Rissa shrugged. "However it may be, Hilaire Gowdy does not allow her private life to interfere with her duties."

"Right. Now then—I've got to do a memo. Designating Craistell and the two men working with her as Hilaire's deputies and department heads." He paused. "You don't think I'm setting up the command, here, too top-heavy with women?"

"Your fleet—with Zelde, Ilse and Hilaire commanding three of the five squadrons—did well enough, I think."

"Yeah. But—the funny part—how *come* I get so many topgrade females on my side?"

Rissa thought, then said, "Because—except at Committee level itself, where *ownership* determines status—UET denies command to women. So capable women, more so than equally capable men, are predisposed toward rebellion. They have more to gain, by Escaping. Is that not so?"

A sharp nod. "Makes sense, at that. I'll keep it in mind."

"Good. Is the truth field equipment ready?"

"By tomorrow it will be. If necessary, the techs'll work late—and that's their idea, not mine."

So the next day Rissa and Tregare proofed the remaining Academy staff; on the average, a third failed the test and were removed. At midday Gowdy called. "Can't make it today— but tomorrow at the latest. And in the morning, with any luck."

"Right," said Tregare. "We'll be looking for you. Tregare out."

By mid-afternoon they had finished with the staff—the one-third average had held, almost exactly. The subject of proofing the entire cadet corps was tabled. "Might's well wait and combine it with the month's deadline," said Tregare, "on who chooses to stay or go. Save time, not bothering with the drop-outs."

"Good. Then we are free until Hilaire arrives tomorrow."

GOWDY landed before mid-morning, and came alone to join Rissa and Tregare aboard *Committee's Fall*. If any had ac-companied her she did not say so, and no one asked.

Over coffee she read the new Regulations. "They'll do the job." Then; "Tregare? Are you going to show me around the place? Or just introduce me to my top people and let them take it from there?"

"Which would you rather?"

"Either's all right. But if you're around for a while, at first, I figure a little of your authority will rub off on me better. You see?"

He laughed. "Sure, Hilaire. I'll go call and set it up."

He left; Gowdy said, "Rissa—you're wondering about El-rain."

"I have not asked, and I will not."

"Tell you anyway—it's a simple matter. He's a good man and competent to take over the squadron. But with me he's ready to settle down and be old—and I'm not." She laughed. "Surprise you?"

"No." Rissa shook her head. "No, I am not surprised."

"No? Then what *are* you?"

"Hilaire, when we met—how many bio-years ago?—you were fat and cared nothing for your appearance. You look younger now, than then. You wasted time being old too soon —now you are making up for it, and I am totally in favor."

Head thrown back, the older woman laughed. "I might've known. Rissa, you—no, here comes Tregare, and you know what I mean, anyway." Briefly she reached and clasped Rissa's hand, then turned and said, "Ready to go, are we?"

Tregare sat. "Give them another cup of coffee's worth of time first; then we'll go. All right?"

TEN minutes later they went groundside and walked to Tre-gare's office. ". . . or rather, yours now, Hilaire."

"Well, it's fancy enough." She sat at the desk. "These

cards—special input codes for the computer terminal?"

"That's right," said Tregare. "Need any help, ask Arden Craistell—she's senior of your three chief assistants. And I didn't keep anybody in the upper echelons who hasn't lost a few objective years, traveling."

Before Hilaire could answer, Craistell entered. "Sorry I'm late—and the other two are held up even longer, I'm afraid."

" 'sall right." Tregare introduced the two women.

Craistell said, "I've heard of you, Gowdy. You were on the ship it's said Peralta took, Escaping."

"With Tregare's help, he took it," Gowdy said. "And Peralta repaid him badly."

"That's old lines," said Tregare. "You rightly named your squadron for him."

Hilaire said, "You've been out yourself, Craistell? Tregare said as much."

"Only twice—once to New Pittsburgh and once on extended patrol. I'm less than twenty years out of objective time."

"You officered?"

"Up to First when I was transferred here."

"Good. Will you show me around the place now? Tregare —Rissa—you don't need to come along if you'd rather not. I think we can manage."

Tregare volunteered to accompany them. Rissa said, "You go—I will return to the ship," and left them.

ABOARD, restlessness overcame her. *I have been too long in this backwater*. She called Zelde M'tana. "What is happening? Is anything new there?"

"We picked up another UET ship." Approaching, hearing on ships' frequencies that there was only one latrine in all of UET, the captain had turned to flee. "Before we could catch up, its drive went dead—mutiny. When Kickem boarded, there wasn't one person left alive that didn't pass truth field on our side."

And otherwise? The captured fleet was wholly screened, cleared of UET partisans—and port personnel were now being checked, all the way down to menial job levels.

"Very good," said Rissa. "Tregare will be pleased. Well— give Jamie my regards." M'tana smiled and cut the circuit.

Still at the console, fingers drumming, Rissa hesitated. What was it she wished to know—and who could most likely tell her? She sat, undecided, and then a screen lit.

"Hagenau calling." Rissa activated transmission. "Rissa— I have word—the *consignments* Tregare mentioned the other evening. They're to be picked up tonight. Does he have any instructions for the scoutships?"

"He has left orders, I know. I will ask—he is not here at present—if he wishes to add to them. If I do not return your call, tell the scout crews to go ahead with their present assignments."

And when Tregare returned he said, "Tonight's job is nothing to talk about over a circuit. Let's go back to HQ—this end is wrapped up, for now."

JEVERS GARN flew the ship and landed it near *Inconnu*, almost on its previous site. Not once had he spoken, and neither Rissa nor Tregare had found reason to question him. Tregare gave orders to reverse the exchange of personnel between *Fall and Inconnu*, then said, "All right—let's go."

Rissa said, "You fly the ship well, Garn. Good-bye." The man smiled as they left Control, to go downship and walk to *Inconnu*.

Aboard, after conferring with Coryle Hagenau before she returned to her own ship, they listened to Markine's taped voice. Some plans for pickup of individual Committee members had been changed slightly; Tregare called his scoutship commanders and made the necessary rearrangements. "And remember—if possible, we want these people alive and kicking. But your lives come before theirs."

An answer came. "That's the kind of orders I like to hear. Both ways, we'll do our best."

WAITING the outcome of Gameel's project, Rissa had expected to help stand night watch. But Tregare said, "They'll be doped or sleepgassed, most of them. We might as well get some rest." Knowing that Tregare kept standing orders to call him in emergencies, she agreed. And once in their quarters she was pleased to find that sleeping was not to be immediate.

Next morning Tregare woke her. "They did it! We've got all the Presiding Committee that's left alive—one was killed; it couldn't be helped. All but the two that're off Earth, I mean—and Gameel brought in *their* representative."

"Where are they now?" She got out of bed. "Shall we go to question them?"

"After breakfast—they'll keep. Except maybe Forbisher—he tried to suicide, and I'm told that he may make it, yet. There's medics with him; we'll see. Anyway—they're in the conference room alongside my office, under guard. I'd half-way thought to question them separately—they're quartered apart—but somebody mixed up the orders and put them all in the room together. Nobody's fault, so the hell with it."

Tregare left. A few minutes later Rissa joined him and they ate, saying little. Then they went downship and walked toward the Headquarters building.

"Tregare! To see these creatures, face to face . . ."

"To have *them* in *our* hands, Rissa. Yes!"

THE room had silver walls and a black ceiling. Guards flanked the doors and occupied two of the room's corners, watching the nine persons who sat around the central table.

And I thought Forbisher was grotesque!

Reminded, she looked and found the man lying on a stretcher; two medical aides attended him. She walked closer. In the tattooed, bejeweled face the mouth hung open. She saw the answer to what had puzzled her—a lower incisor had been ground down to accommodate the ring through its upper counterpart.

Tregare took her arm. "Let's sit and get on with it." Seated, Rissa could only stare at the persons facing her—five men and three women who rivaled Forbisher's bizarre appearance, and one man whose unmarked visage seemed strangely inappropriate.

She heard Tregare's first words. "I'm Tregare; you've called me pirate, but I'm the new boss. Now let's *you* all introduce yourselves." Then Rissa ceased hearing—the names meant nothing to her—and gazed at the members of the Presiding Committee.

I would not have believed it!

One man wore tattoos on every area of exposed skin; through his thinning hair she saw the designs covered even the scalp. Jewels ornamented his nostrils, and he wore a line of them around the edge of each ear.

Gold rings pierced the webs between one woman's fingers; her exposed breasts were several times normal size. Beside her, another woman displayed multicolored gems for teeth, and over most of her face the tattoo of a stylized eagle—the head on her forehead, wings spread from eyebrows to cheekbones, body covering the nasal area with the tail moustaching her upper lip and ending on the lower, and legs curving to each side of her mouth.

And the man with jewels inset in patterns all over his bald skull—and the one with the raised crest of scar tissue, gem-studded, from between his eyebrows up and over and down to his nape—and the woman who—

No! Rissa's eyes clamped shut; she shook her head.

When she looked again, and listened, it was to the one unmutilated man. He said, "My name is Biels Dorning. I represent the two members who are off Earth—the two who, with their proxies of lesser holdings, effectively control this Committee and UET itself."

Tregare said, "I'd like to know a little more about those two."

"So would I," said Dorning. "So would everyone here, I imagine. Myself, I inherited this job; I've never seen either of them, except pictures. Has anyone here? Or had any contact whatsoever, except for their formal reports and directives?"

The grotesque heads shook. Dorning said, "They seldom come to Earth. That's how they managed it, you see—stretching time by traveling space. They're a team, always voting together since they first became major stockholders—oh, fifty-sixty years ago. But every few years one turns up, takes my latest reports and gives me new instructions. Over the special circuit—and on the screen, no face."

"How do you know who it is, for sure?"

"The screen shows fingerprint and retinal patterns—plus some special codes I'm not at liberty to divulge."

"You are if I say so," said Tregare. "But never mind, for now. What I'll settle for is the names. *That's* no secret, is it?"

"Of course not." Dorning looked relieved. "The two women are Tari Obrigo and Cele Metrokin."

• • •

BEFORE Tregare could speak, Rissa clutched his arm. "Bran! The woman, on Stronghold—she may have told the truth?"

He turned to look at her. "You mean—!"

"The one who claimed to be a Committee member—and of course we thought she was lying." She looked to Dorning. "You have pictures of these persons, as well as the identifying patterns?"

"Why, yes—but I don't understand. I—"

"You will, soon enough. But first you will obtain for me copies of those pictures."

"I have them with me."

"Good—let me see them." He rummaged through his brief-case and handed her several photographs. She looked, then nodded. "The one, certainly. The other—Tregare, let us return to the ship and unfreeze the first one. Tomorrow you should be able to bring her here—and then you will learn much more than we can today."

"But—"

"I will remain on *Inconnu*. We must unfreeze the other, also—the one who, even under drugs, could not be made to tell who she is. With the advantage of what we know, I will question her again. For although the picture is not con-clusive—if the one is Cele Metrokin, the other may well be Tari Obrigo."

Tregare grinned. "That might be—it just might. I wouldn't be surprised, come to think of it." He turned to the others. "All right—is there anything more here, now? Before you're returned to your new quarters?"

"If it's all right to ask—" said Dorning. "What's *your* name, the woman who tells Tregare what to do?"

Tregare tensed, then laughed. "Dorning—you just flunked the course in tact. And—well, never mind. You're not old enough to have met my wife—but maybe UET hasn't quite forgot Rissa Kerguelen."

Dorning looked blank. But the woman Rissa had not been able to look at, the one with her ears sliced into drooping fringes and—no, she *still* could not look at the nose—that woman said, "You left Earth the year I was born. But my father told me—'Keep waiting,' he said, 'and someday you'll get her.' "

"It is too bad to disappoint your father," said Rissa, "but the situation appears to be quite the opposite."

"Don't be too sure," the woman said. "This isn't done with, yet."

"No," said Tregare, "it isn't. You'll be back here again tomorrow. Now—anything else?"

One of the medical aides spoke. "One thing. I didn't want to interrupt you, because it wouldn't have helped, anyway. But Forbisher died a few minutes ago." He gestured. "Should I have said something?"

"No." Tregare shook his head. "It was his own doing. He succeeded, and he's welcome to it."

He turned to Rissa. "Let's go—we've got some things to do."

And on *Inconnu*, in their quarters, she put her arms around his neck. "Bran! Do you see it? We have conquered *ourselves*."

TREGARE contented himself with coffee but Rissa took wine. "It is largely Hulzein money, of course—for my own investments, even with the years, could never have built so greatly. Hulzein money and Hulzein maneuverings. Even before I left Earth, Erika must have begun—and since she could not buy UET stock directly, she used the identities she had obtained for me. And Frieda—perhaps thirty-five years ago she received my first report, from Far Corner, and decided to accelerate the program."

She laughed. "At any rate, Bran, it has worked. And we—"

"You're forgetting something," Tregare said. "If the Hulzeins control UET, how come it's running along as rotten as ever?"

"I had not thought—perhaps the control is recent, and there has not been time—"

"Didn't sound that way. Try this for size—maybe Lena Diabla *likes* things as they are."

Rissa shrugged. "It does not matter. For the holdings are in *my* names, no matter who has been manipulating them."

"Yeah." Tregare scratched his chin, rose and poured more coffee. "I wanted to ask you about that? Why Metrokin? And why wait until tomorrow?"

"I cannot use Tari Obrigo because enroute to and on Number One I grew lax—I absorbed her speech patterns as my own, and our mannerisms have merged. And I need the time—today and tonight—for *practice*, since I have not done Cele Metrokin in years."

"Can you remember?"

"Besides the rest of it, I have voice tapes."

"What's she like?"

"She would not attract you." She showed him a picture. "See? Someone else wore the identity, for this, but it is close enough. She should be fatter than I can manage. A drug to retain fluid in the body will give me part of it—for the rest I must make do with padding and thick clothes, and the inserts to puff my cheeks. If I were using the identity fully, in hostile territory, I should have to cut and gray my hair—but for this, the wig will do. When I have added the wrinkle appliqúes to my face, and the two gold teeth and broken-veined nose-piece—"

He looked from Rissa to the picture. "You can make yourself into *this* hag?"

"Hag? She is not so old—biologically fifty, perhaps. She has lived immoderately." She laughed. "It is lucky that Dorning had the pictures—and that the Hulzeins did not insist my doubles follow the disfigurement fads of the rest. Otherwise—"

He put an arm around her. "Otherwise we'd have worked out something else, is all. And by the way—"

"Yes?"

"You mind waiting until tomorrow to pull the transformation?"

"Not at all." She sipped the last of her wine. "But now—Tregare, you must have business to attend. So—"

"You trying to get rid of me?"

"For a time, yes. I need to hear the tapes, and practice being Cele Metrokin."

IT has been so long—I have forgotten so much! She played the tapes three times, taped her own voice in mimicry, listened to short bits of each in sequence. She shook her head—it was going to be a long, arduous time, this . . .

Listening again, trying to engrave the patterns in her mind once more, she sorted through the paraphernalia of identity. Yes, it was all here—and spares for the items that were not reusable. The tape ended; she set the other machine to Record and spoke again. Her accent was better now, she thought—and she was becoming used to the phrasings. *But I must be very careful . . .*

She paused to dine with Tregare, but for the evening again demanded solitude. At the end of it, when he joined her, she said, "I think it will be good enough."

In the morning, after breakfast, Tregare watched her begin the transformation. Already the drug gave her an edemic, bloated look; the cheek inserts and her clothing, only slightly padded, completed the effect. When she spoke, the harshness of her nasal voice owed something to plastic that widened her nostrils. " 'Not *quite* lardy enough, maybe—but 'senough to fool those freaks." She blurred the sibilants, almost lisping. "Gimme the names again. I never seen 'em so I dunno which's which—right? But I oughta know the list, solid."

He read the names; she repeated them. "Okay—I won't forget." She placed the gold toothcaps, then the appliqués that gave her a sot's nose and wrinkled cheeks, streaked with broken capillaries. With her own hair coiled and carefully pinned, she donned the bushy gray wig and painstakingly placed heavy salt-and-pepper eyebrows, holding them until the adhesive dried. Lastly she added Metrokin's fingerprints and retinal patterns.

"Gimme my shoes, huh?"

Tregare started to pick them up. "What—? These things weigh a ton!"

"Two kilos the foot, 'sall. They got lead sheets in the soles." And when she put them on and walked, her heavy, stumping gait satisfied her. "Now the gloves—I got stuff to age the hands, how they look, but takes too long for now."

She stood, posed, and he looked at her. "Peace take me, Rissa!—I mean Metrokin—if I hadn't seen you *do* it—"

"Who knows? Maybe you're lookin' at your own young slut, thirty years along."

"Never!" He shook his head. "Now then—you want time alone with that bunch before I come in—right? So I'll have a guard take you over there. You want him to know who you are, or not?"

"Least knows, the better. 'less you got some clown you can trust—"

"We'll keep it to ourselves, mostly. And I've set up the quarters they'll see you locked into, tonight, and come out of in the morning."

She gave Cele Metrokin's croaking laugh. "What they dunno is, 'sgot a back door to it, as theirs ain't. Well, Tregare— let's get off our ass."

RISSA did not have to pretend nonrecognition of her guard; the man was from offship. *O'course! I'm fresh outa freeze, and this one don't know Tregare's chambers are shot to hell.*

With the guard directing her she clumped downship and across to the building. Inside, her guide became confused; while he led her in the wrong direction, she was hard put to keep silent.

Finally she said, "You dunno, zerchface, why the hell don't you *ask?*" Eyes narrowed, he looked at her. For a moment she expected a slap for her rudeness, but he shook his head and moved her along. Next time they met someone, he did ask directions—and soon escorted her to the conference room.

Inside, she looked at the Committee members. *Remember— I ain't seen these before!"* "Hello, Dorning," she said. Then, "Curse me for a Client! *You're* my goddamn' col- leagues—you bunch of carved-up freaks?" She made her heavy-footed way to a chair and sat. "What in hell got into ya? I heard stuff—sure—but why ya wanna be such friggin' *monsters?"*

Someone—Gemskull, it was—said, "It's a status matter. You've been off Earth; you wouldn't understand. A—a com- petition, with no one else allowed to compete."

Metrokin's harsh laugh. "What I think—you sorta forgot when to quit. No wonder this snotnose Tregare's got his boots up our ass! You'd stuck to business—"

"For that matter," said Fringe Ears, "you're as much a prisoner as we are. So who are *you* to talk?"

"Went into Stronghold, we did—all the signals right. Then we're landed and Police come aboard—only they ain't Police at all, they're Tregare's. How'm *I* supposed to lift ship—stand on the ramp and fart, maybe?" She shook her head, a jerky motion. "Anyway—he didn't take no whole damn *planet* off me, like he did you."

Scar Ridge said, "We're wasting time. The question is, what can we do about it?"

"Dunno about you," said Rissa. "Me, I'm gonna make a deal."

The Dairy Queen's unlikely breasts heaved. "Traitor! If the guards weren't here, I'd—"

"You'd *what?* Smother me with them haybags you got? If you fell over frontwards, your head'd only make it halfways. What *are* those things—plastic or somethin'?"

"They are *not*. It's a glandular treatment—very expensive, too, to maintain."

"Shoulda tried one for your brains—alla ya. But looka here, now—we gotta *try* workin' together. Better chances that way. So—who's top freak between ya?"

"Don't *you* know?"

"Sure—I know it's Hrodicken. But I never seen ya before, any more than you seen me. So whicha you pincushions *is* Hrodicken?"

Gemskull said, "She's dead, I'm told. I'm next in line—after you and Obrigo, of course."

"You gotta name? Or do I gotta read your monogram off your head?"

"Zavole—Aarem Zavole."

"Awright, Zavole. Tregare gets here, you give him the story. All the how-so, *why* we been runnin' things this way, the stuff he's so pissed about."

"Why not you? You're senior to all of us."

"Been off Earth too long—outa touch with all the small shit. Besides, you talk it better."

She pulled at the little finger of her right glove—the sign for Tregare, watching the monitor in his office, to enter. While Zavole still temporized, Tregare walked in and sat.

"Okay—school's started. You been having fun together, kicking old times around? How about it, Metrokin?"

"Har'ya, Tregare? You coulda warned me about the freak farm—some a these, make a maggot puke. They watch the store half the time they spend tryin' to look so candy-ass, you'd be on 'tother end of the stick here."

"Maybe." Tregare spoke quietly. "It strikes me, before I decide what to do with you lot, I'd better hear your side of it. *If* you have one."

"Such a coincidence," said Fringe Ears, "that the idea strikes you when we've just been discussing it here."

"Stuff it," said Rissa. "Any sense at all, he's got eyes and ears on us."

"Yeah," said Tregare. "And what kind of deal, Metrokin, do you have in mind?"

"Shit-simple, Tregare—I play your game, I'm home free."

"Think I'd leave you in voting control? You're crazy."

Rissa said, "Hell with *that*. I mean—you don't punish me for nothin', I live good—and when I want, you let me off Earth. No comin' back, I don't need to—out there I own enough—"

"I'll think about it. *First* you play my game—you do that, you won't be punished. I'll go that far with you, Metrokin."

"And the rest of us?" said Zavole. Tregare shrugged; the man continued. "You wanted to hear our side of it. Do you know how the present system began?"

Tregare leaned back, relaxed now. "What part of it do you have in mind?"

"A hundred and twenty years ago, roughly, this continent had twice its present population and couldn't afford its own government. The system of corporate elections, bidding for the job of governing, saved the economic structure from total collapse. It was supposed to be a stopgap—"

"And it was," said Tregare. "Because after UET'd been in power a while, they stopped having *any* elections."

"Well, yes—but that was before any of *us* were born."

"Not me," said Rissa. "You, maybe."

"Yes—I'd forgotten. But the terrible problem was still over-population—and so many of the people with no work, no way to earn a living."

"So somebody had a bright idea," Tregare said. "Total Welfare."

"Total Welfare, *and* UET's brilliant discovery of star drive." Rissa did not correct the man's idea of how UET had gone into space. He said, "The Welfare system—peace take us all if you succeed in destroying it. Those mindless herds, good for nothing but to *take*—"

"Skip the excuses," said Tregare. "I don't believe them. The way those people are treated, kept ignorant, worked for your gain, not their own—"

"Oh, there's abuse, of course. In *anything* this big—but it works, you see." Before Tregare could interrupt, "Would you rather have what happened in India a hundred years ago? Or China? Africa? Brazil?"

Delicately, careful not to press against the implanted gems, Zavole wiped sweat from his forehead. "Here's what happened. Quarantine of famine areas until the population starved down to fit the food supply. Deliberate introduction of pestilence for the same purpose. Rations withheld from unsterilized men—and since there weren't enough medical people to handle the mobs, like as not the men went to roadside quacks and found themselves castrated instead. Infanticide—enforced by fixing a woman with two touches of a hot iron—so that if she did have a baby she couldn't nurse it.

"I tell you—all these things happened, and worse. But not in North America."

Rissa shuddered. Almost, she forgot Cele Metrokin—but caught herself and said nothing.

Tregare said, "I've read some—not all that, but a little. Here, though—the birthrate was headed off, the way I hear it. So how come—"

"Massive immigration—forced on us by the rest of the world. *We'd* cut back, all right—so we had to make room for those who hadn't. We were at a military disadvantage—treaties that gave us a dubious balance with the Russians but not against the coalition that formed. We had no choice."

"So how—?" Then Rissa nodded. "Oh, sure—once we had spaceships, that crap *stopped*."

Zavole nodded. "You're right. So you see—UET—it's used its power to control population, to extend Welfare and avoid *worse* things."

Tregare said, "Sure. I see it."

"Then you agree we were right?"

"Were, maybe—at one stage. Not now, though. You've *got* it under control. So what's your excuse for keeping seventy percent of the human race—except the part you don't own yet—penned up like animals?"

Fringe Ears spoke. "Because they *are* animals. You should see the ones I use for entertainment at my parties. They—"

Tregare's voice rose. "That's enough. But thanks, whatever you are—you just put this discussion back on track. In perspective, sort of. Because we're done talking about what happened, and why. We're down to what happens next."

Zavole said, "If you don't mind, my first interest is what happens to *us*."

Tregare started to answer, but Rissa cut in. "Gotta remember, Tregare—so you *don't* like how we been runnin' things. But we been goin' by rules that was already set up. Don't we get no points for that?"

Tregare nodded. "Some—but not a lot. All right—here it is. You stay alive—unless you try to act against me. Your power's gone—it was gone when Rissa's brother blew up Newhausen's command ship, you just didn't know it for a while—and most of your wealth, with it. The only question is, *how* will you live? And the answer, for each of you, is anywhere from moderately comfortable to Welfare, depending on how well you cooperate with me."

Zavole cleared his throat. "You want *us* to work for you?"

"You got any objections? Take 'em along to Welfare and be damned to you. Yes—I want your help, and your recommendations of who's capable and who's not, under you. Don't get any bright ideas—you'll be answering my questions under truth field."

Fringe Ears smirked; on a guess, Rissa said, "Tregare—if I gotta work with these freaks, how about you get 'em a little bit undecorated first? Makes me wanna puke, some of it." Fringe Ears's face twisted, snarling. *I got it right! That head hardware fucks up the field!*

Tregare nodded. "You have a point, Metrokin. This—this weird flimflam gets in *my* way, too. Takes my mind off the job too much."

The Dairy Queen's ring-pierced hands tried to cover her outsized breasts. "You—you wouldn't—"

Tregare laughed. "You said it was a gland treatment. We'll just see what happens when it's stopped." He waved her to silence. "Now—I'm setting up teams to work with each of you, get information and check it. But for now, back to quarters while I line up surgery to untrim your Christmas trees." He stood. "You come with me, Metrokin—you're going to sign some papers before you get your lunch."

* * *

IN Tregare's office Rissa spoke little. *Don't* like *bein'* *Metrokin!* Tregare said, "I wish you'd say something, not just nod or shake your head. Anything wrong?"

She restrained the automatic headshake. "Don't like talkin', this one." She put her hands to her face, shut her eyes. Mentally she pushed Cele Metrokin away, saw the fat woman close a door behind her. She said, "Bran—this once and not again, while we need this identity, I speak as myself. It is too difficult—a poor choice, perhaps, but I did not foresee that—I cannot change in and out of Metrokin without great effort, and it strains me to hold the identity at all. So ask your questions. Quickly."

"All right—but *look* at me."

"No. For I—*I*—would see you seeing Cele Metrokin. And that would—*no*, Bran."

Between her hand and the wig his fingers found her ear and stroked it. "Okay. But tell me—do we have them moving? On the verge of stampede, the way we want?"

"I . . . think so." Eyes still covered, she tipped her face up to him. "And when they are stripped of their flesh-piercing ornaments and have only scars to show for them—I cannot, even now, look at that fringe-eared woman's nose, with its nostril flaps cut free and spread like gemmed wings; could not some semblance of normal appearance be restored? But when their pretentious mutilations are stripped of whatever glamour they see in them, perhaps they will become more rational persons. How soon can these changes be accomplished?"

"Not sure. The man who did most of the work is prematurely senile—overdosed on some kind of mindblaster. Two of his assistants are on their way—be here this afternoon. The one I talked to, she doesn't think it's much of a chore—only eight people, after all, and mostly work above the neck. But the tattooing—either we leave it alone, cover it with a solid darker color, or take chances peeling it off in one of several ways—all chancy. You have any preference?"

"Oh, let them keep their foolish colorings, if they like. But the woman who emulates a herd of milk cows—she must cover herself."

"That one bothers you?"

"She ridicules all women—renders a useful, natural function ludicrous—as though her vulva reached to the navel and her labia to the knees. I—*despise* her."

"She'll cover up; I'll see to it. Now—anything else?"

"Yes. Bran—I will stay in the Metrokin identity as long as it is needed, but I hate the role. I had not *realized*—but that is not important. What I would say is—let us use this creature I must be, use her quickly and be done with her. Find a reason why she is no longer available, is not needed—so that I can be free of her."

For a time he was silent. Then he said, "When we don't need her—soon as we can manage that—I catch Metrokin crossing me and I lock her up, solitary, is all."

"When the time comes, Bran, make the betrayal seem most convincing. And until then I will not speak again, as Rissa."

Now in her mind it was Rissa Kerguelen who went behind a closed door. Another opened and Cele Metrokin appeared. After a pause, she opened her eyes, looked up and said, "Awright, Tregare. Stick me back in the pokey and be damned to you."

"But—you don't have to stay there—"

"Hell I don't. Can't hack it, this one, the back 'n' forth."

She saw his puzzlement. Then he said, "Yeah. I see what you mean."

THE next day, Rissa met with Tregare and Biels Dorning, only. "The rest," said Tregare, "they're either waiting surgery, having it or resting from it. And for now I don't need 'em, anyway. Dorning—you explain to me the orders you've been getting, the past few years, from Metrokin and Obrigo. And how well you've followed them."

"But—hasn't *she* said—?"

"I want your version. Crosschecking."

Dorning spoke at length. As Rissa had suspected, the orders were simple enough—try to extend control and don't rock the boat. Only the details would be complex, and for the moment Tregare waved those aside. "And almost every year," said Dorning, "we've advanced our holdings a percentage point or two, even now that we're meeting more resistance."

Tregare said, "No orders to change policies—is that right?"

"When you control most of a world," said Dorning, "you don't tamper with the methods that gained you that control."

"I'd have hoped different," Tregare said. "Like maybe, that making changes was the *object* of getting control."

Rissa gave him a warning glance. "What's to change? All set up—you turn the crank, it works. You—*you're* gonna fuck around with things, make a real puke pile."

"I'll take the chance. Dorning, you get me a full readout— this afternoon—of all major Metrokin-Obrigo operations since the coalition began."

"In detail? But that would take weeks."

"In summary—with coding for *access* to whatever details I might want."

The lone guard took Dorning away. Rissa said, "What else you been doin'?"

Tregare looked at her, then nodded. "All right, if you have to do it that way. Metrokin—a ship of mine, it's spotted a certain scoutship and figures to have the contents here in maybe two weeks." He waited for her nod. "The Academy's shaking down fine, and the port's doing well, too. Upstairs a man named Kybel's doing a good job helping my representative start releasing folks from Welfare—a slow start, but solid. No word from a certain Establishment you know of, and not much more from Australia. Suit you, mostly?"

"You been plenty busy, I guess. Awright—you're through here, I wanna go lie down awhile."

He leaned forward. "You're feeling all right?"

In her cumbersome way, she stood. "Water pill don't help my gut any. What the hell—don't need it no more, is what I think."

Tregare took her to Cele Metrokin's quarters. For a time she rested. Then—before and after her solitary dinner—she worked at a portable computer terminal, screened so as not to be visible from the doorway if a guard or attendant came. Gradually the drug-induced malaise left her; by late evening she was ready to sleep, and slept well.

Two days more of Cele Metrokin, meeting with the Committee members and Dorning and Tregare. She testified under a carefully maladjusted truth field; she watched others speak, and listened, while the field worked properly.

Denuded of their grotesque finery, the eight were much subdued. Where gems and rings had glittered were now only pierced holes or small, healing wounds. Fringe Ears still merited that appellation, but her nose was bandaged; a strip of tape lay flat from nape to eyebrows where Scar Ridge had worn his hideous crest. Ordinary white teeth—dentures?—appeared instead of gems in another woman's mouth. Under the Dairy Queen's robe the swollen mammaries might or might not have begun to diminish; Rissa could not tell by looking.

Late that second afternoon she made her decision. Tregare had left the room briefly; when he returned she made the sign they had agreed on and he strode to face her.

"All right, Metrokin—you've had it!"

"Huh? What's itchin' *you*, Tregare?"

Hard, convincingly, he cuffed her head; she moved only enough to take the sting away. "I don't know how you got to the man—but it won't happen again! He's locked up and you're next. Not here anymore—in the brig on *Inconnu*. You—"

"What you bitchin' about? All I done—"

"All you did was get two coded messages out, maybe more. My comm people unscrambled one of them. It's enough to Welfare you, at the least—after *I'm* done taking your head apart."

She spat in his face—or tried to—he dodged and grabbed a hand, pulling her upright. He twisted the arm behind her and marched her to the door. "Guards—salt these others down as usual, for now. I'll deal with them tomorrow."

BACK on *Inconnu* in their own quarters, Tregare watched as Rissa carefully divested herself of Cele Metrokin. Wig, clothing, appliqués, inserts, gold teeth—all of it she returned to its original containers. She showered and dried herself. Naked, she shook her hair down and loose, and looked in a mirror. Only then did she speak.

"There is still a little bloating, from the drug. Not much—it should be gone by tomorrow or next day."

"You look fine," said Tregare. "What made you decide, today—?"

She sat on his lap, arms around his neck. "We will talk later. First you must come to bed for a time, and convince me that I am restored to myself."

Tregare laughed. "That's the best idea I've heard all day!"

•　•　•

STILL unclothed, Rissa sat and sipped wine. "So, basically," she told Tregare, "I felt I had learned all that would be worthwhile from them, that required . . . that identity. And I had made my evaluations."

"Fine—let's hear them."

"Dorning is an instrument; he will work as well for us as he has done for Lena Hulzein—and he is not vicious. Neither is Zavole—a capable man competing, as he told me once, in the only available competition fitting a man of his caliber. He is also the only Committee member who has cooperated fully enough, in my opinion, to earn him any special leniency or privileges."

She made a sour face. "The others—Maita Pangreen, and cannot *something* be done about those revolting ears?—she is the most total sadist I have ever known; she makes Stagon dal Nardo look like a playful kitten. Things she said when you were not present, of what she had done to Welfare Clients in 'entertainment' at her parties—it was all I could do, Bran, to keep from ending her life out of hand. Scar Ridge—Eloysin, is it?—he is nearly as bad. And the Tattooed Wonder, and the Dairy Queen—and to some extent the woman who wore jewels for teeth. The other two—they seem merely callous, heedless, unthinking—abusing power more by accident than purpose. Worse than Albert Kybel, but not truly monsters."

"You're getting more tolerant," said Tregare. "Kybel got your blood up pretty good, I remember."

"I do *not* tolerate such attitudes. And the two I mention should be Welfared with the rest, if that is what you decide for the group. Simply, it is that I have now seen much worse than Kybel. But at any rate—with all of them, I think there is no more to be learned by subterfuge."

"Right—we know how their operation works and don't need them to help us work it. Any reason *not* to Welfare the whole lot—except Dorning and Zavole—and be done with it?"

She shook her head. "You cannot put those, as they are, into a Welfare Center—unless you intend they die that same day. They have preened their strange appearances before Tri-V cameras; they are known—and hated."

"Do you care whether they live or die?"

"Tregare—if we are to kill, let us do so deliberately and

responsibly, with due grief if need be. Let us not fling them to a mob and turn away.''

He stood and began to dress. "I wasn't planning to, actually. I figured to stick the seven of them into an ex-condominium unit, all by themselves—nobody sees them except people who know how to follow orders—and let them stew in their own sauce.'' His brows raised. "Any objections?''

A moment, then, she thought. "No. In fact, Bran—I rather like it.''

"Good. You want to eat here in your skin, or dress and visit the galley?''

"I will dress.''

DEVEREL joined them at dinner. After greetings, Tregare said, "Any new word, Hain?''

"Yes, skipper—something from the Hulzein group, I think. At least it came over a feedline you thought might be theirs.'' Deverel filled his plate and seasoned the food to his taste. "Pretty badly hashed; Control's still working on the decoding. But the first and last of it's fairly clear.''

"Yeah? Any real information, so far?''

"They know you as Bran Tregare Moray, for one thing. And the last part, if we have it right, reads like a command.''

"Command? Hell—what did it say?''

"Something like—'you will await our further instructions, and be prepared to follow them at once.' ''

Tregare laughed. "Yeah? I guess the decoding must be off a little bit.''

Rissa touched his hand. "From Lena Hulzein? Do not be too sure.''

PLAYING Cele Metrokin, thought Rissa, she had left her own work too long. Next morning she went to Control, and found Albert Kybel there before her. He looked better—still awkward in the Welfare jumpsuit, ears still protruding under the cropped hair—but his face was relaxed and he moved more easily.

"Good morning, Kybel. Have you completed the work I set you?''

When he looked at her, his gaze was direct. "Yes, Ms. Kerguelen. And I added some other material I thought you might want. When that was done I reported to Tregare as you told me to, and have handled his assignments also."

Was it time yet, she wondered? "You seem to have adjusted well, to your new status."

Kybel shrugged. "What else could I do? Kill myself? I thought of it, at first. But then—if millions can go through this and live, so can I. And at least I'm still doing important work—work I'm trained for—not cleaning sewers."

She looked at the stack of reports he had left for her. "This is more than I expected in so short a time."

"I worked overtime. Aiela—Ms. Lindstrom—gave me permission." One side of his mouth smiled. "I like it better here—working—than at the Welfare Center. Even if I do miss an occasional meal."

She paused. "And how do you feel now, about Aiela's having been Welfared?"

"If I'd known what I know now, I'd have fought it. She didn't deserve that." He shrugged. "But we always learn too late, don't we? At least, I did."

It is time. "Perhaps not—though at first I was uncertain of you." Seeing his eyes widen, she said, "You will not have all that you did have, because the excess is needed for others. But your quarters and personal possessions have been held intact for you, and your adjusted salary equivalent approximates the average of what you *used*, of your former quotas. Will this satisfy you, Albert Kybel?"

The man shuddered; one hand braced against a desk so that he did not fall. *"Satisfy* me?" Violently he shook his head. "You take me out of Hell and ask me if I'm *satisfied?"* And now he could smile. "You could keep everything I had and pay me just enough to live, and I'd thank you—so long as you took me out of Welfare!" His face showed puzzlement. "But—*why?"*

"Why Welfare you—or why release you?" She waved further questions away. "Both answers are the same. You are a capable man but were blind to what you were doing. Now I think you have learned why it is important to release from Welfare as many as possible, as soon as can be done. Am I right?"

He only nodded, and she said, "Then at the end of this day

you will be returned to your personal quarters. You may punch the transfer data into the terminal now, if you like, and I will add the authorizing code."

When this was done, he said, "The woman I'm working for—the one in charge of the release program. Is she really—I mean, no offense, but what's a Hulzein doing in Tregare's crew?"

She smiled. "Tregare values his mother's judgment." Kybel's mouth opened but he said nothing. "Well—if you have not met formally, tomorrow I will introduce you to Liesel Hulzein."

As she left, he gestured good-bye, but still did not speak.

IN Tregare's Headquarters office Rissa did not expect the crowd she encountered. Quietly, with a touch here, a word there, she worked through it to Tregare's desk and saw him preparing to activate Tri-V broadcast. "Bran—what is happening?"

He looked up. "Riot in a Welfare Center, Rissa. Rumblings of more on the way. I have to talk to them again, ready or not—I've put it off too long." Indicator lamps lit. He said, "Anything you think I'm missing, tap my shoulder and I'll shut up and let you talk. Okay? Well, the circuit's live, so here goes." He threw the final switch.

One deep breath he took. Then; "Tregare speaking, to everyone I can reach—and especially in the Welfare Centers. D Center—if you're getting tired of breaking up the fixtures, it might pay to stop and listen for a minute. If you don't, you're just hurting yourselves. I don't know what kicked off the riot in D, but nobody's going to get punished for starting it. No Client, I mean."

He looked to Rissa. She said, "Explain as if they had heard none of it before."

He winked at her, turned to the screen. "If you missed it the first time, UET's out of power—the Presiding Committee's locked up. My people are in charge, and our idea is to get folks *out* of Welfare—free citizens again—as fast as we can. But not all at once—we don't have the manpower and there's no place to *put* everybody, on the outside. So you'll have to be patient."

Rissa touched his shoulder; he leaned aside and she faced

the camera. "We are first releasing those who can be freed with the least dislocation. We *must* work this way in order to build a growing base of free citizenry, so do not despair if you are not among the first chosen. At least, the overcrowding will be progressively reduced during your remaining stay."

And for some, it may still be all your lives! But there is no help for it . . .

She stepped back; Tregare said, "We've already eased conditions some—you must have noticed. There's a gripe channel from each Center, and we check to make sure it's kept open. And—"

Rissa whispered to him. "Take a gripe call *now*—from the rioting Center."

"Oh, yeah. I want somebody on the gripe channel from D Center. Whatever your complaint is, there, speak up."

After a pause an auxiliary screen lit—but showed only a masked face. Tregare said, "Hide if you want to—but I *told* you, no retaliations."

The voice trembled. "They always say that. How do we know you're any different? We—"

"Sure," said Tregare. "You don't have to trust me until I prove it. Just go ahead and tell me what it is you have to say."

"It's—you don't know what goes on here! You—"

"*Still?*" Tregare's voice harshened. "I gave *orders*—punishments to stop—"

"Oh, it's stopped, for now, mostly. But for how long? The guards say, 'wait 'til Tregare's in solid, we'll be right back the same as always.' "

Tregare's fist slammed the desk. "*That's a peacefucking lie!*" Rissa saw him fight for calm. "All right—maybe the staff didn't understand, so no retaliation there, either—for anything up to *now*. But no *more* threats, or I wring something. Everybody got that?" No answer came. "Now then—what else you need?"

"Come see for yourself, that's all we ask. What they do—what's *been* done. You come see—you'll be safe—they wouldn't dare—we'd fight 'til we were all dead, like Zed Center in old Britain twenty years back—they don't forget that and they hadn't better—we—"

Tregare scowled. With the voice switch off, he said, "They need this, but I don't have the *time!*"

Rissa flipped the switch. "Tregare cannot come, himself.

An entire continent to bring to order—you must understand. But I will come instead. Do you agree?''

"You? Tregare's the boss. You young fluff—who are *you?* What can you—''

She waved a hand across the screen. "I am Tregare's wife—he will listen to what I say. And I have done what he has not. I spent eleven years of my own life in a Welfare Center, in the Female Juvenile divisions.''

On the screen, fingers reached above the mask to scratch forehead. "That doesn't work. If he pulled you out, you wouldn't have time to grow all that hair so soon." A pause. "And—and you're a young-ass, all right, but no juve any more.''

She laughed. "But Tregare did not rescue me. It was—there were lotteries then, and I won and was released. Nearly sixty years ago on this world. You see—''

A gasp. "You went *spacing.* We've heard—you go to space, you get young. We—''

She shook her head. "That is not correct. One ages more slowly, but one does age. I have *lived* perhaps a tenth of the years that elapsed since I left Earth.''

"Wait a minute. There's an old Underground story—the kid that walked off Earth with twenty million Weltmarks. Around Year Forty, it was—back when a Weltmark was day's pay for a free citizen." The voice tensed. "You wouldn't be *that* one?''

"I would—I am. My name is Rissa Kerguelen.''

After a silence; "You come, then. We'll keep you safe.''

THEY lunched on *Inconnu:* Liesel and Hawkman joined them. After hearing the proposal, Liesel said, "You're going into that place, are you, without protection? Sometimes I think you *like* taking chances.''

"As you, of course, do not. But do not fear for me. Ivan will accompany me.''

Hawkman's brows indicated surprise. "Ivan? Then Ilse Krueger must be—''

"She is," said Ivan Marchant.

Rissa stood and hugged her brother. "Ivan! I did not hear you enter. Tell me—tell us all—the good news of Ilse.''

They sat now; Ivan began eating. "Sorry I'm late—at least

my plate's not cold." Between bites, he spoke "Ilse—she'll do now. Total physical damage, we don't know for sure. Scabs peeling around the edges—so far it's all skin, not scar tissue, and stubble growing from the scalp parts. No way to know yet—how much scarring there'll be in the middle of it, besides the deep slash. But she'll manage now, I think."

"That's good," said Liesel. "She's tough, Ilse is. But how do you know for *sure?*"

Ivan said, "She hit a bad slump. Doctor'd been talking to her, suggesting an electronic bug and a transducer to the left-hand auditory nerve, to give some directional hearing. I thought the idea would *help* her, but after he left she began saying she'd be better off dead. So I—it sounds funny, I guess—"

"Ivan." Rissa pointed a finger. "Working to save the will to live is not humorous. What did you *do?*"

"Oh, sure. Well, I talked rough to her—told her I wanted her to hear something, and to shut up until she did hear it."

"Yes?"

"So I played her the whole battle—the tapes from when she took the squadron in, through the hit we took and the turn-around after, then the part where she told *me* how to take Newhausen, how I blew him to rubble and all the way to when she passed out."

Rissa nodded. "You reassured Ilse of her competence, by objective evidence."

"That's right. Playing by ear and *hoping* I knew what I was doing."

Hawkman smiled. "I'd guess you knew, all right. And what happened?"

"What would you think?" said Ivan Marchant. "For the first time since we caught the hit, she took me to bed—and I thought she'd never stop." He grinned. "Not that I'm complaining, you understand."

"You had *better* not, my brother . . ."

NOT until next morning, after Rissa had introduced Kybel to Liesel Hulzein, did she and Ivan leave for Welfare Center D. Tregare said, "You sure you don't want some troops along—some guns?"

"No," said Rissa. "Hain and Anse will be in the scout—

like old times, is it not? And no Welfare Center has means to defend against a scoutship. We shall have no great trouble, Bran—I am sure of it."

"If you say so. I hope you're right."

IVAN landed the scout to one side of the designated area. "Just in case," he said. Deverel grinned, and made a circle of thumb and forefinger.

"If you come out in a hurry," he said, "stay close to the wall until I blink the staging lights. Then come running, on the high lope—and we go up fast."

"There will be no need," said Rissa. "But, Hain—I appreciate it, that you plan against what we do not expect." The man's smile rewarded her.

Ivan led the way off the scout, across pavement to the Center's guarded gates. The sentry said, "Who are you and what do you want?"

Ivan said, "If you don't know, you're relieved of duty. We're from Tregare."

The man lowered his weapon. "I'm sorry—we're nervous here. Go right on in."

Inside, guards and supervisors seemed civil enough but somehow obstructive. Finally Rissa said, "The man who spoke with Tregare yesterday—where is he?"

A tall woman said, "I'm not sure. It's said, he may have been taken sick."

Ivan moved to face her; she stepped backward and he followed. "That man had better be here, in good health, to talk with us—by five minutes, at the outside." The woman shrank back; he caught her shoulder. "Whatever shape he's in, you bring him here." He pushed her away. "If you want to live this day out, that is."

The woman fled the room; Ivan turned to Rissa. "You'd best talk to Deverel."

She did, ending with "—and should we need a demonstration, Hain, no Clients are housed in the penthouse. It should make a spectacular bit of demolition." She heard his chuckle and signed out, as the tall woman escorted a man into the room.

"Here's the one you want, I think."

Rissa looked at him—standing, wobbling, arms jerking to

keep balance. Above the ragged stubble on his lean, pock-marked cheeks, his eyes bulged.

"*You*—did you talk to Tregare yesterday? And to me?"

From the corners of his mouth, saliva dribbled. "I—yes-herdy? Talk t'ya . . . yeah." He looked haggard; his head shook. "They—gimme shots—I—" He slumped; Ivan sat him into a chair.

No waiting now—two strides and Rissa gripped the woman's neck. Her other hand activated her short-haul voice link. "Hain? It is treachery. If we lose contact, have no mercy on the executive section—but spare the Client dormitories." She heard and acknowledged his answer, then said, "Ivan?"

From flared nostrils his breath snorted. "Rissa? We start right now, we can shoot us out of this trap. Here to the gate, they don't have that many—"

The tall woman snarled, "You don't have a *chance* out of here."

"Wait." Rissa gripped harder, thumb against the larynx, fingers digging alongside the spine. Soft-speaking, she said, "You, woman! Would you die this next minute?"

"I—I—no, wait!"

"Do you have contact—can you influence those outside this room?"

"Yes, but—"

"Then speak, and quickly. Say that this place surrenders —all of it—or all of it dies. I accept that risk. Do you?"

"Oh, God—let me breathe!" Rissa eased her grip, but only slightly. The woman talked at her wristband. "They're crazy—we can't afford to try it—I'm giving up and you can take your own damned chances, Collering—well, the hell with *you*, too!" Gasping, turning back to Rissa, "I did the best I could!"

Rissa released the neck and caught the wrist, shouted at it. "Collering—whoever you are! Surrender now and you live. That is all I promise." A pause. "Answer me!"

A voice came weakly from the wristband. "Collering wouldn't see reason; he can't answer because he just got his throat cut. Tilseng says he sees that scoutship out there and you won the argument. Hold the shooting and he'll be down to give you the keys to the place."

Rissa said, "Be sure Tilseng does it properly. Because Collering ran me rather short of patience."

• • •

TWELVE armed men accompanied Tilseng's entrance. Exasperated, Rissa edged her voice. "You incredible *fools!* Now, listen." She called Deverel. "Hain—very soon a dozen men will come out and leave their weapons on the ground, well outside the gate. If they do not, start blowing this place apart as I have indicated."

The armed men left, running. Now Rissa had time to look at Tilseng. The man made no impression—average in size, neutral in coloring, almost expressionless, he stood as though he were not present. Looking, Rissa said, "I think, Tilseng, that you are the ultimate product of UET's policies."

"I beg pardon?"

"You need not; you owe none. But tell me—who are you?"

"Tilseng. With Collering dead I speak here for the Committee."

"There is no Committee. Who are you, Tilseng?"

"I—there'll be someone I can speak for. Won't there?"

She shook her head. "No. Not until you can speak on your own behalf." To Ivan, she said, "This one is as Welfared as his Clients." And to the tall woman; "I want your name."

"Faris Conichiel. But I cleared myself, didn't I?"

"That is not the point." Rissa gestured toward the drugged man. "Can he be made fit to speak rationally—*now?* If not, find and bring me his deputy."

Conichiel shrugged. "These Underground connections? How would *I* know?"

Rissa grasped the woman's neck again; Conichiel tried to flinch away. "How you know is your problem, not mine. It is also your problem to obey my orders without wasting more of my time about it." She squeezed the neck, hard. "Do you understand?"

Faris Conichiel winced but did not move her head. "Yes. And I'm no good with pain—I never was. So you don't have to touch me again. I know how to find who you want and I'll handle it. Unless *they* get me again."

Rissa said, "You are *that* pliable?"

"They could hurt me right back onto their side again."

"That won't happen," said Ivan Marchant. "I'll escort you—let's go."

• • •

A FEW minutes later they returned; between them limped a young black man. "Here's the man we want," said Ivan. "His name's Brinton, and—"

"Garbatt!" Brinton moved to the seated man; with one hand he tipped up the lolling chin. He looked, then turned to Faris Conichiel. "What the hell you done to him?"

The woman flinched. "*I* didn't do anything. I think he's drugged, but—"

Rissa spoke. "Tilseng! have you *no* initiative? Get a medic here." The man scuttled out; Rissa said, "We will find out, Brinton, about your friend. When he was brought here he still could speak, though not well."

The black man said, "That's Collering's pet trick—dope somebody up so he can't tell anything. I'd like to give *him* a few shots sometime."

"Collering is dead," said Rissa.

"*You* do it?"

"No. His own people did—when he refused to surrender to us."

"Whoever, it's a good thing. Now—what you want of me?"

She gestured toward Ivan. "He and I, we are here for Tregare."

"Yeah? Garbatt said somebody'd come. Me, I wasn't so sure." His eyes narrowed. "Just the two of you—no troops? Hell—where's your *own* guns? Besides those peashooters you got . . ."

"Outside," said Ivan. "Mounted on a scoutship."

Brinton whistled. "And Collering wanted to fight *that?* No wonder they had to wipe his slate." He shook his head. "Well, then—I guess you want I should show you around, let you see the stuff *they'd* like to keep hid. Okay—let's go."

He turned, limping. Rissa said, "Your leg, Brinton—should not someone else guide us instead?"

"Naw—I got clubbed a little, is all. Prob'ly do it good to walk around more, loosen it up better."

As Rissa nodded and began to follow, Tilseng entered. Behind him came a woman carrying a leather bag. "You are the medic?" said Rissa. The woman nodded. "Then see what is wrong with that man—it appears he has been drugged—and try to have him in better condition when we return. His continued good health is of paramount importance."

"In fact," said Ivan, "your own rides with it."

THEY followed Brinton. Occasionally they passed empty-holstered guards, studiously ignoring weapons piled on the floor. As they came to a dormitory, Rissa turned to enter. The black man said, "Don't bother—this part, they'd show you anyway. Standard dorm—no cots, of course, but not even double-decked yet."

They passed a large room; on the floor sat men watching a reading-course presentation on Tri-V. The men were naked. Rissa asked, "Where are their jumpsuits?"

Brinton shrugged. "Economy move, three-four years ago. You don't need clothes in the Client sections, see? You go up to the offices, like me, now, or out to work—*then* you get a jumpsuit."

At the next dormitory entrance: "Here's one double-decked—you wanta see?" He opened the door; Rissa looked. A horizontal partition halved the room; beside the door a ramp reached the upper level. "A meter high, each deck—they say that's plenty. Just don't sit up fast if you're tall." She felt the rubbery floor and peered into the shallow levels. Except for dim lighting and a series of ventilator grilles, she saw only bareness.

She shook her head. "Let us go on." Again Brinton led.

Punishment cells—each a cubic meter with floors of metal grating—except through a slot in the door, no light entered. "They pass food trays in through those—when they get around to it." He grinned. "And they only emptied those hellholes—in a hurry—when they heard you were coming."

Rissa stopped. "You are sure of that? Tregare had given *orders*, long since—"

"You'll see—just watch for guys with a fresh case of waffle ass."

She saw them—new welts and old scars alike, and not only the grating patterns but also obvious whip marks. Ivan said, "Are you thinking the way I am?"

"I am thinking that at the Space Academy, Tregare did well. Before new regulations go into force, the old should be applied to those who have done this." But then she shook her head. "*No*—to see these things—it harms the mind, turns it toward vengeance. I—"

"You're wrong," said Brinton. "It's *not* just getting our own back—it's the only way you'll show 'em they can't get away with it now. And you want the Clients to trust you—right? Well, they see Koster—and Lavitz, maybe a few more—in there getting the ol' waffle: best move you could make!"

Ivan squeezed Rissa's hand. "You mind if *I* snoop around a little, round up the real sadists and give 'em a taste of their own?"

She considered. "A *small* taste, perhaps—hours, not days—and only for the worst among them. But now it seems fitting that Tilseng and the rest move to double-decked sleeping quarters, and draw jumpsuits only when they need to enter the office areas."

SLOWLY, past sights that chilled Rissa, they worked their way down through the Center. At the entrance to the lowest level, an armed guard met them. "Out of bounds."

Brinton said, "If you put that gun down right away, we didn't see it. On account, if we did see it you get waffle ass for about a month." The man looked from one to another of them, put the gun on the floor and walked swiftly away.

Brinton said, "Let's get down there in a hurry. I got an idea I don't like at *all*." He went down the stairs fast; his limp, Rissa noticed, was almost gone.

At the bottom, along a corridor and through a door—they found havoc. Rissa gasped; her eyes clamped shut. When she opened them and could absorb what they saw: "What *happened* here?"

Through the crying and groaning, no one heard her. Some of the naked persons were dead, some wounded, some carrying only old mutilations—but all the uniformed figures were clearly dead. The woman holding the gun—*I must force myself to look at her*—turned and said, "If you're from Tregare, you're a little late."

Still shocked, Rissa looked around and saw no whole, unmarred person. Ivan said, "We are from Tregare—give me the gun and we'll talk about it." He reached, and Rissa thought the woman would shoot, but then Ivan had the weapon. Calmly, as though at a target range, he unloaded it and set it aside. "All right—now tell us what's going on. And first, your name."

Side to side the maimed head shook. "Forget my name —when I didn't look like it anymore, I killed it. Now they call me Ears. Take a good look—you'll see why."

Rissa had seen; of all the woman's scars, these held her horrified attention. One ear retained the inner cup but had been trimmed around, short of the curving fold; the other was gone entirely. "What *happened* to you?"

The answer did not surprise her. "You think Maita Pangreen had herself fixed the way she is, without experimenting first? Do you? If so, you're wrong." The woman gestured around her. "All these, what's left of us now—the Committee's guinea pigs, D Center's allotment."

Rissa shook her head; the woman continued. "Thirty at least—some men and some women—for the ears alone, before she was satisfied. Afterward, you see, they cut the altered parts away completely, so the rest of the freaks won't find out what they're up to, and maybe top it. At least with ears it was simpler for her than killing me—she does that too, sometimes."

Rissa began to speak, but the woman was not done. "And sometimes she doesn't have to—kill, I mean. My sister—when she saw what was left of her face, she drowned herself—wire around her neck so she couldn't pull her head out of the washbasin, turned on the water and threw the faucet handles away. You don't know—"

I must not succumb to the urge for vengeance—but how can I deny it to such as these? Rissa said, "We had thought that Welfaring the Committee members would be punishment enough, but—" She shook her head. "Tell me—these things that were done to you—even under UET's laws, could they be justified legally?"

"No. It was all done secretly. That's why these—" She gestured toward the uniformed corpses. "—why they decided to cremate us alive before you could see us."

Now she told a simple and terrible story. The guards had brought men and women from their separate quarters and herded the mutilated group along, talking and laughing at them, until here—one room short of the cremating furnace— the woman had understood what they meant to do. "Take us in, one at a time, clamp us onto the death trolley and slide us into heat that would melt steel. So I grabbed a gun and turned loose. Jerily—she's dead over there—got one, too. We were all mixed in together by then—no way to keep from killing our own, too, to be sure and get *them*.

"I think—I think it was me that shot Jerily."

Through her horror, Rissa concentrated on facts. "Do you know who gave the orders to kill you? And when?"

The woman shrugged. "Pangreen, I suppose—or some of her clique. Probably around the time Tregare took Headquarters, saying to do it if he sent anybody here. Just to be on the safe side, she'd do that." She looked at Rissa. "Now what happens to us—that hasn't already?"

"Nothing will be done *to* you. I do not know as yet what can be done *for* you. Except that—Brinton? Something is wrong?" She had not seen him leave; now he approached quickly.

He said, "Nobody was doing anything for the hurt ones. I got on the intercom upstairs. Medics coming now."

"Thank you. I should have thought, but—"

The woman gestured. 'First sight of *us*, you wouldn't be thinking too calm. To tell the truth, it doesn't get much easier later on, either."

Rissa groped for speech. "How are you quartered, here?"

"A pair of double-deckers all our own, where nobody has to look at us."

"You will be given more comfortable quarters. For the rest —such things as corrective surgery, cosmetic prostheses—as I say, I do not know as yet, what help we can give you."

But suddenly she knew exactly what to do with Maita Pangreen.

SHE called on the gripe circuit. "It is cruel and terrible, Bran, but it is just. As the woman said—with each of the Committee, have the altered parts removed—using anesthesia, which is more than Pangreen bothered to do. When they have healed they will be effectively anonymous and can be quartered with their victims, subject to the same remedial efforts. But to remain alive they must pretend to *be* victims."

"You think Pangreen can keep up that kind of pretense?"

"If she cannot, her death is her own doing, not ours. And the same for the rest, any who have done similarly."

"You include Zavole in this?"

"So far as I can determine, he used no Clients for experiments. The technique of affixing gems to bone is an old one—perhaps that is why he chose it."

"All right; I'll give the orders. You coming back here tonight?"

"Tomorrow, I had thought—so as to conclude reassignment of quarters, and other matters I have mentioned. Do you approve of these?" She saw him nod. "As to returning—other than our wish to be together, is there cause for hurry?"

"Not really, I guess. But there's something I don't want to discuss in detail, on the circuit."

"Yes, Bran? Can you tell me anything about it, now?"

"Sure. We finally got a solid bite from the Hulzein Establishment." He grinned. "Except, I'm not sure who's supposed to be on which end of the hook."

GARBATT now slept normally; Rissa and Ivan took Brinton to lunch aboard the scout. As they entered, Anse Kenekke said, "You have much trouble in there?"

"Some," said Ivan. "Nothing your presence out here didn't handle."

Kenekke grinned. "Then sit down. Hain and I, we ate already—but he fixed enough extra, just in case."

When Kenekke served the food, Brinton first gulped a huge bite. Then Rissa saw him look at his plate. His next bite was smaller and he chewed it slowly. He looked at her and swallowed. "Food like this—not since I was a little kid, still Outside."

"We know," said Ivan. "We've both *been* in Welfare. Though I suppose the food's got worse—everything else has."

"Pretty bad, all right." Until he was done, Brinton said no more. Then; "How you want to leave things set up here?"

"As soon as possible," said Rissa, "Tregare needs an official representative at each Center, with access to the executive circuits at all times in order to report to Tregare's office at least once a day."

"Report what?"

"Whether operations are proceeding correctly. The representative will appoint assistants to monitor those operations. Brinton—do you want the job for this Center?"

"Should be Garbatt—he's the one got the riot under control, and all. I—"

"If he recovers and is capable—since you vouch for him, he can be the one. You would assist him, then?"

"Sure, that's better. You see—they all *listen* to Garbatt more."

"I will take your word for it. Now, then—besides the things we have discussed, what other immediate changes do you recommend?"

"Visiting." Her brows raised in inquiry; he said, "Men and women, we're kept separate. Saturday nights—that's the only time—five to ten from each dorm, the ones with the best records for the week, can go if they want to."

"Go? Where?"

"To the old gym! Get together and fuck up a storm!"

"You mean—you can meet your lovers only in an open room, among a crowd?"

He laughed. "What lovers? You hardly ever see the same one twice. The only rule we got is, nobody gets left out—you get there at all, somebody takes care of you. It's the only way there is, we can do anything *good* for each other. So—"

She raised a hand. "One moment." Then; "Again, we cannot correct this dehumanizing situation immediately—only one step at a time."

"Forget about privacy," said Ivan, "—at first, anyway. They're not used to it and probably don't care."

"Some do," Brinton said. "The new ones. Some won't go, account of that, or because they still think they'll get back with their own mates sometime."

At least, those will be the first released. Think of the worst cases! She said, "Would the gymnasium accommodate a seventh of the clients in this Center?"

"Empty, it would—easy. Mostly it's filled up with storage."

"Have it cleared; I do not care how it is done. Then—in each dormitory the persons divide themselves among the days of the week. The orders to use names again, rather than numbers, have been followed?" Brinton nodded. "Then *every* night a seventh of those who wish it will have the use of that gymnasium, until releases make more suitable facilities available."

She looked at him. "You guarantee these meetings will be self-policing? No rapes or other violence?"

"To *each other?* We don't do that way. I mean, things are bad enough . . ."

There is hope—even for these, there is hope! "Then—today is Thursday—announce the new procedure to begin on Sunday. That should be time enough to arrange it. So, Brinton—as a stopgap, do you find the proposal satisfactory?"

"Compared to now, anything is. Say—do we have to stay with the day we pick first?"

"What—? Oh, I see—to meet only the same one-seventh, never the rest. No—devise any system you like, so long as it is equitable and provides free choice."

"I gotcha." He frowned. "You really gonna put the staff in double-deckers?"

"For a time. So long as any must experience such discomfort, it is reasonable that staff and guards share it—if only that they may better understand your own feelings."

He grinned. "Hey—do *they* go to the gym, too?"

"Brinton—I do not like your thought, there."

Shrugging, he said, "Thought, yeah—some of those smartasses—but you're right. Things could get bad, that way."

"But for the time," said Rissa, "they will follow the same rules as yourselves. In a place of their own, of course."

Ivan laughed. "Me, I'd put 'em on their *old* rules first."

Before Rissa could answer, Brinton said, "Naw, she's right. Hit 'em too hard, they won't know why. Her way, maybe they will."

She said, "You understand a great deal. Brinton, can you read?"

Shrug. "A little. Just learning when they Welfared us—lost most of it. Been trying, though—watching the new stuff on Tri-V. Getting there a little, but it's slow."

"Keep trying. You will need the ability, to do the work that suits your other talents." He only smiled. She said, "Would you go see if your friend Garbatt is awake and able to talk? If so, tell him what has been decided; then call us here."

"What about Tilseng, Conichiel—those?"

"Tell them you are Tregare's representative and that I will confirm it shortly."

He left. Ivan said, "You've taped all this?"

"Everything since we entered the place."

"You want me to play it off, make a summary for Tregare?"

"There is not time, I would think. We go inside again soon."

Deverel spoke. "If it's not Top Zipper, I could do it."

"Would you, Hain? Thank you. And now, while Ivan abuses his kidneys with more coffee than is healthful, I should like to borrow a bunk, to lie quietly and relax my mind."

She shuddered. "There are things here, I wish I had not seen."

SHE dozed, but came fully awake at Ivan's touch. She put her hand on his where it clasped her shoulder, and said, "Brinton is ready for us?"

"Yes. But no hurry—take your time."

"Two minutes, no more. Excuse me now." And it could not have been much longer before she rejoined him, and they left the scout to enter the forbidding edifice.

Inside, Faris Conichiel met them. "The infirmary—I'll take you there." They followed her.

Garbatt still needed a shave, and his mouth twitched. But his eyes were clear; he sat propped against cushions and answered her query. "Feeling fine now, yeah. Brinton here, he told me what's happened." He squinted against overhead light. "You people really mean it, I guess. I'm glad—you dunno how much I'm glad. Well, then—okay, we'll work it the way you said. Some won't like the part about no getting even, now when we could, so easy. But don't worry—with the Clients, I say beans, everybody farts. And with the staff I talk for Tregare. Good combination—it's gonna work."

"I would think so, Garbatt. Now—would you like a summary of our agreements, for reference, on tape or on paper?"

"Tape. I can read—used to, anyway—but not since they took my contacts. Four years I kept 'em, the guards didn't know, but one time I got caught washing 'em and—"

"I see. In time we can replace such things."

"Sure. Hey—look, I'm sleepy again. Maybe—"

"Certainly. And I will see you on the circuit sometimes, when you report to Tregare."

She shook his hand and led the way out to the corridor.

"Now," she said to Brinton, "before we leave this Center I will see the woman who calls herself Ears."

"Not much you can do for that one. You saw . . ."

"Nonetheless, I wish to see her."

RISSA and Ivan found the maimed ones, with medical personnel attending the recently wounded, in a vacated staff suite. Ears, conferring with a medic, looked up and then came to meet them. She said, "I've seen our new quarters—full height, they are. Thanks. Is it true you're putting staff in our old ones?"

"For a time. I think it is well they have that experience."

"They're not *all* bastards," the woman said. Then, hesitating, she said, "You told me you want to help us. Well, there's one favor—"

"Yes?"

"Couldn't we be all together—men and women both?"

"Have you not been allowed even *that?*"

The scarred mouth twitched. "Sure—just like everybody else—Saturday-night quota to the gym." Her voice rose. "How could we? They see you and look away. I tried once— Jerily said I should—*she* did sometimes, but she wasn't so ruined, herself. They—they tried not to notice me, then three over to one side talked together. I knew why—the rule is, nobody gets left out. Finally one came over to me, looking down and sidewise, anywhere but *at* me. He did it, all right— he was even *good*—but he never once looked at me!"

Now she spoke more quietly. "I thanked him, you know— before he got away as fast as he could. but I never went back. Most of us don't, a second time. Just among ourselves, though—it wouldn't be so bad, I think."

Rissa felt tears welling; she blinked them back. Between her hands she took the ravaged head, palms cupping the cheeks and fingers touching the partial ear and lack of the other. "Of course you can be together! And your hair will grow to cover these, and some scars can be corrected or at least minimized. We will see."

Ivan spoke. "My wife lost an ear—a projector beam took it." He described Ilse's injuries. "She told me—any time the change bothers me, feel free to leave her." He shook his head. "She doesn't believe it yet, but that's never going to happen."

Reaching up, the woman put her hands over Rissa's. "You—you touched me. At first, like everybody else, you couldn't look at me. But now you are." Shuddering, she exhaled. "I don't know what anybody can do about this face; until I see it done, I won't hope for much. But one way, you've already changed me."

"Tell me . . ."

"I'm not going to be *Ears* anymore. I'm Celie Brashean again!"

WALKING back toward the office areas, Rissa unearthed a nagging thought. *Where are the children?* When she found Conichiel, she asked. "—and I suppose that they being smaller, their dormitories are *triple*-decked?"

Conichiel looked blank, then made a hiccuping sound that was almost a laugh. She shook her head. "No—it's the other way around. Welfare gets fewer children all the time, because—"

Rissa waved a hand. "Yes, of course—I should have realized. But where are they?"

"Only two Centers have Juvenile Divisions any more—K and R."

"K?" said Ivan. "Rissa—that's where *we* were!"

She turned to him. "Is it far from here? Far out of our way, going back to Headquarters?"

"Not very."

"Then before we return to *Inconnu*, we will visit that place." And then to Conichiel, "You have reports to show me?" The woman gestured toward a desk; Rissa sat and began inspecting the papers.

After a time she looked up. "Has Tilseng seen these? What does he say?"

"He said just do it and don't bother him. He's holed up in his quarters, while he still has them, floating on a cloud of drug-smoke." The tall woman shrugged. "I don't mind—I'm used to doing his work for him."

"It is no longer his work, Faris Conichiel—it is yours. Assign Tilseng to some job he *can* do—for you are now Chief Administrator here, working with Garbatt who represents Tregare."

"I—" A nod. "All right, I can do it. Except—Garbatt, he scares me."

"He need not. He speaks roughly but displays a sense of fairness. And now—you have done well, and more quickly than I expected. I think I will return to Headquarters today, after all. Is there anything more we need discuss?"

"Well—I see why you're doing it, but do we—the staff—*have* to go sleep in those double-decked chicken coops? And be *naked* all the time we're back there, out of this area? I mean—"

Rissa looked at her. "Yes. You will experience a small part of what you have administered. When congestion is relieved so that *all* may sleep in rooms of full height, then you may also. When all can be clothed whenever they wish, you will have your clothing back. Do you see?"

"I suppose so." Conichiel's arms hugged her breasts, and Rissa thought, *She is aging, and now her body shames her.*

But though she felt pity, she did not change her decision.

K CENTER was a short hop from D and less than fifty miles off their direct line of return. Rissa called *Inconnu*, left a message for Tregare, and got a relay to the Center. The man who answered looked anxious. Rissa said, "Inspection team, from Tregare. We will land inside the perimeter, near Division Female, Juvenile. Advise the gate guards that this landing is authorized." At his nod, she cut the circuit. And soon she pointed downward and said, "Ivan—*that* is the building, where I was."

He landed beside it; the two disembarked. Groundside, she walked slowly, thinking back—*how many years, Earthtime?* Almost seventy, since the small pigtailed girl had come to this place. Like a sleepwalker, she entered the blind concrete hulk, looking from side to side, passing offices whose occupants stared at her.

As Ivan followed, habit found her way to the anteroom that administered Dormitory Eighteen. Inside, behind a desk sat a pale-haired woman, perhaps thirty. The woman said, "You're from Tregare? And who are you, please?"

Unreality, disorientation—*this room!* Rissa suppressed laughter. Once begun, she could not have controlled it.

Carefully she said, "I am the wife of Bran Tregare—but I once lived in this place. You supervise here?" A nod. "Your name?"

"Lanice Teverin." The voice was soft. "Assistant supervisor, actually."

"And in Dormitory Eighteen, Teverin, how many girls do you supervise?"

"Only about forty, now—that's the average. We could put them on cots again, if Supply would release the cots."

"You will have them by this evening. Ivan—make a note?" Her brother nodded, and Rissa said, "I would see these children."

"Certainly." Teverin stood. "There's only three in the dorm itself right now—just back from the infirmary and still resting up from a flu bug. The rest are working or in the gym or the Tri-V room. Which do you want to see first?"

"The three, I believe. Ivan—perhaps you had best wait here."

Teverin led her down the short hall; she peered through the door's glass pane. Inside, three small jumpsuited stubble-headed girls sat in a close circle.

"They are clothed. I had expected—"

Lanice Teverin nodded. "The Adult Centers—I know. But here—with admissions getting fewer all the time—we have suits enough for years to come."

She paused. "Would you look at that—what they're doing?"

One girl held and rocked an armful of air; another imitated her, and then the third. Teverin said, "It's uncanny—this dorm—*only* this dorm, they all do that. And won't tell us what it's about."

Vertigo struck. Rissa's hand caught at the door to keep her from falling. Breathing deeply, she fought for balance. She said, finally, "May I go in—and talk with them?"

Teverin stared at her. "*May* you? I thought you were from Tregare."

Rissa shook her head; now, again, she could think. "I meant—would my intrusion disturb the children?"

"I wouldn't think so. Shall I come with you, or wait here?"

"Wait, please." Rissa entered the dorm and let the door swing shut behind her. As one, the three looked up at her, stared a moment, then resumed their mutual preoccupation.

Rissa crossed the floor and sat beside them.

From the corners of their eyes they looked at her, quickly, looking away again as soon as she caught their glances. She studied the one nearest her—thin of face and body, head crowned with light brown plush, age perhaps six. The child huddled over the emptiness she held, and crooned to it.

Rissa reached a hand—not to touch that space but to define her question. "What's her name?" The child's eyes widened, but she said nothing.

"Does she have a pretty name? You can tell me—because *nobody can ever take her away from you.* Remember?"

"How did *you* know that?" It was another girl—darker, stocky. "Morna—don't tell her anything!"

But the first child, Morna, smiled. "*You* had one, too!" Rissa nodded. "Then it's all right. Luseen—it's all right! She's not like *them*—she's different."

"You sure?"

"I am *very* different," said Rissa. "I believe in pretend dolls."

Luseen gasped. "You won't tell?"

Rissa shook her head. And Morna said, "Mine here—her name's Selene. There's always a Selene, you see—and now she's mine."

Thank you, Uncle Voris—oh, thank you!

ONLY briefly, hugging all three children to her, did Rissa cry. Then she wiped her eyes, petted and patted and kissed the three, rejoined Lanice Teverin outside, and returned to the office. There, on a conference circuit, she gave orders to K Center's Director and to Albert Kybel. "*Top* priority is release and reunion of such children with surviving parents. For orphans, try to locate uncles, aunts, older siblings. Where no one can be found—"

Lanice Teverin said, "If there's a way, *outside* of Welfare, that I could help with the lost ones . . ."

On the circuit, Rissa said, "We will consider these matters further. But quickly."

When the screen dimmed, she turned to Ivan. "How *could* I have forgotten what it is to be a child, alone in this place?"

•   •   •

THEY prepared to leave. Rissa said, "Ivan? Do you wish to inspect Division Male, Juvenile?"

He tensed, then grinned and shook his head. "I'm a little too prejudiced to do the job right."

IVAN drove the scoutship hard—barely high enough to avoid damaging eardrums groundside—and berthed it neatly. He left for *Graf Spee;* Deverel and Kenekke entered *Inconnu* with Rissa.

"If Tregare is in the galley, or in Control," she said, "tell him I will be in our quarters."

But she found him there. After they kissed, he said, "I held off dinner until you got here. You want it now, or fresh up first?"

"You might send for it. I will not be long."

And she was not. While they ate, she made her report. At the end he said, "You're right about the kids; I'll push that, too. For the rest—now we know some of the things to look for, Liesel can send teams to square up the other Centers. Meanwhile I'll amend my orders—put more teeth in them. These new teams, though—you were lucky at D, it could have gone wrong—they'll take more manpower and go fully armed."

"If you wish—though I think that may cause more shooting than it prevents."

"I'm more concerned that *my* people aren't the ones shot." He turned to the relay console and punched access to Control. "Now I want you to hear the Hulzein tape."

"Only hear it? There was no picture?"

"Sort of. The face is a blur—could be anybody."

The screen lit; Rissa peered, then shook her head. It was a face; that was all she could tell. Then, harsh and wheezing, a voice spoke.

"Cousin Tregare." Rissa's brows rose; Tregare nodded. "Lena Hulzein speaking. In two days, at 1800 hours Greenwich time, you will meet me. At my Establishment outside Buenos Aires—the Kerguelen woman knows it. There'll be no more than ten of you in all, and no weapons brought inside. Be on time—I don't like to be kept waiting." Sound and screen died.

"She knows who you are, Bran—and I, also. Did you answer?"

"Tried to—they just reran the tape, was all. And it didn't come over any channel you'd expect to originate in Argentina. Couldn't trace it, though."

"The woman is not in good health. Her breathing—when her voice went thin—"

"That's her doctors' problem. Mine is—where does she come off, giving me orders? I could take *Inconnu*—or even a couple of scouts—and level the place, if I wanted to."

"In all these years, UET has not done so. Perhaps—"

Standing, bringing coffee to pour, Tregare shook his head. "No. She's not relying on physical defenses. I found in the records why the Committee never voted to wipe out the place. First, because Erika took out contingent New Mafia contracts on six Committee members—proved it—and wouldn't say which ones. And later, Tari Obrigo and Cele Metrokin—the Hulzein versions—had enough clout to keep the string loose." He gestured negation. "But I'm not using force—not yet, anyway. For one thing, Liesel still hopes to get cooperation, maybe even reconcile the two branches."

Rissa sipped coffee, then her liqueur. "Is that possible, do you think?"

"Peace, no! I think she's—well, not crazy, seeing it's Liesel—but optimistic as trying to fly a kite underwater. But she wants to give it a chance."

"Well . . ." Rissa thought. "Lena Hulzein—assuming that voice *was* Lena—did not sound irrational. Only harsh, and arrogant—"

"We'll see," said Tregare, "day after tomorrow. 1800 Greenwich—I don't know what time that is in Argentina but I know how long the flight takes, so I don't have to look it up. Because by our time here, that's noon."

"And we have tomorrow to decide, and prepare."

BUT later that evening another call came—again a repeated message, and no answer to questions. Rissa and Tregare listened to the recording.

The voice was the same. "Lena Hulzein to Bran Tregare. I'm told that a ship lifted today."

Rissa looked inquiry; Tregare halted the tape to say, "Routine. Relief crew for the Mercury observatory." The tape began again.

"There'll be no more such liftings without my specific approval until we've met and reached agreement. Listen carefully, Tregare—do not think to flout my orders. Because if you do—well, I don't think you'd care for the results." A rasping chuckle, and then; "That's all. Be here tomorrow, and be on time."

There was no more. Frowning, Tregare shook his head. "What does she mean? What kind of threat does she think she's making, to give me orders like that?"

Memory tugged at Rissa. She quoted aloud, "If Lena Hulzein ever gets her hands on the Australian bomb, Earth may not *be* there when you arrive."

"What?"

"Lircia Gavaine, the Underground woman—on Stronghold. She said that."

"And you think—?" Tregare had gone pale; Rissa's own face felt numb.

She fought with panic. "We cannot afford to assume it is *not* true. Bran—how can we—?"

Now he rose and paced. "Give me a minute—this is too fast. If she—" He shook his head. "No. To think on this, peace love us, I need a drink!" Rissa gestured; he poured for her also.

Now he sat again. "One thing she can't know, is ships' codes. I could give the alert—there's time, just barely, to put it together—*all* ships to lift at the hour we're due to leave for Argentina. Scoutships—low-level flights to round up our people—wouldn't give her any warning. And once in space we're out of reach."

"And Earth, Bran? Still, she could—"

"What good would it do her, once we're clear? Sour grapes? Sheer spite?"

"But perhaps she *has* such spite! Gavaine said—"

"Yeah." His shoulders slumped. "And even if she hasn't, we'd be leaving Earth in her *hands,* just as if we hadn't come here at all." A fist drummed the table. "And maybe on a bluff, at that—a lousy *bluff!*"

Rissa nodded. "You are right, Tregare. We have taken

responsibility that we cannot abandon. We must meet with the woman."

Now the fist beat into his other palm. "All right, peace take it—we *go!*"

"The others, Bran—do we tell them?"

Before answering, he paused. Then; "I wouldn't think so. Because—Rissa, this curdles my spine, makes it hard for me to think straight. What good will it do to demoralize *all* of us?"

She reached and grasped his hand. "It should not make me feel better, Bran, but somehow it does—to know that you are as frightened as I am." She squeezed the hand and released it. "Now—now that we have shared our fears—what can we plan to *do?*"

Cheerless, his grin twitched. "I've been in this *kind* of trap before—just not on such a total scale, is all. I shouldn't let the difference throw me." Now he shrugged. "Well, there's no choice, really. We assume—we *think* on the basis that she really has the handle on Doomsday. That's so we don't make the mistake of crowding her too hard. But we talk and act—as long as we can—as if she's bluffing. And just maybe, push won't come to shove, after all." Head cocked to one side, he looked at her. "What do you think?"

After a moment, she nodded. "Yes—that is best. And our own people will not have to think one way and behave another. Only we ourselves."

"You know? Liesel's the one who could do it best. She's *all* Hulzein."

"Do not forget, Bran—so is Lena Diabla."

THE decisions in council, next morning, largely made themselves. Who should go? Tregare, Rissa, Hawkman, Liesel and Ivan. The latter suggested filling out the quota of ten with combat personnel, but Tregare said, "Five? What's the use? Lena can call on five hundred—five thousand, maybe. And armed."

Ivan shrugged. "Then why go at all?"

Deliberately, Rissa had put from her mind Lena's threat and its crippling terror; to all seeming, Tregare had done the same. Now Rissa said only, "Because, Ivan, we cannot ignore that place."

• • •

AFTER the conference Tregare sent coded orders to Zelde M'tana and to Bernardez. "At worst, Rissa," he said, "we'll save some aces. Should have thought of this last night, but—" He grinned. "They'll have as many ships as possible ready to lift if I send warning. And so at least—well, maybe Number One will rename itself New Earth."

"BUT *why?*" Coryle Hagenau almost screamed it. "Didn't I handle things all right before, here? Why should Ressider—?"

Tregare's voice stayed level. "Ressider has Police administration under control but he doesn't know the details, and Flaer Letiken—the ex-Policewoman—can't do it all by herself. Rocklin Caine, your First Hat, had Police experience before he wangled transfer to space—he can't help a lot. So I want you and Ressider to switch assignments; that's all. You go relieve him so he can be here this afternoon. All right?"

When Hagenau had gone, Rissa said, "I know you, Bran. What is your real reason?"

They sat in *Inconnu*'s Control. Turning back from a report he was reading, Tregare said, "Hagenau's getting temperamental again—throwing snitties, the way she did at first."

"I remember. And I did not understand, and I still do not."

His hand pushed air. "What I think—she *is* capable, but she hasn't got over the years under UET, working with no chance at command, and frustrated about it."

"You mean, perhaps, much the same as—"

"She's not Peralta again, no. But until she steadies down I'm not leaving her here in charge for me. Not while we deal with Lena Diabla."

He handed her the report he had been scanning. "Look at this, will you? It came in through Markine, and if it says what I *think* it does—" He stood. "I'm going into the building, so I can try to reach the man that wrote it—without anyone guessing it's anything more than routine."

He left; she began to read. She found it hard going; occasionally she repeated a phrase aloud. "—mass increase—velocity limit—our present parabolic, *acoherent* drive fields offer no solution—"

Equations filled the rest of that page; their form and content exceeded her grasp of mathematics so she turned to the next sheet. "Now then—" Again she spoke aloud, softly, trying by sound to reinforce what her eyes saw. "—ellipsoidal, *coherent* field—prolate spheroid—subject mass always at one focus—force directed toward the other—accelerations thus derived—"

More equations—she did not pause for them. Now—"—the velocity-derived mass, expanding into parallel continua as shown in equation (34-c)—" No, skip that! She was near the end; the conclusion had to be stated soon. Here? "—aside from effects of the second order, magnitudes only approximately estimated—appears to be no theoretical limit to velocity."

Well! She looked at the undersigned signature: Pennet Hoyfarul. Then she stared. The paper was dated twelve years past.

"No, Bran—I do *not* understand the mathematics. But what else could it be?"

Tregare swallowed the last of his sandwich and sipped whiskey. He stood and paced the length of Control, then sat again. "Faster than light! But like you say—if they had it, why sit on it a dozen years? I wish—*my* math's good enough for navigation and time fixes, but I can only see what he's maybe *trying* to do; that's all. Well, he'll be here this afternoon. We'll see."

IN Tregare's groundside office the three sat and talked. Pennet Hoyfarul, Rissa thought, had once been handsome—his longish gray hair still made an impressive mane. But the jowl wattles, moving as he talked or swallowed, spoiled the effect somewhat. *He must have been fat for a long time, and corrected it too late.*

"All right," Tregare said, as Hoyfarul helped himself again from the snack tray, "I understand it that far, I think. When mass begins to build, these parallel continua of yours absorb the overload. Far as you're concerned, no increase, no time-dilation." Still chewing, Hoyfarul nodded. "So what happens if that excess mass sideswipes something, out there in some other track?''

Hoyfarul paused to swallow. "Impossible. The number of parallel continua is a high-order infinity, perhaps the third or fourth of the aleph-numbers postulated so long ago by Cantor. Whereas the number innately containing or producing matter is of a lower order. So—''

Tregare raised an eyebrow. "You figure that out for yourself?''

"The idea's a century old. You hadn't heard of it?''

"The Space Academy didn't go into deep theory much.''

Hoyfarul raised a hand to his mouth and coughed. "Yes— of course. I'm sorry—you're interested in the practical aspects. Which is why I sent you the paper." He wiped his mouth with a handkerchief. "The facts you want are these. The added mass expands only into matterless continua. Above light-speed other objects do not exist for you, or vice versa— except as detected by gravitational radiation, to enable you to navigate at all.''

Rissa freshened her drink. She said, "I have two questions. How much of this is on paper, only, and how much proven? And secondly—why, after twelve years, have no such ships been built?''

The man stared at her, then nodded. "You're very perceptive. And your two questions are really one." He coughed again. "A little history, if I may. The basic discovery is not mine—my late colleague, Sancia Leckaby, made the crucial breakthrough. We worked on it together and were nearly ready to announce results when—when my dear Sancia was Welfared, by order of Gairn Forbisher.''

He paused. "I've heard he's dead. If there's a tape of that death I'd like to see it. Or if you haven't killed him yet, I want to be there when you do. Is that too much to ask?''

"He killed himself," said Tregare. "Not very efficiently; it took a while before his string finally broke. There's no tape; sorry.''

Hoyfarul sighed. "That will have to do. Normally I'm not a vengeful man—but you see, I saw the tape of *Sancia's* death.'' He shook his head. "May I have another drink, please? Nowadays I seem to need it more.''

His glass replenished, he said, "I tried for Sancia's release, hinting—truly—that her work could greatly advance UET's power. Then she died—was killed, really—so until you came I suppressed the bulk of our findings. As Deputy Director it was simple enough."

"Deputy?" said Rissa. "Who is your superior?"

"It was *Forbisher;* who else?" Hoyfarul drained half his glass. "I've tested as far as could be done without exposing the secret, using only spherical fields that produce no thrust. As predicted, mass *decreases.* I led Forbisher to believe the goal was to circumvent mass-increase to save fuel, only—that the sole obstacle was getting the coherent field to hold together in the presence of the standard one—which, of course, it can never do. What has not been tested—what UET was never told—is the thrust effect of an elongated field."

"But you're telling us." Tregare leaned forward. "Why?"

"Because whatever you are, Tregare—and rumors vary—you're not UET. You know the Hidden Worlds the Committee's never reached—and *that's* where I want this discovery to go."

He shook a finger. "But I'll tell you—I'm old and won't last forever. If you hadn't come—rather than see the human race bottled up forever by light-speed and its limits—no matter how I felt, I'd have *had* to give the thing to UET. In fact, I did—in my will." Now he smiled. "Oh, don't worry—when I sent you the paper, I destroyed all documents that might lead to it."

Now he slumped, almost relaxed. "Have I done right?"

As if for action, Tregare tensed. "Will your drive fit a standard ship—do you know?"

"A standard hull, yes. But it requires—oh, nearly half again the bulk of *your* equipment. You'd have to tear out so much, to remodel—"

Rissa said, "There are ships in progress, building—hulls without much inner structure as yet. Tregare?"

He nodded. "Hoyfarul—I haven't secured the shipyards yet, or your labs. No need, I thought, until later—and my people are stretched pretty thin as it is. The port, now—it's secure as ever will be. If I bring a hull there—can your equipment be moved? And would you be willing to work there?"

The older man thought, then nodded. "The fabrication section—it's less effort to secure it than move it. But the working gear, the model—it's on the ship we tested. And the rest, the instruments and so forth at the labs, can be loaded into that same ship."

"Just a minute." Tregare punched circuit directions. "Get on here, will you? And give the proper instructions."

WHEN that was done, Tregare called Bernardez. "Don't mention my most recent order; this circuit's not secure. But if and when circumstances allow, send a ship to the space labs facility—you have the location. Secure the place—special emphasis on the fabrications area—then wait for further orders. Authorized to speak for me in this is Dr. Pennet Hoyfarul." Turning aside, "Come here, doctor, and look at Kickem Bernardez—and vice versa. Tape him, Kickem—for ID to the ship you send."

A moment later; "With his usual superb efficiency, Bernardez acknowledges. It shall be done, doubt not. All this taped to Zelde, of course, so she's properly aboard." A brief chuckle. "Strange things I hear, Tregare—and some not so strange. You've bottled the Committee so soon? Well enough; tamp the cork firm and tight. Ah, I'd like to add a thump or two from my own sturdy right heel—but 'tis ever Bernardez' misfortune to miss a few of the good things of life. Though not many, mind you—"

Tregare laughed. "Kickem, you better get off here and back to the job—or you'll miss dinner, working overtime."

"There's no poetry in your soul, Tregare. But give Rissa my love—and Aedra's also."

Turning away from the dimming screen, Tregare said, "Don't mind how he talks, Hoyfarul. You just heard a man who doesn't count the odds—he beats them, is all."

Hoyfarul shook his head. "Whatever made you think I object to poets?"

THE three dined aboard *Inconnu*. Afterward, Hawkman and Liesel joined them. Tregare introduced Hoyfarul; the doctor summarized the technical information he had given earlier.

Liesel turned to Hawkman. "You're the science scholar in this family—what do you think?"

Gingerly, Hawkman sipped steaming coffee. "A few questions come to mind, doctor. What happens, say, if you're above light-speed and your drive cuts out? According to some theories, you could explode the entire universe."

"By sudden implosion, in this continuum, of infinite mass?" A headshake. "No. We found—accidentally, as the result of a power failure—that a deactivated field decays in finite time, exponentially. You're familiar with collapse of magnetic field in inductance?" At Hawkman's nod, he said, "Roughly, that's what happens. And since this universe will accommodate only a finite mass increase—well, when the expansion into other continua is reversed, the result is—" He shook his head. "I should say, the result *will* be deceleration of the subject mass at a fantastic rate—sufficient to accommodate the influx of mass."

"By the time the field's totally dead," said Tregare, "you're back down below light-speed?"

Hoyfarul nodded. "According to our calculations, that's correct."

Tregare laughed. "You realize you just doubled the value of this gadget?" At Hoyfarul's puzzled look he gestured and said, "Your figures showed decel taking as much time and power as accel—naturally; that's what we're used to. But what *you* say—we pour on accel all the way until we're near destination, then cut power and drop below light-speed using the energy we've expanded outside this space. From there on, it's just like the decel patterns we use right now." Tregare's brow wrinkled; then he snapped his fingers. "Something else. You just cut travel time—for the above-light part of any trip—nearly thirty percent."

Hoyfarul blinked. "Why—I hadn't thought—but now that you point it out—Tregare, I must modify my proposed designs."

"How come?"

"Because, except for ships designed to explore *far* beyond the volume of space we've reached to date, I've provided nearly twice the necessary fuel capacity."

"So," said Hawkman. "Already we make progress. Now then—doctor, you mentioned second-order effects. Anything more specific that you could tell us?"

"Tentatively, yes. We avoid the mass increase normally associated with velocity, but there is still *some* increase. It seems to relate to the speed—as yet not satisfactorily measured

—of gravity waves. But whereas the usual increase varies as the secant of the arcsine of velocity expressed as a fraction of light-speed, if you follow me—"

"I don't," said Hawkman. "On paper, maybe, and more slowly . . ."

Hoyfarul restrained an incipient pout. "It approaches infinity at light-speed; that's what counts. But this second-order increase is logarithmic. Our extrapolations indicate approximately ten percent at light-speed, and thus you'd reach double mass—and a halving of elapsed time—at slightly over eight lights."

Rissa said, "We travel—I have traveled—at time ratios of roughly twenty to one. With your drive—in theory—what speeds would produce that change?"

Hawkman pulled out a pocket calculator. Before Hoyfarul could answer, he said, "Is ten billion lights close enough?"

The doctor stared at him. "It's probably the right order of magnitude. But—you understand—even with maximum acceleration, before you could reach such inconceivable velocities, you'd be halfway to the next galaxy. Assuming you could carry that much fuel, which you can't."

"Just as well," said Liesel. "*I* haven't lost anything in the next galaxy."

A knock at the door; Tregare answered it. He turned and said, "Dr. Hoyfarul—your transportation to the port—it's ready, whenever you are."

The doctor stood. "Now's as good a time as any. For me, it's getting late. And thank you—all of you—for your hospitality." He sighed. "It's so *good* to start putting Sancia's discoveries to work at last."

As Hoyfarul came to the door, Tregare gripped his shoulder. "We thank *you,* too. And now—at the port you'll be met by Zelde M'tana, my Port Commander. She's alerted; she's assigned quarters for you. You look around—anything you need, don't hesitate to ask. In reason, she'll get it for you. Okay?"

Pennet Hoyfarul smiled. "Oh, I'm easily pleased. Comfort, quiet for sleeping—and never finding that an empty bottle is the last one, late at night when sleep comes hard." He shook Tregare's hand. "Can you comprehend that?"

"Sure. You don't have to tell me you're not a drunk; I can

see that. Just say what you want in the bottles; we have a good selection.''

"I'll do that." Waving a hand, Hoyfarul turned and left.

LIESEL said, "Does he really know what he's talking about?"

"I think so," said Hawkman.

A sigh shook Liesel. "It would be wonderful, of course. But all my life—and before—the Hulzeins have thought in the way we've had to think, to survive. *The long view*—and this may mean the end of it."

Rissa's hand clasped Liesel's. "Or perhaps—only a new beginning."

"Yes—we could go to Number One, and see Sparline and—"

"*If* it works," said Tregare.

"Why do you say that, Bran?"

"Because—Rissa, nothing in Creation stinks as bad as dead hopes." And against her will, Rissa thought of Lena Diabla.

FOR a while they talked of other things—progress in arranging release of Welfare Clients as free citizens—reorganization of the Police from a repressive force to a protective one—Zelde M'tana's bloodless capture of the latest unsuspecting UET ship to land.

Then Liesel said, "Tomorrow we go meet with—my grand-niece, I guess she is—Lena Hulzein. Lena Diabla—not a promising name. Only the five of us, Ivan said?"

"That's not firm," said Tregare. "I turned down only his proposal to fill out our quota with combat types—a drop in Lena's bucket. You have any good ideas? Glad to hear 'em, I'm sure."

"A good thing, Bran—because I had in mind to tell you, anyway." Both smiled. "I have to agree—force is no use there. But misdirection should be." No one commented, so she said, "Rissa—you'd be a lot more use if Lena thought you're someone else."

Rissa shook her head. "I do not see how that could be accomplished. She expects me, and she *knows* of Tari Obrigo and the others. So how—?"

"Let me show you a tape." Liesel inserted the capsule, pushed buttons. The screen lit; Rissa watched and listened.

At the end she spread her hands in inquiry. "If I had ever seen that room I would think that person to be myself—though I do not recall ever speaking those exact words. How did you do it?"

"Alina Rostadt, you saw there. She's Hulzein-trained, but never saw Lena or vice versa. The Underground got her into UET but her programming slipped and the truth field caught her out—I found her one jump ahead of Welfare." Liesel grinned. "She's your size, Rissa, and close enough in age. I saw the possibilities, questioned her—Markine's disguise experts fixed her up to match, no big problem. Three days on the few tapes I could scrounge up of you, and she did what you just saw.

"All right?" Liesel waited.

"It is . . . totally convincing, even to me. But what do *I* do? Lena—"

"You still have all the Laura Konig stuff, don't you? That you picked up on Far Corner? A colonial girl—that'd be a nice touch. Quiet, hard to notice."

"I have it all." She nodded, thinking. "I did not ever have time or reason to formulate the parameters of that identity —speech patterns, mannerisms, and so forth. But as a supporting player, out of the spotlight with little need to speak, these things would not be too important—I can synthesize an average of many people and perhaps not break characterization too badly. Is this what you wish. Liesel?"

"I want Lena's attention and aims spread out, misdirected. She knows you, she knows Tregare. Maybe she knows me and maybe not—and Hawkman. We need a sleeper, though—and the way things are, you're best suited for it."

Tregare said, "I have to go with that. We need all the edge we can get."

"Very well," said Rissa. "Then I shall go now, and become Laura Konig. It will take some time, speaking aloud to myself, to manufacture her as a coherent identity."

"Okay," said Tregare. "I'll see you a little later."

"No. Come with me now, or do not be with me until this episode is done. Because Laura Konig does not yet know you, Bran."

Tregare stood when she did, and took her hand. To his parents he said, "I'll be back in a little while."

Hawkman's smile broadened. "There's no hurry, son—no hurry at all."

AFTER the lovemaking, Rissa said, "I can do the hair faster with your help. Then you should join the others while I take care of the rest—and at the same time practice speech and movements."

"All right." They worked together, and shortly he left. Rissa opened the kit—she made the necessary changes systematically. Dark blue eyes—straight, heavier brows—the first of a series of diuretic pills and a concentrated hormone shot—two tabs of adhesive plastic, and now her earlobes were slightly larger and turned outward—the small blemish high on one cheek, near the eye—the fingerprints—the thin white scar on the forehead, and carefully she parted hair so that the scar continued straight where it marked the scalp. She rummaged—nothing for nose or mouth. Well, Osallin—poor Osallin! how many years ago?—*had* filled her order in a hurry. Face relaxed, she looked in a mirror and tried various minor changes of basic expression until she found one she could hold automatically. The difference was subtle—but definite.

And now, using the mirror as aid, she spoke and moved. *There—that gesture—it is good—keep it.* And gradually the personality of Laura Konig emerged.

When she was satisfied with its structure, its firmness in her mind, she showered. She dried and brushed her hair, and dressed in clothing she considered suitable. She stood once more before the mirror, turned from side to side, nodded and went to join the others.

IN the doorway she posed, enjoying Hawkman's stare. "Well, I guess I'm ready to go with you folks tomorrow. Long as you need somebody that's not too handy at much else, to run the recorder and keep tapes on what's said." She pulled at a tilted earlobe. " 'course, I won't talk all this much, there."

Rissa's dark straight hair had been sitting-length. Laura's

was light brown and so deeply waved that its uncut mass bulked around her head and barely reached her waist.

Hawkman said, "Let me see if I can figure it out. Your face looks smaller, of course. The eyes, the marks—something with the ears. Movement—*and* stance—if I saw you only in silhouette it'd *still* work." He frowned. "And—you're *skinny.*"

She shrugged. "The bra's too tight now, not very comfortable. But pills to get some water out, and a shot I'm glad I won't have to take any more of—I'm not a real busty wench on the records—the damn thing ought to fit better by tomorrow."

Now Liesel spoke. "Where are you from, girl? How long have we known you?"

"I was born in space—I knew the name of the ship, when I was little, but I forgot." In the absentminded gesture she was cultivating, Rissa's knuckle worried the cheek blemish. "My mother got off at Far Corner—that's where I grew up. I worked at this and that, a little of everything, nearly. After she died—in the year of The Sickness—Second Site was too small for me. I don't know why—I'd never been anyplace else—but it was. So I started hanging around when ships came in. I had skills they could use, I thought—but mostly I got the offer for the one I *wasn't* selling."

"Yeah, I remember," said Tregare. "You blacked an eye pretty good on one of my ratings, second or third day you were aboard."

She smiled at him. "I had to be pretty desperate, didn't I, to ship on *Inconnu* as cook's helper?"

"And first chance you had—at Number One—you got off again."

Belligerent, lower lip protruding, she said, "*Sure* I did—and got lucky, too. One day in One Point One, nearly out of Weltmarks and no job yet, I ran into Ms. Kerguelen—Ms. Obrigo, I knew her as. And she took me to Hulzein Lodge with her, and out there—"

"I really wasn't too happy with Rissa," said Liesel, "bringing stray puppies home. But when it turned out you could handle office machines after a fashion, we put you to work. And you did all right, I have to admit it. So when we left Number One we brought you along."

"Sure you did," said Rissa, "and I'm grateful. At first I

wanted to ride in freeze, like you, but I'm glad I didn't. I slept better and warmer and not so lonesome. While it lasted . . ."

"I'm sorry about that, girl," Liesel said, "but we need you here, and Kickem Bernardez won't release the young man from *Hobnails* until he gets a replacement. It shouldn't be long—"

A little out of synchronism, the way she had practiced, Rissa shrugged. "I'll do all right." She looked at Tregare with a side-glance. "Maybe I'll even make a pass at the admiral here."

Hawkman laughed. "You might get away with it, at that— since his wife's unavoidably absent."

"She's not the jealous type, anyway," said Tregare. "But that's enough flying on a loose string. Konig—you know what your job is, tomorrow?"

Thank you, Bran. "Sure. To tape everything important— and to watch out, be ready to act in a hurry. But not unless I *need* to."

Liesel stood. "You'll do, Konig. Hawkman, it's a long day tomorrow. I'm not tired yet—but I don't want to be."

Hawkman joined her; they said goodnights and left. Rissa looked at Tregare; without expression he looked back. Finally he said, "You coming with me, or do you have to sleep someplace else, by yourself?"

"I'd rather be with you, Tregare. One point, though—your wife may not be jealous, but I am. And I can't stand being called by someone else's name."

"All right, I'll remember that . . . Laura."

As they walked to their—Tregare's—quarters, Rissa thought; *How good of them to join in, to help me firm this identity.*

THE next morning, Rissa rechecked her appearance and accompanied Tregare to the galley. Liesel and Hawkman greeted them, and soon Ivan arrived with . . . *why, she is me, to the life!*

The woman—Alina Ristadt, Liesel had said—walked to face Tregare, then hesitated. "Good morning, Tregare. I—"

He stood and kissed her. "Rissa! It's good to have you back. Wish you could have got here yesterday, but I expect Ivan's filled you in okay. Here—sit down."

Seated next to Tregare, she said, "Yes—he and Liesel have told me what my part is to be. I hope I shall perform it well."

Rissa said, "Sure you will, Ms. Kergulen."

Alina Rostadt frowned, touched her high-coiled hair and said, "I am sorry—I do not think I remember you."

"You don't? Laura Konig? Well, I suppose you've had a lot on your mind. And it's been a few years—at Stronghold we didn't see each other more than to say hello once or twice. But on Number One—remember?—you got me into Hulzein Lodge in the first place."

"Oh." The look of sudden recollection was well done. "Yes, of course, Laura Konig." Her hand reached to Rissa's. "It is good to see you again."

"And it is good to see *you*—again." Alina Rostadt's eyes widened; Rissa nodded.

"Now I understand," said Alina. "And—I am truly honored."

"You'll manage fine, I expect." Rissa turned to Ivan. "You're her brother, aren't you? And you look like something's on your mind."

"Yes." Flat-voiced, Ivan said, "Tregare? You're crazy if you don't fill out our quota with combat types. We're allowed ten—right?"

When Tregare nodded, Ivan said, "Six here—that leaves four. Outside I've got two men and two women—even numbers always look peaceful, somehow. But you remember, at Stronghold—Paszacker, with the blade that came out between his knuckles?"

"Not likely I'd forget that. Why? You got more like him?"

"Better." Ivan grinned. "Flip the hand—either hand— back at the wrist. The blade comes out the base of the palm— stab *and* grab."

Headshake. "Lena has metal detectors, sure as peace. And how do I trust these freaks?"

"Truth field says you can. And the blades are organic laminates, not metal."

Tregare hesitated. Rissa said, "Ivan Marchant, your name is? Well, I'm rear pony in this caravan and anybody tells me shut up, I will." No one did.

"This woman down there—she's looking for anything we do. She says bring ten and no more—so she's watching every one of those ten, trying to figure what we're pulling off on her."

Tregare said, "Make your point, Konig."

Rissa double-shrugged; the move came more naturally to her now. "So if only the six of us go in—I expect you'll leave somebody on the ship—"

"Not a ship," he said. "A scout. But I'll have a ship high upstairs. I sent word I needed it for communications relay, and Lena hasn't objected."

"That's your department," said Rissa. "Anyway—just the six of us go in—this woman, first she wonders what's up our sleeves, then she decides we figured the odds and are playing it straight. And then—"

Ivan shook his head, but Liesel said, "I like it."

Hawkman: "Remember the showdown, Liesel? This will be your sister all over again—but worse." *Yes—much worse.*

"No," said Liesel. "Oh, certainly I see what you mean, Hawkman. But this—I think it would get *my* guard down some. And I don't see much in the way of better ideas."

Tregare paused. Then, "I guess it has to be my choice. And where we're going, a little misdirection beats a few blades seven ways from Sunday. Ivan, you lose the argument. You want to stay behind?"

Half-rising, Ivan said, "That's the first time you've ever insulted me!"

Tregare waved a hand. "I didn't mean it that way—just giving you the option, was all." Ivan sat again. "Now then— Konig, you're a colonial, not combat trained or anything. You sure you know what you want, here?"

It is hard for him to talk through these disguises. "I'm sure, Tregare."

He slapped the table lightly. "Then it's set. We leave—let's see—on the hour, straight up. About forty minutes yet. Just the six of us, plus the scout pilot."

"Anybody I know?" said Rissa.

"Probably not—my Third Hat, Anders Kobolak."

"I've heard of him. Pretty young, isn't he?"

"He can do whatever's needed."

"I am sure of that," said Alina Rostadt. Rissa turned to her and smiled. Then, until time for liftoff, the company parted.

•   •   •

ABOARD the scout, still at groundside, Tregare said, "Kobo-lak, this is Laura Konig. She'll guide you in to the Hulzein landing area."

The young man looked to Alina. "I thought *she*—"

"She's got other things to do," said Rissa. "Don't worry; I'm briefed."

"All right." He looked, now, to Tregare. "Ready to lift, sir."

"So am I. Move it, any time now."

Kobolak took the scout up fast and high. Rissa saw him relax as the trajectory firmed. "You fly a good path," she said, and he turned and gave her a brief grin.

After a time the arch of the flight peaked and the scout drove down. Now Rissa looked closely at the screen; finally she pointed. "*There*—past the rounded hill but this side of the buildings." She turned aside. "Tregare—those guard towers, the missiles, they're new since—Kobolak! Ignore the landing circle—come down on this side, as near that steepled building as you can without damaging it—"

The boy looked to Tregare, who nodded and said, "Do it the way she says!" And when they had landed, he said, "From *here,* if you have to lift in a hurry, their own buildings protect you while you get speed up."

A viewscreen alarm sounded; Tregare punched the activating button. The picture wavered, unrecognizable, but the voice came clearly.

"You didn't land as directed; already you inconvenience me." Rissa recognized the harsh voice.

Tregare said, "It's my fault. Things have changed since Rissa was here last; she got a little confused so I told my pilot to set it down right here. Okay? And what do we do next?"

"Wait. I'll send transportation for the ten of you."

"Make it six."

"Six? I told you ten."

"Ten maximum, you said. Six is all we brought. Plus my pilot, who stays aboard."

"Stays aboard? I won't permit that. You will *all* come meet with me."

Tregare shook his head. "You know better than that. I'm willing, if things work out right, to dicker with you for a *real* starship. But for now I'm not leaving even this little scout, unguarded."

Silence. Then; "Starships? All right—your terms don't fit my policy but for the moment I accept. My people will be there shortly." The screen darkened.

Alina said, "I do not think—"

Rissa interrupted. "Your part starts when they get here. For now—Tregare, we have to play this all-hell careful; you know that?"

"I know it, Konig. Anything else on your mind?"

"Quite a bit. Tell you later maybe, if we have time."

TWO groundcars came, each half-filled, Lena Hulzein's minions tried to separate the party, half to each car. Tregare said, "Forget it. You ride your own wagon; there's room for us in this one." And once inside and moving, he said, "Talk nice for the tapes, everybody. We wouldn't want to disappoint anyone." Rissa returned his grin, and for the rest of the ride no one spoke.

When they stopped she recognized the building—Erika's own headquarters. Alighting beside Tregare she whispered, "Before, they didn't have the armed guards."

A tall man approached. "Tregare? I will take you to Madame Hulzein." Tregare nodded; the man turned and they followed him. Inside, Rissa saw well-remembered corridors—how many years?—and then they came to a door. To Tregare she murmured, "Here's where Erika centered her work—her main office." Then the door opened and they entered.

An elderly woman faced them—thin, wearing servant's garb, with long white hair that half-veiled her face. She stood a moment, staring at each in turn, then stepped back and let the group pass.

Rissa's gaze scanned the room quickly, then fixed on the central, standing figure. *Osallin was right!* She gripped Tregare's arm, then realized the act was out of place for Laura Konig and moved aside. Fascinated, she stared and could hardly breathe.

Frieda Hulzein had been a marred copy of Erika. Here, now, Lena was a cruel caricature of Frieda. . . .

The eagle nose a gross vulture's beak—the high, proud cheekbones, exaggerated lumps—the strong jaw grown to extreme and twisted . . .

Rissa shuddered but could not look away. Lena Hulzein

stood crouched and awkward, leaning her unwithered arm on a cane. The two sides of her face—nothing *matched*.

And the woman was half-bald, lank hair straggling over unsuccessful attempt to remove a florid birthmark.

Osallin was right!

The voice was no better; it rasped nerves as well as ears. "Well? Come on in. I have chairs here; sit down, and we'll talk." She herself hobbled to a huge, upholstered chair; a servant helped her seat herself as the group moved forward and found places. Rissa chose a chair toward the front but well to one side.

Lena Hulzein fingered an ornate pendant and the heavy gold chain that held it. Tregare said, "The talk should be easy enough. All these years you've held out against UET. Now you don't have to, anymore, because we broke UET's string."

"You're wrong. Effectively, through the Obrigo and Metrokin identities, I already owned UET. You tore things up there—and for that, before we're done, you'll settle with me. But that's for later."

"Then what's for now?" said Tregare.

The woman scratched her disfigured cheek. "We talk terms."

Tregare hitched his chair closer to the nearest table. "Sure." He looked around. "Somebody get me a drink, or do I have to send back for my own? Bourbon, by preference—and ice." Lena Hulzein gestured; a servant—the woman who had admitted them—left the room. Tregare said, "What kind of terms is it, you have in mind?"

Lena's mouth twitched. For a moment Rissa saw resemblance to Erika's smile; then the similarity vanished into lopsided grotesquerie. The woman said, "The terms under which you administer for me." Her cane rapped the floor. "Don't make any mistake, Tregare—*I* control this planet. Nobody else."

To all appearances, Tregare was having trouble controlling his mirth; finally he succeeded. His drink was served; he sipped it and said, "I've got fifty ships that say you're wrong."

Lena Hulzein's coughing laughter was painful to hear. Finally she controlled her breathing and could speak. "But you're *here*—your lives at my disposal."

Tregare said, "You don't have it right yet, Cousin Lena.

Anything happens to me here—*Inconnu* melts this place down to slag, while *Graf Spee* does the same to your Aussie hangouts we've got a line on. And skip around all *you* want, too—if Kickem Bernardez wants your hide, you won't last a week."

Suddenly Rissa knew their terrible guess had been right—for Lena Hulzein did not flinch. Instead; "If you don't fear for yourselves, fear for this planet. For I've made sure it won't outlive me."

Rissa tensed. Tregare said, "Just what does that mean?"

"Maybe I'll tell you, maybe I won't. I wasn't ready for this, yet—I've got more to say first." She pointed the cane. *Is it a weapon?* But Lena said, "You, Rissa Kerguelen! You admit, don't you, that it's mostly *my* money that controls UET? Even though I channeled it through two identities designed for your use?" Alina Rostadt nodded. "Then what right have you and Tregare to take over?"

Alina looked to Tregare; he said, "When your grandmother fought UET, it wasn't just for herself. Some, sure—but she hated Welfare slavery and wanted to see it stopped. Your mother changed tactics and went after control—and for the same reasons. Now you *have* control—or did have—and how long has it been, now?"

"With a coalition, that hung together on some matters but not on others, nearly ten years. Solidly, only since a few months before my mother died."

"Why haven't you done something about Welfare? If anything, it just kept getting worse."

Lena shrugged; only the good arm's shoulder moved appreciably. "These things take time. Meanwhile the Welfare system makes control easier."

Rissa squirmed. *This disguise has its disadvantages. But we must keep her from the main point.* She made her decision and spoke. "Ms. Kerguelen, you once showed me some pictures from this place. All kinds of people in them—some students, you said, like you—some staff, some servants. They all wore regular clothes. The servants here now—except for the colors, what they wear looks an awful lot like Welfare jumpsuits."

Tregare snapped his fingers. "I get it—Cousin Lena, you're setting up your own version of Welfare, here?"

"That's not true—not *really*. *My* indentured persons have cots in their dormitories. They eat the same food—nearly—as the staff. And I don't restrict their sex lives." She shook her head; it moved at an odd angle. "Not the same as Welfare, not at all."

Tregare nudged Alina, whispered to her. *About time we got some mileage out of that one!* Alina said, "But—these indentured persons—are they free to leave your employ?"

Lena's cane struck the floor. "Of course they are—any time they pay off their contracts."

"And how many of them do so?" Having once spoken, Alina seemed to gain confidence.

"Why—I don't know—I'm too busy to keep track of such things. I—"

Now Tregare took a turn. "Do *any* of them buy out? Surely you know that much."

"Not recently, I believe. But—"

"How long since the last one you remember?"

Lena forced a laugh. "This is ridiculous—questioning me like a schoolgirl, about things that are none of your business, anyway. Enough, I say!"

Alina said, "I, too, feel that it is enough. For I think we have our answer."

A fit of coughing shook Lena. Finally, wiping her eyes, she said, "Whatever you have, it doesn't change anything. I own control of UET and nobody's taking it away from me. My own money . . ."

"Nobody wants to defraud you." For the first time, Liesel spoke. "We'll sort out how much of the Obrigo-Metrokin holdings are your money and how much Rissa's—and mine, for that matter. You'll get everything that's coming to you. Except voting control—you've abused that, Lena, so we—"

"Who are *you* to call me by name?" Lena stared a moment. "You look—a little bit—like my mother. No—more like pictures of my grandmother." She half-stood, lost balance and fell back into the chair. "So that's it! My great-aunt Liesel—you must be! Come to take my Establishment, are you? Well, you won't! I—"

Head shaking, Liesel said, "I claim no part of the Hulzein Establishment on Earth or any offworld branches you may have. I settled for the share Erika gave me—and set up my own dealings on another planet, a Hidden World."

"Then what are you doing here? As they say, who's minding the store for you?"

"Tregare's sister and her husband."

Lena sneered. "You trust another Hulzein that far? Very touching."

With a sigh, Liesel said, "Only half a Hulzein—remember? And I doubt I'll ever see her again, *or* the planet. Anyway, I've a bigger job to do, here. Helping administer UET."

Lena's good hand kneaded her withered one. "No matter what, it comes back to one thing, doesn't it? You're trying to take what's *mine*—and you're not going to. Because if you do, it won't be there any more. Nothing will." And that thought evoked the nearest thing to a real smile that Rissa had yet seen.

"You made a threat before," said Tregare. "Maybe now you'd better explain it." *Yes—since she has brought it into the open, it is best that he take the initiative.*

Lena raised her pendant and lowered it again. "You see this? You know what it is?"

"We are waiting for you to tell us," said Alina Rostadt.

"It's the end of Earth you're looking at," and the harsh voice almost sang. "It's the detonator—a duplicate, rather—for the Australian doomsday bomb. It cost me—oh, how it cost me! But now Earth exists by the mercy of Lena Hulzein!"

RISSA started to move—and Tregare, also—but Lena, teeth bared, gripped the pendant. They sat again. "That's right—you couldn't reach me in time. And I'd better explain why it wouldn't do you any good if you did. The bomb's developed *far* beyond the power of the one that cost Jupiter a satellite. And this detonator—it's booby-trapped, several ways. For one thing, it will operate if it fails to receive my distinctive brainwave patterns. I don't know the effective radius of the receiver—I didn't feel like testing it, just yet. It will also function if the Australians try to tamper with the bomb in any way —they know that, so they haven't tried. Well—you've heard of failsafe devices? This one's different—failure means death, and *my* death means failure." The crooked grin. "Neatly planned, isn't it?"

"So now you see why I will continue to control UET."

"But—" Alina spoke. "—but *you* cannot live forever!"

"No—no, I can't, can I? But as I told you at the first, Earth won't outlive me."

Rissa gasped. The woman was totally insane! She tried to

think of alternatives and could find none. She said, "You're in charge, Tregare—Ms. Kerguelen—but if it was *me* running things I'd say get off this planet. We can't hope to save it." *Warn Zelde and Kickem to lift fleet,* she meant—but Tregare made no move.

Lena peered at her. "I don't know who you are and it doesn't matter. But you're going nowhere—none of you are —until you officially sign over to me, on paper and confirmed on recording circuits at your Headquarters computer complex, total control of UET."

She gave orders for documents to be brought, and view-screen terminals. Then she said, "Cousin Tregare, you'll in-form your people that henceforth their allegiance is to *me*. Explain what happens if I am not obeyed—and that only a small fraction could possibly get off Earth in time to save themselves."

Rissa looked to Tregare; he shook his head. *Checkmate, then. But no matter what she thinks, he can still save the fleet.* Thoughts beating against frustration, she watched as servants brought the things Lena had demanded.

The old woman—the one who had opened the door to them and later had brought Tregare's drink—carried a terminal that looked much too heavy for her. Head bowed, long white hair straggling over her face, she shuffled across the room. As she set the terminal near Lena she slipped—to catch her balance, her hand went to Lena's shoulder. Lena Hulzein snarled—she reached into her clothing and brought out a knife. "You *dare* touch me—!"

The knife flashed, barely missing as the other shrank away. Lena made a lunge—*time slowed*—Rissa was there before the blade could strike, and had Lena's wrist. She gripped it in both hands and braced for effort.

A hand touched hers. "That won't be necessary, Rissa. The drug, that I put into her shoulder—it's taking hold now." And slowly, Lena slumped into collapse.

Rissa turned to see who had spoken. It was the old woman, now standing straight and pushing her hair back. Rissa gasped.

But—it can't be!

Then, voice loud and ringing, the woman spoke. "I am Erika Hulzein, mother of Frieda and—" She gestured toward Lena. "—and grandmother of . . . *that*." Facing the staff group, she said, "I resume leadership of this Establishment and claim your allegiance from this moment!"

Her listeners moved uncertainly; then Tregare stood. "And whether she needs it or not, she has the backing of Bran Tregare."

A man said, "But she *can't* be Erika Hulzein. She was killed —it's been more than fifty years—"

An elderly man came forward. He looked closely at the woman. "That's her, all right—I don't know how or why, but it's her." He reached and took her hand in both of his. "And I was never more glad of anything, in my whole life!"

"Then see that the Establishment is informed. And somebody bring me a drink!"

The woman sat, and only then could Rissa find voice. She heard herself ask, "Erika! How did you recognize me?"

"Had me fooled, you did—I thought that one over there was you. But then Lena pulled the knife and you *moved*. Couldn't have been anyone else, looks or no looks."

"But, Erika—*you* here—how—?"

"A long story, but freeze tells most of it." Erika's eyes narrowed. "But *you* know that—you're the only one I told. Or didn't you get my message?"

Rissa gasped. *Osallin's envelope! No wonder he* . . . But she only shook her head.

"Time and space. Well, no matter." Erika looked down at Lena. "Poor creature. And the worst of it is, she's *my* fault. Liesel—my sister—she tried to tell me. And I chased her off Earth for it. I wish—"

"I *thought* you didn't recognize me." Through the milling group, Liesel came forward. And now it was Erika who gasped; she cried out her sister's name and embraced her. They kissed, then Erika held Liesel's shoulders, gazing at arms' length. They did not, Rissa decided, look like twins; in Liesel's features, Erika's near-harsh handsomeness was somehow gentled.

Erika said, "With your travel and my freeze, the age difference seems about the same. When we've time, you'll have to tell me all about Number One." Liesel's brows raised; Erika laughed. "Oh, I've had time to scan the reports, to ground myself firmly in this time. I've been out of freeze nearly two weeks."

"Yes. We'll talk. Now—do you remember Hawkman?"

"We've never met." She shook his hand. "My—you *are* a fine, big man. But I suppose you two are still monogamous." She shrugged, and stood on tiptoe for his kiss.

"Now where's Bran Tregare?"

He came to her. "A kiss for your pirate nephew, maybe?" After it, he said, "I always wanted to face you. It's a little different from what I expected."

She clutched his arm. "Yes—I'm *sorry*, Bran! My damned Hulzein pride—what it put you through! Oh, yes—I knew—it took time, but I traced you. And by then your ship had Escaped, and later—I was *proud* that my own nephew was the dreaded Tregare!" Now she smiled. "And I haven't thanked you for backing my move here, when things looked a little tight."

"You'd have managed—I speeded it up a little, maybe." He gestured toward Lena, huddled sleeping in her chair. "Do us all a favor?"

"What is it you want?"

"Tell somebody where you want this one kept, and send me some electronics people there. I think I just figured out how to defuse Lena Diabla."

RISSA and Alina rode a groundcar to the scout. The girl said, "I felt out of place in there, disguised as you."

"You did well. But, yes—let us change back to being ourselves. We shall certainly surprise Anders."

They boarded, and indeed he was suitably startled. Then while Alina told him of the happenings he had missed, Rissa carefully removed the Laura Konig accessories. The shower and special solvent washed the dye from her hair; brushing it she found some of the wave would not vanish so quickly, though now the hair lay closer to her head and hung almost its normal length.

Alina in turn prepared to shower. Rissa said, "Shall I wait for you, to rejoin the others indoors?"

"No, thanks. I'm not needed there any more—I think I'll stay and keep Anders company."

Rissa said good-bye and left. From the groundcar she looked, noting things she remembered and also new structures replacing what she had known. She reached the building, thanked the driver, and went inside to where she had left the group. She found all but Tregare sitting to luncheon.

"Come and sit," said Erika. She, too, had changed her appearance. She wore a bright, trim suit; the white hair was combed to smoothness and, as of old, cut squarely around at chin length. She said, "I was just starting to tell why I pulled the disappearing act. You'll recall, Rissa—Frieda, much as I hated to admit it, was getting pretty unpredictable. She kept trying for children—in the Hulzein way, of course—and aborting monsters. She blamed me for it—and with some justice, I admit. I don't know if I was really in danger from her, but a couple of funny things happened. What worried me most—I figured she was stable enough to run things while she lived—but then what would happen? So I decided to go to cover—in freeze, so I could take over again when Frieda died, and train a non-Hulzein successor. Naturally I hadn't considered the possibility, after so long, that she'd produce viable offspring."

"But the report—that UET killed you in Madrid?"

"I'd arranged disappearances before—my own wasn't all that difficult. My false trail, after I was safely in freeze, covered several months and thousands of miles. I paid well for it, and the records show I got my money's worth."

Erika grinned. "My freeze-chamber supposedly contained a wealthy refugee, and I sandbagged the computer's instructions for it against the very best grade of prying. It was coded to open when a non-Hulzein took charge of the Establishment, or if UET lost power—whichever came first."

"So when Tregare took UET Headquarters—"

"That information triggered it. The people who resuscitated me didn't know who I was, of course. Soon as I was up and around I got to a hidden computer terminal—oh, I'd planned ahead, well as I could—scanned the high spots of the past fifty-six years. Surprised—and pleased—to learn Frieda's trouble had been glandular, and cleared up by treatment. Surprised as *hell* by Lena's existence—I thought for certain, Frieda'd taken my advice and given it up. So I coded myself up a servant's identity and assigned me to this building, where I could get to Lena, if need be. And it worked."

"I should say it did," said Liesel.

Before she could say more, Tregare entered. "It's all taken

care of," he said. "Now let's call Australia."

But first Erika insisted he explain. "Well, the detonator's in a vault—plastic—metal would cut off the outside signals. It's listening happily to a recording of Lena's brainwave patterns, and there's two backup units with automatic alarm and switching if the first fails. So now what we do—" He sat and began to fill a plate. "We call Australia and get the signal patterns the detonator needs from *there,* to keep it happy, and duplicate that stuff here, too. Then the thing's a dead issue and we can all relax."

THE picture from Australia came clearly, but the man on the screen refused to summon Kane Altworth. Finally Tregare said, "You tell him this is Bran Tregare, that I'm calling from Lena Hulzein's Argentine headquarters, and that he'll never take a more important call in his life. You got that?"

The screen dimmed, showing only streaks of light. They heard faint voices but not the words. Then Altworth appeared. "Tregare, I hope you know what you're doing."

"So do I." He explained what had happened, what he had done. "I can see why you didn't dare cooperate with me, before. How long has she had her little toy?"

"The day you landed, she called and showed me the thing. I thought she was bluffing, but she sent the priming and test signals, and our unit responded. So you see—I've been handcuffed."

"Sure. Now all we need here is a gadget to feed the signal codes that say you're *not* tampering with the bomb, and you can get into it and fix it so this detonator won't work any more."

Altworth shook his head. "Why would you need such a device?"

"She said the thing blows if the no-tampering signal fails."

"No—that time she lied. Signal failure would only alert *her* to operate the detonator."

"Then start changing your bomb so this detonator won't blow it, and then we can give Lena Diabla back her pretty jewelry. Unless—I don't suppose I can talk you into dismantling the thing altogether?"

Altworth hesitated. "That's exactly what we'd like to do. If

I could be sure—oh, I trust *you* not to come in here as UET wanted to—but to date you really hold only North America. There are other threats.''

"I have fifty armed ships to guarantee your safety—UET took Asia with less than that. And we're about ready to move on the other continental Headquarters centers, to do some reshuffling and start phasing out Total Welfare. In a few days I'm going to speak on worldwide broadcast, with translators. We're keeping the world government idea—and you're welcome to join it if you like—but with a lot more local autonomy, once it's working right. Either way, you won't need your bomb—though there's no reason to tell anyone else, right away, that it's out of business.''

For the first time, Altworth smiled. "It's not a bomb, exactly. It—it releases energies that take advantage of any instability in a large mass, magnify it and—given enough power—trigger it.'' He paused. "Since we won't need it any more, I'll admit something—it would *not* destroy Earth. The designers first thought it would, but later found an error in their maths.''

Palms spread, he gestured. "But what could we do? Our Jovian demonstration had convinced everyone. We could hardly tell UET that our threat really amounted to wiping *ourselves* out and causing major damage—but not total destruction—in a considerable part of the world.''

Tregare grinned. "You *were* flying on a tight string. Well, I guess that's it, for now. Will you call me when your—your gadget's deactivated? And discuss future cooperation, when you get time?''

"Certainly. There'll need to be a lot of natter—I hope you're not in too great a hurry—as to how closely we wish to be associated with your world government. We have a long tradition of independence, you see.''

"No problem.'' If there were one, Tregare's gesture waved it aside. "Long as we can work together, I don't especially care about the fancy legalities.''

"Then I believe we're finished with our business for today.''

Rissa said, "Wait! I would like to ask a few questions, if I may. Not about business—but about your grandmother, Camilla Altworth. Did you know her?''

Kane Altworth smiled. "Knew her and loved her—what a great old warrior!—for more than thirty years. She was fifty, a little more, when I was born. Remarried by then—my grand-father had been killed, a typical stupid error, by Committee Police."

"And was that why she joined the Underground?"

"His death triggered her decision, yes. Uh—by the way, you haven't told me your name?"

"Bran Tregare's wife—Rissa Kerguelen."

The man's smile came again, broadened. "Why—when I was a child, she told me of you! I was twelve when your mes-sage came, from—oh, yes—the planet Far Corner. She was so pleased, I recall—saying how she'd wondered, all those years, how you'd fared. I'm afraid she didn't live to see your next message, though, from the Hidden World."

The long view. "I—I am sorry. She was a fine woman."

"Right enough, she was. Unfortunately a bit given to stub-bornness, as she aged. My father *told* her the horse was too much for her. She was eighty-four."

Unconsciously Rissa smiled, then caught herself. But Alt-worth was smiling, too. "Oh, *she* saw the humor of it. She lasted a few minutes after she was thrown, but knew she'd had it. Said to tell Nielse—my father—the joke was on her."

Seeing Altworth look at his watch, Rissa said, "Thank you for telling me these things. Perhaps sometime, when you are not so busy, we may talk further."

"My pleasure, Rissa Kerguelen." He nodded and cut the circuit.

Rissa turned to Tregare. "It is as Kickem said. I would have wished to see that woman again. Single-handedly, of her own doing, she set my life on this path I have taken. There is no way I could ever thank her enough. But now I have heard that she had, since we parted, a long and happy life. More years than I have experienced, all told." She sighed. "Eighty-four—it is a goodly span."

Erika chuckled. "Not too bad. But our grandmother, Lie-sel's and mine—she lived to ninety-two."

And Liesel said, "Our mother only to eighty-six—but Renalle Hulzein died fighting."

"You folks argue longevity all you want," said Tregare. "I'm going to the scout and brief Zelde and the rest, on what's

been happening. And see what news there is from that end."
As he left, Hawkman accompanied him.

LIESEL and Erika looked at each other. Erika said, "Seems
silly now, doesn't it? My outrage when you had your children
the natural way—the whole business of being unable to share
power? Liesel—do you think we can do that, now?"

Shrugging, Liesel grinned. "Probably—but we don't have
to—you're running the Establishment and I'm helping Bran
handle UET. Of course you've got a whopping big vote in
that, too."

"Yes, but right now I have my work cut out for me—trying
to get hold of all the threads in a hurry, finding out who's to
depend on and who's not, undoing Lena's Welfare setup. Will
you help me?"

After a pause Liesel said, "Sure, why not? As long as our
group stays here, that is."

"Good. Come on—we'll have another run at the records
and plan a schedule."

"Is there anything I can do," said Rissa, "to help, also?"

Looking back over her shoulder, Erika said, "Maybe later,
if you're around long enough. Right now, why don't you walk
around and look over the grounds? There's been changes, but
a lot's still much the same."

"All right. I will see you when you break work for coffee."

"How do you expect to guess that?" said Liesel.

Erika laughed. "She's right. My work habits were always
pretty ironclad."

RISSA went outside into cool air and warm sunlight. She
walked past new buildings to an area that seemed little
changed. As she passed men and women pursuing their own
errands, she found herself looking for familiar faces. She
shook her head—*fifty-eight years; any here were children or
not yet born*. But here and there she saw an older person and
looked in vain for recognition.

She climbed a knoll and sat, comparing the scene around
her to her recalls of it. She fell into reverie; minutes passed un-

noticed. Then behind her she heard a sound, and turned to see an old man standing.

He nodded. "They said you were back. You can't be much older—except for the long hair, you've hardly changed at all. How old are you, Rissa, in bio-years?"

"About—about twenty-three." She stared at him. "I can almost recognize—"

"I doubt it—but maybe you can, at that." He smiled and ran fingers over his sparse white hair. "You and Cecily and I had some good times—and in combat training—"

For a moment she saw the young face superimposed on the old one. "Jorge!" She rose, went to him and gently kissed him.

"You used to do better than that, Rissa." But he laughed. "Oh, I know—seventy-eight's not the same as twenty. Though it's not *totally* different, either."

"Jorge! You must tell me, all that has happened—well, as much as you can. Erika is too busy getting things under control again. Tell me—oh, start anywhere, with whatever is important to you." She hesitated. "Unless—if you are busy?"

He shook his head. "Not me. I'm semiretired—some chores to do, but when *I* get around to them. I'm a very lucky man, Rissa."

She looked her inquiry; he said, "Getting into a line of work that was safe from Lena Diabla's version of Total Welfare. You see—and I believe UET found this out, too—you can't Welfare anyone you have to depend on, not to make mistakes."

After a moment she understood and nodded. "Yes," he said. "She tried it on one of my assistants. The next computer program he set up was Hell's own mess! He was punished, of course, but after a few more similar examples, Lena got the point."

"You program computers now?"

"I instruct, supervise, and make spot checks. Quite a change, isn't it, from teaching sex and combat? But I looked ahead, saw I was in a young man's game and needed a new sideline if I wanted to be *valuable* to the Establishment for the long haul."

He smiled. "So even before Erika was killed—or we thought she was, and isn't *that* a wonder for you?—about the time your brother began to make sense again, in fact, I took new aptitude tests and came out with a ticket for computer work. And trained in it, and gradually phased out of the physical side of my career. As a *job,* that is." He laughed. "I still pursue it as a hobby, though not the combat part. Creaking joints are all well and good, but brittle bones are another matter."

She looked at him and could no longer regret his aging. "Cecily? Is she still—"

"No." He shook his head. "She left the Establishment— how long ago?—say, five years after you were here. Fell tail over turnip in love, took her accumulated bonuses, and went civilian on us in Buenos Aires. With a Tri-V actor. I have to admit she chose well, though I didn't think so at the time—ah, well! To sum it up—the man did reach success, and Cecily became a buxom mother and eventually an alarmingly plump grandmother —and happy in her life. I talked with her only a few days before she died."

"Oh? How—how long ago?"

"Ten years—twelve? At any rate—peacefully, in her sleep."

"Yes. That is one goal."

Now he looked at her. "You have a better one, do you?"

"Better? I do not know. But today I learned the manner of death of one woman, and was reminded of another. Older than you, they were, by six and eight years. One died trying to master an unruly horse—the other, in combat."

"Rissa—do you reproach me?"

"No!" The violence of her headshake made her hair fly. "I only try, Jorge, to define my own feelings." She paused. "I have killed, and found that when I do I must grieve for it. I—"

"You, too? It took me a long, hard time to learn that."

"But you did?" She clasped his hand. "What I mean, I think, is—I have faced death and won. Someday, as with all of us, I will face it and lose. But when that times comes—Jorge, I think I would rather die in daring than in dreaming."

She felt her mouth twist, then straighten again. "Perhaps, as I age, that feeling will change. Do you think it will?"

For a time, he said nothing. Then; "I don't know—I can't know. Some people change, some don't. For me—if that's what you're asking, and it's all right if you are—well, it varies. Some mornings I wake wishing I'd died in Lena's purge. Other days, my liver treating me more kindly, I wish myself another century of life and a warm woman to share every year of it. Have I answered you, Rissa?''

She saw his smile and returned it. "I think so. None of us are the same at all times, you are saying. So that must be true of me, also—I cannot judge my future self by my present feelings.''

"And don't be too harsh with your past self—if you grow and learn, and find you've made some pretty bad mistakes. Because we all make them.''

"I will remember.'' She glanced at her watch. "Oh—it is time to meet with Erika and Liesel, and I did not ever stay silent to hear *your* story. Later, perhaps?''

"Whenever you're free. Anyone in the computer section can tell you where to find me. And—it's been good, very good, to see you again.''

"And you, Jorge. But now I must go.''

SHE found the Hulzein sisters already at coffee; Erika had also a small glass of amber liquid. "Come on, Rissa—sit down. Have some brandy with me?''

Rissa declined and poured coffee for herself. Erika said, "I was about to tell Liesel some things I learned after she left Earth. You might care to hear it, too.''

"Certainly. What sorts of things?''

"About the start of the Hulzein dynasty. I hadn't known before—if our mother knew, she didn't tell us. But prowling the computer banks one time, looking for something else entirely, by accident I ran onto—well, I guess you'd call it our grandmother's personal journal. And the way it began, you see—''

Fascinated, Rissa paid close attention. Heidele Hulzein had been highly intelligent, close to genius, blessed with sound health and long-lived heredity. She married young, had two children and was disappointed in them—for each was given to illness and considerably less intelligent than herself. The fault did not seem to lie with the father—he was Heidele's equal, or nearly so.

"But somehow their genes didn't match up right—a couple of poor recessives that fit together, maybe. Heidele had a smattering of genetics; when she formed her theory she went to a real expert. And the story was—"

Heidele's unique attributes derived from the combinations of *both* halves of her chromosome package; neither by itself could re-create them.

"So her friend the expert devised a way to fertilize one haploid ovum with the nucleus of another. The odds were fifty-fifty."

Rissa said, "I do not understand."

"Out of a binful of identical pairs of shoes pick out two shoes, blindfolded. Keep doing it. On average, a quarter of the time you'll get two left shoes, same for two right ones. But half the tries, you'll get matched pairs. Well, the mismates simply didn't fertilize—no problem there. She got Renalle on the third try and decided she had a dynasty going that would last for all time."

"What happened to the other children?" said Liesel.

"She and her husband raised them and saw them begin their own adult lives. Meanwhile Heidele put her considerable talents to building an empire—the Establishment—for her dynasty to rule."

"And if it had not been for the copy-machine effect—" said Rissa.

"You know where she missed?" Liesel said. "Two generations seems to be as far as it's really safe, but for those two it *did* work well. Right?"

Erika smiled. "*I* think so; I'm glad you agree. But what's your point?"

"That after two parthenogenetic, replicated stages the third should be by normal reproduction. If the woman's not satisfied with the first child, have the next by another father. And so on, if necessary. *Then* maybe another parthenogenetic generation or two, if it seems like a good idea."

She laughed. "As it happened, I was quite satisfied with Bran Tregare and with Sparline, so I didn't need to look further than my first choice—Hawkman."

Erika's brows lowered. "But you would have?"

"Sure I would. I had the Hulzein destiny at heart as much as you did—I just felt it had to take a different path, at that point. But if we'd stayed on Earth . . ."

"If you'd stayed, then what?"

"I'd have advised Sparline to have children *both* ways, at least one of each. The ablest of the lot to inherit, of course."

Erika's fingers drummed the table. "That's a good idea. I'll think about it."

Liesel said, "Isn't it a little late—for the Hulzeins?"

"I wasn't thinking about the Hulzeins. My heirs—well, the Establishment has to merge, eventually, into Tregare's world government. And I expect to live to see that, and a lot more, too."

Erika touched Rissa's hand. "I was thinking about the Kerguelens."

FOR long seconds—minutes?—Rissa could not follow the discussion. Finally she said, "Wait. Erika—you propose that I reproduce myself, as Heidele and Renalle did? But—"

"And as I did, and—peace help her—Frieda, too, neither of us having the sense to quit while we were ahead." Erika waved a pointing finger. "Yes, Rissa, I do suggest this to you—so that you can extend your personality down the years, farther than you yourself can live. Now, before you decide I'm old and senile, let me say *why*."

Erika cleared her throat. "Heidele Hulzein, in effect, has lived for nearly two hundred years. One lifetime isn't enough to accomplish what she and Renalle and I—and Frieda, too—have done, building an Establishment that's stood against UET. And it strikes me that during the next century, that same sort of stability may be needed." An emphatic nod. "At least, *think* about it."

Rissa frowned. "You think all of Earth needs—or would tolerate—a dynasty?"

"Oh, not to own it, the way we Hulzeins have owned our piece of it. But to *be* there—a force, a factor. And of course only the female line can reproduce without change." She shrugged. "Too bad the cloning approach never panned out. But that was before your time."

Head shaking, Rissa said, "If you wish no change, then why me? For I am not a Hulzein."

"Your daughter is," said Liesel. "Part, anyway—and another part yourself." She turned. "Wait 'til you see *that* one, Erika. She—"

Erika laughed. "A mix of Hulzein and Rissa—and Hawkman Moray? I look forward to seeing that child; I'll bet she's a worldbeater. Say—maybe *she* . . ."

"When Liesel Selene is older and well informed," said Rissa, "if she wishes to begin a dynasty, she may do so."

TREGARE, when she told him, said, "I like it." In the quarters Erika had provided, they were reclothing themselves, preparing to meet the others at dinner. "Yes—a new little Rissa—all you, nobody else. Oh, you'd name her something different, I expect. But growing up the way you *should* have done—none of that Welfare crap—real parents all the way. Why, I—"

"Parents, Bran?"

"You'd share her with me, wouldn't you?" She nodded. "Well, then!" Tregare looked at her. "I don't mean right now —or even make up your mind on it, yet. Just leave the idea open, and maybe one of these years . . ."

"Very well, Bran—I will not close my mind. But I do not yet agree to Erika's proposal, either."

"There's no hurry. Hey—let's go see if it's time to eat."

THE dining room, Rissa saw, had not changed greatly. "It is the smaller one," she told Tregare. "I was in the great one only twice."

Even so, at the room's center the table for eight sat small. "—but there's only the five of us," said Erika. Liesel and Hawkman were already seated. "The two on your scout begged off."

"No matter," said Tregare. "All the more for the rest of us." But he ate sparingly, as did Rissa and Erika—only Liesel and Hawkman, in the usual way of persons still recovering from freeze, refilled their plates.

Rissa had finished when a girl entered and whispered to Erika, who frowned. "Well, tell him—he's sitting right there."

The young woman colored and cleared her throat. "Tregare, sir—there's a call—I'll show you—if you'll come with me, please."

He stood. "Sure, thanks." And to the others, "Be back in a minute, I expect."

Liesel said, "I hope nothing's gone wrong."

Erika shook her head. "If it was urgent, the girl would have said something." She sipped at her brandy. "Now then—you were going to tell about your early days on Number One. *That* must have been something—sinking your teeth into a brand-new world."

But Liesel had hardly begun when Tregare returned, grinning. "That was Dacia Kobolak, by relay. The ship picked them up, all right. They're less than two days out."

"But then—" Puzzled, Rissa said, "Then why had they not called earlier? Is something wrong?"

He shrugged. "Transmitter breakdown and out of spares—somebody screwed up. It took the comm tech more than a week to haywire a substitute out of his junk box."

"Did you see Lieselene? Bran—why did you not call me to see her also?"

"She's asleep. This was their first call, as soon as the rig got fixed."

"Two days," said Erika. "You'll be leaving, then. Or could the ship come here?"

"Afraid not," Tregare said. "It has to check in at the port —several reasons. But why don't you come pay *us* a visit? Ride up with us, for that matter. We—"

"Yes!" said Rissa. "How long since you were in North America?"

Erika's brow wrinkled. "Why, that would be—it was the same year you were born, that UET killed Renalle and we fled. Seventy-five years ago. Of course I've lived less than twenty of them, spent the rest in freeze. But why—?"

"Because we shall have a party, a celebration, and you must be there." Turning to Tregare, Rissa displayed her personal chronometer. "We will celebrate my birthday, also—I totally forgot, but it was yesterday. so we can combine the observance with our reunion."

"Wait a minute," said Erika. "You weren't born this time of year, at all."

Rissa shook her head. "I do not mean the Earthly anniversary. It is that yesterday, according to this chronometer that has traveled with me near the speed of light, I completed twenty-three biological years."

Erika grinned. "Of course—no point in your counting by Earth's circlings when you've lived at a different rate. I'm not used to thinking that way—but I'm in the same situation. Born a hundred and thirty years ago, come September—and I'm biologically just past seventy-three."

"It's settled, then?" said Tregare. "You're coming with us?"

Erika scowled a moment, then nodded. "You'll assign me circuits to keep touch here, stay on top of the reorganization? Then of course I'll come. After all, it's Liesel Selene's welcome to Earth—and I'm the only great-aunt she's got!"

KANE ALTWORTH, next day, confirmed that the Australian "bomb" was deactivated and in process of being dismantled. "But as you suggested, Tregare—there's no point in advertising the fact."

When the conversation was done, Tregare said, "Well—are we close to being finished here?"

"There is a man I wish to talk with," said Rissa. "I knew him—and he is quite old now. So—"

"Sure. And I guess we can give Lena back her trinket—maybe it'll make her feel better." He stood. "I'll go get it."

When he returned, Erika accompanied him. She said, "I may as well go with you. Sooner or later I have to decide what to do about . . . my granddaughter."

In her face Rissa saw pain. "But what *is* there to do?"

"Decide whether she has to be locked away or can be trusted with *some* freedom, under watch." She shook her head. "It's hard."

When they reached the place, a guard opened the door; inside sat another. In the middle of a large bed lay Lena Hulzein. Slowly, painstakingly, she sat up and adjusted her robe.

"What do you want *now?*"

Tregare waved for the guard to leave. He approached Lena and held out the pendant. "This thing's been rendered harmless, but it's still a handsome piece of jewelry. So if you want it back—"

The good hand snatched; she set the pendant in her lap and carefully put her fingertips on four jewels. Looking up, she grinned. "You're wrong—there's no way you could deactivate this. So now—*we die!*" She closed her eyes—the fingers stabbed, once and then again. Her eyes opened; she looked, checked the fingers' placement and—tentatively, now—pushed at the jewels. Then, teeth bared, she swung her arm—awkwardly, it seemed, yet Tregare's hand barely deflected the heavy ornament.

"You! What have you done? How did you—*take it all away from me?*" Her breathing rasped; tears started from the corners of her eyes.

He shook his head. "How? It doesn't matter. And we haven't taken everything—just the power. As Liesel said, your wealth is still yours, most of it."

"*Just* the power?" Her good hand clutched the withered one. "Power over life, power of death—what *else* do you think wealth could do for me?" The sound she made was like no laugh Rissa had ever heard. "Could it make me pretty? Could it buy me health? Fertility? Freedom from pain, even?"

Now she breathed in gasps. "Fifty years, almost, I've lived with pain—I don't remember what it's like not to hurt. And in a body that can't know pleasure, the mind's only joy is to share that pain, to *give* it—and to know that all will share my death."

She shook her head. "And now they won't—you've taken *that* from me, too. So—" She stared at him. Rissa wanted to shrink from the sight, but could not—never, even among the Welfare mutilated, had she seen such despair.

"There's still my own death. Give it to me."

"What—?"

"Kill me, Tregare. You owe me that, at least."

"I—I can't do that. I've no reason to want you dead."

"Bran," said Rissa, "it is a favor, that she asks of you. I understand. And if you cannot do it, then I can. For here the death is less to grieve for, than the life."

Hideous parody of a smile. Then, "You're all right, Kerguelen. I wish—maybe, in a different body, I could have been like you . . ." Lena closed her eyes, opened them again. "No —I *want* to see it coming. Just be quick."

Rissa paused, breathed deeply and set her mind. But before she could move, Erika said, "Not you, Rissa—this is all *my* doing. The way Lena is, what she's suffered—all of it. So it's my responsibility to—to end my own line." She sighed. "You and Tregare should go now. There's no reason you have to see this."

Lena said, "I want them here—if they're willing to stay. And—*she* could do it quick, the way she moves. How do I know you won't bungle it—*grandmother?*"

"The way I bungled the rest of your life? No—don't worry —one chop of my hand. I guarantee it."

Rissa nodded. "Less than three of her own bio-years ago, Erika personally gave me my final checkout in unarmed combat. You can depend on her."

Lena nodded. "All right. Kerguelen—would you sit down here, on this side out of the way—and hold my hand? The good one? While—it happens?"

Rissa's tongue moistened her dry lips. "Why—yes, of course." She sat and took the hand; it squeezed hers tightly. Lena's gaze fixed itself to her own; Rissa could not look away. Now, even without adrenaline shock, time slowed. *Will this never end?*

Then Lena's stare flicked aside; Rissa sensed motion. Lena's eyes closed tightly—Rissa's did also. Then she heard the thud and the snapping sound.

The hand gripped briefly, painfully, and went limp. When Rissa looked again, Lena lay on her side; Erika pulled a fold of robe to cover the lolling head.

Erika straightened. "Well, it's done." She flexed her right hand and turned toward the door. "Funerals are out of fashion and I doubt she'd want one anyway. I'll have her buried on the hillside near her mother."

She tried to smile; never had Rissa seen her look so old. "I'm glad we're back to the natural way of things, letting our dead enrich the soil again."

Tregare put his arm around her. "Erika? Do you need to grieve?"

"For the death, no. As Rissa said, it was the life that needs the grieving. And that's not something I'll manage in a hurry, I'm afraid." She patted his hand. "What I need to do now, I suppose, is worry that everyone in the place will think I killed her out of spite."

"Nothing shaken," said Tregare. "Voluntary euthanasia's legal here. As head of the Establishment, you have the authority to grant it. And besides—" He patted the pouch at his belt. "I taped the whole conversation."

RISSA left the others and called the computer section. She had forgotten Jorge's surname, but the young man who answered said, "Certainly I know who you mean—there's lots of Jorges, but only one *Jorge*."

She laughed, obtained her information and met Jorge for

lunch. They talked long; he told her of the years when Frieda's unstable behavior had endangered them all, then of how medical treatment had changed her. "A great lady in her later years. It was a sad loss, when she died."

Of Lena he said very little. "Poor thing—the Hulzein mind trapped in that crippled, painful body. How *could* she be sane?" Then; "And what is to be done with her now?"

Rissa paused—was this event hers to tell? No, she decided, and said only, "Would it surprise you if she were to ask for death?"

"No—somehow it wouldn't. Power was all she had to live for." He stood. "Shall we walk now? And, Rissa—you've told me hardly anything of your own life."

So, outside where chilly air kept them walking fast, she talked. She told of escaping Earth, of Far Corner and Osallin, of going to Number One—she omitted some details of her early acquaintance with Tregare—and events on that Hidden World.

When she came to the duel, and dal Nardo's death, he whistled. "One thing you'd better keep in mind. Here and now, Rissa, *you're* the one who's behind on combat techniques."

She stopped. "Why—I had not thought—you are right, Jorge! Soon as I may, I must find an instructor and learn what has passed me by."

He patted her shoulder. "Meanwhile, if you have to fight at all, stick to weapons. There's never much change in how you shoot a gun."

"Yes. Thank you, Jorge. And now, quickly, here is what next happened." The names would mean nothing so she skimmed, except for Peralta's attack, the building of Tregare's fleet. She deleted the Shrakken from her tale; their existence was not general knowledge. "—so we went to Stronghold and Tregare's plans worked as he intended, and then—" She had just told him of Liesel Selene when she noticed the time. "Oh—Jorge, it is so *late*—I was to have returned before now. Well—then we came to Earth—and you do not need me to tell you what has happened since then. And I *must* go—do you mind if we say our good-byes here and I take a shortcut back, over that knoll?"

"If you must, you must. Good-bye, Rissa—I am so very glad you came here."

She reached up and kissed him, hugged him hard. Then she
turned and ran, not looking back.

DINNER was brief and almost silent; Erika was first to rise.
"You'll excuse me? If I'm leaving with you tomorrow, I'll
need the evening to complete the arrangements."

"You can use some help, I expect," said Liesel, and stood
also. They left.

Hawkman said, "I hope the two of you aren't in a hurry.
We've a bottle of wine, still, and coffee for a dozen."

Rissa smiled. "I am happy to stay with you."

And Tregare nodded. "Anything special on your mind, or
just feeling sociable?"

"A little of both," said Hawkman. He moved his chair
back and turned it to one side, stretching his long legs almost
straight and crossing them at the ankles. "I helped bury
Lena—dug the last two feet of the grave, in fact. But nobody's
told me what happened. Erika may have informed Liesel—but
those two, they've been busy all day."

Rissa looked to Tregare; he waved the question back to her
but she said, "You have the recorder, Bran. We are alone here
—play the tape."

At the end of it, Hawkman's face contorted in pity. "The
poor thing! Whatever hell she visited onto others, she could
never relieve her own." He gestured negation. "A rabid creature is a victim of disease. You may have to kill it but you
don't hate it."

Rissa nodded. "Except, Hawkman, that we hate what we
fear. But once the threat—the detonator—was gone, I did not
hate her."

"And you held her hand while she died?"

"Yes. I did not *see*—when she shut her eyes, mine shut too,
in reflex—I did not see the blow itself. But if Lena made a
sound, then, I did not hear it. Erika struck well."

Hawkman's fist clenched. "There's another I can't hate—
though there was a time she'd have had me killed, and much
of this is her doing. Where's the fault, Rissa—where's the
fault?"

Tregare spoke. "The copy-machine effect, is all. Maybe
Heidele knew the risk, maybe not. Renalle?—nobody knows.

Erika wasn't told, except when Liesel tried—and by then she was hellbent on putting her own ova in charge of the world's destiny, and couldn't change.'' He shrugged. "Either the problem was never realized or the information wasn't passed along. The fault's in *ignorance*, Hawkman—where it's always been and always will be."

"Yes—I suppose so. More wine?" He poured it. "Now, another matter. Left to myself and I'm not really complaining about that, I've been doing a little study from the computer readouts—of the recent history and present state of this planet."

He waited. Rissa said, "What question do you wish to be asked?"

Hawkman laughed. "Well, perhaps, what it is I found, that's worth reporting." Now it was his coffee cup that needed filling, before he said, "You're planning to turn Welfare Clients loose, all over the world, as fast as may be. Right?"

"That is our goal, yes," said Rissa.

"And with what curbs, if any, on their breeding? Once they're free citizens again."

"No immediate problem," said Tregare. "Most are sterilized—and reversible or not, they can't breed without the magnetic consent of a gadget like the one Rissa has."

"I do not think that the immediate future is what concerns Hawkman," she said.

"That's right. What I'm saying, Tregare—you'd better set up some *long*-term policy and make it stick. Or in a few decades—Earth's poorer in resources now than when we left it— you'll have the same problem that UET set out to cope with."

Rissa looked at him. "Hawkman—this will take more than an evening's thought."

"Correct. I merely had the idea that we can't start too soon."

ERIKA, next morning, said she was traveling light. Tregare watched the parade of luggage carriers and said, "I'd hate to see you travel heavy—maybe I should have brought *Inconnu*."

"But I don't know how long I'll be staying. And besides— that's not all clothes and knickknacks, Tregare. More than half's technical equipment—data tapes, scramble gear and the like." Narrowly she gazed at him. "It's not *you* I don't trust, Bran; you know that, I think. But there's other forces—and I'm cutting loose from safe country for the first time in more than fifty years. You can't blame me."

Rissa touched the older woman's hand. "It is all right, Erika. Bran Tregare pretends to believe that one suitcase is sufficient for a star journey."

"That looks like about all of it," Tregare said. "Can we board now?"

On the scout, Anders Kobolak reported in best official fashion. "When the hell," said Tregare, "did we start saluting around here, except to impress the natives?"

Seeing Kobolak look sidelong to Alina Rostadt, Rissa said, "It is good practice, perhaps." She thought she saw gratitude in the boy's smile, and added, "He does it well, does he not?"

"Sure, sure. Now let's see how well he can fly a low airblasting course; the high one, coming south, was good."

Erika tugged at his arm. "Tregare—could a passenger ask a favor?"

He turned to her. "Why not? Ask away."

"If it won't interfere with your training plans, could you fly a high course again, now?" His brow raised; quickly she said, "In all my life I've never been to space. Just a quick hop up there, to see Earth from a distance—it would mean a lot. If it's not too much trouble."

Rissa saw him relax. "Course not. Later, when you get time, you can go out in a ship—get a good look at Mars, even take a real vacation and see Big Jupe up close. But for now—Kobolak, take us up like the fastest bat you ever saw, about twice as high as you did on the way here. Then coast in easy—give the lady time to look, all the way down."

"Yes, sir." Tregare looked hard at him; Kobolak grinned. "Sure, Tregare." The boy thrust hard at the controls; below, Earth leaped away.

As they rose, Erika watched the screens. "Ah—this is *good*." Then; "Tregare—this is a scoutship; the real ships carry them, I know that much. Now, then—what can this scout do, and what *not*? Compared to a ship . . ."

"To tell you so you'll know," said Tregare, "takes a little thinking." Scratching his chin, he paused. "Well—first, scouts don't have ships' power—accel and decel take more time and distance. Next, you've got only so much fuel and supplies. Scouts are designed so these limits all come out close to even."

Erika smiled. "Try me with a few specific figures, why don't you?"

"Sure." He looked to the screen. "We're near peak distance, so watch and don't miss anything. All right—a scout has to be able to decel from light to zerch or it's useless for combat survivors. That's the first parameter, with some leeway to do it slower or faster so that with luck you can reach a place to roost."

He pointed to the screen. "See there? Big storm all across the North Pacific. Well, then—you've got supplies for six people for six months; more passengers or more time means short rations. Maybe *too* short—it's happened. So—"

Erika interrupted. "What I want to know is, what's the maximum start-stop range for this lovely bucket? And don't worry—I'm watching everything down below, and loving it."

"Why didn't you ask if that way in the first place? *That*, I don't have to figure—they tell us at first-snot class at the Academy. Rest to rest, a scout's good for over a trillion miles —between a fifth and a sixth of a light-year. Slowing from light to landing, four times that distance in the same time. More than you'd ever need in a planetary system but useless for interstellar. It's a good design—best you can get and still berth it on a ship."

For a time Erika did not answer; she faced the screen, one palm against the panel beside it. She shook her head. "Ah! Tregare—thanks for showing me this! Now then—for comparison with your trillion miles—what's the range of a real starship?"

"You setting up in the business?" He laughed. "Well, sure you can—you own enough stock to swing a few ships your way, any time you want! Now—one-trip limit, you mean?" She nodded.

"Okay—ships vary. A well-tuned drive, full tanks, theory says fifty light-years—maybe two years' subjective travel, a little more. Longest I ever heard of—and I got it thirdhand —was thirty-six. Answer your question?"

"Yes, and thanks." A sigh. "Oh—Tregare—what a beautiful world we're all setting out to govern!"

• • •

By Tregare's decision they landed at Headquarters, near *Inconnu*. Rissa thought Anders Kobolak was dropping the scout too fast, but when he began decel he brought it to max so smoothly that she did not feel the actual grounding; only the drive's scream rang in her ears. When it ebbed, she said, "Tregare? Will I ever be able to land a scout that well?"

"Probably, if you practice. But I don't know when you'll find time for it."

Then he asked Alina Rostadt where her quarters were. Before she could answer, young Kobolak said, "On *Inconnu*, please, Tregare? She's to be with me."

Tregare looked at the two. "Paired up already?" He turned to Liesel. "You're the one dug her up—you need her for anything?" At his mother's headshake, he said, "Third Hat quarters don't hold two."

"We can make do," said Anders. "We—"

"You listen while I'm talking," said Tregare. "Now then— if you don't mind being quartered below your rank, Kobolak, there's some doubles vacant, downship. Ask Hain Deverel; tell him I okayed it. All right?" The boy nodded. "So get going."

Anders turned to leave; Alina caught his hand. She said, "I don't know who's honored me the most—Anders now, or Tregare for approving, or you, Ms. Kerguelen, for letting me play your part for a while. I—"

"All around," said Rissa, "you have done well. But—" She turned to Tregare. "Perhaps they might wish the ceremonies. Should you not offer?"

"Oh, sure. Rostadt, Kobolak—you want anything official? Old-style, newstyle, freestyle—I've got it all in the files someplace, on *Inconnu*."

"We'll talk it over," Kobolak said, "and when you have time—"

"Well, whatever you want," said Tregare. "Oh—tell Hain you're authorized a groundcar, too—to get Alina's stuff brought over to *Inconnu*."

"There's not that much," the girl said. "But thanks—it's a long walk."

When the two had gone, Tregare said, "Well, we'd better scatter back to our own problems. Right?"

"Not so fast," said Liesel. "While we're here, just the lot of us, let's settle a few things."

"Like what?"

Liesel grabbed his shoulder and shook it. "Like putting a little *structure* into what we're doing. You're the conquering hero, Bran Tregare—and that's truth, for without you we wouldn't be here. But Erika and Hawkman and I know the dull job—except that it's *not* so dull—of managing a going operation. So let's get it set up on a working basis."

"What's to set up? You do it, I'll sign it."

"Bran!" Rissa said it loudly. "If Liesel thinks it is important—"

"All right—I guess we have time. What's the proposal?"

Liesel said, "Let me ask you something. Do you intend to *be* the government, indefinitely?"

"Course not. I said—you set something up, I'll sign it."

"Then here's the main idea. You've put the Committee on ice—except for Zavole, working on a tight string—and I agree with you. But for a corporate system, a Committee structure is the best administrative apparatus."

Tregare frowned. "You want *us* to be a new Committee?"

"Plus others, of course. Oh, we *call* ourselves something different—Board of Directors, maybe, for whatever we decide to rename UET. Then—"

Rissa said, "Certainly, United Energy and Transport is no fitting name for a world government. I prefer, simply—*Earth*."

"Board of Directors of Earth?" said Erika.

Hawkman said, "Not Directors, I think. Trustees? Because as I see it, we hold this power in trust, to use it well."

"That's it," said Liesel. "So I hereby call the existing Board of Trustees of Earth to order in meeting, to elect a chairman." She grinned. "Tregare—you're it!"

Backing away, hands extended, he shook his head. "Not me —not for that job. I run a pretty good war, I think—and kept Stronghold in shape fairly well—but designing a whole new society? I'll keep charge of the space end, if you don't mind—commerce—defense—whatever comes up. Chasing down remaining UET ships, freeing colonies—sure. But the policy end —you people set it up, I'll help on organizing and enforcing." Now he lost tenseness. "You want a Chairman? I nominate Rissa."

She said, "Bran—the functions will not be so separate."

"I should hope not!"

And Liesel said, "Tregare has resigned the chair in favor of Rissa. All in favor?"

Seeing their hands raised, Rissa said, "I think I see why you want me for a figurehead—and that is all, for a long time, that I *can* be. My past—the All-Time Welfare Kid, Markine said—gives me a sympathetic image, with those who wait for freedom."

She smiled. "Very well—but never did I think to see Hulzeins vying to give away power!"

Hawkman chuckled. "You don't know your Hulzeins very well yet. They adapt."

"I do not understand."

He reached to pat her cheek. "Of course you do. Think a moment. In reshaping a world—dealing in total power rather than competition—*individual* power becomes meaningless. Lena showed us that, I think. And from now on, nothing counts for much except what we do *together*."

She rubbed a palm across her forehead. "Yes—of course. Thank you, Hawkman—but how could I have failed, until you reminded me, to see this?"

His vast chest expanded as he sighed. "You've been in the middle of it, Rissa, without time to think. I've been on the sidelines—observing, seeing it happen."

While Rissa strove to find answer, Tregare said, "Just so it works, is all. *I* think we've got a working team. In a day or so we can talk it out, who we want to add to it. I've got a few in mind."

"But not tomorrow," said Rissa. "For then Dacia lands the scout here, and we welcome Liesel Selene."

AFTER so short a separation, Rissa thought, she had been foolish to expect much difference in the child. But it had *seemed* long—so much had happened—and in changing from ship's calendar to Earth's, her time sense had suffered a lapse.

The little girl ran to her; Rissa said, "Welcome, Liesel Selene Moray!" The child paused, blinking. Carefully, clearly, Rissa pronounced the coded trigger words; at the last of them, Lieselene smiled and came forward again. Rissa lifted her to kiss and cuddle, murmuring love into a small ear. "Are you glad to be back with Rissa, darling?"

Laughing, bubbling with pleasure, Lieselene said, "Oh, yes! But Dacia's good!" Then Tregare took the child, and Rissa heard unspacemanlike endearments from her husband's lips.

Now she turned to greet Dacia Kobolak, and here she found change. Not merely the curling red hair now tied severely back, a few shorter strands escaping to wave around her face —that face was leaner and more mature. Rissa hugged the girl and said, "Welcome back to Earth, and thank you for what you have done. Did you have many problems?"

Dacia shook her head. "The scout operated perfectly and the people made a great team. Lisele got homesick for you both, of course—especially the second and third day, along in there. But she got over it—except for asking, every time she thought of it, 'How much *longer?*' Just as though she could count!"

"And she has been healthy? She certainly looks it."

"Oh, yes—no trouble there. She was a little choosy about her food at first, but Creis and Onya—you remember them?— just told her it was space rations, and she came around soon enough."

Dacia grinned. "We had it nervous when we first spotted the ship that came out to meet us, not knowing who it might be. But when we had contact I recognized the woman on the screen—from Stronghold—and she had the right code words, so we all relaxed."

"Right," said Tregare. "Well, we've got one quick job to do—let's get it out of the way."

Dacia said, "What's that?"

"Springing all those hypnotic triggers you won't be needing —yours and the rest of your crew's. Rissa's already cleared Lisele's, in greeting—but we'll check to be sure."

Dacia nodded. "You know? I'd forgotten about those."

QUICKLY the job was done. Tregare did the talking, Rissa monitored the polygraph, and the truth field confirmed the results. Then the group went aboard *Inconnu*, where Dacia enjoyed reunion with her brother.

"—and when I'm off watch, in a few minutes," he said, "I want you to come downship to my quarters and meet some-one."

"Downship, Anders? Aren't you Third Hat any more?"

He laughed. "Sure I am—but those quarters are a little cramped, for two." Rissa could see that Dacia wanted to know more, but Anders only shook his head and smiled. "You'll see, soon enough. I hope you like each other."

THE galley was crowded; while Lieselene napped, Rissa and Tregare lunched in their quarters. He said, "Who all's coming to the party tonight. You know yet?"

"Besides the Board, Hain and Anse, and the Kobolaks?" She counted on her fingers. "Zelde, Hilaire, Kickem and Aedra, Kile Ressider—will there be tension if Zelde brings Jamie?—Terrell Ragan. Bran—we are leaving many key positions unmanned—"

"Not really." Yawning, he stood and stretched. "Every one of those people is backed by good staff, with instant circuit access here if necessary. Zelde's got the port under her thumb like a squashed ant, and—"

"Very well. Oh—you did not tell me—why do you wish some of them here so early?"

"To meet the Board. You said not today, I know—but it won't take long, and this is our best chance for a while."

"For what, Bran?"

"Because if nobody objects, I want Zelde, Hilaire, Kickem, and Ressider on the Board."

"But Kickem is your fleet commander. Soon he will be off Earth."

"While he's here, I think he'll be valuable." He turned to go, then paused. "You didn't say about Ivan. He's coming, isn't he?"

Rissa shrugged. "He does not know. If Ilse does, yes. Otherwise not—and he could not say, yet, what she will decide." She rubbed her cheek. "Bran—should not Ilse, also, be on the Board?"

Tregare's fingers drummed the table. "Before, I'd have said, sure. Now I don't know—if her face is going to warp her thinking . . ." He shook his head.

"If she appears tonight, that should tell us much."

"Yeah, I guess so. Well—I'm going to grab me a shower."

• • •

WHEN they heard the scout land, they got up and dressed. Shortly, Tregare answered a knock and admitted Zelde M'tana.

"Good job, wrapping up Argentina," she said. "And I just got word—I'll match you Hokkaido port, the whole complex. Like you said, Tregare—watched their scramble channels, waited until they had two ships coming in together and caught 'em just grounding. Instant surrender. And groundside, no resistance to speak of—which if I know my strike force commander, means he only had to kill a couple hundred or so."

She looked around. "The baby's asleep, I guess? I hope the drinks aren't."

Tregare grinned and poured her straight spirits, then added ice. The three sat, talking, until the intercom chimed in the next room. Rissa answered it and returned to say, "The others are arriving. I have said we will meet in your office, Bran. You two go ahead, while I find Dacia or another to stay with Lisele. Then I will follow."

WHEN she entered the large office, Tregare was speaking. He paused; she greeted the newcomers, then said to him, "The young couple Dacia mentioned—Creis and Onya Kohler— Lisele is with them." Rissa smiled. "She greets them as uncle and aunt."

"The kind of work schedules we can expect," said Tregare, "she can use some extra family."

"Yes." She sat. "Since the meeting is begun, continue to preside. And I will not interrupt further."

Liesel said, "Do we have any firm idea yet, just how big we want this Board to be? Tregare?"

"I hadn't put a size on it, myself. I don't think the five of us—plus Gameel voting his four percent—is enough. What I'd like to suggest—okay, Zelde, Port Commander—Hilaire, the Academy and related activities—Kickem, fleet chief—Kile, running whatever we call the remodeled Police to take the stink off—I think those four jobs should have votes on the Board. I'm not crowding it—I'll go with a majority—but I *am* suggesting it."

Zelde said, "Maybe you'd like us outside while you talk it over?"

"That doesn't seem necessary," said Erika. "As Tregare

put it, it's *jobs* being represented, that we're voting on. When it comes to your personal abilities, three out of five of us are mostly taking Tregare's word—and glad to. All right?"

Zelde grinned. "You're Tregare's aunt; right? You should have gone to space yourself. I mean, you have what they call the command mind."

"I'd have liked to—but I was on the wrong side. We Hulzeins were trying to lay hands on a starship when UET blasted us out of North America. After that—too busy, for some years, just fighting for our lives."

Tregare said, "Anybody have any points to make, for or against?" No one spoke. "All right—you want to vote all of it, or one at a time?"

"One vote should do it," said Hawkman. "Each case has equal merit."

"Good enough. All in favor, raise a hand." He looked around. "I guess unanimous is good enough. Now, what else is up for deciding?"

"Nothing that I know of," said Liesel. "But while we're all here, I'd like to brief the Board—and welcome to the new members—on how it's going, the administrative setup to start closing down Welfare. We've begun releasing the easier cases, of course . . ."

Liesel's report took longer than Rissa expected, but no one fidgeted.

BACK on *Inconnu*, climbing upship, Rissa said, "Bran? Only one bio-year, a few days more, since we last held celebration on this ship. But that was back on Stronghold and seems a very long time ago."

"By planet time," he said, "it's been ten years, maybe eleven."

She opened the door and preceded him into their quarters. "Do you suppose somehow the mind, the body, *knows* what time has passed, that we have not lived?"

EXCITEMENT gripped Rissa. As the party began, she experienced it only in episodes, vignettes, flashes of vision and concentration . . .

• • •

LIESEL SELENE laughed in delight as Tregare solemnly cut a centimeter from one of the candles on her small cake, then lit all three. "Because you're only two and three-quarters old, Lisele. We want to do this right, don't we?" The child puffed her cheeks out, blew, and the tiny flames died.

SEEING Erika redeyed but smiling, Rissa said, "Something has happened. For the good, I think?"

Erika gripped her arm. "The dam busted. I cried my fool head off for a solid hour, at least. But now—poor Lena doesn't haunt me any more."

"AND who'd have thought," he said after kissing her, "that Bernardez would be fleet commander for all Earth's outgoing ships? Mind, I've never denied the talent of the man—" He laughed. "You're looking exceptionally gorgeous tonight, Rissa. Can it be that Earth agrees with you?"

And Aedra Leng smiled, saying, "It would be well advised to do so."

WILL I ever blow out that last candle? But with a final, creaking exhalation, emptying her lungs to the point of hurt, she did it. And gasped while they sang, again, the ancient ritual.

"A kiss goodnight, before you go with Aunt Dacia—and one for Bran, too." He was talking with Erika and did not hear. "Tregare! A moment for our daughter, please, before she retires."

He turned and held the child, kissed her and nuzzled her neck, then let Dacia Kobolak take her. "You'll be back, Dacia?"

"Oh, yes. But not before this one's safely tucked in."

"—and when I get time," said Liesel, "I'm going to do a computer search. Those first two children of Heidele's—any living descendants would be at least *part* Hulzein. And maybe some of the talent survived."

"At the least," Rissa said, "to find such cousins would be of interest."

"Sure. I could *use* a little more family."

"I CAME alone a-purpose, Kile," said Zelde M'tana.

Ressider spoke slowly. "What about young Pescadore?"

"Jamie's not smallhearted—he knows and he agreed."

Now Ressider smiled. "All right. Later—and where?"

"Your ship. I came in a scout."

"THE Academy's coming fine," said Hilaire Gowdy. "Some of the staff, of course—hopeless drudges, being cruel because it was *expected*—I've got rid of a lot. Bringing in capable ratings from our ships, and promoting them."

To Tregare's question: "The kids? They'll be all right, most of them. A few had their guts tromped out already; those I'll release, come deadline. I had another idea, though—"

Rissa's glass was empty; she moved away to refill it.

"A LITTLE different from Base Two, isn't it, Hain? And yet— a lot the same, too."

"The skipper doesn't change, Anse. Just his situation does. Or rather—he changes it."

"—the one thing Welfare did right," said Liesel. "The experimentation, of course—ruthless! An abomination!" Then she shrugged. "But we can't undo any of that—and in a controlled environment—most of the old diseases wiped out, or almost— I tell you, Tregare, the standard of medical care really surprised me."

"Why did they bother, I wonder?"

"The medics worked with what they had, I guess."

"IVAN!" And beside him, Ilse Krueger. White now, the sunken scar lay like an ivory dagger pressed into the skin, its point near the stretched corner of her mouth. Still a bandage began beside the cheekbone and vanished under her hair. But where scabs had been, new skin—slightly ruddy, yet—was now exposed.

Ilse said, "He decided I could make it, tonight. We'll see." She touched the hair. "It's a full wig, of course. I tried a partial, but it looked like a cat with mange, didn't match. And this one, at first, sat lopsided. So I whacked my own hair, what's left of it, down to bristle length—it helps hold this in place." She looked at Rissa. "Do I pass?"

Rissa hugged her and whispered, "It is so *good* to see you here, Ilse!"

"Did you say something? My ear's on the other side—remember?"

So, face to face, Rissa said it again.

"Thanks. It's good to be here—I *think*."

"Here," said Ivan. "I don't suppose you noticed I was gone, but here's a glass of what's good for you."

They drank a toast, and Rissa thought, *Ilse! She has become herself again!*

"TREGARE," said Bernardez, "Terrell Ragan here, he's after me to be going to space—chase down the rest of UET's ships and free the colonies. After all, he says and rightly, it's a fifty-year job and we'd best get to it. And for all my well-known way with words, I find me at a loss—what am I to say to the good man?"

Standing, leaning one hand on a table, Tregare drained his glass. "Well, let's try the truth. Ragan—d'you know what Dr. Hoyfarul's working on?"

Ragan's tone was cautious. "I've heard rumors. I haven't believed them."

"So start now." Bernardez handed Tregare a fresh drink; gesturing thanks, he raised it. Then; "You have your own squadron; right?" At Ragan's nod, he said, "Kickem, it's time to brief this matter at squadron command level, beginning right here. You'll see to the rest of it?"

"None better."

"All right—Ragan, here's the picture. We don't *know* this thing's going to work—but I'm sending out no fifty-year mission while there's a chance the job might be done in five."

• • •

"I WAS a little worried, Rissa," said Dacia Kobolak. "Anders never had much of a way with girls. So I had my doubts—maybe this is some harpy, you know?—and all that. But she's the right sort. Alina and I hadn't talked five minutes before I knew we'd be friends."

"—quite a few thousand released, so far," Liesel said, "but it's only a small beginning. What I'm doing, Rissa, is shuffling people around so I can convert whole buildings from Clients to citizens—the quick and easy ones first, in a hurry. It doesn't help the crowding much—so to give hope, I have a good dramatic move coming up next week."

"What kind of move? And which day?"

Liesel told her. Rissa turned and climbed—half-jumped—to a table top. She clapped her hands for silence, then picked up her glass and raised it.

"A toast! A toast to Thursday, the fourteenth of this month!" Seeing puzzled faces, she laughed. "That day will see the first *closing* of a Total Welfare Center!"

THE last to leave, Hawkman and Liesel said their goodnights. "It's much the same," said Hawkman, "as when you last blew yourself red in the face, Rissa, blowing out all those candles. And yet so different—for then, at Stronghold, Liesel and I were bound for freeze again, and there was all of UET to face, and none of us could know we'd ever see each other again. While now—"

"Now we've got lots of work to do tomorrow," said Liesel. "Some days lately, peace knows, a freeze-chamber sounds *good* to me."

Rissa said, "Liesel—you must not overwork yourself."

Hawkman smiled. "Oh—she doesn't. Or rather—if she didn't, she wouldn't be happy."

RETURNING to their quarters Rissa held Tregare's arm. Inside, she said, "It was a fine celebration, Bran—was it not?"

"What d'you mean, *was?* Far as I'm concerned, it's just starting. Unless . . ."

"I correct myself. I mean to say—*thus far*, the celebration has gone well indeed."

"That's better."

Now Rissa's work-filled days sped fast, scanning and coordinating Board members' reports of groundside activity. Tregare did the same for space-related work and planning; in the evenings they traded summaries. She had the feeling of reliving a previous time, and finally understood the reason. "It's Stronghold all over again, Bran—only on a much larger scale. Can we ever manage it?"

"We did, before." Leaning across the table he stroked her neck. "And now we have that experience to go on—and a lot more highpowered people to help." She nodded, but still had her doubts.

Erika did take a space junket—but only to Mars, not Jupiter. She returned briefly to her Argentine headquarters, then went to inspect and reorganize the Australian facilities Lena had created. For the first time, data flowed freely between North America and the Hulzein Establishment.

Kane Altworth visited the newly titled Earth Headquarters; in honor of the occasion, Tregare sent a full-sized ship to bring him. The discussions went well. "For the moment," the Australian said, "my country—well, we'd as lief hold the status of close allies, with an eye to possibly joining your government later."

"Fine with us," said Tregare. "I told you we're not picky about the technicalities. Now if you're going to deal directly in interstellar trade—" And they talked of the best site for an Australian spaceport.

That evening, Altworth showed Rissa some pictures. "Now, this is Grandma Camilla not a great deal later than when you knew her. And here—earlier, with my father, before she smuggled him out to safety. And—" Seeing bits of Camilla Altworth's life captured in silent stillness, Rissa felt again the warmth of having known the woman, and thanked the grandson for his thoughtfulness.

One by one the UET bases overseas accepted Tregare's amnesty. Some tried to resist—UET Scandinavia held out until its Headquarters was leveled—but for the most part authority was transferred without bloodshed. The process of releasing Welfare Clients—one bureaucrat called it "deWelfarization" until Tregare told him to talk English or *go* to Welfare—that process accelerated. And within the Centers, the work of reuniting families continued.

Kept busy, Rissa knew she was losing track of some of the many threads she wove. When one day, quickly scanning through a stack of papers, she found a petition signed by Maita Pangreen, for a moment she failed to recognize the name. Then, "Yes, I suppose I must see her. Tomorrow, after lunch."

PANGREEN wore a loose robe and sandals; her walk was shambling. The guard released her arm and stood by the doorway. Rissa looked at her—the ears, fringes gone, were rudimentary cups, like the single one Celie Brashean still carried. Maita Pangreen's nose stood out misshapen and inflamed—the winglike flaps had been sewn back into place before Rissa's decision that the Committee's sadists be trimmed to match their experimental victims, so she had waived further surgery in the case. Looking more closely now, Rissa saw other minor disfigurements that she had not noticed earlier. She shook her head and waited for the other to speak.

Slowly, as though wading waist-deep in water, Pangreen approached. Closer than Rissa would have preferred, she stopped. "Ms. Kerguelen? I asked to talk with you."

"And that is what you are doing. State your petition—and quickly, please."

The woman made a placating gesture. "You hate me, don't you? You're Welfaring me."

"Hate is not the proper word. Loathe? Despise? Either is more accurate."

"I don't understand. You're *that* intolerant? Oh, I admit it was foolish of us, going to such bizarre extremes of personal appearance. But certainly—"

Rissa flexed her hand—talons to fist to talons. "I saw—you would do better not to remind me—some of those on whom you experimented, before you yourself submitted to surgery. You are lucky that I only send you to Welfare."

Pangreen reached and grasped Rissa's hand. "But I can't stay alive there! They know me—they'll kill me!"

"You have killed your share, I think." Rissa pulled her

hand free; as if to wipe away a stench, she scrubbed it against the clothing at her thigh. "And I give you a chance—a new name and identity, not your own which would rightly spell your death."

"*I* can't act like a Welfare Client! How could I possibly?"

"How you act," said Rissa, "is your own concern. You *are* a Welfare Client."

Arms wide, Maita Pangreen stood. "That's your final word? I see it is. Well, then—" Rissa braced herself, but the woman's voice was soft. "—I'll show you how you've misjudged me. You won't forgive me—but I forgive *you*. And I ask only one favor." Gently she reached and touched Rissa's arms. "Give me the kiss of peace—here on my forehead which I've kept unmarked—and I'll go to Welfare without complaint."

Disgust heaved in Rissa's stomach. *But I suppose I must!* She let the woman's arms go round her, felt the other's body warm against her, and leaned to kiss the forehead. The arms clamped tightly then, and—

Pain!—it tore through her chest—breath turned to cough and she tasted blood. She saw Pangreen's teeth-bared grin; with one hand she pushed the face away and the body with it. From below her right breast, blood spurted. Maita Pangreen said, *"That's* one you—" but the rest was lost, for without Rissa's volition her other hand moved, and she heard a dry stick snap.

Then the red haze before her turned to black, and she fell.

PAIN still—and now more widely spread. Someone was talking, but in no language she knew. *No. It is merely that I do not listen correctly.* And now she could understand.

"—the heart, luckily. The lung was bad, but we got to it in time. Sheer butchery, having to work so fast. The scars, I'm afraid—"

"—saw anything like it." *Bran Tregare is here.* "—damned *spike*, organic laminate like Ivan mentioned, bonded to two ribs and sticking straight out, hidden—"

The other voice? Yes. "—served to support the breast from sagging, for one thing. But a hard lunge, compressing the tissues—a good three inches of blade, enough to—"

Sound blurred, then cleared again. "—all right now? Call

me if there's any change. Peace take it, I *have* to get back to the conference . . . Asians get offended and walk out. The Africans, no problem—the leader's a Lombuno, related to my brother-in-law on Number One. But I'll tell them—you just call—"

"—needs another shot now, Tregare. She shouldn't be awake for a while. Not until—"

She barely felt the needle, and then the sounds died away.

SOMETHING squeezed her hand, and again. Her eyes opened. A blur became Tregare's face, in time for her to see his worried expression change to a smile.

"You'll be all right, Rissa. The wound's draining nicely, and your fever's down."

Her lips moved but no sound came. She tried again. "Pangreen—she—"

"I know. Tell you about it later, what we found. Sneaky trick—"

"I—heard. In the breast, she had it. I did not expect—"

"And who would? But the important thing is, she didn't succeed."

Rissa frowned; her head moved from side to side. "I would ask her—"

Tregare reached to stroke her cheek. "You won't be asking that one anything. Maybe you just chopped by reflex—but she died before she hit the ground. Broken neck." He waited, face anxious, then said, "Rissa? Will you have to grieve for her?"

Now her mind cleared; strength came and her voice was firm. "No, Tregare. It is like the policebitch at Hokkaido, so long ago. For the death of an attacking animal, one need not grieve."

SHE healed and soon was up from bed a time each day, though the sawn ribs pained her. The scars she would carry—ruefully, she regarded the mirror. Well, she had never complained of Tregare's; perhaps he would not mind so much, this marring of her own smooth skin.

Friends, when the doctors permitted it, visited her—Liesel and Hawkman, Kickem and Aedra, Zelde and Jamie on a quick hop from the port—others—she lost track. Only when

Tregare came at last to take her to *Inconnu* did she think to ask, "Ivan—where is he? And Ilse? I have not seen them."

Glancing briefly to her as he drove the groundcar—for she was not yet fit to walk such distances—he said, "I guess I haven't kept you up on things too well. A day or two before you could have visitors, they left."

Her silence was inquiry; he said, "Hoyfarul's test ship— *Timejumper*. It's haywired a lot and looks, inside, like a spider mismating with an octopus. But the doc swears the guts of it are solid, and instrument checks bear him out. And—well, we do want to know, soon as may be, whether we *can* beat light."

"So Ivan and Ilse—"

"With a skeleton crew, mostly from *Graf Spee*. And Hoyfarul himself—he insisted. Ilse, see—she needed a special job, I guess, to prove something to herself. And Ivan, of course—"

"Yes. How long a test was planned?"

"Hoyfarul claims his coherent field should give lots better accel than we're used to. Zerch to light in a week or ten days, instead of nearly a month. We'll find out when they get back. The idea was to pass C and go another day or so to see if things are stable above light. Then cut the drive for fast slowdown, do turnover and pour it on homebound. And then—"

She nodded. "Yes, I understand. And when are they due to return?"

"That's the trouble. About a week ago."

Six more days passed before *Timejumper* landed, all personnel in good health. At a closed session the Board took testimony. Hoyfarul spoke first, using terms Rissa did not understand. She nudged Tregare and shook her head; he said, "Step down for a bit, doctor, and let somebody tell it in English first. We'll get to the technical points later." He looked around. "All right, who can say it quick?"

Ivan moved to the chair Hoyfarul, pouting, had vacated. "We got up toward C fast, as predicted. If the thing never does anything else, it'll save time *that* way." He grinned. "Coming up close onto light, everybody walked tiptoe and whispered, but nothing erupted. We passed C all right—no question about that. So we thought we had the galaxy on a loose string. Well, I guess nothing ever works out that simple.''

He shrugged. "What happened, though—above light the drive field couldn't hold coherence; it started to drift frequencies. And an acoherent field can't exist at those speeds, so the drive blew. That slowed us below light, fast—the field-decay thing—and there we were with a dead drive. Took several days—I forget how many—we worked our butts off—to fix it. Then, coming back, it worked fine again up to about the same point and then blew the same way. But Ilse had figured on that—she set accel so the blowup left us the right time and distance to get home quickest. And with a little haywire, all we blew was circuit breakers." He looked to Hoyfarul. "That about right, doctor?"

Pennet Hoyfarul nodded. "Accurate, so far as it goes."

"Where doesn't it go?" said Tregare.

"Why, the *cause* of the failure. The loss of coherence was entirely due to having to substitute existing components, which proved inadequate, for the locking circuits provided in my design. You were in such a hurry for results, I was told, that I was persuaded to install existing hardware in multiple. Well, it's not calibrated with sufficient accuracy; the units did not hold synchronization under stress. So—''

"I think I get it," said Tregare. "We had a problem like that with turret guidance, back when I was in UET. Similar circuit, most likely. Now then—how long you figure it takes to build what you need?"

Hoyfarul paused. "I'll have to consult with Fabrication. The units may be into production—before we left, they were starting to set up for it. Can I tell you tomorrow?"

Tregare waved a hand. "Sure, that's fine. And Dr. Hoyfarul—congratulations, and thanks."

"Congratulations? For this failure?"

"*What* failure? You beat light, didn't you? Nobody else ever did."

LEAVING, Rissa clutched Ivan's arm. "Ilse—where is she? Why did she not come here?"

"Doctor's appointment—finding out what's possible for her."

"She—Ivan, as soon as may be, I wish to see her."

He nodded. "All right. Unless I call and tell you different, come over to *Graf Spee* this evening."

"I shall, and thank you."

ILSE KRUEGER answered Rissa's knock. "Ilse!" She embraced the smaller woman. "And how are you?"

"I was going to ask *you* that, but—come in, sit down. Ivan's upship, checking the log for the time we were gone." Rissa sat. "Now, then—here's a drink, and what's all this about you damn near getting yourself killed?"

Rissa explained. "And we have deduced, from readouts of the Committee's files, that at least twice she had killed that way, successfully. Committee rivals, in intimate situations— she was so equipped on the other side, also—"

Ilse shuddered. "I never considered myself squeamish, but the whole idea give me the cold chills. You mind if I tell you my troubles and set *your* teeth on edge for a change?"

"From the way you speak, Ilse, your troubles are less than they have been. I will gladly listen."

Ilse ran fingers through her wig. "Without this, I'm a mess, currently, so I'll keep it on. But for later, not as bad as I'd thought." She touched the sunken, livid scar. "They can cut this out, pull the sides together, up well past the cheekbone. And the same, if I want to bother, for the other end, starting down the scalp." She shrugged. "It'll leave marks, sure. But I've got plenty of those, elsewhere. A few more—"

"To one who survived UET's Academy . . ."

Ilse nodded. "Yes—you'd know about that, wouldn't you? Well, then—I came out luckier than I expected. Where the ear was—" Her thumb and forefinger made an unclosed circle. "—a patch, about this big, of scar. Around it, good skin— and the part that used to grow hair, still does. One doctor wants to do a skin graft to hide all remaining scar tissue— maybe I'll bother, maybe not. The way he tells it, I'd have a sore belly for a while, where he'd take the skin."

Carefully, "Has Ivan expressed a preference?"

Ilse smiled. "I wish he would—I'd gladly follow it. But he takes great pains to be neutral, Ivan does. He thinks I'm more fragile than I really am, so—"

"Then you must convince him that you are not."

The door opened; Ivan Marchant entered. "Well—who're you two roasting, now?"

"Only you, my brother. And we have decided that you are well done."

WHEN she told Tregare, he shrugged. "It doesn't matter, really. They're going to survive together, anyway; that's obvious."

"Well, it matters to *me*—how Ilse will look for the rest of her life."

"Sure—and to me too—but I don't know what to do about it. If you do, go do it."

Her voice bit. "If I did, I would." Then, more softly; "Ah, Bran—I had forgotten. You married *me* when my face looked like a stomping ground, and you had no way to know what damage might be permanent. So I suppose—"

"Start supposing your brother has as much sense as your husband. And come here, maybe?"

"Not—*oh!*—not until you stop tickling, Tregare!"

LIESEL reported to the Board: "Relocation and release—some ways it's easier than we expected, some ways harder. The hard parts are all the things a lifetime Welfare Client doesn't know —*can't* know. Well—we're working on it."

"What's the easy part?" said Tregare.

"Well, things like furniture. Some never had it, don't need it, don't *want* it. Even for mealtimes—they eat standing up, at a counter. And except for the newer ones, who still have families alive—they don't like the idea of single-family housing, at all. They want housing units for *groups* of adults and children—which makes reconversion a lot cheaper,"

"A different fashion of living," Rissa said.

"Yes, and for them it seems to work. The permanently sterilized can have a share in the kids—the ones existing now and those born later, to reversibles. Generally each group has some fertiles in it—sort of a nucleus."

"That's all right for the present," said Hawkman. "But as I've said before, what about twenty years from now when today's kids grow up fertile? Any policy plans yet?"

Liesel nodded. "It's a little dictatorial, but there's options.

Basically, every woman's entitled to two kids—then she gets a reversible.''

"Why reversible?" Tregare asked the question.

"We want to stabilize the population, not reduce it further. Not all will *have* their quota; to make up the difference we choose from applicants who want a third child. By lottery, maybe.''

Rissa spoke. "Why is it the *woman* who must submit to these things? It takes two to conceive a child." She saw Liesel's grin and added, "I mean, in the usual case.''

"For the pragmatic reason," said Hawkman, "that men don't give birth, and that sterilizing one man doesn't stop a woman from conceiving by another." He spread his hands. "*Of course* it's unfair—but the unfairness lies in our biology.''

Finding no answer, Rissa shrugged. From beside Bernardez, Aedra Leng spoke. "I'm not a Board member—but what about people who feel these restrictions violate their rights?''

"The colonies have no such limits," said Tregare. "Anybody doesn't like Earth's rules—go where they don't apply.''

"But with the ships we have—such a trickle.''

"Now, yes. But we want to beef up the colonies, anyway. So on the boards we're designing *big* ships. There's a point in size where the balance tips—you can carry more people in freeze than awake and eating—and the curve goes up fast. With Hoyfarul's drive we could build *way* past that point—ships built in space, too big to land anywhere. So in the twenty years before the problem hits us, I think we can take care of it.''

Aedra nodded. "You'll never satisfy everyone—but you offer as much choice as possible.''

"Fine," said Liesel. "Now—back to the agenda, maybe?''

Clothes for newly freed citizens were a bottleneck; many were released wearing jumpsuits dyed in non-Welfare colors, and even the suits were in short supply. "Al Kybel's expediting matters, though." Liesel grinned. "Working eighteen-twenty hours a day, he was—sleeping on a cot in his office. Finally had to send him home to get a good night's sleep for a change.''

"Do you have figures," said Rissa, "—rates and totals of Clients released?''

"Not up to date—been too busy. Only that we're making a

dent, especially in the overcrowding.''

"Good. Then if there is no further business before this Board—'' No one spoke. "We stand adjourned.''

WHEN she returned to her work, Rissa found concentration difficult. Thinking to pass a few approving words with Albert Kybel, she went to his place of work. He was not there; Aiela Lindstrom greeted her.

"Ms. Kerguelen—Rissa!''

"You are looking very well, Aiela.'' The young woman's hair, still very short, stood out in pale, fluffy curls; the added bulk made her face look smaller. "And perhaps five years younger than I know you must be. Since you were gone from *Inconnu* when we returned, I assume you have found other quarters?''

"Oh, yes—and nearly furnished them, too. We're a little crowded—'' She laughed. "But you wouldn't know, would you?''

Rissa shook her head. "Until you tell me, I will not.''

"It's Dien—Dien Harbin. We were together—before he was Welfared, to give his job to a Committee protégé. Complaining about that was what got *me* Welfared. Well, Mr. Kybel put in a priority request to Ms. Hulzein, and Dien was released. And next week we're getting married, newstyle. The day New Year 99 begins.''

"Well, I am happy for you, Aiela. And you will be applying for larger quarters?''

"I already have—but not on any special privilege priority. With so many waiting, just to get out of Welfare at all, we can put up with a little crowding for as long as we have to.''

For a moment Rissa was tempted to use her authority to help the couple. Then she thought, *No—the girl is right*. If she began interceding for people she liked, in nonessentials, where would it end? "That is thoughtful of you, and generous.'' Then, "I had intended to give Albert Kybel my regards; I am told he is doing fine work. Will you tell him that I said so?''

"Oh, sure. And—you wouldn't *believe* how different he is, since he came back out of Welfare. Considerate—everyone's a human being to him, now.''

"I am glad. And now I must go. It is good to have seen you, Aiela.''

• • •

RISSA and Tregare were lunching in his office when Liesel entered. Her tight smile betrayed excitement; Rissa said, "What has happened?"

"Tell you in a minute." She sat. "Go ahead eating; I'll have some coffee."

They waited; finally Tregare said, "All right—you're busting with something. What is it?"

"I finally got around to check—remember, I told you, Rissa?—for descendants of Heidele Hulzein's first two children, the ones who were conceived normally."

"Yes—of course. And you have found them?"

"Right, I have. Quite a job—birth registrations not available, some times and places. I got my best confirmation off old *tax* records, listings of dependents for some reason I'm not sure of. But never mind—"

She leaned forward. "The bad mix of genes—Heidele's son transmitted it. None of his children reproduced, viably. But the daughter—she herself was sickly but didn't pass it along. The weak genes got lost in that mating. Happens sometimes, or we'd all be carrying every ailment our ancestors ever had."

Tregare shook his head. "I suppose it's no use asking you to *get* to it?"

"You don't have to—I'm there. I discovered three living descendants—two, fifth generation from Heidele, and one sixth."

Rissa smiled. "And you know where they are? They can come here—we can meet them? Oh—I *hope* they are not in Welfare!"

Tregare touched her shoulder. "Easy, now." Then, "Liesel, you're still holding out. Drop the other shoe, will you?"

His mother laughed. "All right. The three I'm talking about, descended from Heidele's marriage—they are Ivan Marchant, Rissa Kerguelen and Liesel Selene Moray!"

STUNNED, Rissa saw Tregare's face go blank. Then he said, "A cousin marriage? We *inbred*, for Lisele?"

Tension gone, Liesel chuckled. "Not enough to count, Bran. You're half Heidele, twice removed. Rissa's only a thirty-secondth part—and maybe the two don't even overlap.

Some laws permit first cousins—with a possible *fifty* percent in common—to marry. Second cousins, with—let me see—a quarter, possible? That's allowed, almost anywhere. No, Bran —you have no problem."

Liesel grinned at Rissa. "Wait 'til I tell Erika. More than once, she's said you *should* have been a Hulzein!"

Now Rissa laughed. Tregare looked at her, and she said, "On Number One—all that time, during the trouble with dal Nardo and Blaise Tendal. Before I became a Hulzein connection by marriage, I was already one by blood!"

LATER, in their quarters, Rissa stared at a report without seeing it. Something bothered her—nagging in the back of her mind, evading her effort to identify it. The fact of her being a Hulzein? No—she accepted that relationship; it pleased her.

Something about Aiela, then? Not quite—but that was where it had begun. . . .

Tregare said, "You got a problem?" Frowning, she shook her head; she had almost recognized it—or had she? "Planning on a big party for the New Year, so soon after our last one?"

Suddenly, "That's it! No—not the party—but New Year 99."

He laughed. "If you say so. But what's to puzzle about? It's just another year, and UET's power didn't last into three figures, after all. So—"

Preoccupied, she said, "Bran—we will not have New Year 99."

"What? Hey—is something *really* wrong?"

"No. But we have ousted UET—why should we order our years by their numbering?"

"You want to start over? Begin with another Year One? It might be a little confusing."

Impatient, she shook her head. "I am trying to *think*, Bran!" She paused, silent. Then, "No—I cannot remember. Bran—by the *old* way, before UET in its arrogance decided to count only the time of its own rule, what year would this be? I knew the correlation at one time, but I have forgotten."

Tregare shrugged and spread his hands. In one motion, she rose. "I am going upship for a brief time. To Control—the computer has that information."

• • •

AN hour later, carrying a handful of readout tapes, she returned. She sat and looked at one section, then at another. Tregare said, "You find out?"

"I became interested, and learned more than I first intended. Things I recall hearing in vague outline, when I was small and still at home. And, I think, things we must study in order to help plan our future course."

"Sure. Such as what?"

"North America was not always one country—we knew that. The Synthetic Foods Combine used coercion to annex the northern and southern parts. But the largest population was called a United States, and was governed in a way I do not wholly understand. There was a President, who ranked highest over a large Committee called a Congress."

She shrugged. "Well—until it is time for us to devise ways to broaden the base of power, that does not matter. I learned that the last President, before the beginning of corporate elections, had great wealth—the change was perhaps, in great measure, his doing. In the sixth such election UET won power, and held it through ten more—farces, most of them!—before dropping the needless pretense of choice."

"Yeah, sure—I remember hearing some of that. But what's your point?"

"That UET renamed the year it took power, New Year One. And that instead of beginning New Year 99 next week, we will begin Old Year—no, just *Year* two thousand, one hundred and three!"

Tregare grinned. "Now that *does* deserve a party!"

EPILOGUE

Eighty years after Rissa Kerguelen was born . . .

Aged eighty-three, Erika Hulzein signed documents merging the Hulzein Establishment with the corporate government of Earth. Before retiring, Prime Minister Kane Altworth of Australia announced that his country had voted to follow suit.

Rissa Kerguelen celebrated her twenty-eighth birthday, biotime. On her eightieth by planetary time she gave birth to her parthenogenetic, gene-replicated daughter, Renalle.

Director of Relocation and Release Liesel Hulzein, aged seventy-two or thereabouts, reported that less than ten percent of North America's population remained in Welfare Centers —"but now we're scraping the bottom of the barrel."

Dr. Pennet Hoyfarul's ship *Timejumper*, commanded by Ilse Krueger and First Hat Ivan Marchant, returned to Earth. Passengers from the planet Number One included Ernol Lombuno and Sparline Moray. In the cargo were three zoomwombs and three frozen zygotes, consigned to Bran Tregare Moray and Rissa Kerguelen.

Liesel Selene Moray, aged eight and a bit, wondered what it would be like to acquire three more siblings so quickly. She decided it would be a welcome change from studying the calculus.

The Hoyfarul ship *Backspace Key* brought news of the liberation of six more colonies, including Far Corner and the Twin Worlds, as well as several UET ships caught groundside.

Celie Brashean performed a recital of songs and poems—her own compositions—before an audience of eight thousand, with Tri-V coverage. At the end she received a standing ovation.

A third African spaceport was begun.

The Hoyfarul ship *Leapfrog* returned from Stronghold, under the command of Derek Limmer. Accompanying him were his wife Felcie, their son Arlen, and Arlen's two younger sisters. Limmer reported the capture of four visiting UET ships, as well as the expected fleets from Earth. Tregare checked his list against *Backspace Key*'s and found less than a dozen colonies unaccounted for, and fifteen ships.

Limmer also reported meeting a Shrakken ship in space. "... just after we dropped below light. It's not the ship Stonzai had, but she's aboard. A chance rendezvous and she transferred in space, is my understanding."

Tregare sat up straight. "Coming here? What for?"

Limmer's scarred smile. "They're in trouble—under attack from down-Arm. An enemy that simply kills and won't parley. The Shrakken are holding pretty well but the attacks keep stepping up, a new wave every few years. Left on their own, eventually they'll go under."

Rissa Kerguelen looked up from nursing her daughter Renalle. "We *must* help. We owe them that."

Tregare frowned, then nodded. "We shared our weapons; I guess we can share the Hoyfarul drive, too. I'll arrange to send a ship."

"Send? We will *take* it, Bran! *Inconnu Deux* has been tested and waiting for half a year." With its seven turrets—*her* design. . . . *But our three zygotes must now wait longer to be born.*

Tregare protested. "What about Renalle? Or Lisele, for that matter?"

"I?" said Liesel Selene. "Why, I shall tend Renalle while Rissa is busy in Control, just as I did on the shakedown cruise."

"And we do not go to fight, Bran—it is not like coming to

Earth. Though no sublight ship is any great threat to *Inconnu Deux*."

Tregare voiced misgivings, but against his wife and daughter united he had no chance. When the matter was settled, Rissa said, "First, Earth killed Shrakken and stole from them. Lives were taken on both sides; that book is balanced. And now, thanks to Hoyfarul, we have something to *give* them, for what we gained."

Eighty years after Renalle Hulzein's life ended, Rissa Kerguelen's was still beginning.